THE HALFPENNY GIRLS AT CHRISTMAS

As Christmas approaches, Alice, Edith and Marg continue to face hardships growing up on one of the poorest streets in Blackpool. Penniless, their friendship has helped them survive this far, but it'll take more than that to see them through the dark days that lie ahead.

Newly married Alice receives shocking news about her pregnancy that threatens the future she's always dreamed of, Marg is struggling to care for her ailing mother and ensure her little sister receives the education she deserves, and Edith is grieving the loss of her family while preparing to marry her sweetheart.

The Halfpenny Girls once again are faced with a struggle, but with the festive season upon them will family, friendship and Christmas spirit see them through?

MAGGIE MASON

THE HALFPENNY GIRLS AT CHRISTMAS

Complete and Unabridged

MAGNA
Leicester

First published in Great Britain in 2021 by
Sphere
An imprint of Little, Brown Book Group
London

First Ulverscroft Edition
published 2021
by arrangement with
Little, Brown Book Group
London

A catalogue record for this book is available
from the British Library.

ISBN 978-0-7505-4908-0

Published by
Ulverscroft Limited
Anstey, Leicestershire

Printed and bound in Great Britain by
TJ Books Ltd., Padstow, Cornwall

This book is printed on acid-free paper

To my grandchildren who hold my heart.
I am very proud of you all and love you
beyond words.

1

Alice
December 1938

Alice laughed at Marg's funny antics as she hopped about, swinging her arms backwards and forwards trying to stay warm. Her teeth were chattering as she asked, 'By, whose idea was this? It's flipping freezing.'

Edith joined in the laughter, but Alice knew, like her, she felt sorry that Marg's threadbare coat didn't give her the same warmth their own thick coats gave them.

Though none of theirs would fit Marg, the thought of not just one, but three warm coats hanging in her own wardrobe, besides this huge bell-shaped one she wore to cover her seven-month bump, made Alice feel guilty at how her own fortunes had changed. As had Edith's with her fiancé, Philip, to support her. But poor Marg was still stuck in the poverty trap they'd all been in as children.

'Let's get into the warmth and have our chips now, lass.'

'But we're meant to walk along the prom for a while first, Alice. I don't want to spoil that for you two.'

'You're not, I feel the cold an' all. But besides that, me back's aching like mad.' As she said this a gust of wind propelled Alice towards Marg and she landed in her arms. All three fell about laughing.

'Eeh, you're only little, but you're a bundle of trouble; you nearly knocked me off me pins, Alice, and we

1

only brought you because you said you'd treat us to our chips!'

Alice made a face and stuck her tongue out at Marg. 'Ha, not so little now!'

This afternoon was special; it was a rare treat these days for the three of them to be out together. Born within days of each other on Whittaker Avenue in Blackpool, they'd been friends since they were little. This year, in late September, they'd celebrated their twenty-first birthdays.

All they'd been through growing up had drawn them as close as if they were sisters, but their lives now were beginning to take different paths. Gone were the days they would play together, go to school together, and then, later, work in the same factory and end the day sitting on Marg's doorstep drinking cocoa. All that had changed when Alice married her doctor husband, Gerald, and moved to his grander house on a wealthier street.

Sighing the memories away, Alice linked arms with Marg. She wouldn't have missed this walk along Blackpool prom with them for the world. 'I'll be good, but you just have to hang on to me. Despite me bulk, the wind seems to think it can have its wicked way with me.'

They giggled joyfully and it filled Alice with the knowledge that their friendship would always support her, no matter what they were faced with.

As Edith linked Marg's other arm and their laughter died into their loving companionship, familiar sounds came into focus.

'Try your luck at winning an amazing gift! We've clocks to grace your mantelpiece, tea sets to make you feel you could have the King to Christmas Day tea . . .'

2

She loved Blackpool and was proud of its wonderous Tower standing majestic and soaring towards the sky, overlooking its golden sands, the stalls that lined the seafront, and the sometimes angry Irish sea that lashed its shores.

Wanting to get Marg into the warm, Alice told them, 'Come on, let's hurry. And no stopping to talk to Bendy — though it will be good to see him. We can have a chat when we come out of the café.'

Edith gave her a quizzical look. 'By, you've changed your tune, Alice. It's not long since you'd have done anything to avoid his stall.'

'I know, but he did used to go on about me ma a lot and it got on me nerves, him saying he'd been in love with her and how like her I was with me blonde, curly hair and large blue eyes. It used to embarrass me, but he don't do that as much now.'

'Well, it's a good job you don't mind him as he's heading our way.'

Though she'd seen Bendy's contortionist ways many times, Alice was always amazed at his agility. Twisting his body into all sorts of tangles was what gave him his nickname and attracted customers to his coconut shy.

He came cartwheeling towards them, frightening the life out of Alice as they all jumped out of his way. Marg, always the feisty one, shouted at him, 'Bendy, mind what you're doing! The wind has done a good job of knocking Alice about without you having a go an' all! You should be mindful of her condition.'

'Sorry, me lasses, and aye, there are some strong gusts today.' He looked at Alice. 'How are you, love?'

'I'm fine, Bendy, ta, despite the fright you just gave me. We're heading for the chippy, we're frozen.'

3

'Aw, and I thought you were going to have a go on me stall. I've some lovely teddy bears you could win for your babby.'

'I might just do that, after I've eaten me dinner.'

'Here, let me give you a hand. I'll keep the wind from blowing you over. My, you're as dainty as your ma used to be.'

Ignoring this, Alice took the arm Bendy offered. He escorted her inside the café and sat her down with a flourish. She laughed up at him, telling him to stop fussing, but it made no difference.

Now that both her parents were gone, Bendy was one of the few people left who remembered them when they were younger. His memories evoked her own, especially of her da, who, following an accident at the rock factory, was never the same again. He'd risked his life to save Clive, his boss's son, who was now a friend of theirs — well, more than a friend to Marg, though she always insisted that he wasn't.

But for all the hardship she and her brothers had faced because of their father's changed personality, she did have a lot of fond memories too. Like the time when she visited the Tower Ballroom with Edith and Marg and she met her lovely Gerald.

Gerald, a doctor, had tried, but unfortunately not succeeded, to help her da — a time when their initial attraction deepened into a love that consumed her and brought happiness to her life. Not long after she and Gerald had married, they, along with her brothers, had moved to Newton Drive, to the lovely house Gerald's parents had given to him before sailing off into the sunset, as they put it. Now, poverty was a thing of the past for them and they were cocooned in love. How she wished she could make everything

4

right for Edith and Marg too.

Edith was getting there, but Marg . . . Poor Marg.

'By, lass, you're doing a lot of sighing this afternoon. Let's hope a hot mug of tea and the chips sort you out.' Edith smiled down at her. 'I'm ready for mine, I can tell you. I haven't eaten yet today.'

'Me, too, love. Just let me get me purse out.'

'No, you don't have to pay, Alice. I know you said you would, but I'll go halves.'

Marg didn't say anything, and Alice knew she probably didn't have a penny to offer. Wanting to cover up any embarrassment Marg might feel, Alice put on a stern voice.

'I said I'd pay and I will. Now, don't argue with a pregnant lady, it doesn't do her any good.'

Edith's mouth dropped open. 'You're pregnant? I thought you'd just got fat!'

'You daft apeth. Anyway, shush, don't tell everybody!'

'Eeh, Alice, love.' Marg opened her arms. 'You always make me laugh. I just want to hug you.'

'Ha, you'll crush me!'

'Crush you, I can't even get me arms around you. Like Edith says, you've got fat.'

They erupted into a giggling mess then, but were pulled up by Irene, the chip shop owner, shouting at them.

'Oi, you three, are you in here to eat or get warm? 'Cause me café ain't for nowt else other than eating fish and chips.'

They all laughed at Irene. 'Sorry, love, can we have three lots of fish and chips, please, and make them large. Oh, and three mugs of tea as soon as you can — we're freezing.'

5

'By, it's good to hear you can afford that lot, Alice. I remember when you three were ragged-arsed kids, begging for the scratchings. How's things with you all, anyroad? Eeh, I still can't get over what happened to your family, Edith, lass. I were really sad about it.'

Alice stiffened, afraid for Edith that being reminded of the tragedy would dampen her day. But she coped. 'Ta, Irene. I'm all right. It's harder some days than others.'

'And your ma and gran, Marg, how're they doing, lass?'

'Gran gives me the runaround, and me ma, well, she's not too good, but keeps cheerful. Jackie's looking after them to give me a break. I'll tell Ma you were asking after her.'

'Aye, do. By, that sister of yours is a one on her own. She'll go places, she will . . . Well, now, Alice, you've landed in clover, ain't yer? When're you due then? You hadn't better have it on me floor or I'll batter it and serve it up to me customers!'

'Irene!'

'What? I were only having a laugh, Marg. If it happened here, I'd be over the moon. I could double me takings advertising meself as a midwife an' all.'

After the stunned silence of the few in the café, everyone roared at this. Irene was a card, but some of her impromptu remarks were a bit too far off the mark. Alice joined in the laughter, though was glad when the bell above the door clanged, announcing the entrance of the local bobby and taking the attention away from herself.

It was a standing joke that his name was Bob — Bob the bobby — and in true bobby style, he asked, 'Now then, what's going on in here?'

Most laughed, but one chap called out, 'You're just in time to prevent a murder, Bob. One thing about you, you're always in the right place at the right time.'

Alice jumped in. 'Hello, Bob, we ain't seen you in a while.'

'Naw, that's because you've all been good lasses.' He winked at her and then gave them all a wide grin. 'Can I queue-jump, girls? I'm late taking me break and it's left me short of time.'

'As long as we get our mugs of tea first,' Alice told him. 'We're chilled to the bone.'

'Coming up, Alice, lass.'

* * *

As they sat drinking their tea and warming their hands around the hot enamel mugs, Alice began to feel better. She just wished this backache would ease, but it only seemed to be getting worse.

As Edith blew away the steam from her tea, she said, 'So, you've only two months to go now, Alice.'

Alice nodded and tried to smile, but a sudden pain made her catch her breath and she let out an involuntary cry.

'Alice?' This was said by Edith and Marg in unison.

Alice smiled. 'Calm down, it was just a twinge. It happens.'

'Was it the babby kicking? Can I feel? I love to put me hand on your belly when he's moving, it makes him feel more real . . . Eeh, Alice, I can't wait.' With this, Marg put her hand on Alice's bump.

'No, it's not him. He's been good for a couple of days now. Don't worry, you'll know all about it yourselves one of these days; it ain't all plain sailing, knitting and

7

dreaming, you know! Now, do something useful and rub me back for me.'

As Marg did this, Edith said, 'If you're having a girl, she's going to be born with a complex and a feeling that she weren't expected, poor thing. I hope you're knitting some pink things an' all.'

'Lemon and white, to be on the safe side. But, you know, I don't mind what sex it is, I will love it with all my heart. I can't wait for the day it blooming well arrives now. Anyway, Marg, your hand feels warm, but how's the rest of you? Are you warming up, now?'

'Aye, I am. Me belly's beginning to feel less like an ice pit.'

'Marg . . . well, look, why don't you let — '

'I know what you're going to say, Alice, but no, love. You do enough for me and I ain't going to let you buy me a coat, they cost too much. Anyroad, me coat's all right, it were me jumper that made me cold today — I washed it and it didn't dry in time.'

Alice sighed. She so wanted to help Marg more, but knew her pride stopped her accepting anything costly.

Edith must have caught on as she asked, 'How long have you two got? I'm helping with the Christmas fayre at St Kentigern's at three this afternoon and I know there's two coats in what I unpacked for me stall. They looked about the right fit for you and Jackie, love, and those who run the stalls have the pick of the best stuff before the doors open. I could do with some help.'

'I'll help out, but I don't know about buying two coats, I've only a couple of coppers. It'd be good to get Jackie a good warm coat, though. What about you, Alice?'

'I'll be all right now that I've had this rest. You can

8

stop massaging now, ta, Marg, love. Me back feels a lot better.'

Alice caught Edith's eye. She winked at her, then changed the subject. 'Speaking of Christmas, you're both still coming to mine, aren't you?'

'Aye, of course we are. Me and Philip were talking about it last night, and me and Marg have decided we're cooking Christmas dinner, not you. You can supervise the laying of the table and that's it!'

'Eeh, Edith, I know me orders, lass.'

They laughed, but Marg didn't join in. Alice knew it was difficult for her, and this was confirmed when she said, 'Jackie's definitely coming, nothing's going to stop that happening, she so wants to spend it with Harry. But, well, I might not make it. It depends on how me ma is. She's had some bad days since we all made the arrangements. Mind, me and Jackie made the pud, so no matter what I'll send that as promised.'

'Ooh, I love your Christmas pud, Marg. But don't worry, you're coming. Gerald'll fetch your ma in his car, and she couldn't be in better hands than his, as you know. So, all we need to know is will Clive be coming with you?'

'No, why should he? Besides, he has his sons to spend it with.'

Alice wished the pair of them would realise their feelings for each other — well, Marg, at least, as with Clive it was obvious how he felt. But Marg just seemed to want to keep him as a friend, when he'd be so perfect for her.

'Anyroad, if you're sure Gerald wouldn't mind, I wouldn't miss it for the world. Ta, love.'

'He won't, we've already talked about it.'

'Ooh, it'll be grand. When me and Jackie made the

9

Christmas pud the other night, it cheered us up no end as it brought on that Christmassy feeling. But then, Gran had us in tucks when she gave it a stir, as she said, 'I wish John would come home from work and take me to bed for a cuddle and work his magic on me.' Ha! I had to stop her as it seemed like she was going to go on. Jackie was blushing like mad.'

'Eeh, your gran's a one.'

'She is since she lost her marbles, Edith. Though it's easier to cope with her since your lovely ma gave me some tips. Betty was so good with her.'

Marg noticed a change in Edith's expression.

'Oh, Edith, I'm sorry, lass, I shouldn't have said.'

'No, it's all right, I like good memories. Ma was good with your gran.'

Alice could see the relief on Marg's face as she turned towards her. 'It helped an' all, Alice, when Gerald told me that Gran's condition was called dementia, and he explained how it was for her. How she's missing a few pages in the book of her life and gradually losing others.'

'I'm glad it helped you, Marg. I know it ain't easy for you at times, but at least you understand what's happening to Gran. Anyroad, back to Christmas. So there'll be eleven around the table . . . Ooh, I feel so excited. I love Christmas! I loved the ones we used to have when we were kids. There was always a magic about it, even though we didn't have much.'

Their fond memories were interrupted as Irene called out, 'Three times fish and chips! Come and get it, me lasses. I've thrown in some bread and butter for you too.'

'Ta, Irene, I forgot to order that.'

Edith stood. 'Right, I'll fetch them over. Come on,

belly-up-Alice, give me your money.'

This brought their giggles back. Alice handed Edith a shilling and told her, 'I'll have salt and vinegar on mine, please, Edith, love.'

'Ooh, and me an' all, Edith. I'll come with you, lass.'

As they went, Bob passed Alice on his way out, clutching his hot newspaper-wrapped chips. He gave her a cheery grin.

Bob had figured in their lives since they were nippers and supported them through many a crisis. They couldn't wish for a better local bobby.

★ ★ ★

The fish and chips were delicious: lovely and hot and dripping with vinegar. But it was the light, crunchy batter that Alice loved the most. As she bit into it, memories of begging for the scratchings — the bits of batter that had not clung to the fish and had fried in the hot fat until scooped out — came to her.

Irene would put them into little cone-shaped bags and sell them for a farthing, but many a time she'd given the three of them a bag to share and they'd walked along the prom chomping on them and dodging the squawking, hungry seagulls who threatened to steel their prize. Alice smiled to herself at the memory.

When they left the café, they headed for Bendy's stall.

Not feeling up to having a go herself as the chips were lying heavy in her, Alice tapped Marg's shoulder. 'Do you reckon you could win me a teddy, Marg, love? Here, take this change and do your best, eh?'

'Eeh, you make me feel like a kid again, Alice, with buying me chips and giving me a copper or two to

11

have a go on the stalls. All I need now is an ice cream.'

'It's a bit cold for that! Besides, you've always been better at winning than me and Edith, and I know you love having a go . . . Go on, there's a good 'un, win a teddy. It'll be me babby's first present.'

Marg grinned and her lovely freckled face lit up. She wasn't beautiful in the way that Edith was, with her clearcut features, striking large hazel eyes, glossy dark hair and the elegance that being tall gave, but Marg had a nice face framed by mousy-coloured hair that tended to frizz. Her best feature was her lovely dark eyes; her strength shone through them, drawing folk to her.

As Marg tried to win a prize, Alice and Edith huddled together on the bench that stood facing the sea.

Edith found Alice's hand. 'When Marg comes back, we'll go. We need to get to St Kentigern's in good time to grab them coats, and we'll make sure Marg can afford them between us, eh?'

Alice forced a grin onto her face. At this moment she just needed to be in the warmth again.

'You look tired, love.'

'Aye, I am. I've loved it, but the chips aren't settling. I'll be fine in a few moments. I just get a lot of indigestion.'

'Well, you know what the old biddies at the factory always say when anyone's pregnant and suffers that — that babby'll have plenty of hair!'

'Oh, Edith, I hope it has plenty of everything, whether it's a girl or boy . . . Eeh, I didn't mean . . .'

Edith burst out laughing. 'Aye, blessed in every department!'

'Edith!' Shocked, as Edith was the last one to come out with innuendos, Alice playfully slapped her

12

shoulder, though was secretly glad to have made Edith laugh.

When Edith sobered, she said, 'You know, I miss being at yours, Alice, love. Especially when your Gerald's on nights. We used to have such a laugh when the lads went to do their own thing in their rooms and we were left on our own.'

'We did, and I miss you an' all, so much, Edith. How're you finding it back in the old street and living on your own?'

'It's good to be back among them we know, and I've Marg next door for support, but I have to admit, it isn't always easy seeing me old house across the road and imagining me da and ma sitting outside in the sunshine. It's still very painful.'

'I know, love, it will be, but all is coming right now. Well, for us. Me happily married and with me first babby on the way, and you engaged to Philip.'

'Aye, we're lucky, but poor Marg still goes through the mill.'

They had no time to say more as a triumphant Marg called them over. 'I won! I thought you'd like to choose the teddy, Alice, love.'

'Aw, well done, Marg, and ta, love.'

Alice knew the teddy bear she wanted the minute she laid eyes on it: the fluffy yellow one with large button eyes, one of which was half covered with black felt as if winking. He looked adorable with his black and white scarf tied around his neck.

Once Bendy had hooked him off the shelf and handed him to her, she clutched him to her stomach. 'What do reckon to this, little one, eh?'

Bendy grinned. 'By, Alice, lass, you're blooming more than usual. Good luck to you — I hope it's a little girl as pretty as you and your ma.'

Edith put in quickly, 'Eeh, Alice, I love the way you talk to your babby as if he's already here.'

Alice knew she was trying to cover for Bendy having mentioned her ma.

'He is to me, Edith, love, he's part of me — a real little person.'

Bendy didn't seem to pick up on anything amiss as he said, 'Let me get me brother to take you wherever you're going, Alice, he's had a quiet day. His taxi's only just around the corner, and I'll make sure it's a free ride an' all.'

They all gratefully accepted the offer, and as they climbed in Alice said, 'Right, me Halfpenny Girls, let's go bargain hunting, eh?'

'Me da named us that, didn't he, Alice?'

'He did, Edith, love. We were playing out when he called over, 'You three are the Halfpenny Girls,' then said something about us being poor but having the riches of friendship. And that's what we've been called ever since and will always be, no matter how our fortunes change.'

Sitting back, Alice felt a sense of happiness settle in her. Life had dealt them all a bad hand, but it was full of promise now — wasn't it? She quickly dispelled this doubting question as she shifted her body to get comfy and patted her belly.

2

Marg

The church hall looked like a fairyland, decorated as it was in tinsel and paper chains. Marg clasped her hands together. 'Ooh, look, I've got that Christmassy feeling again.'

'Doesn't it look lovely? And Joey had a hand in making the decorations too. All the schoolkids did.'

'Aw, Alice, that's a lovely touch and it's to raise money for the Christmas party and to buy a gift for each child . . . Eeh, look at that!'

Marg looked up to where Edith was pointing. A large bunch of mistletoe hung from the ceiling beam. 'Ha, we'd better watch out, Father Malley loves to grab a peck on the cheek at Christmas time, which is fine, but his breath always stinks of onions!'

Marg saw something different in Edith's face as she said this. She knew the Church and Father Malley meant a lot to her. She and Philip attended church every week, as did her Jackie, but then, she knew that was only because Harry did. She couldn't see anything in it herself and knew Alice didn't either.

Though she did believe, she just didn't think she needed to sit in a cold pew every Sunday morning for God to know that.

Not that she was friends with Him at the moment anyway, the way he sent trouble to their door every five minutes — or so it seemed.

'Right, let's get busy, girls. This is my stall and I've

15

a lot of bags to get through.'

'Eeh, Edith, where did all this come from?'

'It's collected from the posh lot. I even collected from Alice as she's one of them now.'

Alice gave Edith another playful slap. 'I'm not and I'll never be! Anyway, did you keep that blouse aside for yourself like I told you to, Edith? It was Gerald's ma's. She told me to do what I liked with what she left behind. She loved jumble sales and the like, so I give a few of her bits to anyone who comes around collecting for them.'

'I did. It's with a costume I like, but let's find them coats, shall we?'

These were easily located and Marg loved the one Edith had in mind for her. When she tried it on it fitted her a treat. It hung to her thighs, had a huge collar and was a wraparound to keep her snug. The colour — chocolate brown — was just right for her. Hugging it around her, she felt a million dollars, as she'd heard the stars say at the flicks. She did a twirl and snuggled the collar around her neck.

'Aw, Edith, I love it, but they'll never agree to a penny for it. Let's have a look at the one you think will be nice for Jackie and I'll spend me tuppence on that.'

She couldn't keep the disappointment out of her voice, but it helped to see the lovely dark-grey coat and know that it would be just right for Jackie. It had a sort of business-like look, and yet was fashionable too.

Alice asked, 'How much are they, Edith?'

'We're not allowed to price anything for ourselves, love.'

'Well then, take it off Marg and let me take them to who decides.'

Marg had a sneaky feeling that whatever the price, Alice would pay and then tell her the coats were just tuppence. Though torn about this, she so wanted them and didn't object.

Besides, this is how it was with the three of them: when the chips were down, the others propped them up.

But Edith didn't think Alice's idea a good one. 'I'll go, Alice. I'll take them to Maud, she's a good 'un. If you go, she'll know you can afford to pay over the odds. I'll tell her I'll bring the money to her at the end.'

Marg didn't miss the knowing look that passed between them and loved them for the little game they were playing.

As Edith left, Alice said they should get on with emptying some more of the bags, but Marg wasn't going to allow that. She felt worried at how peaky Alice looked.

'Not we. You sit on that chair and sort that bag out there, and I'll go through these.'

As she moved the chair Marg got a glimpse through the window. 'Eeh, it feels like Christmas already with how the ice is shining white on the pavements and clinging to the trees around the church, making lacy patterns out of the webs. And oh, this hall! Look, there's even a Christmas tree, though it ain't decorated yet. I'd love to decorate a tree, but we ain't afforded one for a good while.'

'Won't your da get you one?'

'Don't call him that, Alice, he ain't no da to me. I called him Uncle Eric all me life, and though I did call him Da when I first found out who he really was, I struggle to even say his name now after how he's treated us. Anyway, when it suited him he did buy us stuff at Christmas, but never a tree.'

'So, things are no better then? I know it were a shock to find out he was your da, but I thought with you knowing how he was duped by your ma that you'd accept him more.'

'No, he ain't been back to ours since Ma deceived him by telling him she had cancer when she didn't. Anyroad, I ain't bothered. His way of going on ain't mine, with his rackets and his money lending. Did you hear how he beat Mr Carson almost to death because he missed a payment? It was terrifying, all the street were out. Every time he kicked him he said, 'That's for the pint you had at dinner, and that's for the second one,' and so on, till Ada dashed over with her rolling pin and hit him. Then he stood and turned around, looking at everyone who'd gathered, and said, 'Let this be a lesson to you all. You pay your dues. You don't pee it up the wall after spending it on beer and gin!''

A shudder went through Marg as she remembered how Eric had turned to glare at her. His face had an evil expression as he spat at her,'And that includes you! You owe me, Marg.' His finger wagged at her.'And one day, you'll pay.'

'Are you all right, Marg? Look, I'll tell you what, you can decorate my tree, eh? I wouldn't manage it and the lads don't have a clue. Gerald said he'd try, but I think it needs a woman's touch. How about you do it on Christmas Eve while I help Edith prepare the veg and stuff the cockerel? You can do it just how you want.'

Marg made herself smile as she said, 'Ta. Eeh, I can't believe we have just eight days to go to Christmas

18

Day . . . Alice, one day, I'll repay you for everything.'

'To see that smile's payment enough, love. Anyroad, all I need is to know you're all right. You and Edith. If you are, then I am.'

'Hey, having a sneaky hug while I do all the bargaining, are you?'

They both laughed as they parted. Marg's spirits soared as Edith added, 'There you go, Marg. A penny three farthings, so you've a farthing left to spend, lass.'

She didn't say that she knew what had gone on. She just accepted it as them returning the love that she had for them both.

* * *

Early Monday morning had been busy for Marg and it wasn't yet seven. She fretted over how she'd be late for work again, and for the umpteenth time wondered how she'd hung on to her part-time job at Bradshaw's Biscuit Factory for so long, but she had to — her income and the little money Jackie earned working at Blake's accountants' office was all they had to survive on.

Jackie should be at college really; she was clever enough, and Marg had worked hard to afford tutors so that Jackie could continue her education in the evenings after school, which had resulted in her gaining her school certificate with honours. But the college education and university that Marg had dreamt of had eluded her — it had eluded most girls, but especially those from poor backgrounds.

Even the influence of her tutor hadn't been enough to open doors to a scholarship for Jackie, and Marg's dreams of her making a different life for herself didn't look like they'd ever be realised as she'd settled for a job that she loved, but led nowhere.

Marg sighed in frustration as she thought about how Alice's brother Harry had stood a better chance. He and Jackie had studied together in the evenings alongside Edith. Always a clever lad, but without the chance to shine in the past, he'd come along in leaps and bounds, but had seemed to throw it all away.

Instead of taking the college scholarship that Gerald had arranged for him, Harry had chosen to follow in his father's footsteps and work at the rock factory.

Not wanting to let her anger at this take hold, Marg concentrated on helping her ma to breathe.

For a long time now, she'd adopted the method she'd been taught by Ada Arkwright, who'd been a nurse in the Great War and lived across the road. Ada acted as nurse, doctor and midwife to those who lived in Whittaker Avenue and the surrounding area.

The method was to lean her ma face down over the side of the bed with a bowl under her, and massage her back to aid her in shifting the gunge from her lungs.

This had always helped, more so since Gerald had come into their lives and had given her a regular supply of medication to loosen her ma's chest.

'Eeh, Ma, don't give up. Bring it all out and you'll be better then.'

Ma gasped. The wheezing sound she made frightened Marg. 'Jackie, fetch Ada, will you, lass? Ask her to come in earlier for us.'

Jackie came in from the kitchen, her face ashen white. 'Ma? Ma!'

'Go on, lass. Ada'll soon fix her.'

As Jackie left, Gran came toddling through from the

front room, her long nightie clinging to her with the dampness of her having wet the bed again. Her toothless mouth was slack until she saw what was going on and then the life came back into her face.

'The only thing that'll fix her is Eric coming back. You should fetch him. And who are you? What are you doing, lass? Are you a nurse, eh?'

'It's me, Gran. Marg.' She chose not to comment on what Gran had said about Eric, and instead watched as her gran made her way to her chair by the fireplace, despite there not yet being a towel on it to protect it from her making it damp and smelly.

'I could do with a pot of tea, dear.'

Marg almost laughed. Gran hadn't a clue of the urgency of the situation. 'In a mo, love.'

Relief flooded Marg then as Jackie returned with Ada. But Ada's opening words worried her. 'I'm not a charity, you know, lass. You ain't paid me for last week yet. I've a mind to stop coming in at all.'

'No, Ada, please. We couldn't manage if I had to give me job up. I'm sorry, but the rent man insisted I paid him a bit more of what I owed him. I'll catch up with your payments, I promise.'

Jackie joined her plea to Marg's. 'Ada, please. I'm starting me evening job at the corner shop again soon, Mr Fairweather wants more hours than Marg can give him, so we'll manage your payment better then.'

'Well, all right, but this'll be a tanner extra. Now, let me look at you, Vera, lass. By, that chest of yours sounds bad today.'

Despite her meanness, Marg felt confident that Ada would never refuse to treat her ma. But if Ada decided she would no longer keep an eye on Ma and Gran each morning, Marg didn't know what she would do.

Despite Jackie's brave words, she'd already promised the rent man and the milk man, not to mention the tallyman, that they would have a bit above what she gave them out of the extra Jackie would bring in.

'Ada, I've got to go. I daren't be late again. Jackie, will you see to Gran, love? Will you have time before work?'

'Aye, don't worry. I've an hour and a half before I have to leave. You get off.'

As she made for the door, feeling like a coiled spring of anxiety, Marg was cheered a little as she heard Jackie say in a gentle voice, 'All right, Gran? I'll pour you a drop of tea, love, then I'll fill the tin bath and give you a nice soak. You'd like that, wouldn't you?'

A tear stung her eye as her beloved gran answered, 'Aye, me little lass, I would. And I'm glad that one's left. Why you let her in here when we've got Ada, I don't know.'

Before Marg could dwell on this, Edith came out of her house next door.

Edith becoming the new tenant after old Ethel had died suddenly a few months ago had so lifted Marg. Just to have one of her friends living near to her again filled her with joy. Though Marg knew that she'd never get used to old Ethel having gone. She'd been a one-off character who had many a time threatened her, Edith and Alice with having the piddle pot emptied over them if they didn't stop making a racket.

Marg sighed. There'd been good times despite everything — long summer evenings with her, Alice and Edith sitting on her step drinking cocoa and having a laugh till late at night.

Edith interrupted her thoughts. 'Morning, Marg, lass. Eeh, it's another freezing one. Hey, what's to do?

You're crying!'

'No, it's . . . well, you know. Life. Come on, let's get a move on, lass. The quicker I'm in the hustle and bustle of the factory, the better.'

'You haven't got your new coat on, love.'

'I couldn't wear that for work, could I? Ha, I'd be called all sorts. But I've got me thick jumper on so I'm warm enough.'

'Well, you've got a point there, it is a bit posh. It'll be nice for you when you go out on your walks with Clive, though.' Edith nudged her. 'He'll sit up and take notice then, lass.'

Marg ignored this. She knew it was the mission of Edith and Alice to set her up with Clive and they never missed a trick to hint about it.

When they reached Bradshaw's biscuit factory and clocked in, the usual banter started. Only lately, since it had been made public that Edith was engaged to the boss's son, some of it wasn't so nice. There was usually one who liked to have a dig.

'By, Miss Fancy Pants is still living hand-to-mouth and coming into work then? No rags-to-riches story for you like it was for Alice, is it, lass?'

Marg felt her temper rise. 'Edith ain't no Miss Fancy Pants, Ida. She lives in the same street as us and is the same lass you've always known. You should be pleased for her after all she's been through.'

'Well . . . I am, but better we keep our station in life than look down on them who can't rise.'

Edith, red in the face, went to defend herself. 'I never — ' But before she could finish her sentence, Mrs Robinson, the forewoman — or Moaning Minnie, as she was more commonly known — came teetering in on her too-high heels with her hair piled

23

high. The way she plastered her face with make-up, she looked for all the world as if she was going to make money on the streets rather than lord it over them all.

'None of that, Ida. Edith is the same girl we've always known and isn't about to change. Now, get yourselves to the line and hurry up or the biscuits will be dropping off the end.'

It was Phyllis who changed the atmosphere. Blowing fumes of stale alcohol, she said, 'Ida, you're a nasty bitch. You don't speak for us all. Besides, watch yourself, lass, Edith could be your boss one day and then you'd have to bring your head down from up your arse.'

Ida hurried away, giving a loud *humph* as she went.

When Edith had lived with her family across the road from Marg, Ida had been her next-door neighbour and friend, but that all changed when Ida tried to wheedle a few bits of Edith's furniture for nothing after the terrible tragedy had happened.

Knowing Edith was destitute, Marg had turned Ida away. She'd turned nasty with Edith and had been that way ever since. It made Marg's blood boil.

Linking arms with Edith, she told her, 'Don't mind them lot, Edith. You'll soon be out of here, lass.'

'I will if I pass me exam, Marg.'

'Aye, but you'll do that easily, love. It's just a pity you don't know what happened to your school certificate. Now you've to take the exam again. Can't you apply to somebody to see if it's on record?'

'Philip did say he'd look into it, but as I have to show it as proof of having gained it, I thought it better to take it again, just in case.'

'Well, you passed it once so it'll be no trouble to

pass it again. Mr Grimshaw will see to that. He got our Jackie through hers, so don't worry . . . But, aw, Edith, just fancy, you'll be a teacher one day and Philip's already one, when we all thought he'd remain here till he took over from his da. By, I'm proud of you.'

'Ta, love, but I won't be a teacher for a good while yet, if ever. There's a few stages and, well, I don't hold much to me chances, even though Philip thinks it will happen.'

'He must have some influence, but by, I bet it didn't go down well with his parents, him upping sticks and not following in their footsteps.'

'No, it didn't. His parents haven't forgiven him. To them it was a sudden decision, but Philip had been studying to take his final teaching certificate for a long time.'

'Well, good for him, it's his life.'

'Aye, but I can't fathom his parents. They don't approve of me, nor will they have anything to do with me, but they haven't sacked me . . . Eeh, they take the biscuit, how they can be like they are. After all, they were nobodies themselves who rose up in life.'

'Ha, well, they make biscuits, so they may as well take them an' all.'

They both giggled at this and for Marg the anguish of the morning lifted.

★ ★ ★

When the dinner gong sounded and the whirring of the machinery ground to a halt, Edith came with her to the cloakroom. 'I'll get me sarnies and come out with you, Marg. Have you got to get straight home, lass?'

25

'Aye, I have as Ada came in early. She'll charge me the earth if I keep her late an' all. I'll see you tonight and I'll have tea ready for you.'

'That'll be grand. But don't buy anything for tea; go into mine and you'll find a ham shank on me cold slab. It's big enough to feed us all.'

'Ta, Edith, I was wondering what I'd do, and here were me asking you to share in nothing — or 'nowt', as me gran would say. Eeh, she'll love a bit of boiled ham off the bone. I'll do some chips and egg with it. I've enough money to get half a dozen.'

'No, don't buy them, I've plenty. There's a farm next door to where Philip lives with his sister. You remember, he moved out when life became unbearable with his parents? Well, he gets cheap eggs now and he's always bringing me some so help yourself. Have you got some spuds?'

'I have. A sack full. Clive brought them round.'

'Ha, I thought boyfriends brought flowers, not spuds!'

'Or eggs?' Marg laughed with Edith. She didn't bother denying that Clive, the son of the owner of Barnes rock factory, and now a partner in the business himself, was her boyfriend. No one seemed to understand that a man and woman could be just friends. Oh, she knew that Clive wanted more from her, and was very patient, considering they'd been friends for over a year now. It wasn't that she didn't think a lot of him, but her life was too complicated for a proper relationship. They could never go out — well, not out in the sense of spending a night at the Tower or going to a café or to Leyton Institute for a drink. Though, on occasion, when Gran was in bed and Ma was comfortable, and Jackie, Harry and Edith were in

26

the house studying, they did go for walks together as opposed to just standing or sitting outside her house having a laugh and a natter.

Marg loved those walks and loved to hear Clive telling her about his little sons and his work, and how Harry was doing so well working for him, progressing through all the processes as if he'd been training for years.

Once, when Clive was telling her about his wife dying and the day of the accident in his factory, when Alice's da had saved him from a falling beam, he'd tried to hold her hand, but she'd snatched it away. She regretted that now, feeling sure that Clive had only been looking for comfort. She should have given it to him. He deserved that much from her. He was so good to her, bringing her gifts that would ease her situation a little.

Feeling a little guilty at the memory prompted Marg to promise to herself that next time they walked out, she'd link arms with Clive.

Edith nudged her. 'Are you daydreaming? I thought you had to hurry home.'

'Aye, I should go, love.'

'Well, if you can stay a mo, Marg, you could share me sandwiches, I made enough.'

'Eeh, ta, Edith, me belly feels as though me throat's been cut. But I'll have to eat it on the way, if that's all right.' Sensing there was more to Edith wanting to delay her, she added, 'Is anything wrong, Edith, lass?'

They were outside the factory door. This side entrance opened up onto Mansfield Road and Marg only had to cross over that, nip along to Talbot Road and then she was just a stone's throw from home.

'Well, not exactly, only me nerves. I can't stop thinking that I weren't cut out to be a teacher. Oh,

I've always wanted to be one, but will they accept me? They're all posh, aren't they?'

'Don't be daft, you'll get through this exam and then you can go on from there. Besides, I don't remember all of our teachers being posh; some spoke the same as we do. Don't give up, Edith. And if that's all that's worrying you, well . . . maybe if you learnt to talk like the posh ones, you know, like Philip and Gerald speak, you'd feel better.'

'Aye, one of our teachers did talk like us, and then tried to correct us. We used to giggle at that, but she did stop us saying 'knaw' and 'naw' for 'know' and 'no' and 'nowt' for nothing.'

'Aye, so I suppose me, you and Alice have a bit of a head start, as Jackie and Harry always use the Lancashire version. And knowing you, you'd soon learn the rest of the King's English.'

'I've thought about it and I've spoken to Philip too, but he laughs and says he loves me as I am and doesn't want me to change.'

'Aw, that's nice, but it don't give you the confidence you need.' Not able to resist the sandwich any longer, Marg bit into it. 'Mmm, these sarnies are delicious. I haven't tasted cheese in a long time.'

'Glad you like it, love. And you're right. I could learn, then just speak proper when I have to.'

'Aye, it won't be sarnies, but sandwiches, and no saying 'eeh'. Posh folk say,'oh'. So, not, 'Eeh, lass, it's a grand day and these sarnies are lovely,' but 'Oh, my dear, what a spiffing day it is and I am so enjoying these sandwiches."

Edith burst out laughing at Marg's exaggerated accent, spluttering breadcrumbs all over her. Marg pushed her. 'You dirty madam. You can't go around doing that either!'

They both laughed then, and Marg realised things weren't so bad.

As she walked home, what to do about presents for Christmas occupied her mind and she panicked to think how late she'd left it.

Mulling the problem over, it came to her that she could unravel one of her old cardigans. One was a lovely royal blue and hadn't faded at all. She could knit Jackie a woolly hat and mittens out of the wool as there'd be plenty for that. She was a fast knitter and loved doing it; she could have the hat done in an afternoon using four pins, and that would leave her four more afternoons to make the mittens. With Jackie at work, she wouldn't know anything about it.

The idea pleased Marg. *Eeh, I love giving surprises.*

Gran could do with some slippers, and Ma, some nice-smelling soap. Ma loved the smell of violets. Totting it up in her mind, she decided that she could get the slippers off the tallyman. Though she knew she shouldn't, she also knew he was always willing to give her a bit more credit, and the soap wouldn't be that much. What she'd do for Edith and Alice, she didn't know. They were bound to buy her something. Mind, they wouldn't expect anything from her.

This thought didn't settle her mind, though, and for the rest of her walk she battled with the problem. Then it came to her: there was that box of lace hankies Eric had bought her when she was younger; she'd never taken them out of the box. She could get Gran to embroider one with an 'E' and one with an 'A'. They'd love them.

They'll be something from me that'll stay with them forever.

29

Excitement warmed her as she walked the last few steps to home. For now, she had so much to look forward to and to busy herself with. It all made life seem a lot brighter than it had when she'd left for work that morning.

3

Edith

When Edith arrived home from work at six that evening, Philip's car was parked outside. She knew he would have let himself in. As she entered, he stood from where he'd been sitting on her sofa — the only comfy seating she had, which she'd bought from a second-hand shop.

Her front door, like Marg's and all the terraced houses in the street, opened into the living room. Edith's was sparsely furnished. Besides the sofa, there was a table and chairs and her precious footstool that had rested her late da's feet during all the years he was ill.

In the alcove next to the fireplace stood her bureau, the only other item she'd salvaged from her family home. Always scratched and damaged and used as a dumping ground in the past, Clive, who had an interest in carpentry, had done it up for her. Now it was a beautiful piece and housed all she needed for her studies.

With the downstairs freshly painted and her using the front room for a bedroom, all in all, it was a lovely little home for her, though she longed for the day she and Philip could marry. But many factors held them back — not least her need to recover from the awful tragedy of last year when her brother had caused the deaths of her parents and then taken his own life, leaving her lost and broken.

At first, she'd thought she'd done the wrong thing

31

moving just over the road from her old home, but she'd found comfort in watching the family that now lived there go about their normal, happy life, and she loved being back in her familiar neighbourhood living next door to Marg.

Philip held his arms open to her and she went into the loving feel of them.

'Heavy day, darling?'

'Aye. What about you, you look tired?'

His sigh told her all wasn't well. 'I stupidly went to see Mother. Father was out on business. I should listen to Patricia, but I can't break ties with them; they are my parents and I love them, for all their faults.'

Edith didn't say anything, she just put her hand up and touched his face.

'I got the usual from Mother — how could I do what I had done? That they'd had such hopes for me taking over the running of the biscuit factory, making a good marriage and making them proud. And then the punchline — how could I break their hearts like this? Becoming a teacher is demeaning. They worked their fingers to the bone getting where they are today and they've already had to endure Patricia marrying Wilf, a common carpenter — her words, not mine — when she could have married Derek Farrow, heir to the business empire that his father owns.'

Edith sighed. She'd heard this so many times, but she didn't say so. 'Eeh, Philip. How can they not see that your job is an honourable one? You teach languages at Rossall, a top private school, and one where you have to be very talented to be accepted as one of the masters.'

'I think my father does. He sometimes gives me a look, but he likes to keep the peace. Mother, though, sees teaching as 'beneath' me, something only the working class do.'

'Aw, Philip, you should do as Patricia does and ignore them — I don't mean cut them out of your life, they're your parents, but, well, take what they say with a pinch of salt and don't let it upset you so much.'

'I know. Lodging with Patricia and Wilf, I get preached that on a regular basis.'

'Well, you should take note. Anyroad, love, I'm so glad you're here. Marg's getting tea — I mean, dinner — ready. It's ham on the bone with chips and egg; I'll just nip round to hers and tell her to do an extra egg. There's plenty of ham, and I know she always does a mountain of chips and ends up giving them to the kids in the street in a piece of newspaper — she's like a regular chip shop at times.'

Philip grinned and Edith thought how handsome he was with his dark hair tamed by Brylcreem and his neat moustache. For the umpteenth time she marvelled that he loved her. Her voice sounded croaky to herself as she told him, 'When I get back, I'll have a quick wash and change as I smell of biscuits and must look awful.'

Philip kissed her hair. 'You're beautiful, Edith. You could never look awful.'

She pushed him away playfully. 'You're biased! I'll be back in a mo, then I'll get you a pot of tea.'

'Ha, I'll never get used to you calling a cup of tea a pot. But no, I'll get a glass of water, thanks.'

Edith smiled, but couldn't help but feel stung by his words. She hated any reference to the yawning gap in their social positions. She accepted it, but it still unnerved her. So far she hadn't had to mix with his colleagues at the posh school, but she dreaded doing so. She loved his sister Patricia, and felt totally accepted by her and her husband, Wilf. And their girls, Sophie and Eliza, were adorable. Not that she saw much of them, as they were away at boarding school, and during school holidays seemed to be involved in so many activities that took them away from home.

I just don't ever want to let Philip down.

Sighing, she thought again about taking elocution lessons, as she knew it was mainly the way she spoke that caused her to be looked down upon.

As she opened the door, Philip said, 'Darling, dinner won't be too long, will it? Only, I thought we'd go to the church. You remember Father Malley asked for volunteers to help put the crib up and gather some holly to decorate the church? I've got a back seat full of it from the farm next door, and dripping with berries too.'

'Eeh, that'd be grand, I had thought about it. But them berries don't bode well. You know what they say — laden berries mean a harsh winter as nature's making sure there's food for her birds.'

'Well, it's promising that already. I can't remember it ever being so cold in December. It's like March weather.'

★ ★ ★

As Edith opened the door to Marg's, the delicious smell of the ham cooking wafted over. Marg was busy unravelling a jumper. She was winding the wool around the back of a kitchen chair as she undid it row by row. Gentle snores came from her ma, who looked so peaceful in the bed Marg had brought down for her.

Though convenient for Vera's needs, the room now looked crowded as their huge sofa stood in front of the bed, with Gran's rocking chair to the side of the hearth. Added to this was a sideboard under the window and a table and chairs on the opposite wall. But the room hadn't lost that cosy feel it always had, and felt warm with a roaring fire dancing up the chimney.

'Hello, Edith. Eeh, come in quick and shut the door, it's enough to freeze your lugs off.'

'You look busy, Marg.'

'I am and I ain't got tea done yet, sorry. I got engrossed in this. I've only to cook the chips and fry the eggs. I saw Philip's car so I've done extra — I take it he ain't eaten yet?'

'No, and you've read me mind, he does want some. But don't worry about the time, I've to get washed and changed yet . . . Only, I'd like to fetch ours and have it at home if that's all right with you? I'll bring me plates so I don't have to return them.'

'That's fine, love. I want to get on with this as I can only do it when Jackie's out. She's going to tea at Alice's after work, so I'll be glad not to have the pair of them under me feet and holding me up.'

'Ha, that's a nice way of putting it. What are you up to then?'

Before Marg could finish telling her, her gran came shuffling into the living room.

'Hello, Edith, love. I saw you coming from Ethel's the other day. Is she all right? I ain't seen her for a while.'

This caught Edith off guard for a moment. She picked her words carefully, not wanting to upset Gran by reminding her Ethel had long since died. 'I live there now, Gran. Ethel isn't living there any longer.'

'But she never said goodbye.' Gran's lips quivered.

Marg jumped in. 'I've all your embroidery silks out, Gran. You remember, you said you'd do a special job for me?'

'Aye. An 'E' on one hanky and an 'A' on the other.'

'Gran! It's meant to be a secret!'

Edith laughed at this and winked at Marg. 'I'll see you in a bit, love.'

Philip was curious as to why she was giggling when she came in, but she batted his question away. 'I'll tell you over tea, love. I need to wash and brush up.'

* * *

When they pulled up outside the church, light beamed from every window and the outer door stood open. Their breath made misty clouds as they alighted and unloaded the prickly holly.

Inside was a hive of activity and a lovely atmosphere as those involved in unpacking the crib giggled together, and men up ladders shouted down for what they needed.

Father Malley came hurrying towards them, his long frock billowing behind him. 'Ah, it is yourselves, and how welcome you are. Though it is that your mother has got here before you, Philip. Come, come, unburden your armfuls of the lovely holly it is you've brought.'

Edith gasped. Since the rift, she and Philip had avoided going to the early mass his mother favoured and hadn't thought she would be here because she hadn't mentioned it to him earlier.

Father Malley knew about the situation, but like all priests, believed that some divine intervention would

36

one day mend everything that was wrong in the world.

'Susan! Philip and Edith have arrived.' He clapped his hands as if announcing a gleeful event, but he may as well have told them the devil had walked into the church, as the atmosphere died and a silence fell upon the room. Philip's ma stood glaring at them, her face like thunder.

Recovering, she sniffed. 'Well, get on, ladies, it's not a side show . . .'

Coming towards them, Mrs Bradshaw seemed to sing each syllable of Philip's name, and when she reached them she said in a false-sounding voice, 'How nice to see you, my dear.'

Seeming to ignore Edith's presence, she linked arms with Philip and tried to drag him away.

Philip was having none of it. 'Mother, this is Edith.'

Mrs Bradshaw hissed, 'I know who she is! How dare you embarrass me like this? Kindly follow me and don't make a scene!'

Philip disengaged his arm and turned towards Edith. 'Oh, look, there's a spare ladder, darling. Let's grab it and start putting our holly up.'

Red in the face, Mrs Bradshaw came back with, 'Well!' Then took a deep breath. 'I'll have some of that holly, dear, we need it to go with the laurel around the crib. It's lovely. Clever you, darling. Will you bring it up to the altar for me?'

'No, I'll leave it here, Mother. You take what you need when you need it. Come on, Edith, darling, we've work to do.'

Though Edith was grateful to Philip for sticking by her, she hated to see the effect this rebuff had on his mother. She seemed at a loss, as if something precious was slipping away from her. Edith didn't miss the tear that sprung to her eye. If she hadn't been so afraid of how the woman would react, she'd have tried to smooth things over. But she found herself tongue-tied and glad when Philip took her hand and guided her away.

It was when Edith went to retrieve more holly and became distracted by a little boy humming a tune while running a stick along the ends of the pews that she came across Mrs Bradshaw again. Edith hadn't seen her approaching and only registered her when her voice silenced everyone, 'Do stop that child, he's getting on my nerves!'

The boy's mother came and grabbed his arm, but defiantly he said, 'I don't have to do what she says, she's an old witch, Ma. You told me she don't even like her own kids!'

This seemed to undo Mrs Bradshaw. Her mouth quivered and her hands shook.

The boy's mother grabbed him and walked away, leaving Edith face to face with Mrs Bradshaw. Without thinking, Edith said, 'I . . . I'm sorry, you know what kids are like. Don't take it to heart.'

Expecting a rebuff and wishing she'd simply turned away, Edith held her breath. But Mrs Bradshaw surprised her by nodding her head.

Edith turned to go back to Philip, but as she did she caught sight of the beautiful arrangement Mrs Bradshaw was creating. 'Eeh, that's grand.'

Mrs Bradshaw stiffened. 'For one, there's no such word as 'eeh', and for another, 'grand' isn't what you call something that's small and lovely.'

Edith felt enraged. How dare this woman put her down? 'To folk from Blackpool, it's grand, and the biggest compliment I could pay you. Don't be so rude!'

Mrs Bradshaw swivelled round as if on a turntable, and Edith feared her reaction, but the woman just laughed. 'Well, you've got spirit, I'll give you that . . .' Her voice softened. 'Thank you. I love to work with flowers and greenery.'

Edith smiled. 'The red bow really sets it off; makes it Christmassy. I love Christmas.'

Mrs Bradshaw sighed. 'I used to. Now, I'm looking forward to a very quiet one, because my children . . . Oh, I mean . . . well, you know what's gone on.' Mrs Bradshaw looked around her to check if anyone was listening, but most had gone, leaving only men who weren't interested in their conversation.

'Yes . . . but . . . well, it needn't be like this. I — I mean, Philip . . . he's hurting. He misses you.'

Her face changed. The vulnerability Edith had seen before crept back into her stance as she visibly fought for control. Edith so wanted to reach out to her. 'Eeh, lass, shall we sit down a mo?'

Mrs Bradshaw went to protest, but then with a defeated gesture nodded her head.

When they sat down, Mrs Bradshaw didn't speak for a moment. Edith wondered whether Philip could see them and what his reaction would be, but instead of looking for him she just sat waiting, not wanting to disturb the tentative peace between them.

'I — I only want the best for them.'

'It's all any mother wants, but sometimes mothers don't see things the way their kids do.'

'You've got a level head on your shoulders . . . Edith, isn't it?'

'Aye. Well, I've had to be everything to me family since being little — well, after me da became ill, that is.'

Mrs Bradshaw coughed. 'I heard about . . . well, it was a terrible scandal . . . I mean . . . well, I worried . . . I couldn't see how my Philip could be mixed up in such a thing. I never dreamt he'd ever be dragged that low.'

Anger rose in Edith once more. 'Philip wasn't dragged. He willingly helped me because he loves me and he doesn't look down on folk in trouble. My pain was his, and whatever you think of my family, they were mine and I loved them. Me da was a good man, he could wipe the floor with jumped-up folk like . . . Well, him grafting down the mine to keep the likes of you supplied with coal ruined his health, but even when he saw the signs he kept going, to provide for his family.'

Tears were streaming down Edith's face. At that moment she hated Philip's mother and could gladly have smacked her. How she'd given birth to such lovely children as Philip and Patricia she'd never know — but how she'd even condescended to lie on her back to conceive them was an even bigger mystery.

This thought made her blush, but then giggle at the absurdity of it.

'You're laughing! Are you mad?'

Edith wiped her face. 'Yes, mad at you for being so . . . so bloody stuck up!'

Mrs Bradshaw astonished her then by bursting out laughing. 'I like you. You say it how it is. I like that . . . Yes, you're right. I am, aren't I?'

Edith nodded. 'And it's pushing your family away, bit by bit. It's breaking their hearts, but they can't give up the ones they love. And you shouldn't ask it of them.'

That look came on Mrs Bradshaw's face again and

Edith worried she'd gone too far. 'I'm sorry if I've overstepped the mark. I don't usually do that. Me nature's to be more diplomatic, but —'

'I got your goat? No, don't apologise.' She sighed a huge sigh. 'You're right and I'm realising that I might be wrong, but it's difficult. I can't change just like that, and I worked so hard to make a better life for my children than what I had. It feels as though they are throwing it in my face.'

Edith felt exasperated that Philip's mother still didn't understand the problem, and was about to say so when Mrs Bradshaw said, 'But I can try. I'll extend an olive branch to Patricia to see if she will bring her family to mine on Christmas Day. Would you and Philip come too?'

Edith noticed that Mrs Bradshaw hadn't mentioned inviting Wilf as well as Patricia, as if she still struggled to acknowledge him, but she decided to ignore it. Change takes time.

'Ta for asking, and we would have liked to come, but we can't, we've already committed to going to me friend Alice's.'

'The one who married a doctor? You girls from Whittaker Avenue do think you're —'

Edith felt emboldened now and determined not to let this pass. 'Mrs Bradshaw, you have no right —'

'Susan. Call me Susan, or Sue, which I prefer, and yes, you're right. I told you it wasn't going to be easy . . . I'm me, and I may always say things that upset you. You'll just have to be patient and let me know when I go wrong.'

It was Edith's turn to sigh. She wondered if Susan would ever change.

'Well, dear, how about Boxing Day? Could you

come then?'

'Yes, that'd be grand, ta.'

'And would you help me to get Patricia there? I . . . I shouldn't ask you . . . but well, I — I don't know if she will come if I ask.'

'Ask what?' Both Edith and Mrs Bradshaw were surprised to see Philip appear, as if from nowhere. 'I'm sorry to butt in. I tried not to, but you've been talking a good ten minutes now and my curiosity got the better of me.'

'Ha, it always did.' Sue stood and put her arms out to Philip. He looked bemused, but he held her close as he watched Edith, his face asking, *What's going on?*

'I'm sorry, Philip, I've a lot to make up to you . . . Oh, here's your father — I'll leave Edith to tell you all about it.'

Philip's father stood with his mouth open at their interaction. Philip turned and went to him. 'Hello, Dad. I don't know what's going on, but I think there may be changes in the air.'

As the two shook hands, Philip's father shocked Edith by saying, 'About time, lad. Well, that'd be grand.'

At this, Sue tutted and told him, 'I won't stand for you talking like that and you know it!'

'Meet Edith, Dad,' Philip said in haste, and Edith could tell he was used to batting away any signs of trouble.

'Pleased to meet you, my dear, more than pleased.'

Edith couldn't believe she was shaking hands with her boss, or that she would be going to his house for dinner on Boxing Day. How she'd cope with that she didn't know, but all that mattered was the adoring look on Philip's face.

At that moment, Father Malley appeared — a welcome interruption. 'Well, well. The Lord works in mysterious ways. I'm happy to see you all together like this — it's going to be a merry Christmas for sure.'

But Edith wasn't so sure that it had all come right. Somehow, she felt that Susan had a second agenda and she wondered when that would show.

* * *

Christmas Day had been all they dreamt it would be. Alice's lovely home filled with love, laughter, squeals of delight and carol singing, all around the beautiful tree that Marg had dressed.

Gran had made them laugh with some dubious versions of old music hall songs, and even Marg's ma had been well for most of the day, though she did tire quickly and had slept on the sofa in another room for a time.

Everyone loved their presents. Edith had winked at Marg when she'd presented her with the little parcel, and then gasped in wonder at the intricate embroidery around her initial. 'I'll treasure it forever, love, ta ever so much.'

Alice had loved hers too. She'd bought her and Marg a lovely filigree brooch — Edith's depicted a little church and Marg's a tree. And they'd both loved the violet soap and talc sets that she had bought for them, though Marg had giggled as it was similar to the soap she'd bought for her ma. Gran did very well, with everyone getting her a little something too, her favourite being the pink housecoat from Alice. She'd put it on over her frock and not taken it off again.

Boxing Day, however, started with a strained

atmosphere.

Edith had been astonished by the size of Philip's parents' house, which was situated between Blackpool and Lytham St Anne's. Though large, it had a welcoming exterior as its whitewashed walls reflected the bright winter sun and pretty lace curtains hung at the leaded windows.

The door opened when they alighted from the car. Sue came running out and hugged them both. 'Come on in, my dears. Father is in the conservatory. You're early, which is inconvenient of you, but no matter.'

Edith wondered if everything Sue said would always have a sting in the tail. She also felt underdressed, looking at Sue in her lovely grey satin frock that was almost a gown with how it flowed around her ankles, whilst Edith had chosen to wear a costume in a similar grey that she'd bought at the Christmas fayre and had matched it with a dark blue blouse. But this feeling of not having dressed correctly left her when Patricia arrived as, thankfully, she too wore a costume that wasn't dissimilar.

It was the girls who relaxed them all as they threw themselves at their grandparents, telling them how they'd missed them and going into an excited frenzy over the mountain of presents that awaited them.

'She has to do better than anyone.'

This whisper from Patricia made Edith blush as she was sure it had carried to Sue's ears, but Philip's father coughed and said, 'How about a nice glass of sherry before lunch, eh?' and the moment passed.

How Edith got through the day, she didn't know. By the evening, with Patricia moaning things in her ear, and Sue cajoling them into playing games she'd never heard of, she had a roaring headache and just

44

wanted to escape.

'I'm sorry, darling, that was an ordeal, wasn't it? But maybe if we keep trying, it will all come right.'

They were sitting in Philip's car outside her home. She sighed. 'No, we won't give up.'

Though she said this, she knew it would be a long road to travel and didn't really relish the journey. She couldn't see Susan making much of an effort but could see her returning to her old ways and spoiling everything again.

But then, she was Philip's mother and it made him happy to be on a good footing with her and to imagine that all was well between herself and Susan, so, for that reason, Edith determined she wouldn't give up trying.

She looked at Philip and an overwhelming love for him filled her. He was worth it. Sliding nearer to him, Edith put her head back, offering her lips. His kiss took away all the frustrations of the day, and she knew with him by her side she could get through any-thing — even survive days with his mother.

4

Alice

Alice stood by the sink rinsing the cups, thinking back on the wonderful Christmas Day and the lovely family Boxing Day. She wished it wasn't all over. But normal life was resuming, with Gerald back at work in an hour for the night shift.

She sighed as she reached for the tea towel, wishing their time together could be longer, when a sudden sharp pain shot across her back, forcing her to clutch the edge of the sink to stay upright.

'Are you all right, darling?' Gerald's arms came around her from behind, his hands travelling to her stomach. 'Now, little one, I love you very much, but you're to stop giving Mummy trouble.'

Alice turned into his arms, needing his support, but not wanting to worry him.

He smiled down at her. 'I have more trouble holding you close this way round, darling. Our little one gets in the way.'

'I know. But I like to look into your eyes as you hold me.' As she did, she told him, 'Eeh, I wish you didn't have to go to work, love. It's lonely during the night without you.'

'I know, my darling. But you can think about last night when I snuggled behind you and you were the bus driver.'

Alice burst out laughing. This was a joke between them, referencing her lying on her side with her knees up as he cuddled up to her. The first time it happened, just after they married, Gerald had said, 'So, where are we going then, and can I have a ticket, please?'

She hadn't cottoned on. 'Where are we going? What are you on about?'

'Well, you're the bus driver, aren't you?'

They'd giggled so much that Alice's sides had ached, and they'd ended up making love. The joke had stuck between them, and it was how they often lay, always with the same outcome — Gerald taking her to a place she'd never dreamt of, with feelings assailing her body that took her to another world.

Even now, as heavily pregnant as she was, they made gentle love that way. The thought of this sent a delicious shiver through her. 'Mmm, I can't wait for babby to be born so we can get back to normal.'

His lips kissed her nose. 'Neither can I, my darling love.'

★ ★ ★

The night felt hot and sticky to Alice — she still wasn't used to the central heating that Gerald insisted remained on low to keep them all warm. It was the early hours before she finally dropped off, only to be woken by an intense pain.

Drawing up her knees, Alice thought for a moment that she had cramp, but as she woke fully she became aware of a damp feeling between her legs. A fear gripped her as another, even fiercer pain, assailed her. Her involuntary cry echoed around the still house.

Gasping as the pain clutched her again, Alice switched on the bedside lamp and threw back the covers. In the beam of light splashing across her bed she saw the horror of a bloodied patch standing out against the white sheet.

'No, no, please, God, no!'

Her heart thudded. Panic gripped her as she realised she might lose her precious child.

I can't have my babby now, I can't! It's too early . . . Oh God!

Her thoughts went to how tired she'd been this past week, and the pain she'd felt earlier. Gerald had reassured her that it was all normal with pregnancy; that the weight of the baby often caused a strain on the mother's back. He'd told her not to worry.

'You're a natural mother, darling. Our plans to have lots of babies are well on schedule.'

She'd laughed at him, hit him with the tea towel she'd held and told him she wasn't going through this lots of times, but would consider two or three at the most. But now . . .

No, this can't be happening to me! It can't! My babby, my babby!

It seemed to Alice that their dreams for their child were being ripped to shreds as a pain far worse than the others brought a scream from her, and the certain knowledge that her baby was coming too early.

The bedroom door flung open before her scream died.

Harry stood staring at her. 'Alice, what's to do, eh?'

'Help me, Harry.'

He was by her side in a flash, his face showing the horror at the state she was in. 'What's happening? Shall I get Gerald?'

'Yes, yes, hurry, lad! Run downstairs and telephone the hospital . . . Ooh, no, stay with me . . . *ahh* . . .'

Billy appeared at the open door. 'What's all the

48

noise? It's only six o'clock . . . Eeh, sis, what's to do?'

Harry, his voice steady but firm, answered him. 'Run downstairs and ring the hospital, Billy. Get hold of Gerald and tell him . . . tell him to come home quickly, Alice is having the babby.'

'Aw, Alice . . .'

'Go, Billy! Hurry. Alice needs help, lad.'

Billy was usually the brother Alice could rely on, while Harry tended to be shy and unsure of himself, but the tables had turned now as Billy stood gaping at her.

'Billy, go, please, lad.' Alice gasped out the words. 'Me babby's too early! We've got to do something.'

But as Billy disappeared, Alice knew there was nothing that could be done. Her stomach crunched into a knot of pain that was unbearable, forcing her to screw up her face and strain with all her might. The release of what felt like a huge ball stopped the pain but filled her with anguish.

'Me babby! Eeh, Harry, save me babby!'

Harry dropped her hand, grabbed the counterpane from where it had fallen on the floor and threw it over the bottom half of her.

'Me babby! Aw, Harry, check to see if me babby's breathing. Clear its mouth, Harry, hurry.'

At this command, Harry seemed to regain his wits. He pulled back the cover. 'It . . . it's moving, Alice . . . and it's still attached to you . . . Eeh, Alice, it's a boy.'

The gasp Alice took compounded her agony. 'Hand him to me, Harry. I want me son.'

Shocked at the sight of the little mite, not much bigger than Harry's hand, Alice felt suspended in time. She took her son and held him to her, careful of

49

the cord still attached. A small whimper came from his bow-shaped mouth. 'He's alive! Harry, he's alive! Fetch towels from the bathroom, and bring me warm water, quickly!'

Wrapping the tiny form in one of the soft, white towels he brought, Alice used the second one to dip into the water that Harry held for her. Gently, she bathed the beloved, tiny face, wiping out his mouth and cleaning his nostrils, both of which seemed clogged with blood. Her son didn't stir.

'He's warming up. We can save him, Harry, we can! Look at him, he's perfect, so tiny, but perfect.'

Harry didn't speak as he placed his hand on the baby. His thumb stroked the tiny head. 'He's lovely, Alice, so tiny. Will he be all right?'

'He has to be, Harry. He has to be.'

'While there's life there's hope, as Jackie's gran's always saying.'

'Please God she is right this time, lad . . . Eeh, where's Billy? Did he make that phone call?'

'I'll go and check.'

When Harry came back, he had Joey in tow. Joey, like all of her brothers, showed a maturity much older than his nine years. But then, life had dragged them up through poverty, brutality and sadness.

'It seems Billy couldn't get through, Alice, and so ran out telling Joey he was going to fetch Gerald.'

'Oh, thank God!'

'Are you all right, Alice?' Joey asked, looking as though it was an effort for him to show a brave face.

'Aye, come on in and see your nephew. He's very tiny.'

'Eeh, Alice, me kitten's bigger than him, but he's lovely. Will he make it?'

Harry nudged Joey.

'I — I mean, he's going to be all right, ain't he?'

'He is, Joey. He is!'

Though her voice sounded determined, inside Alice's hope was fading as her child laboured to breathe.

'Alice . . . you knaw . . . well . . . Father Malley preached on baptism a few Sundays ago. He said that if a child was born who . . . well . . . he said anyone can perform a baptism and it would be valid — babby would go straight to heaven . . . not that limbo place.'

These words of Harry's seemed to confirm Alice's worst fears. She didn't want there to be, but knew there was truth in them — her babby could die. She cried out against this thought, 'No . . . no . . . he ain't going to die, Harry!'

Harry put his hand on her hair and stroked it. 'I knaw, but wouldn't you feel bad if he did and we hadn't given him this chance?'

Alice felt her head nodding.

'I'll do it, Alice. I can use this water you washed him in. What's his name?'

As the tears rolled down her face, Alice told Harry, 'Gerald Harry William Joseph, after the four best men I know: me husband and you three, me lovely brothers.'

Harry dipped his fingers in the water and let a drop fall onto little Gerald's head. His voice shook as he said, 'I baptise you, Gerald Harry William Joseph, in the Lord's name. In the name of the father, the son and the Holy Ghost.'

Both Alice and Joey made the sign of the cross. All three were crying silent tears.

Alice didn't react to the sound of feet on the stairs, nor could she look away from her baby when Gerald appeared in the doorway.

'Alice! Alice, my darling.'

He came and stood by the bed and went to lift the baby from her.

'No!'

'Alice . . . The baby . . . our baby . . . he's gone.'

'No! No, no, no!'

'All right, darling.' He turned to Harry. 'I need to examine Alice; just wait outside the door a moment, lads. Alice, I have my bag with me, I'll just take a look at you and see that everything has come away.'

His gasp told her all wasn't well. 'I'm cutting the cord, darling, don't worry.' When he straightened and took off his bloodied gloves, his eyes were full of concern. 'Let me take him, darling, you need urgent help.'

The glistening tears running down Gerald's face told her that this was really happening. She handed their child to him.

Alice watched him snuggle their baby in his arms, then, his voice shaking with emotion, he called Harry in and gently handed little Gerald over. 'Put him in his cot, Harry, make him comfortable . . . Alice, my darling, there's an ambulance outside, we have to get you to hospital. I won't leave you . . . I — I . . . Oh, Alice.' He dropped on his haunches next to her and put his arms around her. His body shook with sobs, but Alice couldn't feel anything.

All her feelings seemed to have closed down.

5

Marg

Marg stood with Edith outside the factory, her shift over for the day. They kept as close as they could to the wall to keep warm and avoid the bitter wind.

'Eeh, these sarnies are good, love. Ta for bringing enough for me again. The leftovers Alice gave me from Christmas Day were eaten up yesterday for Boxing Day, though I've left enough of the cockerel for Jackie to make into a stew, so we're in for a treat tonight. What Jackie can do with a few bits and bobs is good enough for a restaurant.'

'You didn't tell me, did you have a good Boxing Day?'

'Aye, we did, lass, it was really peaceful. Gran and Ma were exhausted from Christmas, but Clive called in for an hour and we went for a walk, then Ma and Gran managed a glass of sherry in the evening and a cosy game of cards around the fire.'

'Better than mine then. I'll tell you sometime, love.'

'Well, you spent it with folk who are so far up their backsides they can't enjoy a bit of fun. Anyroad, love, I've been worrying about Alice since Christmas Day; should she have such severe backache? And look how she was when we went out for our chips . . . Only I was wondering, will you and Philip go round tonight to see how she is?'

Edith went to answer, but suddenly she stared across the road. Marg looked in the same direction and was just as surprised to see Harry turn off Devonshire Road on his bike and almost skid to a halt as he shouted, his tone full of anguish, 'Edith, Marg, can you come out to me?'

They both rushed to him.

'Harry! Eeh, lad, what's to do? You've been . . . well, I mean, you look distressed, lad.'

'I am, Edith. And aye, I've been crying . . . It's Alice . . . She . . . she's lost the babby . . . He was born . . . but he died, and Alice is . . . she's bad.'

'What? No! Eeh, Harry, lad, tell us it's not true. Where is she? What happened?' A tear plopped onto Harry's cheek and Marg felt her own eyes well up.

Edith, always good in a crisis, managed to stay calm. 'Take your time, Harry. Tell us what happened, but take a few breaths first, lad.'

As they listened, Marg felt her heart would break. Not only had Alice lost the baby, but she was in hospital suffering from complications.

'Gerald said Alice lost a lot of blood . . . I — I saw it . . . I thought she was going to die . . . He said the hospital will make her right, but I'm scared. He . . . Gerald came back before I went to work this morning and told us that Alice was a bit better, but that she might have to have an operation . . . But I knaw no matter what, Alice'll never get over her babby dying. She so wanted him . . . and . . . he was so beautiful . . . but he's dead!'

Harry was sobbing now. Marg put her arms around him, heedless of his snotty nose, and held him close. 'Alice'll be right, Harry. She's a strong person. She'll come to terms with this in time. I promise you. How was Gerald?'

'He . . . he was trying to be brave, but I could see he

54

wasn't. I could see he was frightened and that's what scared me the most. If a doctor can be scared and upset, then it must be really bad for Alice.'

'No. Don't look on it like that,' Edith told him. 'Remember, Gerald isn't just a doctor, love. He's a husband who had been looking forward to being a daddy. And he's a big brother to you, Billy and Joey. You have to be there for him as that person and not always think of him as a doctor who can cope with anything. Gerald will be heartbroken and he will need you, Harry. You and your brothers have to care for him, and for Alice when she comes home.'

'I never thought of that, Edith. Billy and Joey were being a pain. Billy wouldn't go to school and then Joey followed his lead, so I left them and went to work . . . I had naw choice, but I'm on me dinner break now.'

'Course you had a choice, lad. Clive would never demand you went into work when you're under such stress. Have you told him what happened?'

'Aye, and he said I needn't go back this afternoon, Marg, but — '

'Then don't, lad. Go back home, take care of your brothers and help Gerald if he's at home an' all.'

'I would rather do that, but I thought I had to go to work at all costs.'

Edith patted his back. 'Good lad. And no, not at all costs, Harry. Look, you get home. As Clive knows what's happened, he'll understand, or you can telephone him.'

Marg nodded her head at this. 'You've no need to worry about your job, lad, Clive's very understanding. Do as Edith says and I'll send Jackie round to yours as she's off work today. She'll help you sort dinner and anything else you need. And, Harry, send Billy or

55

Joey around to tell me what's happening as soon as you know more. I'd go up to the Vic, but I'm best to get home and let Jackie come to help you.'

'Aye, I will. And ta, I'll feel better if Jackie's with me. See you later.'

When he'd gone, Edith turned to Marg. 'Eeh, Marg.'

Marg went into Edith's arms and they hugged — their cure-all and all they had.

'I'll see if Moaning Minnie'll let me off a bit early. She might do when she hears what's happened. You go home, Marg, and send Jackie to Harry like you said, love. I'll come to yours as soon as I get away.'

Marg set off for home feeling as though someone had filled her shoes with lead. Her face tingled as the wind whipped her tears, but she couldn't stop them flowing.

Why? Why?

When she got in, she felt no cheer from the warm glow of the fire, or the lovely smell coming from the kitchen. Jackie stood to greet her, but her smiling expression changed to one of concern as she asked, 'Is everything all right, Marg, love?'

'No . . . it's Alice. Let me sit down a mo, lass.'

'Alice?'

'Aye. Is that tea in the pot hot?'

Jackie crossed to the table where she had a teapot and mugs laid out. 'It is, Marg, I just made it. I knew you'd be in any minute so it's nicely brewed.'

'Pour me one, love, then I'll tell you. I need to thaw out a bit . . . Hello, Ma.' She went to greet Gran too, but saw she was asleep.

'What's to do, love? Come and get warm, lass, then tell us what's gone on.'

56

Ma looked rosy-cheeked. She sat up against her mound of pillows, her hair, which frizzed in the same way as hers and Jackie's did, neatly combed. Marg kissed her cheek. Ma caught her hand and rubbed it. 'By, you are cold, lass.'

Marg's smile at this didn't reach her frozen heart.

As she moved towards the fire, Gran snored and then woke. Her body shuddered, making her chair rock. The shock of this showed in Gran's expression, but that changed as she looked at Marg. 'Eeh, lass, you've come to see me, where've you been?'

'At work, Gran.'

Gran held her arms out. This was so unexpected that Marg broke down. She sobbed in her gran's arms as she told them what had happened to Alice.

Gran patted her back. If she wasn't deep in sorrow, Marg would treasure this moment. Lately, Gran had forgotten her, but this was the woman she adored and who adored her.

Jackie broke the silence. 'The babby's dead?'

Marg got up. 'Aye. Alice had him prematurely during the night.' The words brought the horror of it all to the surface. She swallowed hard. 'When we've had our tea will you go round to Alice's and help Harry with the lads, Jackie?'

Jackie stared at her and nodded her head, but she didn't speak.

A sob from behind her made Marg turn towards Gran. 'It'll be all right, Gran. Don't fret, love.'

'Naw it won't, it'll never be right, Marg.'

Part of Marg felt pleased that Gran still knew her, but this was overshadowed by Gran's grief. She looked towards her ma. Ma shook her head, then said to Gran, 'Come on, Ma, we can't alter owt. Marg'll

57

get you a drop of sherry to have with your tea, how will that be, eh?'

'I'd like that, Vera, lass.'

Marg rose and went to the sideboard.

'I could do with one as well, Marg, love.'

'Ha! Always could!'

This from Gran made Marg hurry along as she didn't want them at each other's throats. 'Well, I'll join you both. It might settle me nerves.'

'I'll leave you to it. I'll see that Billy comes with any news, Marg.' Jackie was already putting her coat on. She swished the lovely blue scarf around her neck. 'Ta for this again, Marg. I love it and it's like you've got your arms around me when I wear it.'

'I have, Jackie, lass. Always did have and always will. Now, put your mitts on an' all, it's cold out there.'

Jackie grinned. 'You'll always mother me, no matter what — even though I'm at work now . . . Eeh, Marg, never stop, though.'

Ma piped in, 'Naw, lass, never stop taking care of me Jackie.'

'I won't, Ma. I'll take care of you all for a long time yet. Now, don't get all maudlin. Here, drink your sherry, and you get off, Jackie.'

With the sipping of the sherry, a calm descended. But then, just as Marg never thought she'd laugh again, a loud noise came from Gran.

'Better out than in, love.' Gran's lips smacked together in a satisfied way before her face broke into a grin.

Marg couldn't help but laugh out loud. Ma joined her and Gran sat with a pleased look on her face. 'Sorrows come and sorrows go, but if we can laugh, we'll win through no matter what.'

Full of wisdom, this from Gran rang true, and yet, Marg wondered if she'd ever see Alice laugh again.

6

Edith

Edith was never so glad as to see Philip's car outside her house when she came home at just after four that evening.

His face held surprise as she opened the door. 'Are you all right, darling? You're home early. I popped round to light the fire thinking I'd have the room nice and warm for when you got in.'

Edith shook her head. 'Something terrible has happened to poor Alice and Gerald.'

He listened in shocked silence as she told him what Harry had told her.

'Oh God, no. We must go to Gerald, darling . . . Oh, but you haven't eaten or had a chance to change out of your work clothes.'

'Marg has stew ready for us, but I can't eat. I'll go round and tell her, and then we'll get off. I'm not bothered about changing me clothes, I just want to see how Alice is.'

'All right, I'll finish here and get the guard securely in place while you're gone . . . Oh, Edith, this is shocking.'

He held her close. She could feel his body trembling. She wanted to stay there forever, but knew she needed to hurry to Alice's house.

★ ★ ★

As Edith and Philip stood on Alice's doorstep, she couldn't help but wonder, *How am I, or any of us, to help Alice?*

Both Harry and Jackie answered the door.

It was Harry who greeted them. 'By, it's good to see you two. Me and Jackie are having a job with our Billy. He wants to go over to the hospital, but Gerald told us we must stay here and wait for him to contact us.'

Edith stepped inside and kissed them both, urging them not to worry. Philip followed her lead, kissing Jackie's cheek, but shaking Harry's hand. Harry blushed, but with a kind of pride at being treated with such respect.

Before Edith could say anything, Billy and Joey came rushing through to the hall, both with an eager, anticipating look on their faces.

'Eeh, what's to do, Billy, lad? Harry tells me you're upset. Well, that's understandable, but look, there's nothing you can do at the moment except keep Joey happy. Why don't you take him out on the lawn and show him a few of the moves you were telling me you have learnt, eh?'

'I just want to see Alice for meself, Edith. I don't think Gerald's telling us everything.'

Billy had a stubborn look on his face, one she knew well. It had been easier to deal with when he'd been a lad, but now, though not that much older, he had the stature of a man. He was what she thought of as an 'in between' — a funny stage that lads went through.

'Gerald has too much love for you as his brothers not to. It is a difficult time for him and he needs to know you're helping to take care of things here. He's relying on you to keep Joey safe and happy . . . Look, me and Philip will go over to the hospital and see how

61

the land lies and I promise I'll come back to let you know.'

Billy was almost as tall as she was and yet, in this moment, he looked like a child, and Edith was at a loss as to how to help him emotionally. She often wondered how these lads had managed to grow so fast in the last two years, as even Joey, the baby of the family, was shooting up. But then, for the first time in their lives, they were having wholesome food every day, instead of once in a blue moon.

Billy's face softened. 'All right, Edith, I'm sorry. I wasn't thinking . . . Come on, Joey.'

Relieved, Edith touched his arm and Billy surprised her by putting his arms around her. She held him close, patting his back.

Not to be outdone, Joey cuddled her too. Edith smiled at Harry and Jackie over Billy's shoulder. 'This is all everyone needs, Billy, a hug. And you knew that I needed one. Ta, lad, you've a special way with you.'

Billy drew away from her, appearing more grown-up once more, his pride restored. He grinned, took hold of Joey and went outside with his arm protectively around his adoring brother.

Edith turned back to Jackie and Harry. 'I will come back, or telephone, once I know what's happening. Will you be all right?'

'Aye, we'll be fine.'

Edith nodded at Harry. She knew they would be, as long as they were together.

* * *

62

At the hospital they were shown to a private wing. Gerald came out of the ward, his face haggard. Philip went to take his hand, but had to quickly support Gerald as his legs seemed to crumble under him.

He clung on to Philip's arm.'I — I can't take it all in.'

Philip guided him to a bench that stood in the corridor outside the ward. 'Sit down, Gerald. What's happened? Is Alice all right? Harry said she'd lost the baby.'

'Yes. Oh, Philip. It isn't just the baby. She . . . she's in the operating theatre . . . They are taking everything away; they couldn't stem the bleeding, they tried, they gave her blood, they stitched her, but . . . Oh God!'

Edith gasped. She couldn't grasp what she'd just heard. 'Eeh, Gerald. No!'

Gerald's head nodded.'She . . . she will never be able to have another baby. Oh, my poor Alice . . . Our baby lived, but only for a short time. I — I went home and brought him here. I — I couldn't leave him in his cot. He's . . . he's downstairs in the morgue . . . I — I . . . Oh God, I can't bear it.'

Edith felt the pain of his words as if it were happening to herself. She knew how much Alice wanted a family of her own. This was cruel. Alice had been through so much. *Oh God, why?* This news and the thought of Alice's tiny baby lying in a cold, heartless morgue shattered her.

Philip's soothing voice helped as he told Gerald,'We're here now, Gerald, lean on us as much as you need to. And don't worry, the lads are fine. Jackie is there with Harry and they are all coping. But, Gerald, you mustn't think of what Alice is losing, but of this procedure as saving her life. She will come to terms with not being able to have children, but if they didn't do this and she died, then she wouldn't ever have the choice of anything ever again.'

This seemed to get through to Gerald. He mopped his eyes with a large handkerchief and took a deep breath. 'You're right, Philip, and as a doctor I know that, but as a husband and the man who loves Alice deeply, I know the pain this will bring her — both of us. For I too so wanted to have sons and daughters.'

'It's every man's dream; it's mine too. But if anything like this happened to Edith, then I would be glad that she was alive and I'd be strong for her. You have to do that, Gerald. You're strong for your patients; you have to be for Alice.'

'I know. Thank you, Philip.'

With this exchange, Edith calmed and found her voice. 'You'll not have to do this on your own, Gerald. Like Philip said, me and Marg and Philip will be beside you both and you'll get through this. You just need to make sure that Alice does an' all.'

Gerald stood and held out his arms to her.

'By, Gerald, it seems we Halfpenny Girls have brought you nothing but trouble.'

'No, that's not true, you brought love into my life. Not that I didn't have any already, and I wish with all my heart my mother and father were here now, but the love you girls give is a special love. Philip will understand what I mean.'

'I do. And for me, meeting you three girls, and especially you, Edith, taught me what the meaning of love is. As you know, I wasn't lucky with my parents in the way that Gerald was.'

Edith held out her free arm to Philip. It affirmed in her that anyone, no matter what their circumstances, had something to give to others.

Gerald drew out of the hug first as the sound of the doors opening took their attention. Two porters came through guiding a bed, and behind them was a doctor in his gown, still wearing a head covering. Gerald rushed forward.

'How is she, Greg, did it all go all right?'

'It did, Gerald. I'm sorry, I did try to save the womb, but it came to a point where Alice would have died if I didn't take it all away and get her closed up.'

'I know you did your best for her, thank you.'

'This won't be easy for her, Gerald. She will need you. Now, let's get her to bed and let the nurses make her comfortable. I will check her over again later. Though I think she will make a good recovery, she is going to need a lot of care.'

Edith had been listening, tears streaming down her face. Now, as Alice's bed was pushed past her and she caught sight of her, always the smallest and the prettiest of the three of them, looking so helpless, she gave way to a sob.

Philip held her tighter.

What would the future hold? she wondered. How would Alice cope? And how did you give comfort, or find the right words for such a tragic happening? Edith didn't know.

As Gerald came up to her, she told him that she'd promised to go back to the lads as quickly as she could, then looked at him appealingly. 'But Gerald, what do I tell them?'

'Just tell them that Alice is all right, that she's had the operation and that's why I haven't been back, but that I'll explain everything to them when I come home.'

Edith nodded.

Philip stepped forward. 'We'll go now, Gerald. You'll need time on your own with Alice.'

'Thanks, Philip. I do.'

'Give her me love, and that of Marg's, the minute she wakes, Gerald, and tell her we'll be there for her. We'll help her through this.'

'Thank you, Edith, she is going to need you both. As will I.'

Edith hugged him once more. 'I'm sorry, lad, so sorry, but you'll be all right, I promise.'

As she and Philip left the hospital, Philip had his arm around her. They didn't speak until they were sat in his car, when he said, 'Oh, Edith, what a dreadful thing to happen.'

'I can't take it in. Alice was so full of joy. She'd planned for the babby; she loved buying all it needed, and this was the first time in her life that she hadn't needed to worry about the money. She read all the books available on pregnancy, ate all the right foods, and kept really well. She was blooming. How could it happen?'

'We may never know, but my grandmother always said that God did everything for a reason. Maybe the baby hadn't formed properly. Maybe there was a defect that would have meant the child couldn't thrive. I don't know, but I think my grandmother was right. I've often felt it was so.'

'I'd like to go to church to light a candle after we've told the boys. The evening mass will be finishing soon and Father Malley will be outside talking to those who linger — he'll let us in for a few moments before he locks up.'

'Yes, I'd like that. Did Harry tell you the child's

name?' 'He did.' The four names came out on a sob. 'Eeh, Philip, to name a dead child seems to make the babby a real being to me, not just a miscarried pregnancy. Little Gerald was real, he breathed, and then died in his mother's loving arms.'

Philip patted her hands. 'I know. I know exactly what you mean; I thought the same as I listened to his names. And Harry was right to baptise him. The baby is safe now.'

* * *

Inside the church, Father Malley listened to their story and told them he would pray for Alice. He left them alone and they sat in the silence of St Kentigern's — a silence that Edith always found more peaceful than any other.

Philip took her hand as they walked forward to light a candle, and then put his hands together and bowed his head as the flame flickered into life. Edith did the same, praying for Alice and Gerald.

After a few minutes, they went back to the pew and Philip took her hand. 'Edith, my darling, I don't want to wait any longer. Please say you will marry me soon?'

Taken aback at first, Edith looked at Philip, but she knew she felt the same. Whether the tragic event had brought on their need to be together forever, she didn't know, but without hesitation she replied, 'Aye, Philip, I will. I cannot wait either. I've been ready for so long. All me past is behind me and I want us to take the next step . . . But, well, there's still the worry about us being able to afford a home, and if we'd cope moneywise an' all.'

'I'm concerned too. I have savings, but my pay is

poor; I don't earn anything near the men in the rock factories or down the mines. But the headmaster told me today that I am being considered for the post of head of year one and two when the current head retires. All the other candidates are nearing retirement so a recruitment drive is to take place, and I am the natural choice to take on the extra responsibility. It will mean a lot more pay for me.'

'Eeh, Philip, that's grand. I wanted to ask you before, but . . . well, what about my house? Would you consider living there so we could marry soon? I know you've witnessed a few fracas in the street, and there's often rowdy behaviour on a Friday night, and, well, last Friday you did see that poor woman running into the street sobbing after her drunk husband had punched her . . . but the folk are all right really.'

'I'd be honoured, but it won't be necessary. I will be given a grace and favour cottage — or a rent allowance — as part of my remuneration, so let's wait and see, eh?'

'By, if I'd have known you'd have been honoured to live with me, I'd have snatched you up months ago.'

Philip laughed. 'You should have asked me! I thought you didn't want to marry yet?'

'I've wanted to marry you since I first set eyes on you, lad.'

'Ha, I love it when you call me lad. I must say, though, that you never gave me that impression, and I held off because of your grief — you needed time, and, well, I have to admit, I was afraid of my parents' reaction and of them hurting your feelings.'

'Well, I feel a lot better now, and I know how quickly life can be taken from you. What happened tonight reinforced that, and I don't want to waste any more

68

time. We should be husband and wife. And as for your parents, well, your ma's coming around, and if she never gets better than she is now, I'll cope. I have a thick skin. Besides, I found that if I stand up to her, she takes it and seems to like me more for it.'

Philip held her hand tightly in his. 'You're so special, darling. If anyone can win her over, it's you.'

As they reached the back of the church, Father Malley called after them, 'So, will you be wanting me to put the banns up anytime soon?'

They laughed and called out goodnight to him. Edith heard his chuckle.

Since she'd started coming to mass, Edith had felt part of a second family. Marg and Alice were her first and most important family, especially since she'd been left alone in the world, but she'd found a community here and most had included her. Something, however, told her it wouldn't be long before she had a single most important family of all — hers and Philip's. The thought filled her with a joy that was tinged with sadness for Alice and Gerald, but as they got outside and Philip took her in his arms telling her how much he loved her, the joy won.

7

Alice

Alice opened her eyes to a bright light shining down on her. She squinted and felt disorientated for a moment, then, as she moved, pain. A pain that gripped her stomach. Her hands went to ease the discomfort and brought the reality of what had happened racing back into her — her babby wasn't there, tucked up inside her . . . He'd gone.

'No . . . no!'

'Alice? It's all right, darling, I'm here.'

'Gerald . . . Eeh, Gerald, our babby.'

'I know, darling. He — he's safe in heaven. Harry saw to that for him.'

'I don't want him to be. I want me babby!'

She knew her voice had risen, but she didn't care. She wanted to shout even louder — to scream and scream — but she knew if she did, she would never stop.

Gerald's head came onto her breast. She felt his sob and her focus went to him. 'Eeh, Gerald, our babby. We had such plans for him. But we'll have another. We will, I'll give you the ten you wanted, love.'

Gerald's sobs became louder, fuelling the despair she held inside her. But she took a deep breath and suppressed her own sorrow as she stroked his back. 'We can get through this together. Help each other. We still have our love. I'm here for you.'

He lifted his head. 'Do you feel brave, darling? Are

you feeling strong?'

Though the urge to scream hadn't left her, Alice could answer truthfully. 'Aye, stronger than I thought I would. I had a dream that our little Gerald was in the arms of me ma. And a peace came over me. Me ma smiled and said,'Ta, Alice. I'll love him for you. You can have more to keep to yourself.' It made me feel hopeful and settled that little Gerald was all right . . . But, ooh, why am I so sore? I feel as though I've been cut open.'

'You have, my darling. Oh, Alice, I have to tell you something that might shatter you all over again and I don't want to.'

The trickle of fear that had entered Alice now flooded her as she looked into Gerald's haggard face.

'We . . . we won't be able to have any more babies, my darling . . . You . . . you lost so much blood and they couldn't stem it, they had no choice but to take your womb away.'

Alice felt herself sinking — drowning beneath a clogging veil of hurt. She felt Gerald's hand grip hers, but it didn't help. Gerald couldn't help her, not with this . . . This would take her away forever. Destroy her.

'Darling, please, scream if you have to, but don't just stare at me like that. There was nothing that could be done. You could have died.'

'I . . . I want to be dead!' The words came out through her gritted teeth. The force of them hurt her throat and scratched the back of her tongue.

She stared at Gerald as if he were some kind of monster who had let them mutilate her. 'I hate you!'

Again, her throat grated these words out, causing her pain, breaking her heart with the truth of them. For at this moment, Gerald was her enemy. His sobs

71

meant nothing to her. She wanted to tear him apart as she felt that he had done the same to her.

Gerald stood, his face aghast as he backed away from the bed. Then he shook his head from side to side, spittle dripping off his slack mouth. When he reached the door he opened it and backed out.

Through the door, Alice saw a nurse grab him. Saw him collapse into her arms. Heard her call out for help. Then feet running — uniformed folk, doctors and nurses, clambering around him, taking him away.

Her screamed words at this further assaulted her sore throat, but she couldn't stop. In her own voice she heard the raw Lancashire dialect as she became Alice again, the hurting, crumbling Alice from Whittaker Avenue. 'Naw, naw, me Gerald, me Gerald . . . me babby, I want me babby!'

Something sharp stuck in her arm. The room and the noises of her mind spun into a peaceful depth.

★ ★ ★

When she woke, Edith and Marg were standing at either side of her bed. Her lips quivered as the blankness cleared and the awful scenes came flooding back to her. 'Gerald?'

'Eeh, Alice, love, Gerald's all right.'

'No, Marg, we must be truthful. Alice, love, Gerald is a broken man. He's at home with the lads and Philip . . . This is a terrible thing that's happened to you both — and it has happened to you both, Alice, not just you, lass. Love is sharing pain, like we've always done. Me, you and Marg. In sharing we've found comfort. We never rejected or blamed. You've done wrong, Alice. Aw, I know you've had a shock and something terrible has happened to you, but those are the times you reach out for one another, not push away the one who loves you beyond all things.'

Edith didn't want to appear angry, but she needed to make Alice realise that she wasn't in this alone. That she and Gerald needed to be strong together and that Gerald was suffering too.

Marg tried to help things by saying, 'By, Edith, hold on, love. Alice has had a massive shock. She were bound to lash out.'

'I know. But to tell Gerald she hated him when he most needed her . . . Aw, Alice, love, whatever possessed you?'

Alice felt the same resentment rising in her towards Edith that she'd felt towards Gerald earlier. She couldn't understand the hate she felt, or why.

The face of her baby drifted into her mind. A beautiful shining picture of a little angel. 'He's with me ma, Marg.'

'Who is, Alice, love?'

'Me little Gerald. He's shining. He looks like Joey. He has his blond hair, and though he only opened his eyes for a split second they were a blue, a very light blue, like Joey's. He was lovely, Marg. I — I loved him. I took him into me heart and tried to save him . . . But when Harry baptised him . . . he . . . he died. Why did Harry do that? Why? He gave him permission to go. I hate Harry, Marg, I hate him.'

'Eeh, Alice, love. You hate who you like. Hate me and Edith, hate Billy and Joey and Gerald and Philip, and me gran, Jackie and me ma. Hate the bloody world, lass, because God knows you've reason to. And I'll hate them all with you.'

'And I will an' all, Alice. I'm sorry, love, I shouldn't

73

have said what I said. I'm sorry.'

Alice looked at Edith. Tears were streaming down her face. 'It's all right, Edith. I know you were only trying to make me see sense, lass, but there is no sense. Where's the sense in me babby dying, and Gerald consenting to have me womb taken away so I can never have babbies?'

'There's no sense, lass, no sense at all, and I were wrong to try to make you see some. I love you, Alice, and I'll always be by your side. I'm so sorry.'

Alice held both of her hands out. Marg took one and Edith took the other. 'With you two by me side, I can make it. I made it through me ma and da dying, and I did that because you two helped me.'

Edith's lips quivered. 'Aye, and I made it through me lovely brother killing me ma and da, and then taking his own life through his guilt, because I had you two.'

'And I'm getting through each day with me gran's dementia and me ma's sickness because I've got the support of you both.'

Alice felt a smile coming to her lips as she said, 'The Halfpenny Girls, eh?'

Edith and Marg grinned back at her.

At that moment, Alice felt a funny feeling. A feeling of loss deep in the pit of her stomach, but it wasn't for her babby, it was for Gerald. A sob tore from her splintered heart, reached her throat and came out as a deep moan. 'I want me Gerald. Aw, Marg, Edith, go and fetch me Gerald. Make him love me again. I love him . . . I don't hate him . . . Oh God, what have I done?'

Marg sat on the bed and grabbed her, holding her shaking body, but nothing gave her comfort. 'I want

Gerald. Eeh, Marg, I've lost him, I've lost him.'

'No, you haven't, lass. Edith's gone already. She shot out of that door. She'll have him back here in the bat of an eyelid. You'll see. But by, me lass, you and him have a long road to travel, and a painful one, but it won't be half so difficult if you travel it together. You, Gerald and the lads, for they are scared, love. They need you. They need you both.'

'Oh, me lovely Harry, how could I have hated him? He did right by me babby, didn't he, Marg?'

'He did. Your little Gerald wouldn't have made it to your ma's knee without Harry's help. So something's come from them all going to mass each week. I don't hold with it meself, but I'm beginning to think there's something in it.'

'Me too. I liked it when me and Edith went after me da died. We only went to hear the prayers for him, but Edith and Harry seemed to get something an' all.'

'Aye, and Jackie, though sometimes I reckon she only goes because Harry does.'

As they chatted on about nothing in particular, Alice's heart was racing with fear and doubt. Could Gerald forgive her? Had she shoved him away for good? She hadn't heard what it was that Marg had said, but burst out, 'I didn't mean it . . . Aw, Marg, Edith will tell him that I didn't mean it, won't she?'

'She will, love, and he'll know. He was more hurt because he wanted to be the one to help you but couldn't. Now lie back on the pillows and relax. You're exhausted.'

'And in such pain. Me stomach hurts so much.'

'It will do, lass. I'll go and get a nurse and see if they can give you something to ease it, eh?'

'Aye, but I don't want to go to sleep. Tell her that. I

75

want to be awake for me Gerald.'

As Marg left her, Alice let go of the aching, burning tears and emptied her heart. In the few minutes that it took for Marg to return with a nurse, she somehow felt stronger. Weak in body, but strong in her soul. This was another mountain she had to climb, and if Gerald would climb it with her, she'd be all right, wouldn't she?

The nurse looked kindly. 'Right, lass, I'm going to give you a sharp prick into your arm. Hold still.'

'Don't put me to sleep, please.'

'Naw. This will make you feel a bit light in the head and take your pain away, but won't make you sleep, unless you want to. Eeh, lass, I wish I could give you sommat for the pain in your heart.'

The nurse, who looked only a little older than Alice, stroked her arm. The gesture brought comfort and it was as if it had lit a light in Alice that gave her a way forward.

She'd had the thought before that she'd like to work alongside Gerald when he realised his dream of becoming a community doctor in general practice, and now this nurse had inspired her. She too wanted to give comfort and ease pain the way she did.

She would look into becoming a nurse as soon as she was well again, and she would get well. She'd do all she could to make it so.

She smiled up at the nurse. 'In some way, you have eased it a little, lass. You've given me a direction. I want to be like you. I want to be a nurse.'

'Eeh, lass, I know that's something you mulled over before.' Marg said this as she stood from the seat she'd taken to be out of the nurse's way.

'I know, but, well . . .'

'By, you'll make a grand nurse, I can tell that. And you'll have a head start on me. It were hard for me to be accepted, coming from a working-class background, but I joined the St John's and got a lot of certificates, and they put me forward. You, being a doctor's wife, will have naw problem. You even speak better than me.'

'Well, we had a teacher who made us pronounce some words in the proper manner, but it's only in how we say them words. We're Blackpool lasses through and through, and have been dragged up the hard way.'

'Well, I think it helps to be. I've seen a lot of women in your position, who've been sent to the asylum from here, poor lasses. We Lancashire lasses are made of tough stuff . . . Aw, I knaw you lost yourself for a bit, it's understandable, but look how you're bouncing back and planning for the future. Mind, you've a lot to face in the coming weeks, so get yourself strong first, lass, then visit your decision again. And if you still want to become a nurse then, well, I wish you all the luck in the world. We need more like you. Folk who knaws how it feels to suffer. Too many of me colleagues have naw feeling. They're kind, and clever at what they do, but they don't knaw pain like we do.'

This further cemented Alice's resolve, but she knew she had a long, rocky road to tramp before it could happen. She would hang on to the idea, though. Make it her lifeline to cling on to — helping others through what she was going through would be her saviour.

When the nurse left, Marg said, 'Close your eyes for a bit, Alice, love. Rest until Gerald comes back, eh?'

'He will, won't he, Marg?'

'He will. Then me and Edith will have to leave you. It's five in the morning, and we've both got work in a

77

couple of hours.'

'Eeh, is that all it is? Will you be all right? Can't you have the day off?'

'Ha, you, an ex-biscuit factory girl asking that? No, Moaning Minnie will have our guts for garters. She's looking for an excuse to get rid of me as it is.'

'She ain't so bad. She'll be on your side when the chips are down. Look how she was with Edith when . . . Eeh, Marg, what happened to me? I love Edith, and me heart bleeds for her, and yet, for one moment I — I hated her.'

'Forget it, love. If you can't hate the ones you love at such a time, then it's a poor show.'

They both giggled.

'Marg, you can go now, love. I'll be all right, I promise. I'll close me eyes and sleep till Gerald comes. Go on. Get back home and have a bit of a kip in the chair or something.'

'All right, lass. I will. Tell Edith I'll see her later, eh?'

When the door closed behind Marg, Alice marvelled at how strong she felt. She just needed Gerald's forgiveness and then she could begin to put her world back together.

* * *

When she next opened her eyes, she felt her hand being held. She looked to the side and saw Gerald smiling down at her. 'My darling, my Alice.'

'I — I'm sorry.'

'No. You were in shock. You saw me as the monster who'd taken everything from you. It was better that I left you for a while, darling. I phoned Philip and woke him up; he went and fetched Edith and Marg, I knew

78

they would help you. Sometimes those who love you most and are involved in your pain cannot give you that help.'

'Where's Edith? I — I need to . . . '

'Edith and I met Marg at the hospital door. Philip is asleep at ours so the boys will be fine if they need someone. And I sent Edith off with Marg, who told her you were feeling mortified about something to do with her. Edith told me to tell you that she loves you and knows you love her, so don't worry.' He squeezed her hand. 'How are you feeling now? Marg said you already had plans?'

'Eeh, I'm so glad Edith forgives me. And, aye, I do have plans, and me first one is to be in your arms.'

'Oh, my darling, Alice.' As he bent over her and held her gently, she could feel him trembling.

'It's all right, darling. We have to grieve. We've lost so much. But not each other. And that's something that's good. We'll get through this, I promise.'

Gerald's body shuddered. 'I — I had no choice, Alice. I couldn't face losing you too.'

'I know, love. Thank you. It must have been an awful moment for you. But with your help, I'll make it. I have to, I've to get on with me plans.'

Gerald pulled back from her, blew his nose and sat down again. He took her hand once more. 'Nothing would surprise me about you, Alice, love, but what have you in mind?'

'Well, you've heard about this one before. I'm going to become a nurse.'

'That's wonderful. I'll help you all I can with your studies, darling . . . Like you say, we'll get stronger together and help each other, and we'll make our little Gerald proud of us.'

They were silent for a moment. Alice lay back look-ing into Gerald's blue eyes, seeing the love there, and the concern. When he spoke, she realised why. 'I need to tell you about little Gerald. Are you up to hearing what has taken place, darling?'

'Yes . . . I — I wish I didn't have to, but it has been on my mind in my quiet moments.'

'I brought him to the hospital, but couldn't rest knowing he was . . . well, it's not a nice place, so I got Harry to help me. He's very special that brother of yours . . . Different, somehow. Anyway, he found that tiny frock you had made for little Gerald, and the shawl you crocheted.'

Alice saw a tear trickle down Gerald's face. She squeezed his hand, afraid to ask but wanting to know where little Gerald was now.

Gerald cleared his throat. 'I asked one of my col-leagues to write the certificate and then Philip called Box Brothers funeral directors and one of their offici-ates met me downstairs here. He helped me to dress our baby. He was so gentle with little Gerald. He took him to the chapel of rest and said that he will order a tiny white coffin for him.'

They were crying together now, but their grief wasn't tearing them apart in the wretched way it had before. They clung to each other, desolate in their loss, and yet forming a bond stronger than any they had ever had.

Alice knew they had many days, weeks and years, even, of grieving to get through, but they would do so knowing their love was strong and would sustain them.

8

Marg

When Marg arrived home after work that afternoon, she felt shattered, having been up for most of the previous night. She hadn't been able to get the picture of Gerald dressing his poor deceased son out of her mind. Now home, she was surprised to see Jackie stood inside the living room.

'Eeh, lass, what's to do? Why are you home from work?'

'Ma's been bad, Marg. Ada sent word to me at the office and Mr Blake suggested I took the afternoon off. Ada's sorted her now and Gran's lying down for a mo. Do you want a pot of tea?'

'Aye, that'd be good. So, is Ma all right now?'

'Aye, she's resting. But, eeh, Marg, poor Alice. I — I just cannot get the little babby out of me mind. Why, Marg? Why does sommat like this happen?'

'I don't know, love. But usually for a good reason. You should know more about that than me, with how you go to mass.'

'I only go for Harry. He loves it . . . You knaw, Marg, I see sommat different about Harry when he's in church. It's like he's transported to another world. He becomes distant. He doesn't have a giggle with me like he used to, but seems as though he's drinking in every moment.'

'Well, if he gets something out of it, that's good, ain't it? He's been through a lot; maybe it helps him

81

to lose himself for an hour. And it's good that you go with him, he can share it with you then.'

'But he doesn't share it with me. He goes very quiet, even after we leave. Almost sullen, and yet, with a kind of out-of-this-world air about him.'

'Eeh, Jackie, you're imagining things, lass. You and Harry will always have your ups and downs in life, it happens in all relationships. Maybe this is just a small down, but it'll pass.'

'There is no real relationship — I mean, not like girlfriend and boyfriend. Me and Harry are just friends. There used to be the odd times when we held hands or he'd kiss me cheek or sommat, but not now.'

'Well, he's a young man, he has feelings that are hard to control. Maybe he thinks it best not to get himself worked up . . . Huh, here comes Gran now.'

Gran came shuffling through. She didn't look at either of them, but went straight up to Ma and sat in the chair next to her bed. It was odd since she usually made for the rocking chair next to the fire, whether it was lit or not.

'She's been doing that ever since Ada left and Ma went off to sleep. I tried to get her to rest, but she keeps coming out every few minutes and goes up to Ma and talks to her, but Ma don't seem to hear her; she's worn out.'

Marg walked slowly towards the two women who meant so much in her life. As she got nearer, she stopped and listened to Gran's quiet words. 'Eeh, Vera, Vera, you took a wrong path, lass, but me and your da, we forgive you. Don't you be fretting.'

'Is Ma all right, Gran?'

Gran turned towards her. 'Aye, she's having a bit of a rest. I won't wake her till her da comes in, he should be here in a moment.'

Marg didn't deny this even though her grandfather had passed away years ago. Gran always thought he would come home any minute and often went looking for him. These times were distressing and frightening as she was so vulnerable and could come to harm wandering the streets. 'Why don't you sit in your chair then, love? You can see her from there.'

Gran didn't protest.

As Marg turned back and looked at her ma, a dread entered her. To see her sallow complexion, her sunken eyes and the shallow, struggling breaths she took made Marg realise that Ma's time was near. With this, her heart became heavy with sorrow.

How was she to face losing her ma? How would her gran cope? Gran had memory lapses about everything other than her daughter and she knew everything about her past.

It had been Gran who had told Marg about her ma's long-running affair with Uncle Eric and how it had been him and not the man she'd thought of as her da who'd fathered her and Jackie.

Thinking of Eric, and the love he had for her ma, Marg wondered if she should let him know just how poorly Ma was. But then, the way he'd looked at her the last time she'd seen him shuddered through her . . . No, he'd made his choice, he'd walked out on them, and that was that.

As if reading her thoughts, Jackie, who'd been standing beside her gazing down at ma, slipped her hand into hers. 'Marg . . . I've something to tell you. I — I . . . well, our da may come to see Ma.'

'Uncle Eric? How? I mean, why? What makes you say that? Have you been to see him, Jackie?' Knowing by the look on Jackie's face that she had, Marg was assailed with mixed emotions. One of these she couldn't understand, but she felt a sense of betrayal by her sister. Jackie eyes were downcast.'Have you? Tell me, Jackie.'

For the first time ever, Jackie had a defiant expression on her face as she looked directly into Marg's eyes.'I have. I've never stopped going to see him. He's me da . . . your da.'

Marg gritted her teeth. 'He chose to walk out of here, we didn't make him, Jackie. He knew the plight we were in. I know Ma deceived him, but that was no reason to walk out on us. We hadn't done anything to him, we were the innocent ones in it all.'

'I knaw, but . . . well, he were hurt bad by Ma. I just . . . well, I liked him. I knaw what he is. I knaw he's a bad person, but he's our da. Ma hurt him by not telling him I was his and by using him just to get her fags and beer.'

'Jackie! Don't say them things, lass. Has Eric put them into your head? He ain't blameless, they used each other . . .

But, lass, all of that isn't of any consequence, it's you deceiving me that hurts.'

'I'm sorry, Marg. I — I just wanted to see him and I knew you'd not agree.'

As a tear plopped onto Jackie's cheek, Marg softened. 'Come here, love. You shouldn't have kept it a secret. But then, that's me own doing . . . I've not had a good word for Eric since he left us. How can a man walk out on his kids, eh?'

'He was badly hurt, Marg, and he didn't think you wanted him around. He has been helping us, though . . . I lied about the food I used to bring when

84

I worked at Fairweather's shop before. Fairweather didn't give it to me, our da did. And I didn't buy that coal we had last winter from me extra earnings I'd made, our da gave me the money.'

'Eeh, Jackie, lass, why did you lie? If we can't be honest with each other, what have we got, eh? Nothing. Our love for each other, the way we depend on each other, it's all worthless if it's built on lies and deceit. No matter what, even if it's going to upset me, you have to tell me the truth. Promise me you'll never lie to me again, lass.'

Jackie burst into tears as she flung herself at Marg. 'I — I'm sorry, I am. Eeh, Marg, I feel awful. I didn't want you upset, I thought I could keep it a secret, but I wanted me da in me life.'

Marg stroked her hair. 'I understand, lass.'

'More than I do.'

They both turned and looked at Gran. She had an angry expression as she asked, 'Eric, you say? That rotter's coming around here? Over me dead body. Me John'll sort him out good and proper. He's naw match for me John, lass.'

'It's all right, Gran. If Jackie wants our da to come around, then we have to let it happen.'

'Well, he ain't going near Vera.'

Marg sighed; it had been Gran who'd said they should fetch him when Ma had first deteriorated so badly. She was about to say so when Jackie forestalled her.

'I'm sorry, Gran. I knaw I've done wrong, but I can't stop him. When I told him how poorly Ma was, he said he'd come and see her . . . He cried, Gran . . . He truly loves Ma.'

'Ha! Love? He don't knaw the meaning of love!

85

Nor do you. What're you doing here, anyroad? Who are you? Nowt but a skivvy. You don't say who comes into me house and who don't!'

'Gran, it's me, Jackie.' Jackie sank down into the armchair behind her. Her sobs filled the room.

'It's all right, Jackie, love.' Marg sat on the arm of the chair and pulled Jackie to her. Gran rarely forgot who Jackie was, and if she did, Jackie always laughed it off. 'It's because Gran's upset. You know how she hates our da.'

'He ain't to blame for it all, you knaw that. But, eeh, Marg, he could be here any minute.'

'I do, but Gran doesn't know that. She only sees a man messing with her daughter's life. But any minute, you say? This afternoon?'

Jackie nodded. 'I saw him when I came out of work. He pulled up in his van to talk to me. I told him I'd been sent for. I'm sorry, Marg.'

'Who's coming here? Not that Eric!' Gran stood and teetered towards Jackie, her distress showing in her face.

Marg stood and gently guided her back to her chair. 'Sit down, Gran, love, we don't want to wake Vera, do we, eh?'

'Why's Jackie crying, lass? Are you the nurse?'

'Jackie's had a bit of an upset, that's all, and aye, I'm the nurse.'

'Funny, she called you Marg. I had a Marg once. I don't knaw where she is.'

Marg held her lovely gran. 'You're upset, love. Why don't I take you into your room for a lie-down? I can bring you a pot of tea, eh?'

'Aye. But will you see to me Jackie?'

'I will. Jackie will be fine.'

86

'You're a good lass. I'm glad you come to see to me Vera, Nurse.'

Marg bit her tongue. She knew she had to hang on to those times when Gran did remember her; all of the lovely memories that Gran gave her as a child. They helped her get through. She had recognised her yesterday, but maybe won't again for a long time.

With Gran settled, and she and Jackie drinking their tea, Marg felt funny about her real da coming to the house again. She wasn't altogether upset by it, more afraid and at a loss as to how to handle it. For a moment she considered going out and leaving Jackie to it, and the more she thought about this, the more the idea appealed.

'Jackie, will you be all right if I pop round to Alice's, love?'

'Naw, don't leave me, Marg. I can't face it alone.'

Marg let out a sigh. 'Why did you do it then, lass? You should have asked me . . . told me.'

'I knaw, I — I . . . I don't knaw why I didn't. Only that I was scared of upsetting you. I tried to stop Eric coming here, but he said he didn't care any longer what happened, or . . . well, how you felt about any-thing, he just needed to see Ma. To make it up with her before . . . Eeh, Marg, Ma's going to die, ain't she?'

'Lass, come here.' As she held Jackie, the reality came to Marg that yes, their ma was going to die, but a rap on the door took the thought away from her as she stiffened with a deeper fear than she'd already felt.

Jackie jumped away from her arms and stared towards the door.

'You'd better answer it, lass.'

When Eric walked in, he stepped gingerly and looked towards Marg.

She stared back at him.

'I'm sorry about the last time we met, lass. I weren't meself.'

Marg nodded. She'd seen this humble side of Eric before. Had even begun to love him at one time. But the Eric who got respect by using violence and was known for his reputation was the one she couldn't get out of her mind now. She felt threatened by him even as he smiled a sheepish grin at her.

'Look, lass, when I walked out I were at a point where I couldn't take any more. I — I, well, I've had news about you from Jackie. I've done a bit for you now and then, but to be honest, I knew I had to stay away.'

'It's water under the bridge now, ain't it? I've got good friends that've helped us, so we didn't need you. Anyway, you've come to see Ma, not talk about how badly you've treated your own flesh and blood.'

'Marg, please don't take that stance. I just couldn't take Vera's treatment of me anymore, but I ain't ever forgot her, nor you and Jackie.' He looked around. 'Where's your gran, then?'

'I've settled her in her room. She couldn't stand an upset like this.'

Eric coughed. 'Well, can I have a few minutes with Vera?'

'Aye, that's what you're here for.'

Marg stepped around him and went into the kitchen. Feeling suddenly hungry, she opened the larder cupboard, then felt despair at there being just a crust of bread. She'd planned on baking the loaf she'd left proving before she'd gone to work, but had forgotten all about it. Getting it now from the bottom warming oven, she put it into the top oven and lit the gas. It had risen nicely, so shouldn't take too long.

In the meantime, she had to eat something as she was shaking. Taking the bowl of dripping down from one of the wire shelves, she spread the crust thickly and tucked in. She'd just finished the last mouthful when Jackie came through.

'I'm going to make a pot of tea, Marg, do you want one?'

'No, I'll go outside for a bit. I'll have one later, lass, ta.'

Just as she said this, the sound of another rap on the front door had her and Jackie looking in bewilderment at each other.

'Go and see who it is and put them off, Jackie. Unless it's Gerald or any of Alice's lads.'

Marg listened as Jackie opened the door, then cringed as she heard her say, 'Hello, Clive. I'll fetch our Marg, only I can't ask you in as we have a visitor.'

'That's fine. It was Marg I came to see.'

Marg checked her appearance in the broken piece of mirror that they kept propped up on the window-sill, whilst quickly undoing the wraparound pinny she still wore. Wetting her fingers, she dampened her hair a little to make it form curls rather than the frizz around her forehead. Then licked her fingers and rubbed them on her eyebrows and wet her lashes, but she couldn't do anything about the bags that lined her tired-looking eyes.

God, I look a mess.

Reaching under the curtain that surrounded the sink, she grabbed the bag that contained her lippy and an almost empty cake of mascara. With her still damp finger she wiped the smooth surface of the black kohl and applied it to her lashes, before drawing in her lips and outlining them with the red lipstick.

'You'll do, lass — you'll have to,' she told her image.

Taking a deep breath and fixing a smile on her face, she grabbed her coat from the hook on the back of the kitchen door and walked through to the front without looking at what was happening in the living room.

Calmly opening the door, Marg stepped through it. 'Clive? I thought you'd be at work?'

'I've taken a couple of hours off, love. I thought I'd come around for a mo, but now as I see Jackie is home with you and Eric's van's out here, I wondered if, with your ma taken care of, you might like to come with me to my boat? I like to tinker with her and the sea air will blow your cobwebs away.'

Clive had bought an old boat a few months ago and, a keen carpenter in his spare time, had been doing it up. He loved fishing and had asked her a number of times to go out with him. At this moment, she could think of nothing better than to sail away into the sunset.

Telling him she'd like that better than a walk, she asked him to wait in his car while she arranged it. Dashing back inside, she motioned to Jackie.

Jackie grinned as she came over to her and whispered, 'If you're going to ask if I'll be all right while you pop out for a bit, the answer's yes. Da wants to stay longer, but he feels uncomfortable with you here, so it'll be a good solution, Marg.'

'Ta, lass. I need to escape. So much has happened since last night. When I come back, we'll have tea.'

Marg winked as she dashed through and ran upstairs where she changed quickly into a pair of slacks, glad that neither Gran nor Ma would see her as both hated to see women in trousers.

Taking a thick woolly cardigan and a scarf from her wardrobe, she put them on, hoping they would help to keep her from freezing. Her new coat wasn't the thing to go messing about on a boat in.

A last glance in her dressing table mirror and she was down the stairs and out the door, not even bothering to say goodbye to anyone, other than blowing a kiss to Jackie.

★ ★ ★

Even though the air bit, there was no wind, and the almost cloudless sky meant the sea was like a millpond: as calm and blue as any pictures she'd seen of the seas abroad. But then, this didn't bode well for the frost that would follow such a day.

As Clive parked the car on the dock at Fleetwood, a small fishing village seven miles from Blackpool, he told Marg, 'Right, lass, you're wrapped up well. I reckon we could go out a little way on the boat. Grab that hat and put it on as this low winter sun will multiply them lovely freckles by the millions.'

Marg laughed as she donned the khaki cloth hat. She felt light-headed with a joyous feeling of freedom, despite all that was going on in her life.

Clive looked at her intently for a moment and said, 'It suits you.' His voice lowered. 'But then, you could wear a sack and look lovely.'

Marg blushed, but made a joke to cover this. 'Aye, over me head and to me feet, then I might.'

His laugh sounded lovely. 'Come on, let's go out in the boat. The tide's in and it'll be easy to launch it.'

'Will we make it back before it gets dark and the tide goes out again?'

'We will. We won't go far, but that sea is crying out to us.'

When they were a little way out, Clive handed her a rod. 'Right, watch me, and do the same as I do. We have a good chance as in this cold, some of the fish prefer to be near to the surface where it's a bit warmer.'

Following his lead, though she hated touching the wriggly maggots, Marg tried to get the bait onto her hook.

They giggled at her attempts and she began to feel more relaxed than she had in an age.

With the floats bobbing up and down and she and Clive chatting, she found herself opening up and telling him everything about Alice's tragedy, and her own feelings where Eric was concerned.

'Sorry to hear all that, lass. Especially Alice's news and your ma failing. I worry that you have such a lot on your shoulders. But you know, from a man's point of view, Eric has done wrong, yes, but he tried. He tried for years, but he had a lot of setbacks and what your ma did in the end, pretending to have cancer, well, that was despicable, and would have tried the patience of a saint — which we know Eric isn't by a long way.'

'I know. But me and Jackie are his daughters and we needed him. Why couldn't he have been there for us, and how could he look at me how he did that day?'

'I don't want to defend such a man, but as he is in your life, Marg, then maybe it would be better for you to find an even bit of ground? Maybe look at it from his point of view? Your ma had him on a string for years, deceived him, extorted money from him. Then he finds the girl he ignored was his daughter too, and that she loves him and shows him that love, while you, the daughter he knew about and made a fuss of all her life, rejected him once she knew the truth about him being her da. You can't have it both ways, Marg.'

Though this stung her, she knew he was right.

'Anyway, let's enjoy the couple of hours' peace that we have, eh? Leave your cares at home, as I do. Though, since we've been friends, Marg, my cares have lessened a lot.'

Marg glanced sideways at him; he was looking at her in a different way to how he had since she'd made it clear she just wanted to be friends.

Turning her head towards him, she held his gaze. The sun lifted the red lights in his dark hair, as it had done when she'd first felt a stirring of feeling for him — a feeling she'd had to deny.

His eyes, a hazel colour, held more than she wanted to acknowledge, and yet a small tingle in her stomach denied this.

'Marg, you know how I feel about you.'

She nodded. 'It's complicated, Clive.'

'I know. I come with two sons and an almost-mended broken heart, but you've had a big part in putting me back together, Marg.'

'It ain't none of that. It's me home life. Jackie needs me, as do Gran and Ma. I'm not free to make a decision about anything.'

Clive leant forward. The boat, now with the engine off and just drifting, rocked in protest, so he shuffled his bottom along to sit beside her on the bench that went all round the outside of the boat. Taking her rod, he fixed it in one of the holding clips and took hold of her hands.

'Marg, I can wait. I don't want anything to happen

to speed your freedom along, but for me the waiting would be so much easier if you told me you had
deeper feelings for me than just being friends.'

As she continued to look into his eyes, so close to
hers now, she found it easy to say what had eluded
her for such a long time. 'I do have feelings for you,
Clive. Strong feelings that lighten me day when I
know you're coming, or send me into a tizzy when,
like today, you surprise me. I've never felt like this for
anyone else.'

'Oh, Marg, Marg! You've given me hope. I — I
want to kiss you.'

Marg wanted him to so much, but her float bobbing up and down caught her eye, and she shouted
out in a gleeful voice, 'I've got one! Eeh, I've hooked
a fish!'

Clive laughed in an ironic way, before putting his
arms around her to help her to draw the good-sized
fish in.

'It's a plaice!'

'Similar, love. It's a dab, but just as creamy tasting.
Well done; it'll make a nice tea for you all.'

Clive didn't take his arms from around her as the
fish wriggled about on the deck, and Marg didn't
want him to. It felt right — comforting, and yet exciting — and somehow gave her hope of a brighter
future.

9

Alice

There was some comfort for Alice in laying the little coffin in her ma's grave, but her desolation was such that she couldn't cry. Ten days had passed and though her physical wounds were healing, she still battled with the mental scars the operation had left her with on top of her grief. Each day from the moment she'd woken with the first pain was etched in her memory, but today, the 7th January 1939, she knew would be there forever.

No New Year celebration had taken place in their house, and to her, every Christmas and dawning of a new year from now on would bring back these memories.

As her and Gerald's handfuls of earth hit the coffin, a pain seared through her. Gasping, she clutched her heart, swallowing hard so as not to cry out. Gerald steadied her. As she leant on him, a picture of her ma came to her. The same mound of curls that she herself had, and the same large blue eyes. But Ma's were twinkly and she was smiling. Alice smiled back.

Take care of me babby, Ma. He's precious and he's the only one I'll ever have.

She fancied she heard her ma's voice. *Me and Da will look after him, lass. Imagine us dancing — you used to giggle when we did. Well, we'll have little Gerald in our arms when we dance tonight, me little lass.*

The unshed tears that had stung her eyes and

95

weighted her heart flowed down her cheeks with these words, 'Ta, me lovely ma.'

'Did you speak, darling?'

Gerald's voice was heavy with emotion. She looked up at him and nodded. Lifting her hand, she wiped his tears with her fingers. 'Aye, I handed our little Gerald over to me ma. She will hold him as she dances with me da tonight.'

'Oh, that's nice. Nice to think of them all together and your father well enough to dance. They say heaven makes people whole again. I don't want to wait that long to be whole again, nor for you to be. We will be all right, won't we, darling?'

They had stepped back to allow other mourners to scatter a handful of earth to send little Gerald on his way. Alice tried to be upbeat. 'We will. Somehow, we will. Marg's gran always says, 'One foot in front of the other will get you there.''

'I see she's here, darling. She's very quiet.'

'I'll explain later; it's to do with Vera. But for now I just need you to hold me. Stop me from falling, Gerald, me love. I need your strength.'

'And I need yours too, Alice. You are strong, you have kept me together this last week. Keep doing that for me.'

Alice felt the weight of this, and yet it helped her too. By being there for Gerald, she could cope better herself. And she would. She would do her crying alone. With this thought she caught sight of her brothers standing huddled together, looking lost.

'The lads need us, love. We can do this for them. They've been through so much and look as though their world has fallen apart again. Let's go to them and get them settled in Philip's car ready for him and

Edith to take them home.'

Alice knew that this would set a precedence for everyone to follow and to start to make their way back to her and Gerald's home where Patricia, Philip's sister, was waiting to take care of them all, having slipped away after the church service as arranged.

As they walked over to Harry, Billy and Joey, she told Gerald, 'I want us to have time alone with little Gerald before we join them, me love.' Then she fixed a smile on her face. 'Harry, I want you all to go with Philip and Edith. Help to look after everyone, lads. Patricia will tell you all that needs doing. We won't be long.'

Harry took her in his arms. Billy and Joey joined him. She felt cocooned in love as she squeezed them back. 'Little Gerald's with Ma. She's cuddling him. He has a heavenly body. The coffin is just a resting place for his earthly body.'

'Do you believe all that, Alice?'

'Aye, I do, Billy.'

A hand came into hers. Knowing it was Joey, Alice looked down at him. His voice quivered as he asked, 'Will you come home, Alice?'

'Me and Gerald just want a minute alone and then we will. You help to take the sausage rolls that we made together around to everyone, and Billy, you offer the sandwiches around, eh, lad? Harry, just see what Patricia needs of you. But be yourselves, lads. Little Gerald wouldn't want you to feel sad. He wants to look down on strong uncles who he can depend on.'

As she said this, Alice felt the pain in her heart again. Gerald took hold of her as the lads let her go and told them, 'See you shortly, boys.'

With Philip steering the lads away, Alice saw Edith put her arms around Joey. The gesture made Alice look around to see where Marg was. She caught her eye and waved. Marg, Gran and Jackie came over.

'Eeh, Alice, love, let me give you a hug.'

Marg's arms gave her little comfort, nothing could, but still the hug helped to steady her. When she heard Marg's sob, she clung on to her as she sensed Marg's tears were for much more than the loss of little Gerald. 'Marg, lass, I'm still here for you. Talk to me later. I'll do all I can for you, lass.'

'Ta, Alice. With all you're going through I don't want to burden you.'

Alice tapped Marg's back. 'You're never a burden, Marg. Never that.'

'Eeh, she can be at times, Alice.'

Alice came out of the hug and smiled at Gran. Gran surprised her then as she opened her arms. 'I need a hug an' all, lass. I'm sorry about your babby. I knaw what it feels like, I have four of them in this churchyard somewhere.'

Marg looked shocked. 'Aw, Gran, I didn't know.'

'Well, it ain't sommat us womenfolk talk about, lass.'

Marg put her arm around her gran. Gran didn't push her away but turned into her and allowed Marg to hug her. Jackie stepped forward and joined in. To Alice it was a lovely sight, as so often Gran rejected Marg, but the thought of Gran going through the same pain she was in hurt deeply. And this was compounded when Gran turned to her once more and hugged her.

'I'm going now, lass. Me John's coming for me.'

For the first time, Alice felt glad that Gran had

98

gone into a different world again — the one that held happiness for her. She wished at this moment she too could do that but didn't imagine that she would ever feel happiness again.

She stood a moment and watched as Gran got into Clive's car, then turned and grasped Gerald's hand. Together they walked over to the open grave.

Alone now, neither spoke as they gazed down. Gerald broke the silence. 'My son, you'll always have a place in Daddy's heart.'

His sob resounded around the almost empty churchyard. Only the men waiting to fill in the grave and the driver of their funeral car stood discreetly a little way away. But to Alice, they didn't matter. Gerald was all that mattered and she knew his pain was increased by hers. He was afraid for her.

Taking a deep breath, she looked down on the tiny coffin and told her little Gerald, 'Ma loves you, darling, with all me heart, and I'm going to make you proud of me. I'm going to help Marg nurse her ma and use it to start me nursing career. I'll visit often and tell you all about it, me little babby. Give Ma and Da a kiss for me, and I hope you meet the babbies that Ma lost and Marg's gran's babbies an' all.'Turning to Gerald, she hugged him. He wiped her eyes with his thumb.

They didn't move for a long time, just clung to one another.

★ ★ ★

On the way home, Gerald asked what it was about Marg's gran that Alice said she would tell him.

'Gran is worried about Vera. Edith told me that

Marg's ma is bad and Marg said Gran's been very quiet for a week now since . . . well, since it became apparent that Vera will die soon.'

'Oh God, you never said. Can I help in any way?'

'We had a lot on our plate, love, and still do, but yes, it would do us both good to help — there's something comforting about helping others. And that's why you must get back to work, Gerald. Your patients need you. The hospital needs you.'

Gerald leant back into the comfort of the thick leather seat of the sleek, black car. 'I know. And I think I can now.'

'That's good, darling. I'm going to throw meself into helping Marg. She has so many problems — not just her ma, which is terrible for her, but I know she's struggling for money too. All she'll take is food as she says she doesn't want to get into debt, but if I could help her to work longer hours, that would ease her situation.'

Gerald just patted her hand and gazed out of the window. His suffering worried Alice. It was hard for him, she knew that. His loss and the need to make everything right for everyone was a burden that he couldn't always surmount, but she would take care of him and help him through this, and she would start by being brave herself.

Little Gerald would help her; he'd be her shining light. She had to look to the future now. She'd long learnt that if she broke, so many around her did — her brothers, and now Gerald. But she would find the strength, Edith and Marg would help her in that. She could always depend on them.

10

Two months had passed and the day had been bright and sunny, though still holding the chill of the usual March weather.

The feeling was that spring was well and truly on the way, giving Edith that sense of hope that something new and better was just around the corner.

Though as she neared home on her way back from work, the thought of Marg's ma did dampen that a little — having rallied well after her last fright, she was struggling again and Marg was distraught.

But as she opened her front door, Edith left these thoughts, discarded her coat and checked on the casserole she had left on a low heat in the oven. Philip was coming to tea.

Opening the stove door caused warm air to waft over her, giving her a delicious aroma of lamb cooking in fresh herbs — a recipe she'd taken from one of her ma's old cookbooks.

Thinking of her ma like this with a smile on her face spurred Edith on. She was on a mission — wash, change, and then, at last, tackle her da's old suitcase, which she knew held all her family's bits and pieces.

Until now, she had shied away from opening it, but she'd just received a boost to her future plans and she knew now was the time.

With everything ready for the evening, and Edith on her hands and knees surrounded by what, to her, were the most precious items, she stared at the piece of paper she held in her hand — her school certificate.

My God, I've been working away to get another like you and I've found you!

Excitement zinged through her as the words of Mrs Wardle, her old school teacher, came to her. They'd met as Edith had walked home from work. Edith had plucked up the courage to tell Mrs Wardle of her ambition to become a teacher, thinking she would laugh at her, but she hadn't. Instead, what she'd told her made this certificate vital to have, because it was the first step. She'd gone on to say, 'And don't worry about your accent. Oh, I know I used to be a stickler for ironing out some of the more, what I call 'raw' words of the Lancashire dialect, but that's because I felt doing so gave more clarity to others, and we Lancastrians wouldn't be looked on as second-class citizens.'

The rummage to find the certificate had been tearful and heart-wrenching for her, and she wished she'd done it a while back to save herself a lot of trouble, but she hadn't been ready then.

More tears flowed now as she looked at a photo of her family: her ma, her da, her brother Albert and herself standing at the door of their house across the street.

She remembered that being taken. The photographer had been to each house and asked them if they wanted a set of photos for a bob. Da had found the shilling for him and he'd posed them all.

Bound in the same elastic band, she'd found one of her ma and da, and one of herself and one of Albert.

Memories were evoked of family life — chaotic and at times stressful, and unhappy in the latter years, but when these photos were taken it was happy and care-free.

Forcing herself to put these photos aside, Edith had delved further. In another bundle she'd found her birth certificate, a tiny Christening gown and this school certificate.

Drying her eyes and closing the case, she shoved it back under her bed. But though memories were painful, by the time she left her bedroom, Edith was smiling again, so thrilled to have found the photos and the certificate. Now she could progress, both emotionally and with her career prospects, as some-how, all the finds had lifted her.

Clutching the certificate as if it were made of gold, she went through into the living room. The smell of the casserole reminded her that Philip would be here soon. Her smile turned to a grin as she knew he'd be hungry for his tea.

Eeh, I need to learn to talk proper and call tea 'dinner'.

Though now the worry about her accent had been lifted and she knew it wouldn't hold her back. It hadn't done for Mrs Wardle.

★ ★ ★

Philip greeted her news with a smile. 'I'm so pleased for you, Edith. And I'm glad you found the courage to look into your dad's memory case, darling. Was it really painful?'

'Yes, but I like how you called it a memory case, as

it is full of good memories. I think it will be less painful for me to go through everything in there thinking
of it like that.'

Philip stretched over the table and took her hand.
He didn't say anything, but she knew his heart ached
for all the loss she'd suffered.

Changing the subject — something he often did
if the moment held too much sadness — he said,
'Mmm, this is good. In fact, I think it puts you in line
for another certificate: the 'Good Enough to Cook
Philip Bradshaw's Meals' certificate.'

Edith burst out laughing. 'Ha, it took a long time
to get that approval! And to my mind it's time you
cooked for us; I don't even know if you can! But I
hope you can as I want to be pampered sometimes,
you know.'

'I can, as it happens, but I prefer to take you out for
dinner, darling.'

'Aye, I know, but the few times we've done that,
I've had to have a jam doorstep when I've got home.
By, you posh lot must be starving if that's how you
eat. Give me the chippy any day.'

They both giggled at this.

'Chippy it is then. Anyway, back to your certificate . . . I've been thinking about what you should do
next. I think you should go to a private tutor, one who
is registered and can put you forward for all the qual-
ifications you will need.

Though, I do have another idea.'

'Oh?'

'Yes . . . to work at my school.'

'What? Rossall? That's not possible. For one thing,
they don't have women teachers and another, I'd
never fit in.'

'Not as a teacher — well, not as such . . . But, look, darling, I haven't mentioned it before, but we have a school matron. She is the wife of the master who is leaving, and if I am promoted, it would naturally be offered to you.'

'But I ain't a nurse!'

'No, you don't have to be. You have to care about the children's welfare, help them to settle in when they first arrive, be a sort of mother figure who they can turn to. And being clever as you are, you can also help the juniors with their homework. It's a lovely job and matrons are well loved.'

Edith couldn't take this all in, and yet, something about it appealed to her. 'But what about the way I talk? They won't like that, nor will the kids' parents. Though I am thinking I need to sort that. I know you like me as I am, but others . . . well, it can make a difference.'

'It's entirely your decision, darling. If it would make you feel more confident, I know someone who could help. He's an old teacher of mine.'

'But that's wonderful. Eeh, I so want to learn. More so that I don't let you down than anything.'

'Darling, I want you to be yourself always. We are not how we speak, we're just us. It's convention that asks those things of us, and I love you as you are.'

'I'd love you to get me them lessons, please, love. Me life is going to change, and I need to adapt to that whichever way I go. Eeh, it would be a start if I were to call me evening meal 'dinner', not 'tea'.'

They giggled together, but that turned into a belly laugh when Edith snorted between her giggles.

When they were able to control themselves, Edith asked, 'When do you think this job that you're talking of will become vacant?'

'I don't know for sure, could be the end of the year. Our year ends when we break up for the summer in July, so perhaps September. That would give you plenty of time, darling.'

Edith hesitated. She wanted things to happen sooner than that. 'Eeh, I don't know, love. It sounds exciting, but my idea has always been to be a teacher to ordinary kids, to help them to get on in life, to give them hope that they can better themselves. To see that I am one of them, and I've bettered myself. These kids you're talking of will have been born with a silver spoon in their mouths, and I'll just be a replacement mother who has no idea of the kind of background they've had, or the way they should behave in the future.'

'Yes, I can understand that. But how will you go forward? I couldn't bear for you to go off to a teacher training college far away from here, and you would have to board. Besides, the cost would be inhibitive.'

'I know. But not all teachers are qualified. I can learn in a post.' She told him then about her conversation with Mrs Wardle. 'I was shocked to learn that she wasn't qualified and neither are her colleagues at St Kentigern's, except the headteacher, Mr Raven. They all have the school certificate and passed an entry exam when they applied. And, of course, they had to be practising Catholics.'

'So, a recommendation from the parish priest would go a long way, I imagine — well, you would get that from Father Malley, without hesitation.'

'I know, and there's more. Something that made me really excited: she said she'd let me know when Mrs Thornton, an elderly teacher at the school, was retiring, but in the meantime, she'd talk to Mr Raven about me and tell him how suitable I would be for the post.'

'That's wonderful, darling. I do know, of course, that there are a lot of uncertified teachers in the system, and doing a really good job too, but I didn't want to suggest it to you and seem like I was undermining your capabilities.'

'Eeh, Philip, you're so careful of the differences between us, and I know you try hard not to offend me, but don't worry. I am sensitive to it, but I know you would never hurt me intentionally.'

'Oh, darling, I'm glad you realise that.'

'Maybe when I'm a teacher and can speak properly I'll feel more worthy of you.'

Philip's chair scraped on the lino floor as he stood in haste. 'Come here, darling.'

Edith stood and went into his arms.

He held her close. 'Never, ever feel you're not worthy of me. I love you, Edith. I fell in love with the beautiful, caring woman you are. I shall always present you proudly as my wife.'

Edith looked up at him. 'Ta, Philip, that means a lot to me.'

'Oh, Edith, you're so beautiful.'

His lips came down on hers in a light kiss that deepened to a passionate one. Edith felt herself responding — not wanting him to stop as they usually did, she pressed herself against him, then cried out his name when his lips parted from her.

Philip's moan as he pulled her to him once more told her of his desire. Kissing his neck, she gasped as his hand cupped her breast. Every part of her wanted them to become lovers, wanted to give herself to him.

She thrilled at the feelings zinging through her as his fingers gently squeezed her protruding nipple.

But suddenly he stopped. 'I — I'm sorry. Oh, Edith, I love you so much. But this is wrong. We must be strong until we are married. We've managed till now to be.'

'I don't want to be.'

'No, I — I . . . Oh, Edith.'

She drank in his kiss, matched the movement of his tongue, and didn't resist as he manoeuvred her towards the sofa. But when they reached there, Philip untangled himself from her. 'Help me, Edith. We cannot do this.'

Seeing his distress, Edith took a deep breath. 'I'm sorry, darling, it was my fault. Oh, Philip, let us marry soon.'

Philip took her back into his arms, only this time in a gentle way. His voice still held all of his need, and she could feel the physical manifestation of that as she snuggled in close to him, but his words reassured. 'We will. We'll post the banns and marry three weeks from now, and I will move in with you until we find a place.'

'Eeh, Philip, are you sure? That would be grand.'

'It will, it'll be more than grand, my darling. Can you get ready in that time? I don't want a huge wedding, do you?'

'No. Just me mates. Let's ask them first before we set a date. Alice and Marg are still going through a rough time, but if I have their blessing to go ahead despite what they are going through, then we will, darling.'

They kissed again, only this time keeping it light.

To lighten things further, Edith said, 'Once we've

done the pots shall we go for a walk, it's a lovely crisp evening.'

'Good idea. And we can call in on Gerald and see if they are all right and tell him and Alice our news.'

★ ★ ★

When they left the house, Edith hesitated. 'Can we call on Marg, first, love?'

'Yes, if you're sure she won't mind. Poor Marg always seems so careworn.'

'She is, and that's why it'd be good to lighten her day a little.'

As they turned to the left, her old neighbour Ida opened her door. She leant on the doorjamb with her arms folded. 'Eeh, I'll tell you sommat for nowt. Poor Betty must be turning in her grave.'

To hear her late ma's name upset Edith, more than what Ida's words implied. 'Shurrup, Ida.'

This came from Ada, who Edith hadn't seen walking towards them.

'Well, have you seen the likes in our street, eh? Naw shame some folk.'

Edith coloured. Philip gripped her hand. 'Ignore her, darling. We've done nothing wrong. Hold your head up high.'

At that moment, Marg shot out of her door and fled across the street. Before Ida knew what was happening, Marg pushed her and sent her reeling back indoors.

'Marg, no! No, lass. Don't . . .'

'She deserves it, Edith. I'm sick of her.'

Ada dashed over to them and took hold of Marg. 'Marg, lass, naw. This ain't helping nowt. You can't paper over your pain by attacking others. Get back inside. Go on, lass.'

Edith wasn't far behind. 'Eeh, Marg. Come on, let's get you inside. You're shivering. How did you hear what was going on?'

'I'd just opened me door. I was going to come round to yours for a mo.'

'Aw, love. You shouldn't worry about Ida, I can take it. I know I haven't misbehaved. It's all in her dirty mind.'

As they went towards Marg's, they heard Ada saying, 'You deserved it, lass. Marg is under a lot of strain and she's a fiery one at the best of times, but now, with her ma failing, well, you should knaw better than to call her mate names. Besides, Edith isn't like that and nor is her young man and you knaw it.'

'Huh, them two are always in that house on their own and you can't tell me they ain't been at it.'

Philip broke away and crossed the road. Edith didn't stop him, but guided Marg to stand inside her doorway. Turning, she held her breath, hoping that Philip managed to handle things in a diplomatic way.

'Ida. I think you know who I am. Well, I am not just Philip Bradshaw, I am an honourable, God-fearing man. What you speak of isn't anything that I would do. I love Edith and I am going to marry her, but I also respect her as she respects herself. We are adult enough to be in a house on our own and not to lose that mutual respect. I would thank you to have respect for my future wife at all times. If you don't, I will speak to my solicitor about taking you to court for slander. I don't want to fall out with you, but I will not stand for any of you hurting Edith.'

Ida's mouth was open but she didn't answer, though

her huff as Philip walked away spoke volumes.

Ada shouted, 'Well said, lad. Ida, you deserved that, you've got a dirty mind. It's about time you let up on our Edith.'

Once inside, Marg broke down.

'Eeh, Marg, lass. You've enough on your plate. Ida isn't worth it, you know.'

'I'm sorry, Edith, I just cracked for a moment there. I'm so weary.'

'Come here, love. We'll help you get through this. We're by your side, Marg.'

As they hugged, Edith told her, 'Look, lass, I've some news that I hope'll cheer you up. But if you think it's wrong for it to happen just now with all that's going on, then it won't. Me and Philip don't want to wait any longer to get married. We want to post the banns and do it in three weeks' time, but we're not moving away. We'll be living next door.'

'Aw, Edith, I — I . . .' Marg sobbed louder and clung to Edith.

This worried Edith; she thought it meant that Marg wouldn't be able to take it. 'Look, love, it'll mean that I won't be moving away, and Philip will be here to help you any time you need a lift with your ma. You'll only have to knock on the wall — we'll work out a code so we know what it is you want and we'll come running to help you, Marg.'

They laughed together at this and Edith felt a sense of relief.

'I'm all right, Edith, lass. I am. And I'm so glad to hear your news. By, that'll be Easter Saturday, won't it?'

'It will, if Father Malley agrees.'

'It's grand news. Any good news is, and this is the

best it could be.' She wiped her eyes and grinned even wider, but then gasped as from behind her came a voice saying, 'You got a good catch, lass.'

'Gran!'

Edith laughed. 'I did, Gran.' Edith went further into the room and looked at Vera. Her heart went out to her as Vera laughed at Gran and went into a fit of coughs. As she calmed, Edith asked, 'How are you, Vera? Nice to see you perky enough to laugh at Gran, love.'

'It's that Eric that done it. What she sees in him, I don't knaw. But they can't get up to their usual tricks anymore, so that's a good thing.'

Gran smacked her lips together as she finished saying this, as if the fact gave her a great deal of satisfaction. Marg looked mortified, but as Philip burst out laughing, she joined him.

This warmed Edith. 'Aw, lovely to see you laughing, Marg. Don't take it all so seriously, lass. We understand Gran and her ways. She's a tonic, not an embarrassment. Must be lovely to be able to say whatever comes into your head.'

'Aye, but I wish that some things didn't pop into Gran's. Anyroad, you two marrying is the best news ever, though it would have broken me heart if it meant you moving away.'

'I know, it seems as everything is changing. We're just going to walk to Alice's. Will Jackie be in from work soon? She started back at the shop, didn't she? You could come with us if she is. Be good for you to get a break.'

'Aye, she will, she'll be here by seven thirty. She did the teatime rush at the shop today. And Harry'll be here an' all. They're planning on studying together, something to do with the stars, but I suppose it's some sort of substitute for them not being able to sit on the step like they did in the summer gazing up at them — simple pleasures, eh?'

'Aye, we all loved sitting on the step. But we'll do it again in the summer.'

'Can't wait. Right, let me pop up and get a wash and change. I haven't had time since I came in from work at lunchtime. I'd love a walk.'

As Marg disappeared upstairs with a jug full of hot water, Philip moved to sit on a stool next to Gran. Edith heard him say, 'So, Gran, how are you?'

'Better for having a handsome young man to talk to. Will you be going to war? All the men did in the last lot.'

'War? That's a funny question. We have the Munich Pact, Gran. Peace has been agreed.'

'Ha!'

Philip looked over at Edith and shrugged his shoulders. Then turned back to Gran as she said, 'You mark me words, them Germans won't ever be satisfied. Look what they're doing in Czechoslovakia. And they've backed them Italians an' all. I don't like that Hitler bloke.'

'Ma, you . . . listen to too many of them talking programmes. You should . . . put the music on more. Eric . . . bought me that wireless to cheer me up, not for you to put the fear of God into everyone.'

'Well, you say that, Vera, but I don't like that Chamberlain, either; he's a yellow-livered sod. There's a lot going on that he should do sommat about.'

'It'll all be all right, Gran, don't you worry about it,' Philip told her. 'Everything will be handled diplomatically, not with fighting. The Great War was the war to end all wars.'

'There was nowt great about it, lad. John were away for five years and I didn't knaw if he were alive or dead. Lads from this street didn't come back, and us at home were starving. I don't want that again, and if we do the right thing, we could stop it . . . Mind, when John did come home, I had to watch meself. He were like an animal. You'll meet him in a mo when he comes home from work.'

Edith saw Philip's face go through many emotions: sympathy, then shock and now grinning. She smiled at him, but her attention was taken by Vera.

'Eeh, Edith . . . that one'll tie your Philip in knots. So . . . you're not studying tonight, lass? I . . . like it when you're all here . . . it's peaceful.'

'No. And guess what?' Edith told Vera about her certificate and possible job.

'By, that's grand, lass.' She was nodding her head, but her weakness was apparent. 'Edith, me Marg will be . . . I mean, you'll look . . . out for her after . . . Well, you knaw.'

'Always, Vera. And Alice will an' all. We're the Half-penny Girls, remember?'

'Aye. Them were the days . . . I smile to think of you all . . . pigtails and plimsoles. Eeh, you're grand lasses.'

Edith's mind went shooting back in time, to her, Alice and Marg at twelve years old, linking arms and singing at the tops of their voices. Carefree and happy. Would they all find that feeling again? Would there be a war as Gran said? No, there couldn't be. Why should there be?

A shiver went through Edith and she prayed: *Dear God, don't let there be, I couldn't bear it.*

114

But then she shook herself mentally and told herself it wouldn't happen, so she wouldn't even think about it. But for all this brave thought, she couldn't help herself.

Marg coming down the stairs looking lovely in a yellow jumper that Edith had passed on to her and black flared trousers made for a diversion to these thoughts.

'You look lovely, lass.'

'That was a bit wistful. What's to do, Edith?'

'Oh, just me thoughts. Your gran thinks there might be another war.'

'Aye, I know. Some of them newsy programmes she likes give me the feeling of doom, but they keep her happy and seem to stimulate her mind so I don't stop her listening to them, even though Ma don't like them. Anyway, let's put it all out of our minds and look forward to seeing Alice.'

'You're right. Whatever happens, we can't alter it.'

'And, like Gran says, half of what you worry about has already happened and the other half probably never will.'

As Marg linked arms with her, Edith felt better. She breathed deeply and determined she would always stay strong, come what may. This is what had got her this far and would help her to cope with whatever was thrown at her in the future.

11

Marg

Thoughts of war stayed with Marg as they walked, and she wished Gran didn't take such a morbid interest in the affairs of the world. There was always trouble somewhere, but surely it would never affect them?

Brushing it all away from her, she determined to enjoy her evening. But then she remembered something she had heard that morning while clocking in at work, which she now couldn't get out of her mind. She knew Edith had heard it too, and wondered if it had fuelled her worry. It had been Mrs Green, a quiet woman who always seemed out of place in the factory. No one knew her background, but they knew she was a cut above them; 'married beneath her', most said.

Mrs Green had nodded her head at Ida. 'Yes, it's looking grim, I think, Ida.'

Marg hadn't heard the beginning of the conversation, but listened after that sentence. 'I think trouble's on the horizon.'

Ida had said, 'Aye, I heard that, but I don't knaw why it should be.'

Mrs Green's answer had been frightening, and much the same as what Gran had said about Hitler's intentions. 'If we make the pact to defend Poland, then our position will be very precarious if Hitler invades them. I think Chamberlain hopes the pact will scare him off, but I don't see Hitler as a man who scares easily — he takes what he wants and sheds blood in the process.'

Marg shuddered with fear and dread as this conversation revisited her. Shaking it away, she concentrated on chatting with Edith as they walked through built-up areas to Alice's home.

Everywhere, folk were out walking or were letting the sun shine in through their open windows, glad to see it after a long winter. Marg couldn't believe the atmosphere; it felt almost like summer, except for still needing a coat.

She wrapped hers around her, feeling how she always did when she wore it — like someone special.

She linked arms with Edith as Philip went after a stray ball some lads were playing with and kicked it to them.

'Eeh, lass, I wish that everything could be like this forever.'

'Aye, I know what you mean, Marg. There's a subtle feeling in the atmosphere that our way of life may change. Have you been thinking about what Gran said?'

'Aye. Daft, ain't it, when you look around? How could anything happen to all of this? But anyway, if it does, we'll never change, will we?'

'Of course not, love, but it's just . . . well, here I am on the verge of something exciting happening, and yet, it all seems to be hanging in the balance.'

'Come on. Let's live for the now, not keep pondering on what might be, eh? I'm having such a good time, Edith.'

Edith smiled and patted her hand. 'Well, if going for a walk is what cheers you, Marg, then I'm glad you're easily pleased, lass.'

They giggled.

117

'No, you know what I mean. I just love being free for a while.'

★ ★ ★

Alice was thrilled to see them. Gerald had answered the door and taken them through to the garden where Alice was planting seeds into the border that skirted the lawn.

'I'll just get up, hold on. Ha, I still feel like everything's an effort, but I'm getting there. These are phlox; multicoloured so they should look nice by mid-summer.'

Seeing Alice's stiffness, Marg moved forward and gave her a hand. Once she was standing, Edith joined them in a hug.

'How're you feeling, lass? You look a bit pale.'

'I feel pale, Marg. Sometimes it's as if I've had all me stuffing taken out of me, but I'm stronger every day and little jobs like this help me no end.'

Gerald stepped forward and lovingly held Alice, guiding her inside. He plumped the cushions of her chair with one hand as he helped her to lower herself into it. 'She's been doing too much. That's the problem with feeling a bit better and the wound healing: folk think they can immediately do what they used to do. Alice won't listen.'

His voice held a mock tone that told them he wasn't really feeling cross, as he continued, 'Right, darling. Now, I'll get us all a drink. We've some lovely lemonade, everyone. Alice managed to make it yesterday. She got a ticking off then for doing too much, but was forgiven when I tasted it.'

As Gerald left them, Alice said, 'It were from his

118

ma's recipe book. She left it with me. It's all hand-written and called *Gerald's Favourites*. Me and her had a real giggle about it before they left; it's all the stuff she made him when he were a lad. I thought I'd surprise him, but it backfired a bit as the taste of the lemonade made him yearn to have his ma and da back with him.'

Marg felt the pity of this. She'd never understood how parents of an only child could go off like Gerald's ma and da had. 'Do they know your news, Alice?'

'We don't know. We write to an agency and they take the mail to them, but it can take weeks, months even.'

Philip surprised Marg then by saying, 'You should both go out to them, Alice. It would do you the world of good, and the boys too, be a good adventure for them, they've been through so much.'

Marg had never thought of any of them going out of the country, let alone to Africa. From what she'd heard at school, it was a place where the sun never stopped shining and they grew exotic fruits and had dangerous animals and snakes. 'Eeh, lass, you wouldn't do that, would you?'

'I'd love to, Marg. Be exciting. And it's funny you should say that, Philip, as we've talked about it. Once I get stronger, we might arrange it.'

Before Marg could express her worry further, Edith piped up, 'Well, don't think about it too soon, lass, as me and Philip want to ask you all something. Anyroad, we'll wait for Gerald to come back to tell you of it, but in the meantime I've other news that I ain't even told Marg of . . . I found me school certificate!'

'Eeh, that's good to hear. But it won't mean you

going away to that college you once spoke of, will it, Edith?'

At this prospect, Marg's stomach turned over. So much was changing and she didn't want it to. She could cope with Edith being married, and wanted that for her, but that had come wrapped up in the good news that she would still be just a wall away.

'No. I don't have to.'

As Edith told of her meeting with their old teacher, Marg felt tears trickle down her cheeks. She hadn't meant to cry, but anything could set her off: relief at Edith not going away, the good news she had of her wedding and her prospects, and for the awful situation Alice was in and how brave she was being, but most of all, fear for her ma.

Edith came towards her. 'Well, I hope they are happy tears, love. Eeh, come here.'

'I — I'm . . . sorry. By, I don't know what you all think of me. I am happy for you, Edith, I just . . .'

An arm came around her shoulder, taking her from Edith. Philip pulled her into his strong body. His shirt smelt of fresh air, and this mingled with a tinge of the smell of the Brylcreem he used to tame his hair. For a moment, the feeling was strange and embarrassment crept up, reddening Marg's cheeks, but Philip's soothing tones helped.

'When we have a lot to contend with, even happy things can make us cry.'

'Ta, Philip, I'm all right now. Stop being nice or I'll blub all night.'

They all giggled and the moment passed. But as she moved away and mopped her face, Marg couldn't shake the feeling the hug had given her and knew it was because she'd never had a strong male in her life

120

who cared enough to offer her comfort. She had Clive now, but he hadn't held her the same way. Philip's hug had been a supportive one — one a girl should receive from a father.

This thought threatened to overwhelm her again, but Alice saved the day as she called over to her, 'Come and sit next to me, Marg, love.'

As Marg went forward, Edith took a chair ahead of her and placed it on one side of Alice. 'There you go, lass, plonk your bottom on that and I'll get another one and sit on the other side.'

Alice smiled. 'Aye, that's a good idea, we can have a good chat then.'

The distraction helped Marg, but as she sat down it hurt her heart to see how tired Alice looked. But her voice was strong as she asked Gerald to take Billy and Joey a glass, explaining to them that the lads were doing a project together in the summer house.

'They're out there every evening. I see them bringing things back and forth, but can't see what they're doing with the summer house being behind that tall hedge, and they won't allow me near it until it's finished.'

'Aw, bless them. Anything that keeps them busy is the best thing for them.'

'Aye, that's what we thought, and they're coping well. Though I don't reckon they fully understand, but I do think doing something for me is helping them. I've an idea that they're cleaning the summer house out and giving it a lick of paint so that it's all cheery for me to enjoy as the weather gets warmer.'

'That's a winning situation for you all then,' Edith put in. 'The lads are kept out of trouble and you'll have a lovely corner of the garden all year round . . .

Anyway, I'm bursting to tell you and Gerald what Marg already knows.'Turning her head to get the attention of the two men who were deep in conversation, Edith grinned as she said, 'Listen, everyone, Philip and I want to get married soon, but, well, it depends on you all, what you think as I know . . . well, it isn't a good time for any of you.'

Marg watched Philip move towards Edith. She held her breath, waiting for Alice's reaction, then sighed with relief as Alice clapped her hands.'Oh, Edith, lass, that's grand, I'm so happy. And it's the best thing to happen for us all. We all need something wonderful to brighten us up and nothing is better than a wedding.'

Philip drew Edith closer and kissed her cheek, but soon went back to Gerald as the girls' talk became about frocks, bridesmaids and receptions, for which Alice said she would love to offer her home.'And the garden. By, if the weather's nice enough for some of the celebrations to be outside, that'd be grand.'

Marg felt lifted from the doldrums. Even more so when Alice said,'Do you know, we should open a bottle of champagne, but I so miss having me cocoa with you two. We had some laughs on your doorstep, Marg. And I ain't tasted another mug of cocoa like yours since I were wed.'

Edith chipped in with, 'I was thinking the same thing earlier, lass, and cocoa would make a fine toast.'

'I'll make some now,Alice, and'll love doing so for you both. I knaw where everything is and I'll make the lads one an' all.'

Gerald followed her into the kitchen. 'I hope you included me and Philip in 'the lads' as I would love a cup of cocoa, Marg, and I'll give you a hand. I'd like to learn how to make it — we never had it in this house. Our bedtime drink was a glass of milk, but I haven't forgotten the mug I had at yours one evening last year.'

'Ha, I'm famous for it . . . Anyway, you get me a bottle of milk out and boil it up for me and I'll get the kettle on.'

'Right. So, then you'll need the tin of cocoa and some mugs. Do you know where it all is?'

'Aye, I do, I found out on the day of . . . Eeh, Gerald, I feel awkward saying owt about . . . well, you know . . . but I need to ask how you are, lad? And how's Alice? Really, I mean. I'm worried about you both. Time's passing, I know, and that heals things, but I feel I want to talk to you both about how you're really coping and if I can help in any way. I feel guilty because I can't be here for you.'

'Thanks, Marg, I understand how it is for you. And for everyone. No one talks about it, but sometimes it helps and, well, things are difficult. I'm worried about Alice: one minute she seems really strong and the next . . .'

'That's how it will be, for you both. I wish that I could help, I really do. I'd like to do something.'

'You can, actually, Marg. Alice wants to help you. She mentioned it just after . . . Well, I think if we let her, it would do her the world of good now that physically she's almost healed. I expect that she's told you that she is going to train to be a nurse?'

'Aye, but that won't be for a while, will it?'

'No, and there could be complications to it, though don't say I told you.'

'She will be able to become a nurse, won't she?'

'I don't know yet, I'm looking into it — ways that she can, I mean. Look, don't discuss my doubts

123

with Alice, and I'll leave it at that for now, but in the meantime, she so wants to practise being one now, but more than that, she wants to ease your situation. She's talking about coming to yours each day to help with your ma and gran, and I think it would be excellent for her. Not only helping you, but to be back amongst her own as well. And Joey too. He could be with his old mates in the street. He's lonely when it's not a school day, and it'll be the Easter holidays at the end of next week.'

'So, you really think I should encourage her? Well, I can't say as I wouldn't be glad of some help, but it's not easy, though Ada's around while me and Jackie are out at work.'

'Yes, I do. You can ease her into it . . . Whoops, the milk's going to boil over . . . Ouch! The bloody handle's hot!'

'Come out of the way, lad! By, if you had the sense you were born with, you'd know lighted gas heats stuff . . . There, got it. Run your hand under the cold-water tap, that'll soothe it.'

Gerald began to laugh. The sound tickled Marg and she burst out laughing with him.

'Medical lessons as well as cocoa ones — is there no end to your talents, Marg?'

They giggled as she showed Gerald how to pour a little milk onto each teaspoon of cocoa that she'd put ready into the mugs, so as to make a paste.

'By, you're a dab hand,' she told him as he expertly followed her instructions.

Marg loved how she felt so comfortable with Gerald — he was like the big brother she'd never had. She hadn't quite got on this footing with Philip yet, but knew she would as the hug had broken through any shyness that had remained in her where he was concerned.

In the sitting room, the mood was as light as it had been before Marg had gone to make the drinks. Marg felt there was a new beginning — well, not exactly new, but going back to how things were, with Alice back with her on the street sometimes and Edith next door.

Alice looked pleased as she turned to Marg. 'Eeh, Marg, Gerald just told me he'd had a word with you. You will accept me help then, lass? Not that I know much about nursing yet, but I can learn from Ada.'

'Aye, lass, it'll be grand to have you. And an extra pair of hands, and to not have to pay Ada as much. I know without doubt you can care for me ma and gran. Ta for suggesting it.'

'What about next week? I'll be even stronger by then and can do any light lifting so could do quite a lot for them.'

'That'd be grand, though you can come around in the afternoons before that if you want and bring Joey. I'd love that. Gerald says he's off school then. He'll love being back with his old mates.'

'Eeh, I'd love that an' all, Marg. Ta, lass.'

'You make me envious, both of you. I feel left out now. But work calls.'

Alice turned to look at Edith. 'If Gerald's on late shift, I'll still be there some evenings when you come back home, Edith. We can sit on the step together again.'

'Ha, I might not join you. I might hang out me window and tell the pair of you to shut up or I'll empty me piddle pot over you!'

They fell about laughing at this.

'Oh dear, poor old Ethel, we did give her a time of it, didn't we, but she never did empty the pot on us!' As she said this, Marg caught Gerald's eye and saw him smiling at her. He nodded his head as if to say thank you, but he had no need to; he had done so much for her, giving her this chance to have Alice back in Whittaker Avenue with her, that she felt it should be her thanking him.

As if Edith had had the same thought, she said, 'Eeh, Alice, we'll all be together again.'

'Aye, and giggling like kids. Ha, we were always in trouble for giggling at school, do you remember? Me da used to call us giggling pins ... ' Edith's laughter stopped abruptly as she said this. Philip stepped forward as if to catch her, but Marg, seeing the frightened, unsure look flash across Alice's face too, realised that both of their grief had been triggered, and so, finished the sentence. 'And that made us giggle even more. And you, Edith, used to snort so we stood no chance.'

They were all laughing now and the moment passed, but Marg wondered if they would ever be that way again, without sadness marring their days. Because they had been carefree as young lasses — often hungry, often cold, but carefree and happy for all that.

★ ★ ★

On Alice's first day of helping to take care of Marg's gran and ma, Marg almost skipped home from work, but as she turned into the street, she was surprised to see Gerald's car parked outside her home.

A small worry niggled at her. She quickened her steps. When she entered the house, she was shocked to find Gerald examining her ma. Ma lay almost listless and didn't answer the questions Gerald was asking her.

'Eeh, is Ma bad?'

Alice got up from the sofa.'Marg, love. Eeh, it's good to be back here with you.'

As she went into Alice's hug, Marg's fear deepened. 'Alice? Ma . . . is . . . ?'

'She's all right, love. Gerald's helping her.'

Gerald turned.'Hello, Marg, don't worry, nothing's amiss, but have you any more pillows or cushions? Your mother should be sat up at all times. It will help her breathing.'

'I've some cushions in the front room that we don't use now; Gran has it for her bedroom.'

When Ma was propped up, she looked a lot better and some of Marg's fears left her, but they came back tenfold when Gerald asked her to follow him outside.

'Marg, your mother is very ill, but at the same time, I think . . . well, I think she is capable of more than she is doing.'

Marg didn't feel affronted by this. It was something she'd thought herself and knew her ma to milk a situation in the past. A part of her felt angry that this behaviour was confirmed by a doctor.

'Look, my dear, I would suggest she is taken to hospital, where they will assess her better, but I don't think you would want that, would you?'

'No. I want her to stay here. I've long promised her she'd . . . well, it's an understanding we have.'

'As long as you're prepared. I'm not minimising what her problems are, but it isn't good for her to coddle herself, nor for you as you're doing a lot more lifting than you need to. Moving about will help your mother to clear her own chest more. And, as ill as she is, to be inside all the time isn't good either; she needs fresh air. I'll help you to get her outside now if you like, and I'll see what I can do to get a wheelchair for her, and then you can take her for walks.'

'By, that'd be grand, Gerald, ta. I think underneath it all, she'd love to be outside a bit, but why didn't Ada say owt? She must have known.'

'Tending to patients is money to Ada, as I understand it.'

Anger seethed through Marg. Not only had her ma deceived her, but Ada too.

'Don't be too harsh on your mother, Marg. If Ada has kept her thinking she couldn't move about, then she will have succumbed to that and built up a fear of moving. Anyway, start afresh from now, as recriminations aren't helpful. Get your mother out whenever it's warm enough, even if it means you have to wrap her in a blanket. Especially here in Blackpool, where our air is of such good quality. But in any case, sitting outside chatting to neighbours would help her. People give up if they don't feel part of anything.'

'I'll see that she gets out, I promise. So, there's hope then?'

'I can't say that, Marg. It's right that you should be ready for the worst, but I do think your mother could enjoy a better quality of life for her last weeks.'

'Weeks?' A pain sliced Marg's heart.

'I'm sorry, Marg. So very sorry, but yes. I don't think that your mother has got a lot of time.'

Marg gasped, her fear of losing her ma outweighing her anger now. Even though she'd known it was coming, hearing it spelt out floored her.

'Come on, it's not too bad out today. Let's do it

128

now, shall we? I'll show you how to support her without hurting your back and in a way that's safe for her too.'

Ma was outside in no time, and was soon joined by Gran, who looked as happy as Larry to be sitting with her daughter. Both were on kitchen chairs with cushions on and wrapped up snuggly in blankets.

Marg hugged Gerald as he went to leave. 'Ta, Gerald. I've never liked to bother you over Ma, as it would feel like I was taking advantage, but this, and them pills you get for her, have changed things for me.'

'You can always call on me, Marg, we're family.'

This warmed her heart. 'You know, I thought the other evening in your kitchen that you were like a big brother, and you are. Ta for everything, love.'

'It's good to hear you say that. I did worry I had somehow broken up something precious when Alice and I got together. It's what prompted me to urge you to help Alice by letting her help you.'

'Eeh, Gerald, I'm sorry. I know I give that impression, and I am sad to lose what we three had, but, well . . .'

'Marg, you haven't lost it and never will. All that is happening is that you're moving to the next stage of life, but nothing — not husbands, or even a volcano — could ever change or spoil what you three have. Yours is a special friendship, but you have to adapt, allow for changes, embrace them even, because not to do so might be the only thing that will spoil it.'

This shocked Marg, mostly because she could see the truth in it. 'I've been daft, haven't I? Well, I won't be from now on. I'll accept everything and do as you say.'

'I think you'll find it easier and nicer and that it

129

will help you, Marg. No one, as much as we all want to, can cling on to the past, but we can make a better future by taking the past along with us — the good bits, anyway. Now, I'll be late for work if I don't get a move on. Take care of Alice for me and I'll be back for her later.'

As Marg turned to go back in to Alice, Gran said, 'He's nice, duckie. Is he your boyfriend?'

Marg burst out laughing. Gran wasn't Gran anymore, but Marg would do what Gerald had said and take the best bits of Gran forward with her — the times she had with her as a kid, and the love she'd felt from her and had for her, these she would treasure forever, as she would her loving friendship with Edith and Alice.

12

Jackie walked down the steps of Blake & Partners accountants' office on Talbot Road, a road that ran from the North Pier to Layton, doing up the buttons of the coat Marg had bought her. Somehow, she felt years older than sixteen.

Her full-time work and all that went on at home had matured her before her time. She enjoyed her job, as long as she managed to ignore the little voice inside her telling her that this wasn't where all the studying had been meant to lead, but then, she was a girl, and that was that.

At least accounts were fascinating, and she loved working with figures and entering everything neatly into ledgers. And she always felt that sense of satisfaction when everything balanced.

She felt tired, though, mentally, and this made her body weary, which no one seemed to understand, goading her about sitting down all day.

Sighing, she knew she had to surmount the weary feeling as she was to go to Fairweather's now and work in the shop for another couple of hours before she could rest. But at least her mind was easier about the situation at home now Alice helped them out.

It was good, too, that she had a nice, understanding boss who she liked very much.

Donald Blake preferred the informal approach to work. He was chatty and made the day go by a lot quicker. Married, with a lovely family, who she knew from the photo on his desk and from them calling in occasionally, he seemed to have all that a man could need in life.

Other than him and the two elderly partners, Mr Jones and Mr Brown, there was an older, lady clerk, Miss Robbins, who was nice, but liked Jackie to keep her place. Even though her work wasn't as skilled as Jackie's as she only typed letters and filed folders and ledgers when she and Mr Blake and the others had finished with them, Miss Robbins considered herself the senior. But Jackie didn't mind, and felt the older woman deserved her respect as she had worked for the firm for years.

Today, Donald had surprised her. It had happened after he'd returned from his lunch. He'd told her that he would be required to go away on government business in the next couple of months. That he'd been put on alert. She had no idea why, except a worrying feeling that it might have something to do with the prospect of war. But the bigger surprise had come with him saying that as young as she was, he needed her to take charge of a few accounts, which his older partners weren't up to including in their already heavy schedules.

'Until I go, I will take your training forward, Jackie,' he'd told her. Then he'd confirmed her thoughts by saying, 'I cannot tell you where I have to go as it is top secret and involves something I was trained in during the Great War.'

This had unsteadied her. Until now, the odd talk of war hadn't worried her as it was all 'what if 's, but this was real — a preparation for the event. War could really happen! Donald's newspaper, which he often

132

passed over to her to read, was full of the unrest in Europe. She'd read this part of the paper at first but had soon begun to skip this section and read the newsy bits, as it was all speculation to her.

But it had stayed with her. Not that she'd talked about it. She'd vowed weeks ago not to talk about all she knew of current affairs to anyone, especially not Marg. It was all too frightening.

As she walked along Talbot Road in the direction of Whitegate Drive, she was surprised when the door to a car parked ahead of her opened and no one got out.

When she neared it, she heard a voice say, 'Can I give you a lift, madam?'

'Harry! What are you doing? You gave me a fright.'

Harry laughed as he stepped out of the car. 'Me early birthday present from Gerald . . . well, his da really.'

'His da? Has he been in touch?'

'Naw. But when they left it seems he put it in a lock-up and gave the keys to Gerald, telling him that he could do what he liked with it. Gerald decided that it should come to me for me eighteenth birthday.'

'But that ain't till August.'

'I know, but Gerald seems to want me to have everything sooner. He's one of these who thinks there might be trouble for this country in the future, so thinks us young 'uns should enjoy life as much as we can.'

Not wanting to talk about this, Jackie asked, 'Eeh, Harry, can you drive it?'

'Aye, Gerald took me around the block a few times and that was it, I'm the best driver in the world.'

'By, Harry, that's boastful, but so good to hear you cheerful. I — I well, you've been different lately.'

133

'Aw, I knaw. Get in, lass, eh? And I'll talk to you as I take you to Fairweather's.'

Jackie couldn't contain her excitement as she climbed inside what to her was a beautiful maroon car. 'What sort is it, Harry?'

'It's an Austin 7 and it ain't hardly done any miles, according to Gerald. He says the furthest his ma and da went in it was to their holiday home in the Lakes.'

'Eeh, Harry, what it must be like to be able to afford a car and a holiday home, besides that beautiful house you now live in, I can't imagine. One day I want the same, Harry.'

'I knaw, and you're disappointed in me for not grabbing it all when I had the chance — well, at least taking the first step and accepting Gerald's offer to help me to university. But all that ain't for me, Jackie.'

'Well, never mind that, get going or you'll never get me there, and I want to hear about what's been troubling you.'

'The newspapers.'

'Oh, well, I understand that, as I was just pondering it all when you surprised me.'

'But it's likely if there is a war, I'll have to go . . . I — I've been trying to make you fall out with me, as I'd be able to leave you easier then.'

'By, Harry! You daft apeth, I'd never do that, naw matter how horrible you were, and you weren't, you were just distant. I thought . . . well, I wondered if you had designs on being a priest as you seemed so . . . I don't knaw . . . taken with God and all that.'

'I am taken with God. And aye, it did cross me mind until I found out that you have to go to college. You can't just say you want to be a priest, there's years of training.'

'Really? You really were thinking along them lines?'

'Jackie, I still am, but I love you.'

'Oh?'

'I mean, love you in that I want to marry you, and priests can't marry.'

'By, Harry! I don't knaw what to say. But won't the Church always be a pull on you? And, besides, we're so young . . . I mean, I want to, but . . . '

'That's all that matters. All the thinking I've been doing and all me pushing you away has been because I've been confused. I've been wanting you so much, and yet, I might have to leave you, and that would be unbearable. So, I made me mind up, I'd have it all out in the open. I love you, Jackie, there'll never be anyone else for me, and if I do have to go away to war — if there is a war — I want to knaw you'll be waiting for me.'

'I will, Harry. I've loved you forever.'

Harry turned the car into the gateway of Stanley Park and pulled up. Jackie looked around her, surprised at where they were. She hadn't been looking where they were headed.

'Don't worry, lass, you've got plenty of time, but I wanted to kiss you. Can I?'

She couldn't answer. She slid along the bench seat of the car and into Harry's waiting arms. Her head leant on his shoulder. He looked down at her, his lovely blue eyes misted over, his face holding an expression that she'd never seen before. Then as he lowered his lips to hers a wonderful feeling consumed her whole being.

A loud banging on the car made them shoot apart.

'Now then, young Harry Brett, what's all this?'

They looked up into the face of Bob the bobby.

'Such lewd behaviour ain't allowed in the streets, lad, and where did you get this motor then? By, you've gone up in the world, but that don't give you permission to behave in the manner you have.'

Bob was leaning through the window now. 'And you, Jackie, I'm surprised at you.'

Jackie was so shocked she couldn't speak.

'Right, now, what punishment to give you both, that's the question?'

'I — I'm sorry, Bob, I didn't knaw, and I so wanted to . . . I mean . . . Eeh, I'm sorry.'

'Aye, you wanted to kiss your lassie. Well, it ain't done, not in the street it ain't, lad. And you should have a bit more respect for Jackie. What do you think her gran would say to this, eh?'

Jackie's nerves made her want to giggle at this as she had a good idea what her gran would say, but she forced herself not to think about it. 'Bob, we didn't knaw it weren't allowed, we'll never do it again. It's the first time we've ever kissed. It was because we'd been talking about the possibility of war and Harry might have to go away and we forgot ourselves.'

Bob took his helmet off and scratched his head. 'The first time, you say?'

'Aye, we've never kissed before.'

'Well, it's right that it might come to you young 'uns going off to foreign parts as we did in the last lot, but lassie, you should never let this behaviour happen to you. Not in a public place. And I can see the circumstances and the car and everything got you carried away, so we'll let it go this time . . . Now, this is Dr Meredith Senior's old car, ain't it? It's a beauty. You do have a right to have it, don't you, Harry?'

Bob stepped back and Harry jumped out. 'I do, it's

a present from Gerald.'

'Well, it were a good day when that young man fell in love with your sister. Alice is a lovely lass. I was sorry to hear what happened to her babby.'

'She was glad to see you at the funeral, Bob. Ta for turning up. You should have come back to the house.'

'Naw, I didn't want to intrude. But you tell Alice that I send me regards and if ever me and Mrs Butcher can do owt for her, we will. Mind, I've done her a favour this very moment as I could have had you in court, so think on, lad, and behave well in public.'

'I will, Bob, ta.'

'Right, now get on your way. You're a lucky lad, but by, you had some good luck coming to you and that's for sure.'

Bob mounted his bicycle and went on his way, wobbling as he waved to them.

Jackie burst out laughing. 'Ha, we won't forget our first kiss in a hurry, Harry.'

Harry's face shone bright red and he looked as though he felt a bit silly for a moment, but then he burst out laughing with her.

As he came back into the car having cranked the engine, he looked down at her. 'By, it were worth the scare, lass. I'd do it again right now if I dared, but Bob'll be hiding somewhere and'll pop up and nab me if I do.'

'Aye, it was grand, and I want to feel it again, and again, and again, but you'd better get me to work.'

As they drove off, Harry said, 'How about Sunday after church? I'll ask Alice if I can pack a picnic. I won't care what the weather's like, it can snow if it likes, it won't stop us. We'll take off and go for a drive. We could make it to the Bowland Hills if I carry a couple of cans of petrol with us, and find a nice secluded spot.'

'Eeh, that'd be grand, Harry. Grand.'

★ ★ ★

When she came out of the shop hours later, Harry was waiting for her. She ran gleefully to him and jumped in beside him. 'By, it's like having me own personal taxi.'

'At your service, ma'am.'

They laughed out loud, and Jackie thought that she'd never felt happier than she did at this moment.

All of that changed when she reached home. An ambulance was parked outside their house. 'Oh, naw. Ma, Ma . . .'

Jumping out of the car, Jackie ran to Marg. 'Marg! What's happened? Why didn't you send someone for me?'

'It was all too quick, lass . . . Ma . . . Ma's collapsed, Jackie. She went blue then blacked out. I — I . . . Ada couldn't bring her round, she sent one of the lads in the street to phone for an ambulance. It was all happening . . . Oh, Jackie, lass . . .'

'What do we do, Marg?'

Jackie's fear was compounded by Marg's, and by her inability to tell her what they should do. Marg just stood staring. Her body trembled.

Deciding she would take charge, Jackie went over to the ambulance. 'I'm her youngest daughter. Can I come to the hospital with her?'

'Aye, you can. Hop in. You can hold her hand, lass.'

'I'm going with Ma, Marg. You and Gran get in with Harry and follow behind.'

138

With this, Marg seemed to come back to life. 'Aye, all right, lass, I'll see you up there. Tell Ma I love her.'

Jackie jumped up the steps. One look at her ma told her that this was the end. She couldn't bear the thought, but a strength came to her. She turned and shouted to Marg, 'Fetch our da, Marg . . . Please, fetch Da.'

Relieved that Marg didn't protest, Jackie sat on the bench opposite her ma and took her hand. 'Ma, I'm here with you. You'll be all right, Ma.'

Ma looked shrunken. Her nose looked bigger and her eyes were sunk into their darkened sockets. She opened them and Jackie smiled at her. 'You'll be all right, they'll fix you up. I promise, Ma.'

Ma nodded, but didn't speak.

'I love you, Ma. Don't leave us. Don't die, Ma.'

* * *

Ma didn't open her eyes again until she was in a ward. A black oxygen mask covered most of her face. Eric had taken her hand. 'Eeh, me Vera. I could have taken care of you, lass, but he were always between us.'

Tears streamed down Eric's face. Jackie knew he referred to her ma's late husband, his brother, and her imposter dad.

She knew her own face was wet with a river of tears and could hear Marg and Gran sobbing. How was she going to live without her ma?

Harry's hand came into hers. She looked up at him. 'Fetch Alice, love, and Edith should be home from work now; fetch her an' all, Harry. Marg needs them.'

Harry squeezed her hand and nodded before he left.

As the curtain swished back after him, Jackie saw Marg move forward. Eric stood aside. Marg took Ma's hand and Jackie took her other one.

Gran plonked herself on the bed. She looked desperately lonely. Jackie put her hand out to her and she took it in her tiny, cold one. Then, she warmed Jackie's heart as she offered her other one to Marg. 'We lasses face things together . . . Oh, me Vera, me lovely Vera.'

Ma's eyes flickered; her breath released on one whispered, hardly discernible word: 'love'. She didn't take the breath back in but became still. Very, very still.

A sob broke the silence. Jackie felt held in a cocoon of sorrow, too deep to physically cry and yet she knew her heart was breaking as before her eyes, her beloved ma became a relaxed, beautiful impression of someone much younger.

Gran's hand tightened in hers. 'She's gone. Me last babby's gone. I want to go with her, Marg. I — I can't stay, lass.'

Marg turned her head away from Ma and looked at Gran. Snatching her hand out of Ma's, Marg grabbed Gran as she fell backwards. 'No, no, Gran, don't go. Stay with us, love.'

Jackie heard her own voice scream out, 'Nurse! Doctor! Someone help us!'

Gerald came through the curtain. He looked at Ma, and then at Gran. 'Move away, please, Jackie, and you, Marg. I've got Gran. Just step outside the curtain a moment and let a nurse come to help me. We'll take care of her.'

As they stepped outside, Eric didn't. Jackie saw him move to the head of the bed and take Ma in his arms.

140

Gerald didn't object and Jackie was glad that Marg didn't either.

She turned to her sister. 'Marg, eeh, Marg.'

Marg's arms enclosed her. She didn't speak, just rocked her backwards and forwards.

Words were spoken behind the curtain, but they couldn't see what was going on.

'What happened, Marg?'

'I don't know. It was sudden. Ma had some tea — well, a bit of mashed spud in gravy — but she seemed too weak to manage. So, I fed her. She kept smiling, but not talking. Then suddenly, her head flopped forward. I — I did that blowing thing that Edith once did, and she started to breathe. I — I screamed in the street for Ada. But then . . . it was all confusing. Next thing, the ambulance was there and you . . . I just don't know.'

'Oh, Marg . . . she's gone.'

Marg crushed her to her. 'I'm here, Jackie. You'll be all right, you'll always have me, lass.'

Jackie's sobs broke and though she knew she was making a noise, she couldn't stop herself and despite Marg holding her tightly, she still felt as if she was sinking to the floor.

When the curtain came back, Gerald patted them both. 'Your gran's all right, she's recovering. It was the shock, she fainted. But . . . well . . . ' His arms came around them. 'I'm sorry, so very sorry. I — I don't want to say the words, but I think you know that your ma has passed. Very peacefully, and with all her family around her. Try to think that she is out of pain now. And of how her last days were happy ones, as Alice told me that you managed to get her out in the sunshine a little and that she loved it.' His arms held them tighter. 'Now, do you want us to keep Gran in to keep an eye on her? We will if you like, but I think if you can be strong for her sake and take her home, it will be for the best.'

Marg lifted her head. 'We'll take her home, Gerald, ta.'

To Jackie, Marg seemed like a tower of strength as she came out of Gerald's arms and went behind the curtain.

Gerald still held Jackie and she knew she needed him to; she clung on to him. His hand patted her. 'You'll be all right, and so will Marg and Gran. I've never met stronger women than those who come from Whittaker Avenue.'

He'd hardly said the words than Harry turned up with Edith and Alice. Gerald released her into their arms. Then kissed Alice's hair before stepping back behind the curtain.

Marg came out and joined the hug. She looked so in control, so strong and brave.

None of them spoke, and Jackie thought, yes, Gerald was right. The women from her street were strong and she would be like them.

Breaking away and leaving them in a huddle, she went back in. Gran was sitting by the bed looking at Ma.

'Gran, we're going to take you home, your Vera said we must. She is happy, very happy, free from pain and cares, and you have to take care of yourself.'

'Aye, that were my Vera. How she was before she started her games with that oaf.'

Eric looked at Gran. 'Sandra, I loved your daughter. For some reason she preferred me brother. A waster, a gambler, and a lying, cheating sod who used her.

It weren't me as used her, but him. He used her to get me money, but not for her and the kids, to fund his gambling. Yet, you've always admired him, just as she did. All right, I ain't the best of characters. We were dragged up in far worse conditions than any of you lot knaw of or have experienced. I got meself out of that. I ain't proud of what I do. But I am proud of the love I had for me Vera, all me life. She were the only one for me, but I suffered for it. You have naw idea. You hate me, but I'm telling you now, if ever you want owt, it's there for you. You only have to let me knaw. Vera loved you, and that's good enough for me.'

Jackie ran to him. 'Da, it's all right. Gran has things fixed in her head. She says anything that comes into it. I'll come and see you tomorrow.'

Her da's arms enclosed her. 'But for you, lassie . . . but for you . . . '

Marg came through the curtains; she must have heard it all. 'Hold on, Gran, Jackie, love.'

There was something in Marg's voice that compelled Jackie to do just that. Marg went towards Eric. She opened her arms and her da sobbed as he took hold of her. 'I'm sorry, lass, I should have handled things in a better way.'

'You had no choice, Da. I know what Ma did. But we have to forgive her now. We'll take Gran home. Come and see us tomorrow night after nine, as she's in bed then. She's confused. It's probably your brother she hates, not you.'

'All right, me lass.'

With this, they helped Gran into the wheelchair that a nurse had fetched for them. As Marg wheeled her out, Alice and Edith were each side of her, and

143

Harry walked with Jackie.

Her hand was in Harry's and at this moment, she never wanted to release it. Harry was her rock.

13

Marg

Gran fell asleep in the back of Harry's car, but woke when they arrived home. Marg looked out as Harry parked and saw that Edith and Alice were pulling up in a taxi behind them. With them by her side, she knew she could cope.

Her mind would give her no peace. Had she really been hugged by her da? Somehow, she felt compelled to call Eric that now. It was as if a light had been turned on and all she'd learnt about him two years ago felt different. He'd had no option but to stop coming to their house, but she could have done as Jackie did and gone to see him. He would have refused her nothing. He was just unable to take any more from her ma, and Marg knew that included her too, as she'd also treated him badly. Well, she would see to it that there were changes, and she would learn to love her real da and forget his rotten brother whose memory she'd once held so dear.

A little voice inside her head belied all this and asked of her: *What about his ways? What about how he looked at you and threatened you?*

This unnerved her, but she swallowed hard. She was daft to keep carrying doubts about her da. He was what he was.

She had no time to deal with the sense of unease she felt as Edith and Alice quickly appeared by her side.

'Let us help you, love.'

Marg could only nod, suddenly drained of energy.

Alice, with Harry's help, gently coaxed Gran out of the car, giving instructions as she did.

'Edith, love, fetch the wheelchair that Gerald brought round, please. It's behind Gran's bedroom door. Jackie, go inside and put the kettle on, lass. And Harry and Marg, I'll hold the wheelchair when Edith brings it and you two can help Gran into it. You get behind her, Marg.'

Everyone did as they were told. Marg knew Alice would take care of everything, but Gran wasn't having any of it.

As they went to push her inside, she said, 'Naw, I want you to take me for a walk, Nurse. Take me to me John. I need to tell him about our Vera.'

Gran had taken to calling Alice 'Nurse' so nobody corrected her, and Alice had said that she didn't mind — she liked it — and Gran thinking she was dealing with a nurse made her easier to handle.

Feeling unsure, Marg asked, 'What should I do, Alice?'

Alice bent over Gran. 'Wouldn't you like a nice cup of tea first, and then we'll all take you for a walk?'

'Naw, it's getting late and it'll be dark soon. It ain't far, I just want to go to the cemetery.'

Marg couldn't believe this. Never since she'd lost her marbles had Gran acknowledged that her husband had passed away.

'What do you think, Marg?'

'I think I should take her. Well, me and Jackie, but if you all want to come, it would help.'

'I'll sort things out here, lass,' Alice replied, 'and have the kettle on for when you get back. I can only face the cemetery with Gerald by me side.'

'Aw, Alice . . . I . . . When will it end, lass?'

'It will, love. No matter what, I'm here for you, Marg. Hold it together for Gran. And, if you like, I'll stay till late and we can sit on the step together, eh?'

'Aye. We'll do that, Marg,' Edith smiled at her. 'We'll keep warm by wrapping ourselves in blankets. But I'll stay and help Alice. You three go and take Gran.'

As they walked through the darkness, Marg could feel her strength ebbing, but she kept going.

Gran was quiet. She sat forward in the wheelchair, looking straight ahead. Jackie and Harry walked in front, holding hands. This warmed a small corner of Marg's heart; she'd never seen them this close before. *I wonder if something more has happened between them?*

'Are you all right, Gran?'

'Aye, you should have let that nurse bring me, lass.'

'She couldn't, love. We're all right together, ain't we?'

'Aye.'

When they reached the churchyard, they found it well lit with good street lighting. They walked by the most recent graves; among them was little Gerald as well as Alice's da, and the double grave of Edith's ma and da, and behind the tree, but out of sight, Edith's brother, Albert, buried in unconsecrated ground due to him taking his own life, but near to his ma and da, which had helped Edith.

Granddad's was further back amongst the much older graves — some leaning a little; others looking as though they may fall over. Granddad's looked fine and stood on the edge of the path so they didn't have to push the chair over the grass. As soon as they stood in front of the grave, Gran surprised Marg by getting up out of the chair in a way that belied the weakness she'd shown earlier.

'Now then, John, our Vera is coming to you, lad. Take care of her, and I'll not be long joining you all. Marg and Jackie are here, so when I get up there we'll have the job of looking after them, as things ain't right down here, John.'

To hear Gran recognise her and speak with such an understanding of everything broke Marg. She fell to her knees on the ground and sobbed. Jackie joined her.

Two gnarled hands came onto Marg's shoulders. 'It'll be all right, lass. You're a good girl, you looked after your ma well.'

Marg looked up at her beloved gran. 'Don't you go as well, Gran.'

Gran smiled, but then her eyes veiled. 'Am I your gran, love. What's your name then, eh?'

Marg and Jackie rose. Marg took hold of Gran. 'Eeh, love, let's get you home.'

★ ★ ★

When they got home, Marg was shocked to see that her living room had returned to how it used to be before Ma had needed her bed downstairs.

A fire roared up the chimney.

'Eeh, me lasses, ta. I don't think any of us could have coped with seeing Ma's bed there how she'd left it, but how did you do it?'

'We fetched the street in, Marg. They all came willingly. The bed is back upstairs in the little bedroom.'

'Ta, me lasses, from the bottom of me heart.'

Edith and Alice hugged her. In their arms she felt

148

safe. 'What do you think, Jackie, love?'

'Oh, Marg, it's grand. All the way home I were dreading coming back in here. Now, it's easier to do.'

'Aye, well, you'd all better watch out as when me John finds out that you've taken his bed, he'll have sommat to say. He liked to cuddle me on it.'

'Right. Time for a cuppa, Gran. Let's get you in your chair, eh?'

Gran didn't protest.

'You look so tired, Marg. Have you had your tea? We couldn't find any evidence of it.'

'No, Edith, lass. None of us have eaten.'

'Well, Harry, be a good 'un and nip to the chippy, eh, lad? I bet you're hungry. And get enough for Billy and Joey, and call round and pick them up. We'll all have supper together.'

Jackie piped up, 'I'll go with you, Harry.'

'That's a good idea, Jackie, love. Now, Marg, I'll get Gran ready for bed, then when she's had her piece of fish, we can get her settled and sit out together, eh?'

'Ta, Alice.'

'And I'll pour that tea, or it'll be stewed.' Edith was already making for the kitchen as she said this.

* * *

Just under two hours later, with the street all quiet, Harry having taken the lads back home, Jackie asleep on the sofa and Gran in bed, the three young women sat on the step as they had done umpteen times during the years they'd grown up together.

Huddled in blankets, they talked, giggled, reminisced and drank cocoa. And Marg reflected on their lives.

'Eeh, me lasses, we've been through so much since the days when all we had to worry about was what there was for tea and who could win at double skipping.'

'Aye, we've all been through the mill, but we got through, and you will an' all, Marg.'

'You know, as awful as it sounds, I actually feel relieved at this moment. Ma was suffering badly and I was finding it difficult to cope.'

'It was hard for you, Marg, I know that, lass, and Vera couldn't have gone on much longer, love. You did her proud.'

'I know. I feel guilty for feeling relief, but at the same time I know she's safe now. Gran put her in the care of Granddad and I believe she's with him and happy. I don't know how I'll cope with not being able to see her and talk to her, but I'm glad she's resting.'

'Don't feel guilty, Marg. That feeling ate away at me for a while after what happened.' Edith looked wistfully across the road to the house that was once her family home. 'I felt that I should have done more, been more patient with Albert, made things better for him somehow, so he wouldn't have become bitter and blamed me ma for everything. But then Philip said to me that none of us can walk in another's shoes. All we can do is our best. And you did that, Marg. You've sacrificed so much to take care of your ma, and to put Jackie through her schooling and extra tutoring. You should be proud of yourself, as me and Alice are proud of you, lass.'

'Edith's right, we are, but I know the feelings of guilt an' all, so knaw what you mean, love. After I lost me babby, I tortured meself trying to understand what I did wrong. Did I do too much? You were all always telling me to slow down. Did I eat the right things? It went on and on, but the truth is, no one knows the reason why these things happen. It isn't our fault and we mustn't let the guilt take us over.'

Marg listened, then said, 'I tell you something: no one would want to walk in our shoes. But you're right, Edith, we should be proud. We do the best we can and we stick by one another. I'm proud of us Halfpenny Girls.'

As she said this, she wiped away a tear.

Alice reached for her hand. 'I'm proud of us an' all. And I know you'll move forward soon, Marg, as Edith and I have. You'll rise to the challenge of taking care of Gran, and then you and Jackie can get on with your own lives and hold your heads up high knowing you did your best.'

'Ta, Alice. Eeh, I love you two. It's all I could want in all the world on such a night, to be sitting here with you both.'

'Ha, and without the threat of Ethel saying she'll empty her piddle pot on us.'

They all laughed at this from Edith. Marg felt good being able to laugh. It made her feel that everything could be all right again.

★ ★ ★

Jackie woke her the next morning. 'Pot of tea, Marg. Come on, sleepyhead, Gran's up and fretting about you, but she's had a good bowl full of porridge and she hasn't mentioned Ma.'

A heavy, clogging sadness gripped Marg as she faced the reality of what had happened yesterday. 'Eeh, lass, are you all right?'

'I am. I'm not going into work and neither are you. Edith will tell them at the factory.'

Marg took her tea and gulped down a mouthful of the scalding liquid. 'Aye, I know, I gave Alice a note for Harry to pop through the letter box of your office, but I was going to go in. What time is it?'

'Eight o'clock. And I know about your note, Edith told me.'

'Eight o'clock! How did I sleep that long? Is Gran all right?'

'She is, as I just said. She's up, hasn't mentioned anything and has eaten well. Now, enjoy your tea and I'll go down and watch her.'

'Jackie?'

Jackie stopped by the bedroom door and looked back.

'Are you really all right, lass? You sound bright and breezy. I didn't expect you to.'

Jackie turned and came back to sit on the bed. 'Aye, I'm all right for now. I keep making meself think that Ma's in a better place, then I can cope.'

'It's a good way to look at it, love, but we do have to let our grief out an' all.'

'I did when I went to bed. I cried meself to sleep. And I woke in the night with a feeling of dread in me, but then I had a lovely dream. Ma was all better and she had hold of Granddad's hand and she was happy. She was laughing and she looked like the photo we have of her wedding day. Somehow, I felt better because, though me dream kept changing, Ma was happy, laughing and dancing, and that gave me a good feeling.'

'I'm glad, lass. I didn't dream at all. I just went to sleep and conked out good and proper. And now I

152

need to pee, so mind yourself and let me get out of bed, lass.'

When she stood up, Marg said, 'Mind, even the urge to pee can wait till I've given you a hug. Aw, Jackie, while you can cope, lass, I can.' As they hugged, Marg told her, 'We'll be all right, Jackie, and we'll cope with all they throw at us, because while we stick together, nothing can break us.'

★ ★ ★

The day had been a lot better than Marg had thought it could be. Gran had been away with the fairies most of the time, and though Marg had wished she remembered her and the good times they had together, she was glad for her being in another world as it meant she didn't feel the pain of this one.

With Jackie helping, the two of them had busied themselves cleaning the house, doing the washing and ironing, and had been strong as they'd talked about the past — blocking out bad memories and laughing over good.

And so, when their da arrived, they were ready for him. It was easy for Jackie as she had long accepted him, but Marg was nervous about what his expectations would be of them — her especially. Last night around Ma's deathbed, caught up as she was in the emotion of everything, she'd hugged him and it had seemed the right thing to do, but now she wasn't so sure, as old feelings of anger towards him kept creeping into her.

When he tapped on the door and walked in, Gran had the first say. 'By, it's you, is it? Haven't you done enough damage?'

'You and me both, Sandra. Here, I've brought you a stout.'

Gran smacked her lips. 'Only one?'

'Naw, you daft old bat, I wouldn't dare, would I? I've bought a couple more for you an' all, but this will do you for now.' He took a bottle opener out of his pocket. 'Here, wet your lips on that, Sandra, and behave a moment. I've come to see me daughters, we've a lot to talk about.'

Gran slurped the stout, but didn't look happy.

'Right, me lasses, don't your da get a hug?'

Jackie ran into his arms with such carefree abandonment that Marg felt she was missing out on something.

'Come on, Marg. Put it all behind you, lass. You were wronged, but not by me. You knaw that, lass.'

Marg wanted to retort that he was a large part of her hurt. He knew he had been used. He could have walked away, but no, Eric took what was offered by her ma — paid for it knowing where the money was going, but only thinking of his own need and the result was her and Jackie and the years of deceit they had suffered.

Eric put his head on one side. 'Marg, I can't undo owt, lass. I can only offer what I am and what I have to give.'

Seeing the plea in Jackie's face, Marg relented and went into Eric's free arm and allowed him to cuddle her without resisting.

'Eeh, Marg, you'll take time to heal, I knaw that. Maybe I did wrong, walking out when you'd only just found out the truth about me being your da, but your ma broke me heart. I missed her and I missed you, Marg. I know how much she put on you — far from me speaking ill of the dead, and me heart breaks that Vera has passed, but there were naw need for her to take to her bed and burden you like she did. She weren't that bad at first.'

'Don't. Please don't try to rationalise anything by blaming Ma. I knaw what she did to you, and I knaw she gave me a twisted view of you, and yes, even Gerald said these last two weeks that she shouldn't be in bed all the time as it worsened her condition, but at the end of the day she were me ma, and I loved her, and . . . now she's . . . gone.'

'Eeh, lass. You cry all you need to. I get the message. And I'm a lot to blame.'

A tear plopped onto the top of Marg's head, followed by another, and she felt the heaving of her da's body.

She looked up. His face was awash with tears. 'I — I did wrong, Marg. I did.'

Jackie's pleading voice came to her. 'Naw, Da, don't cry, Marg's all right with you, she's just upset.'

Marg put her free arm around Jackie. The three of them formed a hug, and Marg thought it felt good. Her da did love her. He'd acted like a thwarted lover instead of a responsible da, but then, he'd never been allowed to be the latter. She tightened her grip on his waist. 'We'll sort it, Da, it'll just take time.'

He took his arm from around Jackie and wiped his face with his hand. 'Aye, well, we've got that. And, lass, you'll want for nowt now. I shouldn't have punished you for what your ma did.'

'Come and sit down . . . Jackie, put the kettle on, lass.'

When they sat on the sofa, Da said, 'We have the arrangements to talk about. Are you up to doing that,

Marg? I know you've a lot to sort out.'

'Aye, I haven't thought through what I've to do. Gerald said something about the certificate and when I've got that, I have to register the death and arrange with a funeral director.'

'I'll help you. I'll fetch the certificate — it should be ready — and I'll pay for the funeral. What would you like for your ma, eh?'

'I'd like her put in with me granddad.'

'Not her husband, me brother?'

'No. He don't deserve to get her back; me grand-dad will look after her.'

'Right . . . Ah, here's the tea. Ta, Jackie, love. Me and Marg were just talking about the arrangements, are you all right with that?'

'Aye, I am. It has to be sorted.'

'Right. Me and Marg think . . .'

Marg couldn't believe how gentle her da was with Jackie.

This pleased her, but the adoring look that she saw in Jackie's eyes worried her too. What if this was all a sham? She shook herself mentally.

Eeh, I must forget all the evil I've seen where Eric's concerned, and think of him in a different light.

Her attention was brought back when Da said, 'Now, what about we have the wake at the Layton Institute, eh? Naw need to worry about the cost, only I don't want you two having to do a lot of work. You've done enough. I'm proud of you both.'

Jackie nodded, but Marg didn't agree. 'Ta, for everything, Da, but no. I'll do a few butties here for them as were close to Ma. I don't hold with big wakes where people who haven't given you the time of the day get drunk under the pretence of feeling sorry that

156

someone they didn't care for has died.'

'Aye, I get your point, lass. Well, how about I give you a fiver and you get a nice ham on the bone in, and a few bottles of beer, and a couple of bottles of sherry, eh?'

'Aye, that's all that's needed.'

'Get some stout for me, lass.'

Marg laughed. 'I will, Gran.'

Jackie's hand came into Marg's.

'You all right, lass?'

Jackie nodded. 'I'm just glad we're going to do the wake for Ma.'

'Look, Jackie, anything you want to happen, just say. Your da's only making suggestions, love.'

'I knaw, Da, but I don't knaw what I want . . . I don't want any of it . . .'

'Aw, me little lass.' Marg put her cup down and gathered Jackie to her. She rocked her backwards and forwards. 'Be strong, love, we've a long way to go, but we'll be all right.'

Though these were brave words, Marg wondered how much more they had to face. It wasn't just laying their ma to rest, but Gran was frail too, and the whole world seemed a bit shaky at this moment.

It felt that with Ma's passing, the bottom had dropped out of everything, but no matter what, Jackie needed support and Marg would be there for her.

14

Edith

Edith hadn't been able to settle all week. Not even the excitement of the new furniture she and Philip had ordered beginning to arrive — a new sofa with a winged back in moss green and a matching chair, the lovely rose-coloured velvet cushions she'd chosen to grace them, the light green rug and the heavy velvet curtains — could erase the feeling she had that this day was marred.

Vera's funeral had been a week yesterday and now here it was, her wedding day and Easter Saturday, just eight days later.

She couldn't help thinking that it wasn't right for them to have gone ahead at this time, and she worried what the folk in the street would say. Did they think she was rubbing their noses in her newfound wealth, as they saw all this grand stuff arrive?

Sighing, she sipped the hot tea she'd made and set about laying the table, which now occupied a large space in the front room as she and Philip had moved the bedroom upstairs.

A thrill, tinged by fear, went through her as she thought, *Tonight's the night* — something she'd longed for was really about to happen. She smiled through the blush that had crept over her cheeks and got on with the task in hand before everyone arrived.

Marg was cooking breakfast and bringing it round. Gran, Jackie and Alice were coming too, an arrangement to help her not to dwell too much on her family not being there to celebrate with her.

Trying to dispel any thoughts of sadness, Edith stood a moment gazing at her cream frock draped over the back of the sofa — simple, yet elegant in style, it had a square neckline and a sleek bodice with pearl buttons running to the fitted waist, which flared into the long skirt.

She thought herself so lucky to have found it in a little back street in Lytham St Anne's, a small town not far from Blackpool. The shop was owned by a young seamstress, who'd taken measurements for Marg, Jackie and Alice and, in a couple of days, had run up the two rose-coloured frocks for Marg and Jackie, and a cream one for Alice, her maid of honour. Alice's had a matching rose sash. The effect was stunning.

As she gazed at the frocks, Edith felt calmer.

Whatever the folk in the street think of me, this is my special day and I'm going to enjoy every moment.

It was then that her guard fell as she caught sight of the family photograph she'd had framed, which now stood on the mantelpiece. There they all were smiling down on her.

A huge sob caught in her throat.

Ma should be here with me today, helping me get ready.

She pulled herself up, determined not to give in to her heartbreak. But then another thought came to her.

Ma is with me, I can feel her presence . . . Eeh, better hide the sherry bottle!

This had her bursting out laughing.

Deciding she needed music to stop any further thoughts taking her back into the doldrums, she turned on the old wireless set. Music, light and bright, filled the room.

Picking up her frock, she held it next to her bare skin and danced around with it as her partner. At last, as she twirled around the sofa, the feelings of joy she should feel on her wedding day filled her and she felt able to cope.

A knock on the door hailed Alice arriving.

'Eeh, you're rosy-cheeked, lass, and dripping from the rain. Did you walk?'

'I did. Gerald wanted to bring me, but he was called out in the night and hasn't had much sleep, so I made him go to bed. Have you seen Marg? Is she all right?'

'Not this morning. We sat chatting till late and she was fine.'

'That's good, love. Give us a hug. Warm me up a bit.'

Edith was glad when Alice caught sight of her dress and changed the subject. 'Aw, Edith, that's beautiful. Eeh, love, you're going to look stunning.'

'Ta, love, and I'll have three stunning maids to attend me. What about all you have to do to get your house and garden ready? Not that I can see us being in the garden much, but we shouldn't have taken your offer, it's too much for you.'

'No, love, it helps, you know that yourself. Grief has to be worked through, and distractions help you to do that. Anyroad, it's all done and we've opened up the conservatory to make more room. The lads have made the summer house look lovely, so if the weather doesn't improve, and anyone wants to escape there for a bit, they can. The folding tables are in place, so we only have to put the food out when needed, then all can help themselves. Now, Cinderella, all we have to do is get you ready for the ball!'

160

'Aw, Alice, thank you. I'm still not sure how many guests there'll be. Philip has given out invites to all of his friends and, most scary of all, to the headmaster and his wife. I just hope Philip's mother behaves herself! She's upset Patricia again.'

'Oh dear, Patricia will have to get used to it, like you have. She seems like a strong woman, like she can cope with anything. I like Wilf too, he was lovely at . . . Oh, well, you know.'

Edith didn't comment. She knew Alice had been about to mention little Gerald's funeral, so she jumped in with, 'So, what do you think to me furniture?'

'By, it's all grand, lass. Though if Philip gets this job that he was telling us about, you'll be moving, I expect?'

'That's the plan, but I don't want to.'

'It is hard to do, but once you make the break your new place soon becomes home. Me heart's never left Whittaker Avenue, but me body don't want to come back.'

Edith laughed at this. 'Well, that don't make a lot of sense, but I actually know what you mean. I think my heart will always be here an' all, but maybe it would be easier to live somewhere else.'

The door opened. 'Eeh, I ain't standing on ceremony and knocking in this rain. And I saw Alice come in, so knew that meant you weren't in the bath. Fry-up's ready!'

'Marg, come in out of the cold, you never need to stand on ceremony, lass! Ha, well, I mean, that's now; I don't want you barging in unheralded when I have me husband in situ, though.'

They all laughed as Marg said, 'Not flipping likely, I don't want to catch you at it!'

161

Marg headed for the kitchen. 'I'll just light the oven and then fetch it all round. It'll keep warm while we make the tea.'

When the door closed behind her, Alice turned and looked at Edith. 'Eeh, lass, we're going to have a job with Marg's hair. It looks like she's washed it and left it. It's frizzier than ever!'

Edith smiled. Marg had resembled a tangled mop. 'Don't worry, I told her to do that because I have the very thing to sort it. I bought you all one, but with Marg and Jackie in mind. What do you think?'

Edith showed Alice the satin bands with a little veil in cream, with a silk rose attached. It had a crocheted pouch hanging down. 'You clip this on then tuck the rest of your hair into this elasticated pouch.'

'Aw, they're perfect, I remember seeing your idol, Rita Hayworth, in one of these.'

'That's where I got the idea. The lady at the shop where I bought my frock told me where I could buy them.'

'By, lass, I feel excited now.'

'Don't start, me tummy's got a million marbles juggling about in it as it is.'

'Come on, let's get the kettle on.'

★ ★ ★

The chatter around the table was hilarious as Marg teased Edith. Edith knew that Marg was trying to help herself in playing the clown, and not only because of her recent bereavement, but last night she'd confessed to feeling left behind and was worried she might spoil things by being tearful.

Edith had told her it was understandable and

they'd all be there for her and Jackie. But as Marg now said, 'Right then, lasses, we ought to get ourselves ready — it's ten o'clock and the wedding car will be here at eleven thirty,' it was obvious that she was taking charge as a way of coping. She soon had the dishes in the sink, and ordered Edith to carry on putting her lippy on and Alice to dry the pots.

'You take Gran back home and get her ready, Jackie. Me and Alice will help Edith to get ready when the clearing up's done, and then we'll all help you into your frock, lass.'

Edith thought how well Jackie was doing too. She soon had Gran outside without any fuss.

★ ★ ★

By the time they were ready, Edith was near to tears again. They all looked so lovely, and she felt like a princess herself.

Outside, despite the rain, the whole street was out to cheer her and this warmed her heart and settled her earlier misgivings.

It distracted her, too, from looking longingly at the door of her old house. When she did take a quick glance, she fancied she saw her ma waving to her. She lifted her hand and waved back.

'Ha, you look like a princess and you're acting like one, waving to the crowd, Edith.'

The moment passed into a giggle, but Edith felt stronger now as she sat in the front seat of the car Philip had arranged to take her to church. Marg, Alice and Jackie got into the back seat.

They were to meet Billy at the church. She'd asked Billy to give her away as he'd always held a special

163

place in her heart when he was growing up. Always making her laugh, she'd admired his strength, the way that he would stand up to his da to defend Alice or Harry, despite only being a young lad at the time. He'd been thrilled and full of pride, drawing his four-teen-year-old-self up to stand tall.

It hadn't been a difficult choice for her. All of Alice's brothers had been like brothers to her, but Harry understood as she'd put it to him that he'd done the honours for Alice, and now that he had a car, he was useful in giving lifts. He followed behind with Gran and Ada, who was attending to watch over Gran.

The rain stopped as they drove to St Kentigern's church on Newton Drive. Billy stepped forward from where he stood outside the church, looking so hand-some in his grey suit. His blond hair, normally curly like Alice's, was tamed with Brylcreem, making him look really grown-up — something she suspected Gerald had had a hand in.

'Aw, Edith, you look lovely.'

'Ta, Billy. Can I take your arm?'

Almost as tall as her, Billy proffered his arm. 'Do you know, when I were a little lad, I used to tell every-one that I was going to marry you one day.'

'Aw, Billy! You never asked me!'

'Ha, naw, I fell in love with Gracie Beldon and for-got all about it.'

They both laughed. 'So, are you in love with anyone at the moment?'

'Aye, her name's Annie Bothford. She likes footie and is always at the game. She helps me take the water out for the players.'

'Aw, you're missing the game and the Tangerines are doing so well.'

'I knaw . . . But I don't mind, you're worth it.'

They'd reached the church door. Talking about football was the last thing that Edith expected to be doing, but somehow it had calmed her more than the attempts of anyone else. 'Let's hope they win, Billy.'

'Aye, I shouldn't be talking about them really. If our Alice heard me, she'd skelp me lugholes.'

Edith laughed out loud at this. The church was only half full and her laugh echoed around it.

'Well, the moment is on us and you're looking as happy as I feel to have the honour of joining you in marriage to Philip, Edith.' Father Malley smiled at her as he stepped forward from where he had been waiting just inside the church. 'And who do we have here?'

'I'm Billy, Father. I'm a friend.'

'And a very good one, I am thinking. One with the honour of giving Edith to Philip. Well now, you escort her to the aisle and then when I ask, 'Who gives this woman to be married to this man?' you answer, 'I do'. And then you step back and take your seat. Is that okay?'

'Aye.'

'And do you have your speech all ready?'

'Naw, Edith let me off that bit. Gerald's making the toast.'

'Ah, lucky you.'

Billy carried out his duty with a flourish, almost presenting her as if she were a star he'd led onto a stage, and she felt like one at this moment as Philip turned, and the love he had for her filled his eyes.

Edith held his gaze, implanting it on her mind. She never wanted to forget this moment as long as she lived.

When they walked into the vestry to sign the register, Edith was happy to see that Philip's mother had a smile on her face as she walked with his father behind Alice and Billy. Alice, as matron of honour, and Billy were to be her witnesses.

As Edith smiled at Sue, Sue stepped forward. 'My dear, I want to welcome you as my daughter-in-law.'

Sue's tone suggested she would rather be doing anything but that, which made Edith shake with nerves. 'Ta . . . I mean, thank you.' She looked at Philip, but he had no time to react as Mr Bradshaw stepped forward and took her hand. 'Welcome, lass, you look very beautiful.'

Edith could smile easily at him as his was a genuine and heartfelt welcome.

* * *

With the ceremony behind them, Philip sat holding her hands in the back seat of the car.

'My darling, you look beautiful. My lovely, lovely bride — my wife.' 'And you do an' all, Philip, love. I love you more than I can tell you.'

He kissed her lightly then as the car drew away and the congregation waved them off. As she sat back, Philip said, 'Mother didn't upset you, did she, darling? Only she seemed very cold in her greeting.'

'She threw me for a moment, even though I had prepared myself after you told me how much she disapproved of us marrying so suddenly.'

'I reminded her this morning that it wasn't sudden, and her thoughts were wrong, that we were always going to marry, we just decided not to wait.'

Edith coloured. *So Susan thought they'd had to get married!*

She was about to blow her top when she saw the look on Philip's face and burst out laughing.

'You don't mind?'

'No. I shall enjoy seeing her count the months and looking at my tummy.'

'I think Mother was right — she has met her match!'

Philip was beaming now and that was all that mattered. It took the sting out of what his mother had said. 'Anyway, lad, this is our day. And we're going to enjoy it, nothing can spoil it.'

'Ha, I am your lad now, darling, and nothing will ever change or spoil that.'

Philip's gentle kiss held a promise of all that was to come and awoke an eagerness inside her. All the nervousness she'd felt left her and she couldn't wait for the moment they would be alone together.

* * *

The sun came out while they had their food — Alice had made lovely platters of daintily cut sandwiches and sausage rolls, which she'd baked herself, and Jackie, an excellent baker, had made little meat patties and a variety of tiny cakes.

It was a bit of a phenomenon, but the whole country was experiencing a lovely warm Easter and this meant they could go into the garden for a surprise that Alice had arranged — an Easter egg hunt.

She'd boiled eggs in water reddened with cochineal to turn the eggs pink, and had drawn faces on them. 'Whoever finds the ones with the bride and groom's names on will win a chocolate egg!'

What followed surprised and overjoyed Edith as all, including Susan and Philip's headteacher and his wife, who she'd only formally shaken hands with and said hello to, joined in.

The laughter and cries of 'I've got one!' and 'You cheated, you saw me going for that one!' and 'I'm a winner!' filled the air.

Edith stood watching, holding Philip's hand. Her love for him swelled in her as his laughter and shouts of encouragement rang out. He looked so handsome.

Then came the mock presentation as she and Philip had to give out the prizes to the winners. And another surprise for them as Alice gave them a lovely egg, intricately made in blue porcelain and decorated with gold filigree. 'It's a replica of the real thing, which Gerald tells me is called a Fabergé and would cost thousands, but comes with our love as a momento of today.'

'It's beautiful. We'll treasure it forever. Thanks, Alice, lass, you've made our day perfect.'

'And I made you these, Edith, to keep yours and Philip's eggs warm.'

Marg gave her two knitted egg cosies, made from the same blue wool she'd made Jackie's Christmas scarf with. 'And Gran embroidered a 'P' on the one for Philip and an 'E' on the other one.'

'Eeh, Marg, they're lovely. I'll treasure these an' all.'

She opened her arms to them both and they hugged. Then something strange happened as the sound of clapping could be heard, just one person at first and then everyone joined in.

Edith knew tears were beginning to prick her eyes as she thought it was an applause the three of them deserved — they had all shown courage and strength no matter what had been thrown at them.

She didn't know if that's why they were clapping, but she suspected so as most knew how hard it had been for the three of them to get to this stage.

An arm came around her and drew her away. She went into Philip's waiting embrace and saw Gerald do the same with Alice. Clive stepped forward, and Edith's heart sang as Marg didn't reject him but went into a cuddle.

It was Susan who made the first step to break this up as she came forward and tapped Edith on the shoulder. With this, others broke the circle they'd formed and all began to mingle and chatter.

'Ta ever so much for coming and for welcoming me into the family, Sue.'

Philip moved away. Edith wanted to hang on to him, but she knew this chat had to come. Though, in a million years she didn't expect to hear what Sue said.

'I've been a foolish woman, Edith. I don't know why, but seeing you girls together and knowing your stories suddenly made me realise what I am missing in life — *friends*. All that socialising and trying to be top dog has wasted my life and caused me to lose sight of what is really important. I know what that is now. I want to help others . . . I know, I'm shocked myself, but there must be so many like you three in Blackpool who I could help through charity work. I — I never even helped at the church fundraisers. Oh, I gave money and things for stalls, but I didn't muck in and offer my labour. That's going to change. And I think you'll be the one to help me to make these changes.'

Edith couldn't help herself, she took Sue in her

arms and hugged her. When they parted Sue had tears in her eyes, but she quickly dabbed at them, looking embarrassed.

'Hey, a ma-in-law is meant to cry on her son's wedding day, you know.'

Susan smiled.

'I can make changes an' all. I'm going to learn to speak properly, so when we do have to be with your business associates, I won't let you down.'

'Don't do that. I tried to be what I'm not and ended up a sad woman. You be proud to be a Lancashire lass. I like the accent, always have, just didn't let myself. Well, more fool me. And in future, I won't be correcting Tom . . . your da-in-law, as you will call him. Poor thing has struggled to speak correctly.'

'I'm glad. Eeh, you've made me feel at home with you and boosted me confidence.'

'Well, it's Father Malley we have to thank as he sowed the seed.'

'Oh?'

'Yes, when you were hugging your friends and everyone was clapping, he said, 'Now, that's real love, God love them.' I hmphed.' She grinned a quirky little grin. 'Well, I hadn't had my enlightened moment then. Anyway, he told me that if I didn't accept God's children for who they are, how can I expect God to accept me? And that shook me. No, you be you, Edith, my dear, and show this silly woman the real way to live life.'

This gladdened Edith. 'Ta, Sue, for accepting me and I'm glad you've stopped me from trying to be someone I'm not.'

'Well, you have an ally in me, and I won't let you make the same mistakes that I have . . . Ah, here's

Philip. He looks like he may take you away from me, as he has his headmaster in tow. Now, remember, my dear, be yourself.'

Edith kissed Sue on the cheek. 'Thanks, Ma.'

An almost triumphant smile lit Sue's face as she looked over at Philip.

Philip's expression was a picture. Edith knew he was bursting to ask what had prompted her to kiss his mother, but that had to wait.

'Edith, Mother, I've brought Mr Cartland, my head-teacher, over to meet you properly.'

Sue held out her hand. 'Delighted to meet you and I hope you're keeping this son of mine in line.'

Mr Cartland took the hand and kissed it with a flourish. 'Indeed, my dear, though I haven't found the need to as of yet. How very nice to make your acquaintance. And this is your beautiful bride, Philip? Lucky man. Edith will grace your side and together you will go far in life. How do you do, Edith?'

The moment was on Edith. She'd practised several answers to various questions she might be asked. To this one, it should be, 'Very well, thank you, how nice to meet you.' But what she said was, 'I'm well, ta, and it's good to meet you an' all.'

Mr Cartland looked astonished, but recovered. 'My, a good old Lancashire lass, eh? I'm very pleased to meet you.'

'Aye, and a true Sandgronian, Blackpool born and bred.'

For a moment, Edith could feel the tension and had the sinking feeling that she'd let Philip down, but then Mr Cartland burst out laughing. 'Well, meet a Yorkshire man by 'eck. You're a red rose to my white, but I think we're going to get on, young lady.'

They all laughed at this.

'Philip tells me you want to take up teaching?'

'Aye, I do, and I might get me chance soon.'

'Well, I wish you luck, my dear, I am sure you will make a good teacher. You will change lives, Edith.' He turned to Philip. 'You must keep me informed of how Edith gets on, and we must make a date when you and Edith can come to dinner. My wife would love that. Besides, you and I have a lot to talk about.' He turned back to Edith. 'My wife was a teacher, but she gave it up for my career. She'll be able to give you some tips, dear. Now, enjoy this special day. I will take my leave now, but I look forward to seeing you both in the near future.'

When Philip came back to her, after seeing his boss and his wife to the gate, he took her in his arms. 'There, haven't I always told you to be yourself, my darling? Oh, I love you so much.'

'And so you should, Philip. You are a very lucky man to have found Edith.'

'Thank you, Mother.' With this, Philip put his arms out to her.

Susan had to let go of the hands of Patricia's girls, Sophie and Eliza, who had run over to her and seemed to want to be near their grandmother all day, but she went to Philip with tears once more glistening in her eyes.

As Philip hugged his mother to him, he said, 'I have the best wife and mother in the world.'

'And nieces!'

'Yes.' He hugged the girls. 'The very best nieces who I miss so much when they are at school, and whom I am so proud of.'

Patricia tapped him on the shoulder. 'And don't

forget your best sister, either.'

Philip laughed as he turned to Patricia. 'No one can surpass you, sis. You've stood by me through everything, thank you. Your strength has got me through a lot.'

When they came out of the hug, Patricia said, 'That's because I take after Mother.' She smiled at her mother and was rewarded with a hug.

Edith felt so glad that Patricia had been thoughtful enough to turn Philip's words around as they might have upset his mother, and she least wanted that to happen. She couldn't believe this turn of events, but she loved it, welcomed it and thanked God for it.

15

Alice
August 1939

Almost five months had passed since the wedding. It had been a lovely summer with many gatherings in the garden, but today was another special one and everywhere looked lovely for it.

She stood back and admired the picture it all made.

It wasn't just how the phlox, roses and so many flowers she'd planted in her darkest days had bloomed, but the excitement that the bunting, fluttering in the warm breeze, generated. It made the whole setting perfect.

Joey, always the creative one who loved to draw, had made the bunting by joining pages and pages from his drawing book together and crayoning a huge, 'Happy Birthday Harry'. It had really amazed her and thrilled Harry, who'd picked Joey up and swung him around above his head, making Alice realise just how big and strong this eldest brother of hers was. He towered over her now.

This Friday evening, the 25th of August, was to celebrate his eighteenth birthday and it was going so well. Everyone's chatter and laughter created a lovely atmosphere.

She looked over to where Gerald was serving drinks from a tray. As he approached her he asked, 'Well? Is it all to your liking, darling?'

'It is. Eeh, Gerald.'

'And Harry's really happy and enjoying the attention, which is why we did all of this. You know, he's like a brother and a son to me . . . Oh, I mean — '

'It's all right, love, you don't have to be on your guard. I promise not to shed tears over you thinking of Harry and the lads as the sons we can never have. Besides, we've both shed enough of those over the last months to fill a river. I just want us to feel happy and at peace. We can do that, can't we?'

Gerald pulled her to him; she could hear his heart beating steadily in his chest. He didn't speak, just held her. It was all she wanted. In Gerald's arms she felt safe.

When he released her, Alice caught sight of Marg standing with Clive. Nothing had changed with them, they still only behaved like friends — though inseparable ones, as they were always together.

As she reached them, Marg giggled. 'We were just watching Harry with Jackie. After it all going quiet when Ma died, we think things are moving on again.'

Gran answered. 'Course they are. I told him that if he didn't marry our Jackie one day, then I'd marry him. Then I told him he'd have to fight me John first, as he wouldn't let anyone take his girl off him . . .'

Alice laughed and moved away to speak to Harry. She'd heard lovely Gran's tales about her John so often, though she wondered whether she'd missed something new as the group were laughing hysterically when she reached Harry's side.

He greeted her with, 'By, is that Gran and her stories? She can tell them, but whether they're true or not is another matter.'

'As long as they are to her, Harry. Anyway, lad, I hear you aren't doing so bad, you have two girlfriends now. So, which is it to be, Jackie or Gran?'

'I'd marry Gran every time.'

Jackie hit him on the shoulder.

'Naw, Jackie's me girl and always was.' With this, Harry caught hold of Jackie and drew her to him.

Alice felt a surge of love for Jackie, 'Eeh, lass, you've always been like a little sister to me — now I know you will be one for real one day and that's grand, just grand.'

Jackie came out of Harry's arms and hugged her. 'Ta, Alice. It took a long time for that brother of yours to see that I should be his girl.'

'It was Gerald giving him that car that made him realise he was a man, and what a beautiful girl he had who loved him.'

'Aye, well, I have to keep him in check. He nearly got us into court when he took me for me first ride!'

'What?' Alice coloured. She hoped that Jackie wasn't going to tell her anything she couldn't cope with. Harry might be classed as a man, but he was still her little brother.

She listened as Jackie told her about their encounter with Bob the Bobby. 'It . . . it were the day me ma were took ill.'

Alice jumped in to counter this memory. 'By, Jackie! Bob would have been pulling your leg, but don't chance it. Make sure any canoodling you do is in a private place, lass.'

'I will. I never knew it was an offence. It shouldn't be, it was the best thing that ever happened to me.'

'I know, lass. You've loved Harry since you were a young 'un, knee high to a donkey. And I'm glad for you. I can think of no one better to be me sister as I know one day you two will marry. Me, Edith and

176

Marg have always known it.'

Billy interrupted them. 'I take it from what Alice just said that you and Harry are going out proper at last? Well, I'd like you for a sister an' all . . . well, me second sister.'

'Ta, Billy. Where's Joey?'

'I'll take you to him, Jackie. He's sitting in the summer house. You knaw, that'll be somewhere private for you and Harry.'

'You heard?'

'Aye, but I knew Harry were going to kiss you, I heard him practising asking you. It was right funny. Anyway, let's go and get Joey, he'll be reading a book. By, he don't knaw how to enjoy himself that one, he's like a sort of professor or sommat.'

Alice walked away, leaving them to it. She was almost up to where Gerald stood with his back to her talking to Philip when she heard Philip say, 'What a time for such as Harry — for all of us with how things are escalating. What do you think of it all, Gerald?'

Curious to know, as Gerald hadn't spoken much about the threat of war that hung over them all, Alice hesitated then held her breath as he said, 'I'm still hoping war won't happen, but I think it will. What will you do? Have you thought about it?'

'I have. I think I'll wait a while to see what happens. It might be all over in a flash, but if it goes on, I don't see that we'll have a choice in what we do.'

'I feel the same, though if they need doctors . . . Oh, I don't know, I hate thinking about it, much less talking about it, and yet, I have a compelling urge to talk to anyone and everyone, hoping that someone will tell me it won't happen.'

To Alice it was as if a cold hand had clutched her

heart. Suddenly, she remembered all the tales of the last war that she'd overheard from the women on her street, telling of the men going away for years, of their fear that their man wouldn't come back, of the not knowing if they were safe or not, and of the hunger through the shortages.

Please God, don't let it happen. I couldn't bear Gerald going away!

'Are you all right, Nurse?'

Gran taking hold of her hand brought Alice's attention away from her feelings. She looked down at Gran, not realising she was so close to her. 'I am, Sandra, love. Are you?'

'Aye. Me daughter's not here. She went off with me John and they've not come back.'

'Ha, they'll be having a whale of a time. John'll have Vera on the big dipper and she'll be squealing with laughter. Can I get you another drink, love?'

'Aye, see if they've got a stout, eh? I ain't much for this fizzy stuff, it goes up me nose.'

'I know what you mean. I never thought I'd drink champagne, and now I do I don't think I'll ever get used to it. I prefer a sherry.'

As she moved away, Alice saw Clive join Gerald and Philip and heard him say, 'I heard you talking about the possibility of war? I, too, think it will happen. I don't think Hitler can keep his hands off Poland. It's a worrying time.'

Suddenly, it didn't seem like merely men's talk, but as if it would truly happen. She jumped when Marg linked arms with her. 'I heard what they were talking about, Alice. Eeh, it's frightening. Clive says he'll join up if they need him. He's already volunteered himself as a lifeboat crew member. He says that until he might

178

be needed, he'd like to help to protect our shores that way and help save anyone in distress. He gave me the willies as he thinks Blackpool is a likely landing place for invaders.'

'No! Aw, Marg, just when we were getting on an even footing. Now I feel as though we are doomed, and I'm cross with Gerald, he promised to keep it all light-hearted tonight.'

'Lads will be lads, love. I'll help you with the drinks. No doubt nothing will happen and we're worrying needlessly.'

Though Alice smiled, she wasn't convinced, but she didn't say so. She made herself brighten. 'Anyway, we can keep tonight fun if the men can't. We need a laugh or two, don't we?'

'Don't get me started. And don't ask me how I am, lass, as I still blubber at the drop of a hat.'

'I know that feeling. Come on, Gran wants a stout, we got some in for her.'

With Gran settled, Edith came over to them. 'Do you know what I feel like doing?'

Alice and Marg looked at her, unsure of what she was getting at.

'I feel like us three having our own little party. A sort of crowning of the happiness — or lack of sadness that life has dealt us for five whole months. I mean, there's been no terrible things happen since before me wedding day and that's allowed us to get some normal life back. Does that sound daft?'

'No, it sounds grand. When?'

'Why not tonight? After everyone goes, we'll take a bottle of sherry into the summer house and have a good old chinwag, eh?'

Edith appeared to be a little drunk. Alice laughed

at her. 'Not sherry, cocoa. If I have any more alcoholic drinks, I'll wake with an awful headache, and I have a secret to reveal about tomorrow yet.'

'Eeh, tell us, lass.'

Edith leant in a little too far and nearly toppled over. Marg caught hold of her.

'No, I'll keep it. Now, I'm going to make you a cup of tea, Edith, you're all over the place.'

'Ha! I just felt like letting go of everything. It's overwhelming me — talk of war, mainly.'

'Edith! Don't cry, love. Come on, sit down a mo, and I'll make that cuppa and bring it out to you.'

As she went to the kitchen, Alice had the horrible feeling that, in Edith, she'd seen a flash of Betty, Edith's late ma, who had a drinking problem. But when she went back with the steaming drinks, Edith had sobered a little. 'Eeh, I didn't like that feeling. Whatever possessed me? I only had one sherry and that champagne.'

'Well, maybe you shouldn't drink at all, love. Some people can't tolerate it.'

'You're right. I'm teetotal from now on.'

Relief flooded Alice and she told herself how silly she was being. Edith had hated her ma's drinking, there was no way she would go down the same path.

★ ★ ★

By the time they sat in the summer house, all was quiet. The party had gone on and on, and Alice couldn't believe it was now one o'clock in the morning. Harry had taken Jackie and a singing and dancing Gran home, and the other two boys had gone to bed. There was mess everywhere but they decided they would all tackle it tomorrow. They soon regretted this decision when the rain that had threatened in the last hour began to fall, sounding loudly on the glass roof.

'I hope the men go inside. They'll get soaked sitting in the garden with their nightcaps.'

'Eeh, never mind them, Alice, they're old enough to look after themselves. Now, tell us what's happening tomorrow?'

Alice grinned. 'By, I can't wait to tell you, Edith. Are you both ready?'

'Stop teasing and get on with it. But make it something good — I only want good news from now on.' Marg blew the steam from her mug as she said this.

'Well, I'm really excited about it. I only go and start a new job as an orderly on the wards at Blackpool Victoria tomorrow!'

'Oh, really? I mean, that's wonderful, lass. Eeh, give me a hug.'

'Ta, Marg.'

Edith joined in. The three of them giggled as they hugged how they were always used to doing.

'But listen, Marg, it's mornings only, so I can still come to yours in between to look after Gran. How will that be?'

'Well, actually, I've got news on that front. Me da's going to help us out with paying Ada, so we'll be fine. I'll keep to me part-time, though, as Gran needs her own around her for most of the day. But I want to hear more. Will this job lead to your training, Alice?'

'Well, not exactly. Sadly, I won't be accepted for training to be a nurse as I'm married — but I'm really hoping it gives me insight and experience. But as well as the job, I'll be joining the Red Cross. Even though they don't train married women, they do teach first aid to a high standard, though I'll have to pay for me certificates.'

They were sitting back down when Edith said, 'It seems like everything is working out for us. I know we've been dragged through the grinder to get here, but, well, I have a good feeling about every — '

Her words were cut short by an enormous explosion that shook the ground beneath them. The colour drained from their faces as they stared at one another.

The door opened and Gerald stood there in shock. Alice almost didn't want him to answer the question that came to her. 'Is . . . is it the Germans?'

'No, darling, I doubt it very much. Probably a gas explosion, or some such.'

But though he'd tried to sound reassuring, Gerald's voice shook and Alice could see that his body did too. His fear intensified hers.

The clanging of bells suddenly filled the space around them. The sound seemed to help Gerald as he shifted into his doctor role.

'That's the ambulance. Hold on.' He was back in a second. 'I can see it heading this way. I'll get the others and we'll follow it as we might be needed.'

'No, Gerald, no!'

'Stay calm, my darling. Be strong. I'll be fine. But there may be people hurt.'

'We're with you, Gerald.' Clive appeared by Gerald's side. He looked over at Marg. 'Stay here, Marg, I'll come back for you.'

Edith was on her feet. 'Philip!'

'I'm here. It's all right, darling, stay with Alice and Marg. We'll be back as soon as we can.'

With this they were gone.

Out in the garden, Billy and Joey stood in their

pyjamas. 'Has the war started, Alice?'

'No . . . I mean, I don't know. Come on, let's get inside. It's pouring now, you'll get soaked. Is Harry back?'

As Billy shook his head, Harry's car pulled into the drive. He jumped out. 'Sommat's happened to the town hall. I thought I'd drive back along the prom, but I saw police everywhere and then, *boom*! I managed to turn around and come back through the back streets. I've never seen so many police and ambulances rushing towards the sea.'

'But you don't know what happened?'

'Naw, except, well, I think it were a bomb from what I did see. By, me ears!' Harry patted his ears. 'They're all blocked.'

Inside the house they stood in a huddle in the kitchen. Marg did what she always did and made more cocoa, as the others speculated in frightened voices.

★   ★   ★

It was two hours later that the men came home. All looked tired and pale. Gerald was the one to tell them. 'No one hurt, but the town hall is in tatters. Bob the bobby said he thought it was IRA because other bombs were found before this one went off. One was outside Woolworths. The police had all been looking to see if there were others when this happened.'

There was a silence. All Alice could think of was why? She knew about the troubles over the water, but why come across the sea just to ruin their lovely town hall?

It was Edith who asked this question of Gerald.

'Well, it's all about disruption. Papers will be

destroyed, as will records, and the IRA will get publicity out of it too.'

Although Alice could see this, it still seemed senseless and dangerous.

Clive at least put this in perspective. 'Well, thank goodness they chose to do it at night when there weren't any workers involved. Now, I for one need my bed. It's been a lovely, but eventful night. Are you lads all right?'

The boys all nodded.

'Well, I'll see you in work on Monday, Harry, lad.'

'Ta for coming, Clive. See you Monday.'

With Marg and Clive making for the door, Philip and Edith decided to go too. But this time as they hugged goodnight, Alice felt there was something different in how they did so as in each hug there was a sense of fear, mingled with the need to give reassurance and comfort.

★ ★ ★

Once in their room, Alice couldn't keep still. She sat on the end of the bed and Gerald came and sat on his haunches in front of her. 'It's all right, my darling. It won't happen again. They never strike in the same place twice.'

'But the war will.'

'Oh, my darling, come here.'

Held in his arms, Alice didn't feel safe like she usually did. Instead, her fears deepened. 'You'll go, won't you? Oh, Gerald, I'll not be able to bear it.'

He didn't deny the truth of her statement, but lowered his lips to hers. 'I'm here now, my darling. Kiss me, Alice.'

184

In his kiss, Alice felt an urgency, a seeking of normality. She gave that back to him, letting her fears go from her. Her Gerald was here. Here in her arms and she wasn't going to waste this moment worrying about what might lie ahead.

16

Just over a week later, Marg sat on her step hugging her knees as the simple six-word sentence 'Britain is at war with Germany' raged around her head.

What now? How would their world change? Already, the men of the street were carting sacks of sand back from the beach to stack around their doors. They'd all been taking measures to black out the windows too, but like everything that took money, Marg had put off doing hers.

Bob had knocked a couple of nights this week to tell her she must sort it out, but she just didn't know how she was going to be able to. She wondered whether she could use the four heavy candlewick bedspreads that Ma had bought a while ago from the market.

Jackie plonked down beside her, interrupting her chain of thought. She rested her head on Marg's shoulder but didn't speak, and Marg didn't know how to comfort her. They sat in silence like this until Clive's car pulled up and Marg felt a glimmer of hope surge through her.

Jumping up, she didn't stop to think what she was doing, but went into his open arms for the hug he offered. Since that afternoon in the boat many months ago, they'd returned to their usual banter and friendly ways and hadn't progressed from a quick hug and a peck.

'Not good news, Marg, but we did expect it.'

'Oh, but you, Harry, Gerald and Philip will have to go! It's unbearable . . . '

'I know, but it won't happen overnight. Conscription has only just been passed, and there's a lot to put into place before the forces can cope with an influx, so it appears that we have to await our papers arriving to give us our orders. We'll all have time to adjust.'

No length of time was enough time to Marg.

'Anyway, I've come to see if I can help you with your blackouts. I've done mine, and I've been busy organising for the factory to be done too. I hadn't time to give thought to how you were coping, but I expect Bob has given you a couple of friendly reminders. He's taking his new duties very seriously.'

'Aye, he has, and I were just thinking about what to do. I've some old candlewicks, but I don't know if they will do the job.'

'No need for that. I checked and I've enough black canvas left over to make blinds for all of your windows. But it isn't an easy job so we best get on with it, love. Is Gran all right?'

'Aye, she is, she's taking it all in her stride. She's made of tough stuff. I thought I might lose her after Ma passed, but she's bounced back.'

'Well, that's good, only I did worry as she was very quiet yesterday.' He spotted Jackie then, looking like a ball of misery as she'd remained curled up on the step. 'Hello there, Jackie. How are you after your couple of sherries at the wedding? You made me split my sides with laughter at some of your sayings.'

Jackie smiled. 'I had a headache the next day actually, and a heavy feeling of doom.'

'Like us all, love. Now, let's see how we're going to

187

fix these blinds. I've brought tools and some wooden poles. I've also got a bag of curtain rings, so once we have our lengths, Jackie can set about sewing the rings onto the tops of the canvas, as I'll need you to help me, Marg. How does that sound?'

'Ta, Clive, aye, I think that'll work grand. Jackie and Gran are better at sewing than I am anyway.'

As they cut the lengths, Clive explained that he hadn't any rolling mechanisms. 'I brought this roll of chord with me. I thought, Jackie, if you can make loops out of the canvas that's left over and sew one each side of the bottom, then I'll attach one end of the cord to the wood that I make the baton with, and then when you want to raise the blinds, you can pass it through the loops and pull it up that way. Hopefully, it will go up far enough to give you daylight.'

Leaving Jackie and Gran to it, Marg told them, 'Once we have all the fittings in place I'll come and help you finish the blinds. Is that all right, Gran?'

'Aye, that's grand, I like a bit of sewing to do. I were a good seamstress in me day, you knaw, I — '

'You can tell me all about it later, love. I have to help Clive now.'

'Well, while you're at it, you make a man of him, lass.'

Marg coloured, but Clive just laughed. 'Nice to see you back on form, Sandra, love.'

Before Gran could answer, Marg said, 'Right, let's get on then, shall we?'

★ ★ ★

Almost two hours later, they'd finished the downstairs and had rattled on with the top windows. The work went much quicker now they knew what they were doing.

'Well, the last one to do is this bedroom, lass.'

They were outside the door to Marg's bedroom. It used to be her ma's, before they'd moved her downstairs when she'd become weaker. Marg hadn't bothered to move back to her old room as she felt close to Ma in here, and it was bigger. She'd been dreading taking Clive in there; not that it wasn't tidy, but there were her own personal things around — her make-up and a jar of cream on the dresser, her dressing gown on the back of the door and her folded nightie on the pillow.

Clive sensed her discomfort. 'Is there stuff you want to put away before I go in, love?'

Feeling silly, she shook her head. 'I've nowhere to put them, and there's nothing really embarrassing, it's just . . .'

'Me being in your bedroom? I understand that. But the windows have to be done, and I'll be respectful, lass.'

Marg wasn't sure she wanted him to be. Since the incident on the boat, he'd kept his distance, when she'd wanted more. But she knew he'd taken a step back because of her grief. This only made her want him more strongly, though she didn't know if her feelings for him were love — well, at least, not the kind of love Alice and Edith had found — but she did think a lot of him.

'It's fine. I had a daft moment of embarrassment, but it's passed. Come on.' It hadn't all passed — not the feelings of the intimacy she knew the room would give her.

Clive behaved matter-of-factly, laying down his

189

tools and the wood he would need and then fetching his ladder from Jackie's room and propping that up. 'Right, we'll get the fittings up and see if Jackie and Gran need help, and then a nice cup of tea'll go down well, lass.'

'Oh, I should have offered you one before now! What am I thinking? Do you want to break and have one?'

She was holding the ladder and he'd just stepped on the first rung. When he looked down at her, his face was very close to hers. Their eyes met. Marg knew that, like herself, Clive had felt the heightened feeling between them. She didn't look away as Clive's eyes held love and were like a magnet to her.

'Lass, I have to speak up.'

She nodded.

'I love you, Marg. I know you have problems, and I wanted to wait until you felt stronger, helping you all I could along the way. But now, with war upon us, who knows what the future holds? I feel as if there's no time to wait, I have to ask you . . . Is there a chance that you feel anything other than friendship for me?'

Again, Marg nodded. Her throat had dried, her senses were heightened, and suddenly she knew she did love Clive. It wasn't all-consuming, but a comfortable and yet exciting love.

'Oh, Marg.'

She couldn't have said how it happened, but she was being held in Clive's strong arms, and it felt good — safe, and the right place for her to be. She looked up at him and then accepted his lips meeting hers. She wanted to deepen the kiss, but she waited, enjoyed the gentleness of it, as if Clive was still afraid that he'd overstepped the mark.

After a few seconds he took his lips from hers, looked quizzically at her, then kissed her nose.

Marg knew that any deeper feelings had to be shown by her, that Clive still wasn't sure how she felt, so she put both of her hands up and cupped his face, bringing him back down onto her lips, before sliding her hands to the back of his head and deepening the kiss.

It was then that a more intense feeling for him burst inside her, and she knew his passion to be released. His kiss became something that consumed her with pleasure and lit in her a yearning for more — for Clive to take the whole of her.

When they came out of the kiss, he gazed down at her. His eyes filled with tears. 'I love you, Marg.'

The deep emotion in his voice made her realise that he was, and had been, fighting a battle inside himself. He had loved his wife dearly and this must seem to him like a betrayal of her.

She stroked his cheek. 'It's all right to love again, Clive. I love you and will be mindful of how you still hold feelings for Harriet. She were a lovely lass and we will always honour her memory.'

'Eeh, Marg, thank you. Thank you for loving me and for understanding. The love I have for you is as strong as the love I had for Harriet, but it doesn't replace that love. Is that all right by you?'

'It is, lad. To be given the same love I know you had for Harriet is more than enough. I don't think any man is capable of giving a love deeper than that.'

Clive held her to him in a hug that Marg found undemanding and yet full of love. It gave comfort and sought it, and it gave friendship too — a friendship that she knew would sustain their love.

A stomping on the stairs drew them apart. Jackie

191

seemed to be warning them of her approach. They giggled. But Marg blushed as she wondered if Jackie had been up once and decided to go back down and make a noisier entrance.

When Jackie did open the door, Marg felt convinced of this by the cheeky look on her face. 'What took you two so long? I don't knaw, but by, I've been waiting for this for a long time.'

They all laughed as Jackie flung the blackouts onto the bed and told them the ones for this room were ready. She then rushed at them, encircling them both with her arms as much as she could. 'You daft pair of apeths, I've felt like banging your heads together many a time!'

They extended their arms to take her into their embrace, and the three of them hugged.

'I'm happy for you, and feeling happier for me now, Marg, as I'll have a big brother to turn to.'

'Hey, hang on a mo, Clive ain't asked me to marry him, we've — '

'Well, I'm asking you now, Marg.' Clive left their hug and went down on his bended knee. 'Will you do me the honour of marrying me, Margaret Porter?'

Jackie coughed. 'Er, time I left,' and scurried out of the door.

Marg looked down into Clive's lovely, smiling face and her heart swelled. 'Aye, I will, lad. You'll do for me a treat.' She bent over and kissed his lips. She loved kissing him and wanted to kiss him all over. The thought made her kiss deepen and she sunk down beside him, steadied by his strong arms.

Clive's moan told her his feelings were the same, but he took his mouth from hers on a gasp. 'Let's make it soon, Marg. There's so much for everyone to face, I can do that with you by my side.'

'Aye, let's make it soon.'

Clive rose then and pulled her up too. As he held her, she could feel his need. Her own matched his, but this was something she couldn't take the lead in — or even knew how to — so she accepted it when he said, 'I think you should go and make that pot of tea, lass. Give me time to calm down and get on with what I'm supposed to be doing. I can manage on my own, I just wanted you with me so I made up the excuse that I needed help.'

Marg laughed at him. 'Aye, I know. I were the same, I just wanted to be with you. I'll give you a shout when tea's ready . . . and, ta, Clive.'

'For what, love?'

'For loving me. For taking me on when I ain't of your station. For not taking advantage of me and the feelings that you know I have for you. All of that makes me love you all the more.'

She didn't say it, but the thought came to her that she didn't think she could love him more, and yet, as she walked down the stairs she couldn't help but feel that what they had wasn't the all-consuming love that Alice and Edith had found. Hers and Clive's was a love that had grown, whereas theirs had hit them smack in the face.

Telling herself not to be so silly, she shook off the feeling and clicked the latch to the door at the bottom of the stairs.

Though happy a few moments ago, Jackie now looked like she was about to cry. 'Harry will have to leave me, and . . . and, well, Clive will have to leave you an' all. They said eighteens to forty-ones for conscription.'

193

'I know, lass. But you know, us womenfolk have to be brave at such times. We have to show our men that yes, we're sad and will miss them, but that we'll cope, and keep the home ready for when they return.'

'I know, but it's all so sad and frightening.'

'It is, I know, but we'll get through it. Now, my man is asking for a pot of tea so I'd better show what a good wife I'll make and get it for him. But, Jackie, lass, I know it seems like you're catching up with me, but I'm still your big sis and I'm always here for you. Like everything else, we'll face what we have to together, eh?'

'Aye, we will.'

Jackie wiped her eyes, but didn't find her lovely smile until Gran said, 'Eeh, I could do with a man.' Then Jackie burst out laughing.

'That's the spirit, love,' Marg told her between giggles.

* * *

By the time Clive was ready to leave, he'd made arrangements for them to go on a proper date. He'd said that as they both liked dancing, he would take her to the Tower Ballroom the following Saturday, but would come around a few times before that.

'By, I love it there, Clive,' she told him. 'And I ain't been for nigh on two years now. It'll be grand . . . But they won't close it, will they?'

He'd assured that they wouldn't do that. 'As you know, my dad's on the council; well, he told me that there's plans for Blackpool. We'll have a large influx of servicemen — airmen and soldiers. They'll be doing their training here and be billeted in the guest houses, so they'll need some entertainment.'

This news took them all back to chatting about the war, so to combat that Marg changed the subject to talking about his sons. 'Why don't you bring Carl and George with you on your next visit? It would be grand to get to know them.'

'I'd love to, thank you, Marg. I could do so later this afternoon, if that's all right?'

'Aye, then if the weather brightens, we can take them for a walk.'

Clive smiled down at her before kissing her cheek.

As she waved him off, another vehicle turned into the street. She put her hand up and waved at her da. His face was full of concern for them as he stepped onto the pavement. 'Was that Clive? Did I see him give you a kiss, lass?'

'You did, Da, and no doubt you'll get a visit from him soon.'

'Oh, aye? Well, you could do a lot worse, lass. Let's give you a hug.'

As she came out of the hug, which now seemed so natural to her, Da said, 'So, me lasses, it's going to be happening then?'

'Aye. It is.'

'And have you got everything ready, eh? Do you know where your nearest shelter is?'

'We do. It's just at the top of the road next to the bus stop.'

'Well then, at the first sound of the siren you get down there. Have your gran's wheelchair ready and have no cotter from her — just lift her and dump her in it — for knowing her, she'll have a lot to say and will only hold you up. In the meantime, I'm getting someone round here to dig the yard up. I've come across a few Anderson shelters and one's earmarked for you two.'

'That's grand, Da, ta very much.' Marg didn't ask how he'd come across them as she knew it wouldn't be honestly, but then, she wasn't about to look a gift horse in the mouth.

'So, how are Philip and Edith taking the news?'

'I don't know,' Marg replied. 'Philip's car's gone now and they didn't come out of their house when it was announced. We've been busy anyway — Clive fixed our blackouts.'

'Aw, I should have done that, but I've been tied up. Look, girls, if you want anything, come to your da. I can get owt, and I might be useful to Clive an' all. He's going to need a supply of sugar as there ain't going to be a lot of any stuff that comes from abroad, I'll tell you.'

Jackie, seeming to want to change the subject, asked, 'Do you want a cuppa, Da?'

'Naw, ta, Jackie, love, I ain't stopping. I've a lot to do. I just wanted to let you knaw about the Anderson and the workmen coming. I've a lot of deals going on, but listen, me lasses, don't tell anyone about what I get up to from now on. Here's one who's going to profit from this bloody war, and that means you will an' all.'

When he'd gone, Jackie sighed heavily. 'I wish Da didn't do shady deals. I feel as though it will land him in big trouble one of these days and it ain't right to live how he does.'

'I know, lass, but we'll never change him, so just accept it, eh?'

Marg couldn't believe she'd said this. It had taken her a long time to accept Eric as their da, and she wasn't about to start fighting him about his way of life. Besides, on the practical side, they were going to need what he could get hold of for them.

She smiled to herself as she brushed these thoughts away. She didn't want to think of anything but how Clive loved her and they were going to be married.

This thought had her hugging herself. *He really does, Clive loves me!*

17

Edith

Edith had woken that morning feeling afraid of what the Prime Minister's announcement would bring down on them.

Philip had put his arm around her and held her close. She'd lain curled in his arms, and he'd kissed her hair, telling her he loved her. He then had surprised her by saying, 'Pack an overnight bag, darling. I'm taking you to the Lake District. I've booked us into a hotel in Windermere for the night. The head gave me tomorrow morning off, but I have to go into school in the afternoon for a meeting with him.'

Now they were on their way, having hardly spoken about the horror of what was to come. Wanting comfort, Edith sat close to Philip on the car's bench seat. He reached for her hand. Squeezing it gently, he'd told her, 'Everything will be all right, my darling.'

'Eeh, love, it won't, we can't pretend . . . I — I'm scared out of me wits.'

Philip pulled the car into a layby and turned to her. His dark eyes held love and concern. 'Darling, I felt just like that too the moment the words were uttered.'

'Aw, Philip, me love. You'll have to leave me and I can't bear it.'

Philip drew her to him. 'Oh, Edith.'

When he kissed her the tension between them eased, and the raw passion, evoked so often, raced through them both.

'I have a blanket in the boot.' Philip's voice had taken on a throaty sound that enhanced how Edith was feeling. His eyes misted over. 'That gate looks like it leads to a field. Shall we?'

Edith couldn't speak, her throat had tightened. Her breath came in short pants as she nodded her head.

The grass felt damp around her ankles, but she didn't care. Once they were behind the hedge and shielded from the road, Philip laid the blanket down, held her hand while she lowered herself onto it, and joined her and took her into his arms.

His kiss was gentle, and yet more demanding than she'd ever known as his tongue parted her lips and thrilled her by touching hers. His hands removed her cardigan and then unbuttoned her blouse.

Taking his cue, Edith unbuttoned his shirt, and so each garment came off as they kissed, touched, caressed, until, naked, they entwined their bodies.

'You're so beautiful, Edith, my darling. I love you.'

Edith cupped his face and looked intently into his eyes. 'I love you with all of me, Philip, and all of me wants to be yours.'

A small moan came from his throat. His body rolled with her until he was between her legs.

Their fears dissolved as they gave themselves up to their lovemaking.

Edith felt as though all she'd ever been was changing at this moment. She didn't recognise herself as the passionate being who called out Philip's name, seeking what she knew he could give her. When it happened, he shattered her as wave upon wave of exquisite feeling zinged through her body. She clung to him and heard her own guttural cries. She knew she was crying, knew she was being released and yet captivated by this man she would love forever.

They lay without speaking. Letting their touching hands say all, looking up at the clouds — some dark, some fluffy, all witness to their love joining them forever.

Philip moved first. He turned his head and looked at her. She turned hers and gazed into his eyes. He moved towards her and she went into his arms. They curled their naked bodies around each other. They kissed, they touched, they explored, then the magic happened again and they were in a frenzy of giving, of loving, of crying out their joy of one another, until spent, they lay and sobbed in each other's arms.

After a moment, Philip said, 'I don't know why I am crying. It isn't sad crying, it's thankful, a joy-filled release.'

Edith knew. She knew exactly what he meant, as there was no sadness in her, just a feeling of being home. Of being loved and safe.

It took a while for them to dress. They were reluctant to do so. When they were clothed, Philip picked a crushed daisy from under the blanket and handed it to her.'Dry it out, darling, by pressing it in one of my heavy books, and we'll keep it forever as a reminder of how it held us as we came together when we most needed to.'

Then as they walked back to the car, he laughed a small laugh.'Oh, and the second time too.'

Edith felt a giggle rise up inside her. When it burst from her it was full of her joy. 'This will always be our very special place.'

'It will. We'll visit it on our anniversary each year and do the same.'

They both laughed then as Philip added,'Not that we'll wait until then to do it again.'

When they checked into the hotel, this became a reality as they soon found themselves back in each other's arms.

It was turning on the wireless set provided in the bedroom that brought them both down to earth, as the news was full of that morning's announcement. Philip turned it off and they sat in silence for a while, in the two beige-coloured velvet armchairs set in the bay window. They'd put them together facing the view over the sparkling Lake Windermere to watch the swans glide along. Their hands were joined; each had their own thoughts, fears and, for Edith, a sadness that what they had was to be so fleeting.

This turned to a deep pit of agony that took her world away as Philip said, 'Edith, I have given this situation a lot of thought. I have mulled it over and over, how I would feel, how I would react if war broke out and I only have one way of dealing with it . . . I must offer my services. I have to put myself forward as a fit young man, who can speak several languages, in the hope that I can do the right thing for my country and my fellow men. And yet, I have tortured myself with the thoughts that in doing that, I would be doing wrong by you.'

Edith knew the moment was on her. She was to rise to it, as she too had rehearsed this moment. She'd never spoken of it, and had begged of God to take it away from her, but she knew Philip more than he knew himself, and she'd known in her heart that this would be his reaction if what they dreaded became a reality, and it had.

She'd questioned herself: should she protest, get

angry? Should she cry and tell him he was being self-ish, ask how could he do such a thing, why he couldn't wait like others would until he was forced to go? But in the end, this was the man she loved. This courageous, strong, loving man who also loved his country and his fellow man. A good man, God-fearing and kind. A talented man, whose talents would be called upon. And she'd concluded that she must be strong too. 'I will support you in anything you want — need — to do, my love.'

'Oh, Edith, thank you. I have been so torn. But to go with your blessing will be so much easier. I would like to ask Father to fund me to go to Sandhurst initially, to train to become an officer. Once they bring out the best in me, they will know the direction in which I am most needed. My language skills will be useful, I'm sure. Especially my German and French, and I have a good knowledge of the geography of each country too, and I have studied everything about them: their customs, their beliefs and myths. I know if called upon to, I could pass myself off as a countryman in either land.'

Though she felt like screaming in protest at everything he was saying, Edith asked calmly, 'How do you see your talents being used, love?'

'Well, in intelligence gathering, mainly. But it won't be up to me. I have given it a lot of thought, and I don't see myself in trenches, or commanding men to go over the top, but in working to undermine the enemy, and gathering information that would help our strategic planners.'

Somehow this didn't seem so frightening to Edith. She guessed it might mean him going into dangerous places, and possibly posing as a citizen. If that was the case, then he wouldn't be found out, she was sure of it . . . But what if he was? Didn't they torture and kill spies in the last war?

Edith's heart began to race.

'Don't be afraid, darling. I will be safe. I promise you that I won't be in danger. I'll have the very best looking after me — anyway, we don't know yet that I will be accepted for such work.'

'I know that you will, love. But if you're determined and are so brave about it, then I will be. I can't bear the thought of you going, but me heart will go with you, and you'll only be a thought away from me.'

'I will. Touch your heart at any given time and you will be touching mine.' He kissed her then, a gentle kiss full of love.

'Now, shall we go for a walk and enjoy our day here? This is my favourite place in Britain.'

'From what I've seen so far, I know I'll love it an' all.'

★ ★ ★

They walked along the towpath, hand in hand, avoiding any more conversation about war. They bought hot potatoes from a stand and sat on a bench, enjoying what they ate, but throwing some to the swans, who, eager for more, surrounded them. Philip, a keen photographer, snapped away with his camera, mostly shots of her.

A gentleman walked by and stopped to talk to them. 'Enjoy your day, my dears, and remember every moment of it.'

Philip answered him, 'Thank you, sir. I wonder if I could trouble you to take a photo of us, please?'

'I would be delighted to. Look, I'll show you one I took with a delayed action camera set on a tripod in this very spot. It was taken on the thirtieth of July, 1914.'

The photo was lovely. Edith gazed at the beautiful, serene young woman who sat with a younger version of the gentleman, who she guessed was now in his fifties.

In the eyes of the beautiful lady, she saw the same pain she herself was feeling, hidden behind the smile — unusual to see a smile on an old photograph, and she'd always wondered why. But this smile told of courage, and strength.

'By, it's a grand photo. Your wife is beautiful.'

'Was, my dear, she is no longer with us. And not my wife but the love of my life. Sadly, her parents wouldn't consent to us marrying in a rush before I left to go to war — we'd only been courting for two months.' The gentleman swallowed hard, but still the tears glistened in his eyes.

'Typhoid fever took her before I returned.'

'Eeh, I'm sorry.'

Philip took the photo. 'She was very beautiful; may she rest in peace. I am so very sorry, sir. I shouldn't have asked you to — '

'No, it is fine, and my pleasure. Eloise hasn't left me, she's still in my heart. Which is where I carried her throughout my time as an officer in the British cavalry. Right here in my top pocket, and where she always stays.'

'You commanded from the back of a horse?'

'I did, poor, magnificent animals. They had courage, you know. They never baulked at charging and weren't easily spooked. They suffered too. We lost

204

some good horses.'

'My hat off to you, sir, you're an example I shall follow.'

'Yes, young man, I know that. It is why I stopped. What are your plans?'

When Philip told him, he surprised them by saying, 'Well, our paths will cross. I won't say any more, except to say that the first lesson you will learn is to never tell anyone, not your wife, and in particular, a stranger, as I am, anything. I could be a German spy.'

Philip looked taken aback. 'Oh, I've failed at the first hurdle then?'

'Yes, but a lesson that I know for certain you have learnt, so don't look so defeated. Now, I will take that photo for you and I want you both smiling. For my Eloise, and for the times in the future when you will need to look at it, make this the best damn photo in the world.'

Edith did her utmost. Meeting the gentleman had seemed to make Philip's hopes a reality and left her feeling cold and empty. But she would behave as Eloise had. She would remember the face of this strong, young woman who never knew the completion of the love she had for this gentleman.

After taking a couple of pictures, the gentleman shook Philip's hand. 'Well, young man, we will meet again, and then you will know who I am.' He turned to Edith. 'But I want you to know that along with Eloise, I will carry you with me, praying that, like her, you have the courage to send your man off with a smile. Good day.'

With this, he bowed and walked away from them. Edith felt as though she'd met a being from another world, it was all so surreal. How could they bump into a man who was going to be instrumental in Philip's life and yet she would never see again?

'Can you believe that?'

'No, Philip, I can't. It was the strangest thing ever. Who do you think he was?'

'It was strange, and I have no idea. Obviously, someone involved in our intelligence service, but how much of a coincidence is it that he should be walking along this same towpath at the same time as us? In fact, too much of one.'

'What do you mean?'

'Well, from things that I have read — and there's very little material on the Secret Intelligence Service — they know everything about everyone. I don't mean they spy on us, but they make it their business to know about certain people — enemies of the state as well as those of use to their mission. I am a language teacher, they will need people who speak languages, where else would they look? They probably know what paste I use to brush my teeth with and when I go to the lavatory!'

'Eeh, you're making the hairs stand up on the back of me neck.'

'Mine too . . . Wait a minute . . . Something the head said is coming back to me. It's what set me off thinking about doing intelligence work — he said, 'Think carefully about your future. You have many talents.' I thought he was talking about my promotion, so told him that me accepting was not now possible as I intended to go to do my bit in the war. Instead of protesting he said,'I know. I need to see you on Monday afternoon.' Then he looked at me intently and said, 'I have an idea that you know what I refer to.' Now, I think he may have been involved in this in some way.'

Edith was lost. It didn't matter how or why it happened, it just meant that her lovely Philip would leave her soon. She sought his hand. 'Let's walk, me love.'

Philip stood and steadied her as he helped her up. Linking her arm in his, he clutched her hand at the same time and pulled her body close to his. Like this they walked on, noticing wonderous things: a heron looking magnificent as he gracefully dived, flapped his wings, spraying water, then took off with a fish in his beak; geese waddling and making a clatter as they moved in a group on the edge of the water; swans gliding like skaters on ice, hardly disturbing the water; and weeping willows dripping their tears into the lake.

'There's a café, darling, would you like a cup of tea? My parents always took me there; they make scones to rival those in Cornwall.'

Edith nodded. She didn't think she could eat a morsel, but then found that the scones were wonderful and tucked in, spreading the strawberry jam thick and making Philip laugh as it stuck around her lips when she bit into it.

He wiped her mouth on his hanky and had them giggling, and Edith had the thought that this was what she wanted to happen. She couldn't change the fact that Philip was going, or that he would be in danger, and her heart would be breaking every minute he'd be gone, but she could change the mood now. She could make this day and every day that they were together count.

* * *

With everything that had been going on, Edith hadn't given much thought to what Sue had asked her to help

207

her with on the Monday afternoon. Even Philip telling her he would have her back in time hadn't really brought to the fore the sadness of the task.

Sue had joined the WRVS and was to help to supervise an influx of evacuee children. She'd asked Edith to bring along Marg and Alice to help too.

Still in a daze, trying to come to terms with what had been a wonderful overnight stay but had changed her world, Edith smiled at Sue's greeting.

'Oh, you've come here! I thought we were to meet on the station, Edith, dear? Are your friends going to be there?'

'Alice will be, but not Marg as she has to look after her gran, but she will help at the weekends.'

'Good. Both she and Marg — when she can — will be needed, I am sure. We're only just getting organised ourselves, but we'll soon need all the extra hands we can get.'

'Ha! Can I get a word in? You ladies haven't given me a chance.'

'Sorry, Philip, dear, of course, it's good to see you.'

'It's good to see you, Mother. I just wanted to say that we came early as I want to talk to Dad, and then to you both afterwards.'

'Oh dear, that sounds ominous. But then so does everything at the moment.'

They followed Philip's mother inside the hall, which, on first seeing it, had surprised Edith. It was smaller than the grand house's exterior suggested, though the stairs to the right were in keeping: they swept beautifully around in a curve and were adorned with delicately carved balustrades. The chandelier, however, was all too huge and elaborate for its setting.

'Father's in the conservatory with his papers, dear.'

Sue ushered them into the living room — a long room with a floral carpet and three cream sofas that looked as though they would swallow you up when you sat on them.

'Now, my dear, I'll go and organise some tea and biscuits for us, we've plenty of time. Sit yourself down.'

When the door closed on her, Philip kissed her cheek. 'If it's all right with you, darling, I'll leave you to it while I seek Father out.'

'Aye, it's fine. Good luck.' These were the last words that Edith felt like saying, but no matter what, Philip would be going to war, so better that he went to Sandhurst, which sounded like the safest option, initially.

As she waited, Edith looked around her. She hadn't made many visits since Boxing Day, and the room had looked so different then with the over-the-top decorations and huge tree, but now she could take in how regal it all looked, with its striped wallpaper, deep mahogany furniture, pale green drapes and cushions, and walls adorned with the loveliest paintings she'd ever seen. Again, huge chandeliers hung from the ceiling and elaborate china ornaments adorned the occasional furniture. To Edith it was all so beautiful — she felt as if she were in a palace.

As Sue came back into the room, she was already talking, giving the impression of someone whose nerves were on edge. But then, she must have been speculating as to what Philip was going to tell her.

She sat down heavily on the sofa opposite Edith. 'He's going, isn't he?'

Edith nodded.

'Oh God! I can't bear it!'

Edith's heart went out to her. 'We'll get through it somehow.'

209

Sue straightened herself, and to Edith she suddenly looked every bit like the backbone of Britain that was always being talked about.

'Anyway, what about you? Have you secured a teaching post?'

They talked for a while about Edith's possibilities, but were interrupted when Philip and his father appeared through the French doors.

Though Sue was prepared for what was to come, she was devastated when Philip told her that he would be applying for Sandhurst.

'But you will be a soldier, dear, and likely . . . Oh, I can't bear it, I can't.'

Tom's voice shook with emotion as he told her, 'Come on, Sue, stiff upper lip and all that, eh, lass? Philip needs us to be brave. Besides, as an officer he'll stand a better chance of surviving all of this — not that that is the reason he's chosen this path. He has the right qualities to lead and he would rather join now and be of the most help he can be than wait to be conscripted to the ranks. I'm proud of the lad.'

Sue rose and went towards Philip. Edith was glad to see him open his arms to her. 'It will be all right, Mother, I will be highly trained.'

'Come on, old girl, we've all got to face the future with a brave face and support our young people. They've a lot to contend with. I know, I've been there.'

'You never talk about your experiences in the Great War, Father.'

'There was nothing great about it and it's best forgotten. We had to get on with life as you will do too. Aye, and Wilf, as no doubt he'll have to go at some point.'

They all fell silent. Sue's small sob broke it.

Tom moved towards her. 'Now, now, that won't help. People like you will be needed. You're the strongest woman I know, and you'll not only cope, you'll help others to. You'll have your charity work, your WV . . . whatever it is, and you'll do a lot of good and keep spirits up.'

'You're right, dear. I will cope; it's the initial shock. I knew you would have to go, Philip, but hoped it wouldn't be for a while yet and by that time Hitler would be beaten. I didn't think you'd run headlong at it. After all, what about Edith?'

'I'm all right. I'll support Philip in anything he wants to do. I — I'm frightened, like you, but Tom's right, we have to do our bit at home, and you'll be the one to guide me in that, Sue.'

'You put me to shame. But, yes, we can do this. Now, as you are so early, will you stay and have lunch?'

Sue had transformed in a bat of the eye. She was once more in charge and everything in her world was normal enough to start organising routine things again. This helped Edith — if women like her cracked, then none of them stood a chance.

18

Alice

Alice breezed around the ward but didn't find anything she needed to do; everywhere was tidy and most of the patients were snoozing. The poor things were woken at the crack of dawn so the nurses could begin the ward routine — bedpans, temperature taking and dressings — before breakfast was served. Then came bed-making, done so precisely that the patients who were allowed out of bed were banned from sitting on them, and those who weren't hardly dared move for fear of disturbing the neatly tucked corners.

When Alice arrived at the bed of the appendectomy patient in the corner she seemed unsettled.

'Can I help you in any way, lass?'

'Aye, take away this pain. Eeh, it's worse than when me appendix were raging at me.'

'Here, have a couple of sips of water. That's right, lass. Now, let me go and seek help for you, eh?'

'Ta, Nurse.'

Alice loved the sound of anyone calling her Nurse, even when Marg's Gran did so in her confusion. Sadly, it wasn't ever to be real, but this job at least gave her satisfaction, something to help fulfil her, and she had her interview with the Red Cross to look forward to tomorrow.

With them, she would be trained in first aid, and basic home nursing and hygiene, and then would be considered qualified enough to go with them on any mission they undertook. With the two irons in the fire, she felt they would be enough distraction to help her to cope with her loss and . . . well, she wouldn't think of Gerald going to war. She couldn't.

She sighed. The loss of her child still ground a deep pain into her, but didn't appear to mean much to others now — except Gerald, of course. Everyone seemed to think they were over it, or didn't like mentioning it. But she knew they would never get over losing their little Gerald; they just had to carry on as best they could.

Hurrying along the corridor, Alice was relieved to see Gerald walking briskly towards her. 'That's a worried look, darling.'

'Gerald! I thought you were off duty?'

'No, there was an admission and I was called to do the assessment. I was just on my way to the ward. I need to check on the patients before I leave for home. Is everything all right? You look anxious, darling.'

'l am. I'm worried about the appendectomy patient. She seems to be in a lot of pain and looks very pale. I was on my way to find help.'

'Oh? Right, take me to her and I'll check her over.'

★ ★ ★

As she walked home, Alice felt a wonderful sense of satisfaction, that what she did was worthwhile. She may not be a nurse as she'd dreamt, but she had still made a difference — without her fast action the young woman may have died, as it turned out she was bleeding internally and in danger of peritonitis.

With Gerald held up by the incident, he wasn't able to drive her to the station to meet Edith. Sighing,

Alice wondered if there was a bus, as her legs felt too tired to walk.

With this dilemma, she made her mind up to learn to drive. Gerald had said he would teach her and even buy her a small car, but it just hadn't been something that she'd ever thought of doing and had seemed a frightening prospect. But now her confidence had grown and she felt capable of doing anything, and learning to drive would be her next aim.

The exhaustion left her as she spotted Edith. The station seemed crowded with women, and there was an air of expectancy, and yet confusion, as more than one of these women seemed to think they were in charge, which only meant they all countered each other's orders.

'Edith! Over here!'

As Edith came towards her, her cheeks were glowing with the redness borne of frustration.

'What's to do? It all looks a bit chaotic, love.'

'It is. The train's delayed, which is a good thing as there is no organisation. I have been pulled from pillar to post, as one lady tells me to do one thing and then another tells me different. Sue is doing her best, but there doesn't seem to be a clear leader.'

'By, that's not good. What are the things they have in place?'

'There's a table over there with huge urns on it. Some have hot soup in and others tea, but the mugs haven't arrived. The stationmaster is furious as he doesn't want his station turned into a soup kitchen, and no one knows if anyone has organised a coach to take the children to the Salvation Army hall where the distribution is to take place.'

'Oh dear. By, it looks a shambles. Surely, the best

thing would be to get the children to the hall, then to feed and organise them?'

'That's what me and Sue think, but I think she's reluctant to assert herself.'

'Well, we'll have to do it.'

'Aye, I'm up for that, but you know what they're like with the likes of us.'

'The likes of us? I'm a doctor's wife, and you're the wife of one of the masters of Rossall School, where most of their kids go. We're as good as them, and it's time to show them that.'

'You're right. Wish me luck.' With this, the teacher Edith wanted to be came out in her as she turned and clapped her hands and shouted, 'Quiet, everyone!'

Everyone looked at her. Edith reddened, but stood her ground. 'Who is meant to be in charge here?'

Sue answered, 'Iris Middleton, but she has been taken ill. She does everything and never delegates until we are in situ. But I am sure, ladies, that the refreshments were meant to be taken to the hall.'

One or two murmured their dissent to this, but Edith nipped this in the bud. 'Serving the kids food when they get to the hall makes a lot more sense. They're going to be tired and probably upset at leaving their families. We'll only add to that by making them queue up here and cope with standing and eating.'

More women agreed than disagreed, but Edith kept hold of the reins. 'Arguing about it is making things worse. Who brought the food here?'

When the ladies came forward, Edith soon had them taking it away again.

This calmed the stationmaster, and as he thanked Edith, he asked her if he could be of any further assistance.

Alice jumped in. 'Aye, you can allow us to use your telephone, please. Does anyone know the number of the coach company?'

A woman put her hand up. 'The owner is a friend of mine.'

With the woman dispatched to ring her friend and get him and his bus here as quickly as he could, everyone became calm. A few thanked Edith, asking who she was. Sue took great pride in introducing her as her new daughter-in-law, adding that she was going into the teaching profession.

Alice giggled at Edith's wry smile. 'You've got to allow Sue her moment, love.'

Sue breezed over. 'Edith, I'm very proud of you, dear. My, I'd love to be a fly on the wall when Iris is told how you sorted everything out.'

'Eeh, I'm shaking in me shoes, though. It were Alice who prompted me, but now I think I've made a few enemies.'

'Oh, who cares, up their own ar . . . bottoms most of them.'

Alice and Edith burst out laughing and Alice thought how nice it was to see Sue changing from the person they'd first met — even if she couldn't bring herself to say 'arses'.

When they calmed down, Edith asked, 'What happens to the children once we get them fed and watered, Sue?'

'Oh, there will be officials waiting at the hall, they'll sort that out. The WVRS job is to assist where we're needed, we can't take charge of anything — as you can see, it's a good job we don't. This organisation needs more women like you and Alice, but I fear snobbery keeps them away — something I admit I was once a part of. I hope you two are prepared for a few rebuffs?'

'We'll give as good as we get. Though I'm not sure I can be fully involved as I need to work more than anything now that Philip's going.'

Alice was shocked to hear this. 'Philip's going?'

'Yes, he's going to apply to Sandhurst. He could have gone there before from the school he attended — it was almost a natural progression for a lot of his mates — but he had . . . Oh, I mean, well, his family business was important.'

'I know what you were going to say, my dear, and you're right. I did wrong in insisting that he joined his father's business.'

'Eeh, that's all behind you now, Sue. I shouldn't have mentioned it. Philip didn't come to any harm, it did him good to see how the business was run.'

'Anyroad, Edith, I'm sorry, love. You must be devastated?'

'I am, Alice, but we have to have courage. The men'll need us to.'

There was no time for any more chatter as the train could be heard approaching the station. When it arrived, it belched out smoke, covering them all in a cloud and starting up a racket of coughing and protests.

'Filthy things!'

'Disgusting!'

Such comments had Alice and Edith giggling.

Edith whispered, 'How they come to think of themselves as charity workers, eeh, I don't know.'

As the doors opened, the sight of the motley crew of children climbing down from the train touched Alice's heart, as she could see it had Edith's. Most were bedraggled, dirty and looked very afraid. A few were well dressed and looked more assured. It sickened her to see that most of the volunteers made a beeline for those.

Alice and Edith looked at the poor mites, who'd obviously come from poverty, and put out their arms to them. 'Eeh, me little ones, welcome to Blackpool. You're safe now and we'll take care of you.'

A little girl with pigtails, her coat tied with string, stared up at them. The smudges on her face showed that she'd been crying and had wiped her tears and snot over one side of her face, where it had dried in a dirty streak. 'Will you be looking after me and me bruvver, lady?'

Alice's heart melted, but she knew she wouldn't be able to take them on. 'No, lass, just till they get you sorted, that's all, but you'll find a good home, I'm sure. Where's your brother?'

'He's 'ere, behind me. He's me twin, but me mum says he's the weaker of us. He didn't come out for a while after me and then he 'ad the cord around his neck and it nearly strangled him . . . Come 'ere, Alf. Don't be scared.'

Alf appeared from behind his sister's coat. His eyes were like saucers, his nose was running, and large tears stood poised to trickle over from his eyelids. 'I want me mum.'

The girl answered. 'I know you do, Alf, but she ain't 'ere, is she? I'll look after you.'

Alice swallowed the lump in her throat and looked around for Edith.

Edith was talking to the woman who'd accompanied the children. A little boy with bright ginger hair was looking up at her as if she were his saviour. She felt near to tears, but before she could give in to that emotion a voice shouted, 'The coach is here, Edith!'

Edith immediately took charge again. 'This is Mildred Thompson. She's in charge of the children until she formerly hands them over to the officials at the hall. Now, if everyone could please take the hands of two children and take responsibility for seeing them onto the bus safely.'

This was quickly accomplished. But once they arrived at the hall, it was chaos once more until Edith instructed the children to form an orderly queue to get their soup and a chunk of bread.

By the time they'd eaten, the officials arrived and most of the women made themselves scarce. One or two had obviously been told they were to take children in as they were frantically trying to pick the best of the bunch and put themselves forward as a good match.

'Eeh, Edith, it's like a cattle market.'

Edith nodded. 'I can't do anything as it's all out of me hands now. The officials have informed all the families who have to take the kids in, and they're beginning to arrive. I don't know what the system is, how they're chosen or if they can pick a kid they take a fancy to.'

The little girl who'd first spoken to Alice came over to her with her brother in tow. 'Don't let us go with them women, miss.'

'Eeh, lass, I can't help who you go to, it ain't up to me. I'm sorry, love. What's your name?'

'Mandy . . . Well, Amanda, after me gran, but that's too posh so we're both called Mandy. Me gran didn't want us to leave her.'

Alf piped up then, 'Nor me mum.'

'Huh, Gran said Mum can get on with her tricks

without us so weren't sorry to see us go.' She turned to Alice. 'She earns her money on the streets as a prossie.'

This shocked Alice. 'How old are you, both?'

'We're nine. But Gran says I'm more like twelve, but he's more like seven.'

Alf hung his head.

'You know, Mandy, if you keep telling him and everyone else that he ain't as good as you, then he's never going to be. You should boost your brother up a bit, make him feel worth something.'

'You talk funny.'

'Aye, and so do you.'

'I talk like all Londoners do.'

'Aye, and I talk like all Blackpudlians do, except for the posh ones.'

'I don't like the posh ones, but I like you. Please take us and look after us. We'll be good, won't we, Alf?'

Alf nodded. His nose was running still, so Alice got out her hanky. 'Here, blow your nose, Alf. You're a little man who'll grow into a big man one day, so square your shoulders and take care of your sister, eh?'

Alf seemed to grow in stature. 'She's a bit of an 'andful for me, miss. Me gran says that too, only she says Mandy's got to be tough enough for us both.'

'I do, as he ain't strong, miss.'

'Well then, take care of each other, eh?'

Alf almost ripped Alice's heart out then, as his little hand came into hers. 'I wanna go with you, miss. Me and Mandy both do.'

Alice went on her haunches. 'If it was up to me, I'd take you home with me, lad, but it ain't. Them women with the clipboards are sorting you all out, and I reckon you'll go to someone who's really nice

220

and'll love you. There's some good folk in Blackpool.'

Alf's lip quivered. Neither of them had mentioned a father, so Alice suspected that this little chap was domineered by women — from Mandy to his gran — who all thought he needed mollycoddling, but they were making a weakling out of him.

As he looked into her eyes with his huge, dark, tear-filled ones, Alice felt her heart breaking. How would it have been if her little Gerald had had this to suffer? A shudder went through her.

Edith brought her out of the feeling that threatened to engulf her as she came over to her with the little ginger-haired boy. 'By, Alice, lass, it's hard. I've got little Ben here hooking on to me. He lives in the same street as Mandy and Alf in the East End of London. I've heard tell how poor it is there, it breaks your heart . . . Eeh, lass, you're crying. Come on, I think we should go, there's no more we can do here.'

Alice nodded. Wiping her eyes, she bent down and hugged Ben and then Mandy and Alf. 'Be good, kids, and you'll be grand. If you play up, you'll get nothing but trouble, so be helpful, do as you're told and cheer up, eh?'

She watched as Edith did the same, and really admired how good she was with them and how she managed to convince them that everything was going to be all right.

Walking away was difficult for Alice. She felt as though the three of them were hers and she was abandoning them to an uncertain fate.

Outside, she breathed a sigh of relief, and yet wanted to run back and grab the three children and take them home with her. 'Do you reckon there'll be a way that we can find out how they're doing, Edith?'

'I don't know, but I did hear one of the officials say that there'll be a person assigned to look after the welfare of the kids and the families. He said that if anyone needed any help, they were to go to the council offices and ask for the person in charge of the evacuees.'

'I wonder who'll take our three?'

'Don't call them that, lass. They're not ours. Anyroad, how's work going down? I ain't had time to ask you yet.'

Though Edith's words sounded harsh and she'd changed the subject, Alice knew it was just a front, and that Edith was suffering as much as she was at leaving Ben, Mandy and Alf.

'It's grand, but not as I want it to be. I'm hoping that the Red Cross will fill the gap for me. I want to help to heal people, to . . . well, to be a nurse.'

'It's rotten that married women can't be nurses; there's a lot out there like yourself who can't have children and would make wonderful nurses. Philip reckons the ban is because people say 'A woman's place is in the home having kids.' They seem to think that's all we're good enough for!'

Alice took in an involuntary gasp.

'Eeh, Alice, lass. I'm not going to apologise for mentioning having kids . . . I — I, well . . . you have to talk to us, lass. Me and Marg know you're suffering, but you seem to want to pretend it never happened.'

Alice felt the tears spill over, but they were now from a mixture of grief and relief.

'Eeh, lass . . . Alice, love, bottling it up won't help.'

'I know, but I thought you wouldn't want me to keep going on about it.'

'You don't have to; but treat it as something we can talk to you about. Don't shut us out. Don't make us

222

be on our guard all the time. You don't have to always be on top form with us, love.'

'Ta, Edith. There's a tight knot inside me and I know there's one inside Gerald an' all, but we hardly talk to each other about it and it began to feel as though everyone had forgotten and expected us to have an' all.'

'That's because you both seem to be treating it that way, as if it happened, it's passed, and that's that.'

Alice turned towards Edith. Edith put out her arms and she went into them. 'We're here for you, lass — the Halfpenny Girls.'

Alice swallowed hard. 'Have you got time to go up to the cemetery with me, Edith?'

'Aye, I have. Sue left a while back so there's no one that I need to say goodbye to. Let's get going, shall we?'

When they reached the cemetery, Alice found a small bunch of roses on the tiny grave. She picked them up. A card dropped out of them. Lifting it, she read: *From Daddy, son. Love you always.*

'Oh God, Edith. I have to go home. Gerald needs me.'

'You need each other, love. Do as I say and talk, eh?'

'We will. I promise.'

★ ★ ★

Gerald was sitting as if studying a book but staring into space when Alice arrived home. Alice didn't think he'd heard her come in, as he didn't move.

'The roses are beautiful, love.'

'Uh? What . . . Oh, I . . . um, maybe we should have

taken them together, I'm sorry.'

'Don't be, love. I — I know, we haven't shared . . . Oh, Gerald, I love you.'

'Oh, Alice, Alice.'

He rose and scooped her up, holding her close to him, then slowly lowered her. 'We'll be all right, Alice, love, we will. It just takes time.'

'I know. Let's start by visiting little Gerald's resting place together as often as we can, eh?'

'Yes, there's a peace there with him.'

'And let's talk about him and help each other. I'm suffering so much and have felt so lonely.'

'Me too. It's a cloying pain. Like you, I've tried to keep busy, filled my hours when I needn't have done — avoided you, even. But that has been a lonely place too.'

'I know. I knew today that you didn't really have to do another ward round.'

'That's what it's been like, staying at work for longer hours — going to the graveside on my own. Anything, to keep me strong for you, my darling.'

'Well, you don't have to be. We'll do this together. If we want to cry, we'll cry with each other.'

Gerald smiled down at her. 'I love you so much, Alice.'

'Ta, love.'

He kissed her nose. 'Come on, I'll make you a cuppa and you can tell me all about your adventures with the children.'

When they sat with their tea, they didn't immediately talk about the evacuees, as now they'd broken through the barrier of talking about little Gerald, they both needed to say more. They spoke of the hopes and dreams they'd had for him and for other children they thought they'd be blessed with. They cried, they held each other and gradually came to a healing of the void that had been between them.

After a while they just sat holding each other and Alice told him about Mandy and Alf and Ben.

Gerald sat in silence for a moment, before saying, 'I think they'll send them all to families whose menfolk won't have to go to war. Otherwise, it will be too much for women on their own.'

'I don't think so, love. There was a widow waiting — a lady from the next street to us. Mind, she's no children at home, so it might be good for her. And that spinster from the sweet shop near to me old house. She added to me worry about the kids as me heart sank when I heard her say she wanted someone who would be useful, not a snivelling kid.'

'Hmm, they're not picking and choosing, are they?'

'No, a few tried it on but they got who was assigned to them, but eeh, Gerald, little Mandy, Alf and Ben were poor mites, and they begged me and Edith to take them.'

Gerald sighed. 'I fear this is just the start, darling. Did Edith tell you about Philip going? Typical Philip. Always full of courage . . . But, Alice, well, you do know they're going to need doctors too, don't you?'

Alice didn't answer for a moment. Her heart thudded in her chest. Taking a deep breath, she said, 'Aye. But nothing's happening yet, and besides, we know that doctors are exempt from call-up.'

'We are, but with Philip doing what I think is the honourable thing, I feel a need to help too.'

'No, Gerald, please.'

As soon as she said this, Alice felt guilty for doing so. Gerald was a man who cared deeply, and he had the relevant surgical skills. He'd be a great asset to the war. But she couldn't help herself as she pleaded, 'You'll be needed here. Look how the talk is of providing beds for military personnel. I don't think I could bear it if you went away.'

'You're stronger than you think, Alice, darling. I don't want to leave you, it would break my heart, but I feel that I should be there, helping men to survive so that they can get home to their wives and children. I'm young and so many older doctors can fill the gaps here.'

Defeated and with tears rolling down her cheeks, she asked, 'When?'

He hesitated for just a moment and then shattered her as he answered, 'I want to volunteer for the Medical Corps as soon as possible.'

Against all she wanted to do, Alice nodded, and more tears spilt from her eyes.

'Oh, darling, please try to understand.'

'I do. I do understand, and I wouldn't have you any different. I am crying for all the might-have-beens that we're losing — our own GP practice, with me working as a nurse alongside you, adopting children . . . but most of all, I'm crying for all the times we would have spent together that will be snatched away.'

'Alice, my darling, you didn't say anything about adoption before.'

'It was being with those children today. It made me realise that there are children who need me — us. It was something I was going to talk to you about.'

'Well, when the war is finished we'll talk about it again. Oh, Alice, it is an amazing idea. I really want to do it too . . . Look, darling, we're only doing what millions are having to do, putting our lives on hold until we have beaten Germany.

If we don't, life as we know it will be gone, and there will be nothing to put back together — no safe home for our adopted children, or for your brothers. Everyone who can has to do their bit.'

This sunk in and took root. 'You're right, love. I'll not hold you back. And I'll do me bit an' all. I want to learn to drive.'

'What? Where did that come from, I thought — '

'I know, but I've changed me mind. As a driver, there'll be a hundred and one things I can get involved in.'

'Right. I think it's an excellent idea. We can start right now. Let's go for a drive this minute. Come on.' Gerald pulled her up off the sofa and hugged her to him.

As they went through to the hall, the afternoon post plopped through the letter box — one letter, and so distinguishable with its foreign stamps that they both stood and stared at it. Gerald spoke first. 'It's from Mother and Father.'

'I know, love, pick it up. I can't wait to read their news.'

After ripping the envelope open and reading a few lines, Gerald said, 'They're coming home! Oh, Alice, they're coming home.'

'Eeh, that's grand. When?' A picture of lovely Averill and adorable Rod came to her and Alice felt excited at the thought of seeing them again.

Gerald turned the letter over. 'Oh . . . it looks like this was sent before they received our letter.' He read further. 'Docking on the first of December! And they want us to pick them up at Southampton. Oh . . . '

'What?'

'Oh, my darling, Mother says that she cannot wait and that . . . they . . . Well, they don't know what happened, darling.'

'She thinks she'll be able to greet her grandchild . . . '

Gerald opened his arms. 'Darling, we'll have many setbacks like this. Let's keep strong, eh?'

She went to him and his arms came around her. She clung on to him for a moment, wanting to remember every part of how this felt, store it for when he was gone. The thought nearly undid her, but she took a deep breath.

I can do this — Edith can, so I can too. We'll support each other. The Halfpenny Girls can take on any challenge.

19

Jackie

At work, Jackie was taking on more responsibility and enjoying doing so. Donald Blake spent a lot of his time away, but when in the office, he concentrated on showing her how to handle the different clients' accounts and prepare them for the partners to do the consolidating and final tax accounts.

'I will leave completely next week, Jackie, but though you will have a lot of pressure in the first instance, we are in talks with a retired accountant who would very much like to take up a post as assistant to Mr Brown and Mr Jones, so that will ease your responsibilities. I cannot tell you how grateful I am to you, and you will be helping your country in a round-about way by facilitating me to take up my post.'

It was a mystery to Jackie, but already the sayings were going around — 'careless talk costs lives' and 'walls have ears' — so she didn't ask any questions, just felt glad to be assisting him to do whatever war work he needed to.

She had an urge to be more involved in the war effort herself. She'd thought through several options and of these, joining the Women's Land Army really appealed, but anything would do. She just didn't know how she would cope when Harry got his papers — she wanted to be so busy that she didn't have to think, but then, she couldn't leave Marg and Gran.

As it was, she was less occupied after her job at

Fairweather's shop had come to an end once more, though they were coping moneywise as Da and Clive helped out: Da by giving them a bit of money now and again, and Clive by always seeming to have something or other for them — potatoes, eggs and, the other day, three lamb chops. Jackie couldn't remember ever tasting meat like it in her life.

Clive's boys were adorable and would be there this evening when she got home as Marg had them for the afternoon. Carl, eight years old, was as bright as a button, and George, six, melted your heart.

Jackie sighed. Everything was changing: Marg was thinking of marrying Clive soon, but couldn't make her mind up about when. There was no room at theirs for Clive and his two boys, and though apparently there was room at Clive's, Marg couldn't even think about moving Gran, it would upset her too much.

'Have I caught you daydreaming, Jackie?'

'Sorry, Donald, yes, me mind was elsewhere. It travels many roads at the moment, with everything so topsy-turvy.'

Donald got up from his desk and came to look over her shoulder. He'd never been so close to her in the two years she'd been there, and Jackie didn't feel comfortable. 'Now, then, let me see.'

He leant over and ran his pencil down the columns of figures. His body was leaning on hers and she could feel his trousers against her arm. She wanted to move, but there was nowhere to go as she was sitting close to the desk.

His sleeve brushed her hair.

The moment held tension. The clock's ticking seemed to fill the room, emphasising that there was no one here. The other staff all worked upstairs.

230

The strange sensation of having Donald's body so close to hers made Jackie's skin prickle. Fear gripped her.

'Are you all right, Jackie? You seem tense.' His hand came onto her shoulder. 'I'm going to miss you, my dear.'

His voice was no more than a husky whisper.

'Donald, I — I — '

'You feel it too?'

'Naw. I . . . Please move away a little.'

'Oh? Sorry, I hadn't realised. Oh, Jackie, you know there's something there between us — has been since you arrived here — but I was waiting till you were older. Now I have to go away and I can't think of going without speaking — '

'Stop! Naw, please don't. I didn't knaw. You . . . you're me boss. I — I just . . . Please, stop.'

Donald moved away. 'I'm sorry. I thought — '

'You have a wife and kids . . . ' Jackie felt the tears pricking her eyes. How could this be happening? She'd never have guessed something like this was on Donald's mind.

'Can I go, please?'

Donald barred her way. 'No. Not like this. I'm sorry, I just find you so beautiful, so innocent. I think a lot of you, Jackie. Would one kiss hurt?'

'You touch me and I'll scream.' Jackie didn't know where this strength was coming from, but she had to escape. 'Get out of me way. I'm going and I ain't coming back.'

'There's no need for that. I'll be going soon and I'll be away for a long time. I just thought . . . Look, stop this pretence, you know you've been making eyes at me.'

231

He moved closer to her and Jackie backed away. She knew she'd done nothing to lead him on. She had Harry and he was all she wanted.

Grabbing her bag, she pushed past him. 'I'm going!'

He caught her arm. 'Breathe a word of this and you're done for — that Carter account don't look right to me. Have you been at twisting the books then? Is that why you tried to keep me sweet? Well, it's back-fired, hasn't it, madam?'

'Naw, all the books are straight. I've never done anything like that.'

'Well, I can soon make it look like you have, so if you tell anyone about this, you'll end up in prison, young lady.'

'Naw, why? I ain't done anything.'

Sheer panic took Jackie. She ran for the door and was out in the street, running as if the devil were after her — and to her mind he could be.

Gasping for breath as her fear clutched at her, she stopped and looked back. Once she saw that Donald wasn't following her, she leant heavily against the wall of the men's barber shop.

How did that happen to me? Why?

'Are you all right, Jackie, love?'

Jackie looked into the kindly face of the barber who always greeted her morning and night as she passed his shop. 'Aye. I have to get home. See you around, Joe.'

Walking swiftly away, Jackie tried to think what to do next. She could never go back there, but if she told Marg, she would likely confront Donald. She couldn't risk that. She couldn't risk telling anyone.

By the time she got home, she still hadn't thought of an excuse for why she couldn't go back to work at the accountants'. She hated Donald now, after liking him so much for over two years. But the hate didn't help.

Marg needed the money she brought in. And where would she get another job? What would everyone think of her if she told them she'd packed in such a good position without having another job to go to? And would Donald blacken her name amongst the other accountants, making it impossible for her?

These questions raged around her brain as she opened the door to her home.

'Eeh, lass, what're you doing home, eh?'

'I'm not well, Marg.' She greeted the boys who'd come running towards her, ruffling their hair. The action made her feel better, but Marg wasn't leaving it.

'By, you do look pasty. It ain't time for your monthly, so what ails you, lass? Has something happened?'

'Naw. It's just a headache, I think I'm coming down with sommat. I'll be all right, only they sent me home as I couldn't concentrate and kept making mistakes.'

How easily the lies tripped off her tongue.

'Well, go and lie down for a while, eh?'

George caught hold of her skirt. 'No, don't go to bed, Jackie. Will you play ball with me, please? I like it when you throw the ball and I have to catch it, then if I don't, I have to go down on one knee, it's funny.'

Carl tutted, probably considered himself too old to play such a game. She laughed at him. 'Come on, the pair of you. If anyone can get rid of my headache, you can, lads.'

Carl grinned and followed them out.

As the game got underway, everything felt better, but she still worried about how to tell Marg that

233

she'd lost her job. And doubts began to creep in as to whether she'd even get her last week's wage that she was entitled to.

A voice called out to her. Edith had arrived home.'Hey, you're an unusual sight on a Monday. Why aren't you at work?'

Although what Edith said compounded her situation, it also lifted her a little as she knew she could talk to Edith. Edith always knew what to do.'Carl, lad, carry on playing with George, only keep your ears and eyes open for a car coming. I'll be back in a mo, I just need to see Edith.'

'Eeh, Edith, I need to talk to you.'

'Are you all right, Jackie?'

'Naw.' Though she hadn't meant to, she burst into tears. Through her sobs she told Edith what had happened. 'I don't know what to do, Edith. If I tell Marg, she'll go mad at Mr Blake, then he'll do as he says and accuse me of fiddling.'

'Aw, Jackie, I can't believe this has happened to you, lass. What a rotten character. And he'd never before shown any signs of thinking of you in that way?'

'Naw, he's always been friendly. Really friendly. It were nice, made me working day go by and made me feel of worth, but he said he couldn't leave without telling me . . . He wanted to kiss me and touch me . . . Eeh, Edith, what am I to do?'

'Well, Marg has got to know, but I'll tell her. I'll convince her that she can't do anything about it. I can handle Marg. Then, once she knows, she can be your ally in whatever story you make up to tell your da and Harry.'

'I don't want to lie to Harry. Will you tell him an' all? Only I knaw I'll cry and that'll upset him, and he'll feel like defending me.'

'All right, lass. I'll make him see that it's best left alone. But can your boss make such an accusation stand?'

'Aye, on some of the accounts — those for the small businesses in outlying villages — we do the banking an' all. Mr Blake could make it look as though I entered less takings and pocketed the rest. Most clients don't know the balance of their banks, and if they do, they wouldn't generally get a statement until the end of the year so wouldn't notice it till then, by which time, anyone who'd embezzled could have made the accounts tally.'

'In that case, lass, it's better to keep everything quiet as I can't see how you'd have a leg to stand on otherwise. That rotter could be preparing a set of books right now to make his story stand up . . . Look, don't worry. It's unfair, I know, and he'll get away with his behaviour, but you'll come out better for not making a fuss. Mud sticks and he has standing in the community, while the likes of us don't stand a chance. It's the way of the world, love. What he don't have is friends like you've got. His'll be the false, buttering up sort who think they can benefit from knowing him. Nor can he have a happy wife and family as this won't be the first time he's preyed on young girls. Didn't you say that you got the post because a young girl had left? Well, the reason may have sounded good to you, but I wonder what the real cause was.'

'Aye, and he'll be in a mess as I'm supposed to take the brunt of the daily accounting when he goes away on war business.'

'Well, at least he'll soon be gone then, so he won't be a threat to you. Look, love, I'll just open me post, go for a pee and I'll be round to talk to Marg. Carry on playing with Carl, lass, as if nothing's wrong, and I'll sort this — though you'll need to sort yourself out with another job. Any ideas?'

'Come to think of it, there is. One of the clients was always saying she wished I'd come and work for her. She has a millinery. She said I could do her books and look after the shop at times to give her a break as with paying for her accounts to be done she can't afford help as well.'

'That sounds grand. It sounds as though she sees you as the whole package Why don't you go along and see her, eh? . . . Mind, it's tricky as Blake ain't going to be too pleased about losing a client, let alone you being the one responsible.'

The hope that had filled Jackie died.

'Mmm, wait a mo. Look, I know who can help with this. Father Malley. We can go and tell him everything, and he'll understand about not getting the police involved. Then ask him to speak on your behalf to this lady you know. I think that'll work, lass.'

The hope came back, as to have a priest speak for you was the very best recommendation you could get.

'Ta, Edith.' Jackie flung her arms around Edith. 'I knew you would find a solution for me. Eeh, I love you, lass.'

Edith laughed. 'And I love you an' all, but if I don't go to the lav, I'll pee right here. Buzz off and leave it all to me.'

Sighing with relief, Jackie went outside. 'Right, lad, throw the ball.'

When Carl did, she pretended to miss it so that she had to go down on one knee. This made George double over in a fit of giggles and earned him another look of disdain from Carl, but that turned to a look of admiration as Carl retrieved the ball and threw it towards George, who caught it and then bounced it and kicked it deftly back to his brother.

'Shall we play football instead, George?'

With George agreeing, Jackie joined in with the changed game, feeling happy to be with them. She loved these little boys as if they were her brothers.

'Right, I've had enough for a while. You carry on, but mind, do as I say and watch out for cars . . . Oh, and windows, or someone might skelp your lugs for you.'

'What's 'skelp my lugs', Jackie?'

Carl answered. 'It means box your ears. Don't you know anything, George!'

Jackie was laughing as she went inside but that changed as she caught Marg struggling to put a sheet she'd lifted out of the dolly tub through the mangle.

'Aw, Marg, you should have called me.'

'No, you were doing me a favour looking after the lads. It gave me a chance to tackle this. It's been in soaking all morning.'

Jackie didn't have to ask; she knew it would have come off Gran's bed. 'Marg, I reckon we should out Gran's mattress an' all. The stink in her room knocks you backwards. She could have mine and I could sleep on the sofa, then we could ask Gerald if he could get us one of them rubber sheets that they use in hospital to put under the sheet on Gran's.'

'By, that's a grand idea, lass. Though I were thinking of putting your mattress in the Anderson shelter when it's built and moving you in with me. So, you can do that now, lass.'

'I'd like that, especially in the winter; you keep me warm . . . But when you marry we'll have to think of sommat else.'

'Eeh, lass, that won't be for a while. I ain't free to go and get married.'

Jackie felt the pity of this. Marg deserved to follow her heart and be happy, but she knew no argument she could put up about taking the responsibility for Gran herself would change her mind.

'Anyway, you look better. Has your headache gone?'

'Aye, it has, ta.'

'It weren't just a headache, were it, Jackie, lass?' Jackie paused, unsure of what to say.

Luckily, Edith saved the day as she burst through the door shouting, 'Where are you, Marg?'

'Coming, Edith, what's up? Is someone after you or something?'

Jackie took the sheet. 'I'll go and get this on the line.' Just as she went out the back door, Jackie heard Edith say, 'I've got it!'

She didn't wait to hear what Edith had got, but hurried into the backyard and set about battling with the dripping sheet. The struggle to get it pegged into place didn't quell her nerves, though, as she feared Marg's reaction to Edith telling her all that had happened.

* * *

When she went back in, Marg was hugging Edith. 'Eeh, I'm glad for you, lass.'

'What's all this about? Have you won the pools, Edith?'

'No, but I have been invited for an interview at St Kentigern's School! I can't believe it. Oh, I so want this job. With Philip going it will be a godsend!'

'Philip's going so soon? He's not volunteering, is he?'

'Aye, he is.'

Jackie felt the guilt of putting her troubles on to Edith as she listened to what Edith faced but Edith dispelled this by saying, 'It's just something we all have to deal with, so let's not dwell on it, eh? Let's be just be glad this has happened for me.'

To Jackie, Edith was a hero, and someone she wanted to be like. She smiled and went towards her to hug her, but before she could, Edith signalled with her eyes for Jackie to make herself scarce.

Gran woke from her doze at that moment and burst into tears.

'I'll see to Gran. You pop round Edith's, Marg, and have a cuppa with her. You've loads to talk about, and the break'll do you good, love.'

'Ta, Jackie, I could do with five minutes. Poor Gran. No doubt she's been dreaming again.'

Going over to Gran, Jackie went down on her haunches. 'What is it, Gran, love?'

'Eeh, Jackie, love. It . . . it's, me John. He's dead, ain't he?'

'Gran, he's with Ma, your lovely Vera. They're looking after each other. You wouldn't want Vera to be on her own, would you?'

'Naw. You knaw, it's funny, but everyone calls me Gran. No one calls me Sandra or Mrs Bird anymore. All them as did have gone now. Mind, I'm glad as Mrs Bird sounds like I'm going to peck everyone.'

Jackie giggled at this.

'I never liked that name, you knaw . . . Me John always called me his 'little lass'. Eeh, I loved me John.'

Knowing where this was leading, Jackie distracted

Gran by making tweeting noises and flapping her elbows. As she bobbed her head like a chicken, Carl and George came through the door. George squealed with laughter, but Carl looked quizzically at her. Gran caught on to the giggle and went into her cackling laughter, showing her one tooth.

This set them all off.

Gran's sad moment had passed.

'All this giggling is making me want the lav! Will yer give me a lift up, Jackie, love? Me legs ain't working.'

As Jackie took Gran under her arm, Carl said, 'Hold my hand, Gran, I can help too.'

Gran smiled her lovely smile as she took Carl's hand. 'That's better, I feel as though I'll make it with your help, lad.'

Carl's face was a picture of determination as he held Gran's hand. George, not to be outdone, took her other one. 'Come on, Gran, me and Carl are strong, we'll get you there.'

'Eeh, me lovely lads.'

Gran's voice held such love for the boys. She adored them. But her weakness worried Jackie. She looked heavenward. *Please, God, don't take me Gran an' all. I couldn't bear that.*

It seemed to Jackie that suddenly everything was changing, and they stood to lose so much of what they knew and loved. Already they were going to have to say goodbye to Philip. How long before the others went? Weeks? Months? Would they all be gone before Christmas?

With this thought, tears pricked her eyes as even though it was still September and the sun was shining, they would usually be mentioning Christmas and beginning to think about putting a bit by for the extras they'd need. Before she left her job at the shop, customers were already asking about the savings club that Mr Fairweather always ran.

Jackie sighed. She had a feeling that Christmas this year would be a ruined, lonely and fearful time.

Once more she prayed. *Let us all have a good Christmas, please, God. Don't take any of our men away from us before that, and please, don't take me Gran. I promise, I'll go to mass every Sunday, if you'll just do this for me.*

20

Edith

Marg had the look on her face that Edith had seen often.

'Marg, you have to listen to me, lass. I know how you feel, I felt the same. Jackie's scared, love. We have to protect her. She could end up accused of something she hasn't done. We need to help her, Marg.'

Marg took a deep breath. 'I've looked after me sister all me life, she's everything to me. I can't bear anybody hurting her or frightening her, Edith.'

'I know. But if you want to look after her this time, you've got to hold your temper.'

Marg's expression changed. 'But what if she gets this job and he does what he threatens? Jackie'll be better off taking your job at the biscuit factory.'

'Actually, that's not a bad idea. It's not what any of us want for Jackie, but she'll be safe there. At least until Blake has gone. But will she agree?'

'Aye, I think she'll feel safer all round being with me in the mornings, and the others an' all, when I've gone home.'

'Do you want me to put it to her?'

'No, I will. I'll go now. If I know Jackie, she'll be worrying, and I want to check on Gran anyway.'

'All right, love, good luck.'

Rushing around, Edith managed to cook some chips and had eggs ready to fry. She was buttering the bread when she heard Philip's car. He was in the doorway by the time she whipped her pinny off and straightened her hair. His arms opened and she went into them.

He kissed her hair. 'I've news, darling. I've been released from my contract at the school, but my job will be kept open for me.'

Edith gasped. Philip held her tighter.

When he released her, he said, 'Shall we sit down, darling? Will what you have cooking wait a moment? I'm afraid I'm not very hungry.'

'It will. I'll just put the chip pan on the side. Would you like a pot of tea?'

'No. I just need to talk.'

Edith's heart thumped against her ribs. Her mind screamed at her that she couldn't take whatever Philip had to tell her, but she gripped the towel rail in front of the stove and breathed in deeply.

For Philip, she had to be brave.

When she went back to him, he was sitting on the sofa patting the seat next to him.

His arm came around her the moment she sat down.

'Darling. The gentleman we met — I still don't know his name and may never do so — has visited the school.'

'What? You mean . . . he was looking for you?'

'Checking me out. It appears he was sent on a mission to do this of all the known linguists in the country. I have been chosen to join the Intelligence Service.'

'And Sandhurst?'

'That is where you must tell everyone I have gone. You must keep to this, Edith. I shouldn't even be telling you, but I trust you with my life. However, after tonight, I cannot tell you anything about what I do.'

'Oh God! Philip, I can't take it in. When will you go?'

'I don't know, I have to await instructions. I only know that I'll be based in London for some time. To this end, darling, I am going to order a telephone to be put in. I want you to stay living here. I want you with Marg and your neighbours who all love you. I will think of you in this house, and I will telephone you whenever I get the opportunity, but don't ask any questions of me.'

Edith felt stunned. It all sounded like they were part of a film, but she knew this was truly happening.

'Edith, tell me you will be all right, darling.'

Edith forced a smile onto her face. 'I will, love. I have a chance of becoming a teacher!'

'That's wonderful! When? How?'

Glad to have something to distract from the dreadful news she'd just heard, Edith told him her news. 'You know I told you that I'd met my old teacher? Well, she kept her promise and I've had a letter from Mr Raven, the head-teacher at St Kentigern's.'

'Well, darling, it sounds to me like you've got the job. Heads don't usually send invites in this way. They sift through those who apply.'

'Really? So, this could mean I have a good chance?'

'I think so, darling, especially as Father Malley is likely to be on the panel, and even Mother could be as she is one of the trustees. What does the letter say about the post?'

Edith read it out:

'If you are successful, you will be required to take up the post as soon as possible, and will initially work alongside our excellent staff and learn from them. We hope to have the successful candidate ready to take over from one of our

244

most respected staff members when she retires at the end of this term.'

'Excellent. It sounds like they have decided that you are the one. You can give your notice in now.'

'No, I daren't. If I'm left without a job, I'd never cope, not being around here all day.'

Philip was quiet for a moment. When he spoke, he said, 'When is the interview?'

'The day after tomorrow, which I thought were very quick. By, me nerves won't have time to settle.'

'That will be because of us being at war. My head said today that a few teachers will be recruited, even though the profession is exempt from call-up. He thinks there will be a shortage and is asking the head of department who was about to retire not to.'

'So, you really think I have a chance?'

'I do, and I will pray that you get it. Then you will be exempt too, because there's always a possibility that womenfolk will be called up to do war work, particularly because there will be a shortage of manpower to do the jobs they are doing now. Already the Land Army has reformed, but I see women taking on many roles they wouldn't have dreamt of doing. If you are a teacher, they won't call you away from home to get involved.'

This pleased Edith. She knew that she would hardly cope without Philip, but didn't relish going away to somewhere strange. At least here she would have Alice and . . . 'Do you think Marg could be called up? Will they take into account her responsibilities to her gran?'

'I don't know, darling. I think all single girls may find themselves called upon, and married ones too, if they've no children.'

245

The mention of children brought Mandy, Alf and Ben to her mind and she wondered how they were faring and who'd taken them in.

'But I don't think Alice would be called as she has a child to care for in Joey. But then, her Red Cross work could lead her into volunteering locally, so you should always have her with you, darling, only . . . well, Gerald is talking of going.'

'Eeh, no. Why? Alice never said anything. I mean, she's worried about it, but is it definite? Poor Alice will be lost without him.'

'The thing is, darling, that as young men, who are fit and healthy and love our families and our country, and seeing all of that under threat, we feel we have a duty to do what we can to defend it all.'

Edith sighed. Philip was a principled man and this was part of what she loved about him. And though she screamed against it, she had to try to accept what was happening and to help Alice to as well.

Wanting to change the subject, she rose. 'I know and I will support you, love. Let me get your tea on the table. It's a simple meal as when I came home, I was delayed by poor Jackie.'

Philip listened to what happened to Jackie. 'That's a travesty, what a rotter . . . But is there no hope of Jackie getting a job to fit her skills? I'm not putting Father's factory down, of course, but Jackie's special, and doesn't seem to be made of the same stuff as the women who work there.'

'By, that's a bit much.'

'No.' Philip laughed. 'I didn't mean anything other than how strong they are. Strong in character, I mean. You can all take the banter and the odd fallout that happens, and stand on your feet for long hours, but I

246

don't see Jackie like that.'

'I know what you mean, and you're right, but it seems the only solution.'

'What if we had a word with my father? He might be able to use her in the accounts department. I think I could tell him what happened. He knows Blake anyway, so will probably know about his character.'

'That'd be grand. Would you do that? Eeh, when?'

'This is why we need a phone. If we had one, I'd just pick up the receiver and ask now. What about after tea? I'll pop round to him then.'

'Ta, love.'

'Right, I'm starving. You've worn me to skin and bone these last two days.'

Edith laughed as she got up. She went to say there was plenty more in store for him, but there wouldn't be, as he'd soon be gone.

Brushing the emotions away that assailed her with this thought, she hurried into the kitchen.

* * *

It was gone eight when Philip returned. 'Father said he'd be delighted to have Jackie. And he wasn't surprised at Blake's behaviour, only that it took so long for it to come out. He is known in their circles for being a womaniser and has upset a few of the waitresses at the club they both use.'

'Someone should do something!'

'Well, he'll be gone soon. Anyway, Father is worried about how many staff he will lose, as many of his male staff, including his chief clerk, could be called up too. He's also worried there will be shortages of everything that comes from abroad — you know he relies heavily on sugar.'

'By, it's all these things that you don't think of. But let's go and tell Jackie and Marg, this'll cheer them up no end.'

When they got outside, Marg and Jackie were sitting on the step.

'Are you both all right? We've got news that'll cheer you.'

Marg answered. 'Aye, we are now. Gran had a turn. Clive came to pick the boys up and she cried her eyes out because they were going. We've never seen her like this.'

'She's off her legs again an' all,' Jackie put in. 'Me and Marg had the biggest job getting her to her bed, but she's exhausted.'

'Eeh, you should have knocked, love.'

'Well, Philip had just come home and we didn't like to bother you, lass.'

'Always bother us, Marg,' Philip said. 'We want to help. Gran's only tiny, I could probably lift her into bed for you.'

'Aye, and she'd do one of two things: she'd either drag you in with her or clock you one!'

They all laughed at this and the mood lightened.

'Anyway, Marg, get another couple of chairs out. It'll be nice to sit with you a while and tell you our news.'

Both Jackie and Marg were over the moon that Jackie could start work on the accounts at Philip's father's factory.

'I like your da, Philip. He chatted to me at your wedding.'

'Yes, he remembered. He said he's very happy to have you working there.' Philip told them then what his father had said about Blake. 'So, no smearing of your name will be tolerated by him. Don't worry about it anymore, Jackie. Put it down to experience and look forward to your new post.'

Marg put her arm around her sister. 'Eeh, lass, you'll be working in the same factory as me, but not grafting on the factory floor. It couldn't be a better outcome.'

Jackie leant her head on Marg's shoulder. 'Now, can you fix everything else, Philip? Can you make this war go away and Harry not have to go?'

'I will try to make it as short as possible and do all I can to stop it, Jackie.'

As he said this, Harry's car turned into the street.

Jackie jumped up. 'Eeh, he's here! He said he wouldn't come around tonight as Gerald's on nights and Alice needs company when he's gone.'

Harry earned himself a slap when, after Jackie jumped up excitedly to greet him, he grinned and told them he'd only fetched her as Alice wanted to play cards and they needed a fourth.

When they pulled away, Edith told Marg about Gerald's plans.

'Eeh, no, not Gerald an' all?'

'Aye. He wants to join the Medical Corps, or, if not that, volunteer with the Red Cross, as they're organising sending doctors to the front lines.'

'Are there any front lines? I haven't heard of anything involving our soldiers.'

Philip answered. 'No, but there's bound to be preparations for such, and the papers are full of talk about us needing to defend France to stop a German invasion. But I don't think Gerald's thinking of going immediately, he's just making enquiries at the moment.'

Edith realised that Philip was already being cagey and knew more than he could tell them, but Marg accepted it.

'It's like living on a knife edge. Clive is worried an' all. He needs to work all night getting some rush orders done.'

'He's maybe stockpiling all the rock he can so that he has something to sell.'

'Aye. He thinks they may make lifeboat men exempt. Not that he wants to be, but I told him that rescue work will be important an' all.'

'It will. And I hope they do. At least the three of you will have one of us to watch out for you.' Edith felt a shudder zing through her. 'Let's not talk any more about war. I think it's cocoa time.'

★ ★ ★

When the day arrived for her interview, Edith felt like a bag of nerves, and yet, on the surface was coping well. The forelady at the biscuit factory had been all right about her taking another morning off, but the other women didn't let her off lightly. Ida seemed back to her old self as she'd sniped, 'By, she can come and go now she's married to the boss's son. One rule for her and another for us.'

Others had joined in and Edith had felt glad to go home. A big part of her hoped never to have to go back.

This wish seemed a reality as she got through the maths, English and catechism exams with flying colours, and then found out she'd breezed through the interview.

She was asked a few questions by a daunting panel,

made a little easier by the kindness of Father Malley spouting her virtues.

'From the Church's point of view, there is no better candidate than Mrs Bradshaw. For sure, she is a good Catholic girl, and her exam results prove that she's a clever one too.'

Mr Raven nodded his head, and Sue smiled at her.

By the time she came out of the headmaster's office, Edith had her verbal confirmation that she'd be offered the job and felt like joining in the skipping that was going on in the playground.

It was then that she spotted Mandy as one of the girls turning the rope. Her heart filled with joy as she ran down the steps and called out to her. 'Mandy, how are you? My, you look happy enough, lass.'

'I am at school, miss, but not at the place they sent me. I don't know where . . . 'The little girl's eyes filled with tears. 'They took me bruvver and Ben some-where different.'

'Eeh, that ain't right. I'll see what I can do, lass. I'm going to be one of your teachers and I'll see you here in just over a week, so I want you to be brave until then. Can you do that, love?'

'I don't want to be another week without Alf.'

'If I get answers before, I'll come here to see you then. How would that be?'

As Mandy nodded, her tears spilt over, cutting Edith's heart in two.

'Is it just missing your brother that's making you unhappy, lass?'

'No. The woman I'm with don't want me. She tells me all the time that I'm just a nuisance that she has to put up with, but if she can find a way of getting rid of me, she will. She has other kids, and they bully me, but I give them a good kick and shut 'em up.'

Edith wanted to gather her up and run away with her. 'I promise, I'll sort something out. Don't kick anybody again, as that sort of behaviour is no better than them and can get you into trouble. Besides, it isn't the way to deal with things. Try to ignore them and keep out of the way as much as you can, lass.'

An authoritative voice calling out made Edith stand up and look around. An older woman came over to them. 'Is there a problem, Mandy? And who are you, miss?'

'Sorry, I have just been with Mr Raven. I'm Edith Bradshaw. I start here as a student teacher in just over a week. I met Mandy when I was with the WRVS helping with the arrival of the evacuees; I were just having a chat with her.'

'Oh? Well, she can be a nuisance that one, as no doubt you will find out. Mandy, stop your snivelling and get on with things. Go on.'

The woman turned back to Edith. 'There's a few of them here; they're from the poor end of London and I reckon they've been dragged up. They all give us trouble, but we'll knock that out of them in due course. They won't get away with it. Now they're in the North they'll behave like we do or feel the consequences.'

'But it's all strange to them, they need help to settle in. They've been taken from their parents, friends and their homes and they need careful handling.'

'Oh no, you're not a bloody do-gooder, are you? Not that I care, I can't wait for the end of term when I can say goodbye to snotty-nosed kids forever.' With this she turned, lifted the whistle that was on a band around her neck and blew a shrill, ear-blasting sound that hurt Edith's ears.

The noise of the playground stopped immediately. The children stood, as if turned to stone in the last position they were in. One more blast on the whistle and they marched in silence into lines, waiting to be told when they could file in.

Edith was taken back to her own school days. Nothing had changed. The kids' feelings were not considered, nor their circumstances taken into account. They reacted to a whistle as if they weren't human. But then she realised they weren't treated as such, and for the first time Edith doubted her ability to do the job as she could never treat children that way, and yet, she worried about rocking the boat.

When she left the school, her dreams feeling crushed and her heart heavy, Edith briskly walked the two miles or so to the prom.

The sea air cheered her as she breathed deeply. It was as she turned to walk home that she changed her mind. She wouldn't go yet, but jump on a tram going south, stay on to the terminal and then make the ten-minute walk to her in-laws'. Her hope was that Sue could advise her.

Sue greeted her with surprise, but in a welcoming way, which settled Edith's nerves. She'd had her doubts about turning up unannounced, but she'd stuck to her plan, hoping the new Sue would accept her dropping in like this.

'Oh, my dear, how nice to see you. And congratulations, you did so well. I was very proud of you. Ooh, I can't wait for you to get a telephone installed. I wanted to be able to ring you to tell you how thrilled I was, and that you had it in the bag the moment you answered the first question. I nearly came around to your house — besides wanting to congratulate you, I'm longing to see it.'

Edith was surprised as she'd never wanted to visit them on such a lowly street before.

'You're welcome anytime we're in, Sue, but thinking about it, why don't you come for your dinner on Sunday after mass?'

As soon as the words were out, Edith wanted to snatch them back. What would Sue and Tom think of her house? What if there was trouble — a street brawl, as often happened when the men came home after a Sunday lunch drinking session in the Layton Institute?

But it was too late now and Sue clasped her hands, saying, 'That will be wonderful. We'll do that and we'll really look forward to it, my dear. Now, to what do I owe this impromptu, but very welcome visit?'

Once sat in the front room, Sue scurried away to get a pot of tea. This she served from a beautiful china teapot in a matching bone china cup — similarly designed to the tea set they had given to her and Philip as part of their wedding gift, along with a very generous amount of money. The china was now stored in Edith's sideboard, only to be brought out on special occasions, but such was the difference between them that Sue had bone china for everyday use too.

'I so admire you, Edith. I know it's said that Tom and I came from nothing, but it wasn't quite like that. We didn't have the disadvantages that you had. You should pat yourself on the back.'

'Ta, I am pleased . . . only, well, it's all been tainted a bit by something that happened in the playground.'

Edith told Sue about Mandy and the elderly teacher who she was certain was the Mrs Thornton she was to replace.

'Oh dear. I can see why you're upset, and my own previous attitude is visiting me again with hearing the way this teacher reacted — that could have been me a couple of short months ago.'

'Eeh, I didn't mean for that to happen . . . I just wondered if there was a way you could help?'

'I do know one or two influential people that I could speak to, but not as it happens on the school board, which is what I expect you think I could do. You see, they are sticklers, and of the same school of thought as the elderly teacher you told me of — though Mr Raven himself isn't, he is strictly governed by them. What do you think is the best thing that could happen for the children, if I can get help?'

'Getting the children placed together, or if that isn't possible, arranging a time for them to be together each week — or . . . well . . .' Without thinking the idea through that had occurred on her walk, Edith blurted out, 'I'd like to take on the three I am speaking of. Could you find out if that's possible?' Having said it, she warmed to her theme. 'With me new job, I could have them at the school with me. Mandy's a Catholic, so her brother must be and it's a fair bet Ben is an' all. This means the other two might not be getting a Catholic education. Besides which, as I am to be a teacher at the school, I will be home with them whenever they are.'

'Good gracious, Edith, that's asking a lot of yourself with Philip going! How would you manage?'

'That's just it. The children would benefit from being with someone who wants them and cares about them, and I would benefit from their company and how they would fill my hours . . . I — I could be looking at years of being on my own.'

255

'Hmm, yes, I can see that. And I could help out. You know, I was never happier than when my children were little. I loved being a mum and now love being a grandmother and I'm a very lucky one too, given how I . . . Well, that's by the by. But I could be a surrogate grandmother to the children — yes, I can see this working.'

Edith thought this wonderful and knew it would help her quest. But then a wistful thought took her about being a ma for real. She would so welcome finding herself pregnant. To have a piece of Philip with her always. His child. She longed for it to be so.

Sue interrupted these thoughts. 'My dear, I will do all that I can, I promise. And I think we have a good chance — I'm owed one or two favours.'

'Ta, Sue. It would help, even if I only got Mandy and Alf as then I could make friends with the woman who has Ben and arrange to have him for tea and to sleep over now and then.'

'Well, I'm sure that whoever she is, she would be agreeable to that. I know I would. I was only glad to be let off and not assigned anyone; a lot of my age were. But though we older women love children, we like to be able to hand them back. Not that I arranged it that I didn't get a child . . . Well, I did put forward that with so many going to war from the factory, I would have to work.'

This, Edith let go. She understood. Sue could never cope with a small child and it wouldn't have been beneficial for either of them.

Edith felt full of hope as she left, and couldn't wait to share her news with Alice and Marg.

Where the idea to take the children herself came from, she didn't know, as it had occurred out of the blue as she'd walked, but she knew it was the perfect solution for the twins, and for herself and Ben, too. She couldn't wait to see Philip later to tell him, but she knew he would be in agreement with her.

As she walked back along the road towards Blackpool, she drew in a deep breath of the fresh Irish Sea air — not that she could see the sea, as in this part of Blackpool it was hidden behind mounds of sand dunes. But she could smell it and hear it crashing its waves onto the shore and felt better for its familiar presence.

21

Marg

Marg did a twirl for Jackie. She loved the bridesmaid's frock that Edith had bought her and thought it the perfect outfit for the Tower Ballroom, where many wore ballgowns for an evening of dancing.

With the extra money they had coming in now, she'd managed to buy a lace bolero in navy and navy shoes and gloves, which made the dress look perfect for the new occasion.

'You look lovely, Marg. Let me take the pipe cleaners out — they should have tamed your hair by now.'

'Ta, let's hope it works, Jackie, lass. I didn't really want to have to wear the net we had on for the wedding; it looked lovely, but I'll feel like a bridesmaid again.'

'We could get Gran to crochet a plain one for us. She were saying today about how she used to do her knitting, and things. If we bought a pattern, we could help her to follow it.'

'Better that you get her to teach you. Let her think she is making them, but learn from her how to crochet — we missed out on those skills with Ma how she was. Mind, Gran taught me a few — I can knit like the rest of them and do the household chores with skill.'

'I know, I love all the things you've knitted for me, but I never thought of learning meself. I reckon I'd be good at it and enjoy doing it an' all ... There, ooh, Marg, it's coming along lovely; we should have thought of this before.'

'It was Ida who suggested it to me. I thought me hair were curly enough, but she said I could tame the frizz with these pipe clips. She had one in her hand-bag — don't ask me why. Anyroad, she dampened a strand of me hair, then curled it around the pipe and twisted the pipe to clasp it. It was like magic.'

'As it is now, only . . .'

'What?'

'Eeh, Marg, I've got this one stuck!'

'No, you haven't! Aw, Jackie, get it out, it'll spoil everything.'

'Naw, it won't come. We'll have to cut it out — I'll go and get the scissors.'

'What! No, you're not cutting it out!'

'Well, you'll have to go with it in then as it's proper stuck, lass.'

Marg looked in horror at Jackie, but then saw a little smile on her face. Picking up the pillow off the bed, she threw it at her. 'You rotter! You had me going then.'

They both laughed. Marg dabbed her eyes. 'Good job I haven't put me mascara on yet, you little devil.'

'Sorry, I couldn't resist. I'll finish it off now . . . There, you look lovely, Marg.'

'Ta, love, I feel like a princess.'

'Well, you deserve to. Don't worry about us, I'll get Gran to bed later. Harry's coming round and she likes to sit with him a while. Just have a grand time. A time to remember when —'

'No talk of war! Shut up, I'm not listening.'

'By, you made me jump then. Naw, you're right, the less we talk about it, the less it's likely to happen.'

Marg wanted to say that it has happened, but she knew what Jackie meant. It made it real when they spoke about it.

When Clive arrived, he looked so handsome in his grey suit. His face lit up as he greeted her with a kiss on the cheek, whispering, 'You look beautiful, Marg.'

Marg couldn't speak, her heart was thumping in her throat.

How could this be happening to me? For two years, I've kept Clive easily at bay, loving his company without hankering after more. But now I want him to hold me, to kiss me and to make me his.

She knew Clive felt that too; she could see it in his eyes and it thrilled her.

In the car, he held her hand. She slid along the bench seat to sit close to him.

'I have a present for you, Marg. It's a token of my love for you.'

The little box gave Marg a feeling she'd never had. She opened it gently and gasped at the gold locket inside.

'By, it's grand! Ta, love. I'll treasure it. Help me to put it on.'

As he did, Marg thought she really was a princess now, never had she thought to own such a thing.

While they drove along, he told her, 'I've booked for us to have our photograph taken in that booth next to the Tower, darling. He said he can reproduce them the same size as the locket, and one for my pocket watch too so that I only have to open it to see you.'

'Aw, that's lovely. I'd like one framed of us an' all for me dressing table.'

When Clive reached the shop and pulled up, he leant over and kissed her. In a soft voice he said, 'Is there any chance of us sharing a dressing table soon, darling, and having our own sideboard to display our photos?'

'I so wish there were, love. I love you, Clive, and I want to be your wife, but Gran . . . Oh, it's hopeless. I can't move Gran, it would kill her. The only way is if you move into ours, and I couldn't ask that of you. Besides, we've no room for the boys.'

'I might have a solution. Oh, Marg. I can't wait any longer, I love you . . . I need you. Things may change rapidly, I . . . Oh, Marg, let me hold you.'

She rested her head on his shoulder. It all seemed an impossible dream. Whatever Clive's solution was, she couldn't see a way forward until her Gran . . . But no! She wouldn't think of that time, she couldn't bear to lose her.

'Anyway, let's go and look pretty for the camera. And I'll see what I can do.'

★ ★ ★

'Right, they'll be ready next week. I can develop the sizes you need, but I'll need you to leave the locket and the watch with me. You can collect them next Saturday.'

'Oh, can you add two of the best ones of us together so that we can frame them, please?'

'I can add a frame for you. Silver, gold, light wood or dark wood?'

They both chose silver, though the cost was enormous, but Clive didn't mind that at all.

Marg had never thought about how well off Clive was. To her, he was just Clive, but these photos and the locket brought home to her the difference in their circumstances and reminded her how much he must love her. He could have his pick of the women of his own standing, and yet he'd stuck to her all this time, accepting her friendship and waiting till she was ready.

Outside she told him, 'You're a good man, Clive.'

'Well, is that all I get for lavishing my last penny on you?'

'You daft apeth! No, come here.' Taking his cheeks, she pulled him down to her and kissed him. 'That's for starters, as folk are looking, but later I'll give you a proper kiss.'

'I look forward to that.'

* * *

It was a magical evening, with Reginald Dixon on the famous Wurlitzer, and the beautiful, elaborate ballroom lit up like a golden grotto, its many balconies adorned with golden carvings and its magnificent paintings of mythical women on the ceiling.

They danced almost every dance, from the Viennese waltz to the quick step and the progressive waltz, during which they tried to keep eye contact as they parted to take different partners whenever Reginald called out, 'Change your partners, please!'

They giggled when a rhumba was played as neither of them knew how to do it, and instead tried to follow an older couple who were obviously still so very much in love.

Panting for breath, Clive caught her waist and said, 'Let's sit this one out, darling.' Thanking the couple, they made it back to their table.

They found it surprisingly easy to chat, despite the music, chatter and laughter going on around them.

Clive took her hands in his. 'Darling, about what I said earlier. I have a sort of solution. It isn't ideal, but I so want to be married to you.'

'I want that an' all. Do you reckon it can be done?'

'Well . . . Look, this is only an idea, but how would it be if we married, but you stayed at home, except for a few days and nights a week?'

'You mean, leave Jackie to take care of Gran? Eeh, no, Clive, I couldn't do it.'

Clive looked down at their hands. When he looked up, he said, 'I'm sorry I asked. I'm just desperate to be married to you.'

'I know, I feel it an' all. What about if we did it the other way around? You come to stay with me for some nights a week and me stay one with you? Would the lads be able to manage without you? I mean, they can come an' all, they love it with us and we love them, but I know it's not the best thing for them to move them about like that.'

'No, they are used to staying with their granny — Harriet's mother — two nights a week, and my parents for two because I can't see to them and get to work in time. But I always tuck them up into bed and pop out of work to see them at their breakfast time, then have a later start on Friday and Saturday so that they can sleep at home with me and spend Sunday with me. Anyway, this arrangement would suit us all very well. We'll keep it like that until such time as you and I can live our lives together. Would you accept that arrangement, my darling?'

'I would, me love. Nothing we can come up with is ideal, but we could make this work. For Gran, the lads and Jackie. But I would love it if me night with you could be when the lads are at home, so we can

263

spend time as the family we'll eventually become.'

'That's a smashing idea, Marg, that means a lot. We can make it work for us all, my darling. Many husbands and wives have to live apart for weeks — soldiers, travelling businessmen, even night workers don't get to spend many nights together with their wives. And I wouldn't even suggest we live like this but for the war.'

'I know. Mind, I want to see you every day. By, I couldn't live without that.'

'Oh, Marg, I can't believe that at last you love me so deeply. I have waited so long for this. I loved you from the moment I met you at Alice's da's funeral, only at that time I didn't recognise it as that, as I was deep in grief. Yet, somehow I knew I had met the person who was going to be the saviour of me.'

Marg couldn't speak. Her eyes filled with tears. To have found this kind of love — a solid love that she knew would last a lifetime — was wonderous to her. Yes, it was true she hadn't been swept off her feet in the way that Alice and Edith had, but she knew now that what she had with Clive was the kind of love that would last forever, and could surmount all that life threw at them.

'Are you crying, Marg?'

'Tears of joy, lad, tears of joy.'

Clive smiled and squeezed her hand. 'They're playing another waltz — would you give me the honour?'

They glided around the dance floor as if they were one. Marg moulded her body to Clive's, felt the thrill of being this close to him, of him planting little kisses on her neck, of his breath on her cheek, and wanted this moment to last forever.

★ ★ ★

264

When they arrived home, having driven through darkened streets with shrouded lights on the car, Whittaker Avenue was in complete darkness. The moon was just a bright crescent in a blackened sky. Marg shuddered.

'Eeh, it feels eerie, like the world's come to an end.'

Clive put his arm around her and snuggled her to him. 'I like it, it's as if we are the only two people in the world.'

'Aye, and the curtain twitchers must have heard the car and be frustrated at not being able to take a peek.'

'Ha, I bet they are. They'll miss me kissing you goodnight, darling.'

Marg lifted her lips to his. When his covered hers and his arms encircled her, she longed to stay like this forever. To stop the world and all that loomed in the future and to spend the rest of her life in this beautiful, safe place.

When they came out of the kiss, Clive whispered her name. The sound was full of emotion. 'I love you, Clive, and always will.'

'Let's set a date, darling.'

Marg did as all the young women she'd ever known to get married did: she calculated quickly when she would be on her period for the next two months — no one got married when their monthly was due. Being very regular, she knew that her next one would be exactly three weeks away.

'Marg? Are you having doubts?'

'No, there's nothing more certain than me wanting to marry you, love. I were just thinking a few things through. How about five weeks today? I don't know what date that is, though.'

Clive counted on his fingers — today is the ninth,

265

so . . . October the fourteenth? That sounds wonderful. That will be our happiness day — the day you become mine, darling. I'll come to yours tomorrow and then we can make all the arrangements.'

'What I'd like you to do, Clive, is to arrange to see me da. He's never been allowed to do anything that das do, and I'd like him to be asked, as should happen.'

'Oh? I didn't know . . . I mean, you've always hated him. I know things have been better since he reappeared, but . . . anyway, I'm glad. For whatever Eric Porter is, he's your father, and that's all that matters.'

'We'll go to his house tomorrow, eh? I ain't been there very often. I never wanted to, and now, with Gran taking a lot of me time, I just haven't got around to it, but I'd like to.'

'That sounds like a plan. I will have my boys with me, remember?'

'That'll be grand. Da'll be able to see for himself how much I love the boys and so won't be worried about that.'

'Do you think he will object, Marg?'

'No. He's already said you're a good catch. But this will be his first real fatherly role, so he might milk it a bit.'

'Well, I can see that. Now, Marg, we'd better say goodnight, but remember, soon, we won't have to leave each other. Well, not on most nights . . . Oh, Marg, I can't wait, and I want to make next Saturday another definite date — an afternoon one as I want to buy you your rings. An engagement one to wear now, which tells the world you're promised to me, and a wedding ring in readiness for our big day, then I will take you and my boys to tea — a 'tea and cakes tea'

266

at the Imperial Hotel — if the government don't beat me to it and take it over again.'

'The government? Why would they do that?'

'They did in the Great War. It was used as a hospital for officers.'

'Well, there's nowhere better, right near to the sea. It's a grand place — too grand for the likes of me. I'd rather go to the café on the prom in South Shore, Clive. I'd enjoy that better. I'd feel like a pig in a palace in the Imperial.'

'Ha! Well, I haven't heard that one before, and it's not true, your beauty would grace any place on earth, but I don't want you feeling uncomfortable on our engagement day, so café on the prom it is, darling.'

'Ta, Clive. I'd love that. They make lovely doughnuts.'

Clive squeezed her. 'Never change, Marg. I love you as you are.'

This to Marg was one of the nicest things he could say. Though she would always feel comfortable in her own skin, she did worry what his parents and friends would think of her. But if she was good enough for Clive, then they'd have to accept her, or not, as they wished.

* * *

Marg linked arms with Jackie as they walked to work together for the first time the following Monday, thrilled that all had worked out as it had and feeling helped by Jackie's presence, as today was to be the start of factory life without Edith.

Edith had for the first time taken advantage of her position as the boss's daughter-in-law, and had asked to be let off working a full week's notice.

When Alice had left, it had been a hard blow, but for a long time she'd put off thinking about what it would be like when Edith left too. Now that had been cushioned in the most unexpected way.

'Eeh, Marg, fancy you getting married. By, it'll be strange having you and Clive in Ma's bed.'

'Aye, but we won't be, we'll buy a new one, and it ain't been Ma's room for a long time. Though we'll have to see to getting you a bed an' all, now Gran's got your old one. And I'll speak to Clive about decorating that room. Aye, the more I think of it, the more I want to do that, then it'll be our room, not me ma's old one.'

'But that'll be like turning Ma out — the bed she had downstairs has already gone.'

Marg felt terrible as she heard the distress in Jackie's voice. 'Don't worry, love, I won't do that if it will hurt your feelings.'

They were quiet for a moment, then an idea occurred to Marg. 'What if me and Clive have the front room? We could put a bed in the living room behind the sofa for Gran, like we did for Ma. It'd be easier all round as she'll be in a central place — you'll be able to leave the bedroom door open when I'm not there and then you'll hear her if she moves around — not that we have any difficulty now as she usually makes a lot of noise and wakes us immediately.'

'Aye, that's a grand idea. Edith made a lovely bedroom of the front room of her house until she married.'

'She did. Anyway, it'll all work out; it has to, love. Da didn't like it. He wanted me to put Gran in a home and get wed properly — he said you could go and live with him, Jackie, but that ain't going to

268

happen. He took it all right when I told him frankly that it wouldn't. He wanted to arrange everything for me wedding an' all, but I wouldn't let him. He'd only cook up something whereby all his cronies could get drunk, but he did give me twenty quid to spend on me frock and me bridesmaids'.'

'That's grand, Marg . . . Aw, why don't you do as he says, at least the bit about living with Clive? I'd manage.'

'No, love, I won't so don't even think about it. It'll all work out, and if you like, you can have Harry over for the night when I'm away at Clive's.'

'Naw. That wouldn't be a good idea. Harry . . . well . . . you know.'

Marg was shocked at the implication of this as she still thought of these two as young 'uns. But Harry wasn't . . . well, not altogether. He was a young man, and young men had a job controlling their urges. 'He don't bother you, does he, love?'

'Harry? Naw. But, well . . . Eeh, Marg, I'm blushing now, but both of us . . . we find it difficult.'

Marg knew how difficult it was, but found it even more so to accept her kid sister had those feelings. But now she found herself jolted into a different world, one where she had to look on her little sis as a young woman in all things. And the young were impetuous. They acted on their feelings.

'Right, I understand. No sleepovers for Harry then. Eeh, lass, just another couple of years and you'll be of an age where it won't be frowned upon if you marry, and this war will most likely be behind us, and . . . well, all things will probably be different. Harry'll be twenty and back working with Clive, and you'll have your job, then you can set out on your life together.'

'That's how I see it — well, both of us do — so we have to try not to get into . . . well, situations.'

Marg felt uncomfortable discussing this with Jackie, and yet recognised that Jackie needed someone to talk to. 'Why don't you chat to Edith, lass? You did when you lost your job and that horrid thing happened. Edith's easy to talk to and always has a solution.'

'Aye, I might do that. Ta, Marg, for not getting all cross and wanting to have a go at Harry.'

'Is that what you thought I'd do? . . . Aye, well, I can answer that one meself. Anyroad, when you're older we'll chat about everything, and some of the things'll make your hair curl!'

'Ha, curlier than it is now?'

Despite it being early morning, they laughed out loud and Marg knew the awkward moment had passed, but she wondered if this was a changing point — a time when she had to look differently on her little sister.

She sighed heavily. She hated change and everything she knew was changing, or was about to, and more may be taken away from her. She prayed to God that wouldn't happen, but couldn't deny the feeling of doom that descended on her.

22

As Alice walked home after her interview with the Red Cross on Thursday afternoon, she felt good about the outcome, particularly since they intended to provide help in so many areas of medicine — ambulance drivers, nurses, first aid, and wherever else they might be most needed.

It was this that made her decide she'd offer her services full-time and leave the hospital job.

The training she would receive would be intensive and would give her a good base knowledge for what to do for almost any trauma she may come across.

'Our local branch will primarily be assigned to incidents in Blackpool and the surrounding towns, but if needed, we will send our workers anywhere. We are part of the international Red Cross, and must be willing to help where help is needed,' Miss Tenby, head of the local organisation, had told her.

A stout woman with a mop of black hair, and brown eyes that seemed to read everything about you, she'd then asked, 'Would you be willing to travel?'

Alice had hesitated for a moment as she had to consider Billy and Joey, but she didn't want her inflexibility to spoil her chances.

'I don't mean going abroad, but to any of the cities nearby. Manchester, for instance, if we were needed on a short-term basis?'

271

Alice felt she could commit to that as she knew Edith or Marg would be willing to look after the lads for her — well, Joey, as Billy could take care of himself. So, she'd said that she could and had told Miss Tenby that she was learning to drive, so could transport others too.

'In that case I might earmark you as an ambulance driver. Anyway, I am putting you forward for first aid training — a six-week, full-time course. After that, you can put in for the advanced course and then you will be qualified to work on an ambulance. How does that sound?'

'Grand, ta, though I'll need a week before I start as I have to give me notice in at the hospital.'

This was then agreed, and Alice walked out of the office feeling as if she'd found the niche she needed; the salve that would help her pain and fill the void inside her. As well as help her to cope if Gerald did volunteer for overseas work.

She thought about her driving lessons — she'd had three so far. The first had ended with her and Gerald in such fits of laughter that they'd had to call it a day. It hadn't furthered her skills, but it had gone a long way towards making them both feel better.

But with Gerald no longer avoiding coming home since they'd been able to talk more about little Gerald, he'd been able to take her driving twice more, and so now she felt she'd really mastered the art.

All she had to brave was going out in the car on her own; she intended to do that this evening and go along to surprise Edith and Marg, as neither had a clue she was learning to drive.

She also wanted to know how Edith had enjoyed her first couple of days at school, and how Jackie had fared in the factory office, and, well, just to be with them.

She'd take Billy and Joey, as they loved to be back in the old street, though she knew it would be difficult driving them for the first time. Any mistakes and they'd pull her leg forever more, or probably demand that she stop so they can walk.

Thinking about the lads, she dwelt on Billy for a moment and her worry of how sad he'd become since his dream job at Blackpool Football Club had folded. Even Blackpool finishing top of the league wasn't any consolation for him. She couldn't imagine what Billy would do now, but knew she had to find some way to help him as he was in the doldrums enough over not seeing his friend, Annie, so often — Annie had got a job in a shop, and her parents were strict about her leaving the house in the evenings. And Harry's prospect of being called up had left Billy envious and wishing he were older.

For her part, Alice was glad he wasn't. Billy was made of the stuff of heroes, whereas, whilst Harry would be brave and do all he was called upon to do, he would obey rules, and she felt this gave him a chance. Billy would wade in with no thought for himself, as he had done so often to try to save her from a beating by their da. She only hoped this war would be over before he became old enough to enlist.

★ ★ ★

The noise she made honking the hooter when she turned into Whittaker Avenue brought everyone out. Old neighbours were laughing and waving when they saw who it was.

Billy slid down on the seat. 'By, Alice, you're embarrassing us.'

'Aw, Billy, lad, I'm only having some fun,' Alice laughed at him; Billy was easily embarrassed these days.

When she parked outside Marg's, she and Edith were clapping their hands. Both rushed at her as she alighted. Their hug brought tears to her eyes.

'Eeh, lass, I hope they're happy tears. When did you learn to drive then? By, I'm proud of you, Alice, lass.'

'This is me fourth outing, Marg — me first on me own, though. I love it.'

'You beat me to it, lass. I was telling Philip that he had to teach me before he goes.'

'Aye, do it, Edith, it's liberating — gives you independence an' all.'

Billy tutted and went off with Joey to join the lads who were all crowding around. She could hear them ribbing him about being driven by a woman, but he held his own and stuck up for her, telling them, 'Our Alice can drive as good as any man.'

Alice swelled with pride at his praise — it had been hard won, but meant the world.

Philip came out then. 'Well, Alice, clever you. I love the way you've parked in the middle of the road — if we get another car turn into the street, they can pass either side!'

They all laughed as Alice hit out at him, 'Cheeky!'

'Ha, I'm only kidding. You've done very well, and you've given me a push to take Edith out for lessons. It's going to be useful to you both when . . . Well, I'm glad you've mastered it. I'll leave you girls to it and go and read my book, before I dig myself too deep a hole.'

Edith let out a sigh.

Alice ruffled her arm. 'It'll be all right, love, we'll be here for you. We'll all be so busy with our jobs that the time will go by quickly, eh?'

Marg took their attention. 'Aye, and I've news that'll top any that either of you have. I've been saving it till we could all be together.'

This surprised Alice as Marg was the last one she expected would have news — at least, not good news — but she could tell she was bursting with something exciting.

They all did a jig with Marg when she told them. 'Good job I'm last to wed, as I didn't give much for me chances if one more person asked me to be bridesmaid.'

Jackie popped her head out of the door. 'Ha, that's an old wives' tale — at least I hope it is, as you'll be me third!'

Marg hugged Jackie to her. 'By, I never thought of that, lass, but you'll be all right, you've got your Harry.'

'Aye, Harry won't let you slip through his fingers.' Alice put her arms out and Jackie came into them. When they came out of the hug, saying their hellos, Jackie asked if Alice would teach her to drive one day.

Alice said, 'Of course I will. Just let me make sure that I've got the hang of it first, I'm still learning meself. But if I were you, I'd get Harry to give you some lessons. He'd make a good teacher . . . Anyway, how's the new job going?'

'I love it, ta. I were nervous as the work's so different, and yet the same, if you knaw what I mean? But I soon got the hang of things. It's seeing the book-keeping in progress instead of the end result.'

'That's grand, and so that leaves you, Edith. Our very own teacher! My, we've travelled far, the three of us.'

As she listened to Edith, Alice felt the quietening of so many niggly worries she had over Mandy and Alf.

'So, Mandy's all right, but what about Alf?'

'She's not exactly. She doesn't know where Alf is, but I've found him and Ben and neither are happy, nor are the folk that have got them. They said they'd let them go tomorrow, so won't object to me putting in for them.'

Alice couldn't believe what she was hearing. 'You mean, you'll take all three on? By, Edith, will they let you?'

'I should know in a few days, but keep your fingers crossed for me. I so want to do this. They'd be happy with me and be the saving of me an' all. The council are meeting with officials this week to see if there are any complaints or problems. Sue has someone speaking for me at the meeting and the current hosts are attending to give reasons why they cannot carry on with taking care of the children.'

'And Philip don't mind?'

'He's fine with it, Marg. I didn't tell you of it, love, 'cause, like you, I wanted to keep all of this till we were together.'

Alice had them giggling then as she took the chair. 'Right, let's bring this meeting to order. I'll be chairman, and I say we hear more about the wedding first — the best news of all.'

'I agree. Come on, Marg, you take the stand, lass.'

This news of Marg's was what they'd been waiting for for a long time, though Alice thought it a little tainted by how she and Clive would have to live. It wouldn't feel like a proper marriage to her. She didn't voice this, but knew it hung in the air between the three of them. She caught a glance from Edith that held the pity of Marg's and Clive's situation and wished she could do something about it.

'Will you get a couple of days away together, love?'

'Just one night, and that's why we're having the wedding early in the day. Me da wants a big do, but I'm having none of it. There'll be a small reception in St Kentigern's church hall and then me and Clive'll leave for a trip to I don't know where yet, and be back on Monday morning. Jackie'll cope with Gran, and I know she can call on you, Edith.'

'And I'll pop in for an hour on Saturday and Sunday, Marg.'

'Eeh, Alice, that'll be grand. Ta, love.'

'No problem, I'm just so happy for you, Marg, and you'll make a beautiful bride . . . My turn now. My last news is . . . I've joined the Red Cross!'

★ ★ ★

It was an hour later, and with darkness falling, that Alice set out to go back home. Driving in the dusk with shielded lights was a different experience and she was shaking by the time she put the key into her front door.

The silence of the house struck Alice. Not that it was quiet, but without Gerald being there it was not home. Whittaker Avenue was home, and she so longed to be back, not living in this lovely house without Gerald, as she knew that this was how it would feel once he went away.

'Get all the blackouts down, lads. Where's Harry?

277

'I thought he said he'd be in tonight, but his car's not there?'

'He put it in the garage earlier. Maybe he's in bed, he wasn't feeling well.'

'What? He didn't say — though, he didn't eat much of his tea.'

'He got — '

'Shut up, Joey, Harry said we weren't to tell!'

'What? What did Harry get? Tell me, Joey. Billy, you go and do the blackouts at the back of the house so we can put a light on . . . Ouch! That's the second time I've hit me shin. Eeh, why didn't Harry shut the black — '

The sound of Harry vomiting cut Alice off.

She groped her way to the stairs, pulling the landing window blind down as she passed it. 'Harry, lad, what's to do? Eeh, I'll be with you in a moment, I'll just finish the blinds so that I can switch a light on.'

A few minutes later, with several bruises on her shins now, Alice switched on the landing light. It flooded the darkened bathroom where Harry was on his knees bending over the toilet.

'Harry!'

Alice gently rubbed his back, not liking the green-brown colour of what he was bringing up. His moans told of his pain.

'Billy, fetch a drink of water, lad . . . Harry, try to swallow. Nothing's coming up now, it's just reflex.' In no time Billy was back with the water. 'Take a sip, Harry — gently — just a tiny one.'

With the spasm passed, Alice felt her heart sink at the colour of Harry. His skin looked ashen white.

'Me stomach, Alice. Oh, I can't stand it!'

'Try to get up, Harry, love. Let's get you to bed.'

278

'I can't, I can't . . . Help me, Alice.'

'Billy, go and ring for an ambulance, and then ring the number we have for Gerald.' Rubbing Harry's back once more, she told him, 'I'll just go and get a blanket, you needn't move, lad.'

As soon as she switched the light on in Harry's room, Alice saw it. A brown envelope with MOD stamped on it.

No, not me Harry, not yet!

Not stopping to read it, Alice dragged the eiderdown off his bed and ran back to Harry. Covering him, she resisted asking the question of what the letter contained, but instead concentrated on helping Harry to take another drink. The exercise was useless as Harry brought the water straight back up.

Being so near to the hospital, it was only minutes before the ambulance arrived.

'Billy, did you get hold of Gerald?'

'Aye, he said to come to the hospital with Harry and he'll meet you there.'

The ambulance drivers had to literally lift Harry, as he couldn't straighten enough to help himself, such was the intensity of his pain.

Alice felt fear zing through her as she watched this.

At the hospital it was a relief to see her Gerald. As always, he was calm. 'Now then, Harry, you're all right now, we'll take care of you.' He looked to Alice. 'Darling, wait here, I'll come to you as soon as I can, I promise.'

Alice caught his arm. 'Gerald, Harry's had a letter from the Ministry of Defence.'

'Oh God, has he been called up?'

'I didn't read it, but yes, that's the likely conclusion. The lads didn't utter a word about it to me as Harry has warned them not to.'

'You don't think he's . . . I mean, Harry will be able to face it, won't he?'

'Aye, why, what . . . Eeh, no, Harry wouldn't do anything to harm himself.'

'I had to ask, and we will have to check, Alice, there have been a few cases reported nationally. Some poor lads are just not able to face going to war or becoming conscientious objectors.'

'No! Harry would never do that! There's something wrong, Gerald, please find out what it is. Don't let anything happen to him.'

Gerald squeezed her hand. 'We won't, darling, I promise. We will investigate all probable causes and then, if not them, we'll look into . . . Well, you sit down on the bench. I'll try not to be long and you try not to worry.'

★ ★ ★

The ticking of the clock on the wall sounded to Alice like it was counting down to doom. Another lady sat a little way away from her quietly crying. 'Can I help you, love?'

'Naw one can, lass. Me husband of thirty years has just passed. I'm waiting to be able to go back in when they've washed him and before . . . before they take him to the morgue.'

Alice moved along the bench to her. 'Eeh, I'm sorry, love. Can I get you a cup of tea? I work here, well, until the weekend, and I know where everything is. I could do with one meself. Me young brother's not well, he's being assessed.'

'Ta, if you could, it would be welcome. I've been

280

here since this morning. He had a heart attack.'

Alice patted her shoulder then ran in the direction of the kitchen that served the wards nearby.

'Well, if it isn't miss tell-tale tit.'

Alice recognised the young nurse who was supposed to have been on the ward the night she found the patient with internal bleeding.

'Got me in a load of trouble, didn't you? Well, that kind of thing don't go down well around here, so watch yourself.'

'It weren't on purpose. I came looking for you, but I bumped into my hus . . . Doctor Melford, and he took over. I'm sorry if you got into trouble.'

'Aye, well, sorry don't always put everything right, but I'll get me own back.'

Alice felt her blood boiling; she had enough on her plate without this playground-like talk. 'Well, you won't get your chance, love, I'm leaving.'

'Good!'

With this parting shot the girl left. Alice was left shaking, but pulled herself together. She wouldn't cry over the silly incident. She had so much worse than that to cry over.

Back with the grieving woman, Alice listened to the woman's tales of her time in the last war. 'He was brave, me Harold was. He got a medal, you knaw. He ran across no man's land and shot the gunner who was mowing them down one by one.'

'That's a grand thing to remember about him. What was it like without him? When he was at war, I mean.'

'Are you facing that, love? Is your hubby a soldier?'

'No, a doctor, but he wants to go to work with the Medical Corps.'

'It weren't easy, lass, but you get used to it and learn

to cope. Your friends, family and neighbours help, and most will be in the same boat. You need to be busy. There's loads they will need us women to do.'

Alice slipped her arm around the woman. 'What's your name, love?'

'Heather. Me ma were from the Scottish Highlands and said the name reminded her of home.'

'It's a lovely name. Mine's Alice. Have you any family?'

'Naw, it never happened for us, but I love little 'uns. I put meself forward to have an evacuee, but they said they would only come to me as a last resort. I'm glad now, but it would have been lovely.'

This gave Alice an idea, and by the time Gerald came back she had Heather's address and promised to contact her soon. She said it was to make sure she was all right, but different ways Heather could be of help were occurring to her, and, importantly, they were ways she thought would help the lovely lady too. Somehow, she felt a deep connection to her — the childlessness, facing being apart from her hubby. Alice felt she'd found a friend.

She jumped up to meet Gerald.

'Darling, he's all right. He's very poorly, but all should be fine soon.'

'What is it? What's wrong, he didn't . . . ?'

Gerald took her arm. 'Let's go to my office, darling. Brian isn't on duty so we'll have it to ourselves.' Gerald smiled and nodded at Heather.

'Oh, this is Heather, we've made friends. Poor Heather's hubby has just passed away.'

'Oh dear, I am sorry.' Gerald went to Heather and squatted in front of her, taking her hand. 'He is in a good place now, dear. Will you be all right? Have you someone to help you?'

'Naw . . . well, I have me good friends.'

'Look, I'll see if the almoner is around, she will give you some help, but if not, stay here and we will be back.'

'Ta, love, you're very kind. I just want to see me Harold before he's taken down to the morgue.'

Gerald patted her hands.

When they reached his office — more of a general office, but where he spent a lot of time going through case notes and writing them up — Gerald located the almoner before taking Alice in his arms.

'What is it, love? Is Harry going to be all right?'

'He is. But it will take a long time — weeks, maybe months.' He stood back from her and looked down into her eyes; she saw the love and honesty in his. 'He has a burst appendix and that could lead to peritonitis — an infection, a serious one. The surgeons are operating now, and I think we caught it in time, and if we did, then six weeks from now, he'll be . . . oh, I was going to say . . . well, fit enough for anything. If an infection takes hold, then he could become very ill, but we'll face that if it happens.'

Alice knew that Gerald had been about to say 'fighting fit' but had thought better of such an apt phrase for the situation they all faced. 'He will get better, won't he? I — I mean, if he gets the peritonitis?'

'He will, he is very strong. But he will have a fight on his hands. But let's hope that doesn't happen. You will have to read the letter he had and we will have to deal with it, or he could get into trouble, but we'll send evidence to show that he isn't absconding. As I think we can assume these are his call-up papers.'

Alice went in close to Gerald once more. 'Don't let

him die, Gerald.'

'Be strong, Alice, my darling. Show Harry all the strength you have had over the last few months.'

Alice went cold. 'Eeh, Gerald, you're not going soon, are you?'

'Possibly, darling. The hospital posted a communication from the War Office about doctors and nurses volunteering their services. I have replied to it, offering mine . . . We had talked about it and I . . . well, I had no idea this would happen. I was going to tell you when I got home. I'm so sorry, darling, but, well, I have to do this, Alice.'

'I know. It breaks me heart, but I do know, and I will cope, me love. I promise, I'll be caring for the sick and injured, just like you, only at home.'

'And then, when it is all over, we'll start the general practice we've always talked about, and you will be my nurse.'

Alice couldn't wait for that day, but neither could she think about it, just in case . . .

'Now, get home to the lads, darling. I'll see you in the morning, but I promise you that I will ring you if there is anything to worry over.'

After kissing her — a sweet, gentle kiss — Gerald took her by the arm and led her into the corridor. Heather was no longer there, and she hoped the almoner had managed to help her.

When they were nearly at the door, Gerald said, 'I'll leave you here, darling, as I was about to do my round when Billy rang. Try not to worry.'

She watched him walk away, his white coat flowing behind him, his elegant stride taking him further into the distance, and her body released a shudder that resonated through her. Taking a deep breath, she told herself, *This is where it starts for me, seeing my love walking away from me, as one day soon, he will do that, and I may not see him for years. I have to bear it, I have to.*

With this last thought, an inner resolve began to form; it shored her up and gave her courage. She would do this, and she'd do it by helping others more stricken than herself.

23

Jackie sat on her bed putting her shoes on. She was up early for a Saturday morning, but for some reason had felt restless all night; a feeling that something was wrong. Now, with the early morning sun splashing across her, she reasoned that everyone had felt like that lately. As if a storm cloud hovered over them and would at any minute break.

She thought about her new job and how she was beginning to settle in, and how the office no longer felt a strange place, even though she'd only been there for a week.

She'd even got used to it smelling of delicious biscuits, instead of paper, ink, and, well, that distinctive 'office' smell that her last place of work had had.

Her new colleagues had made her welcome — Rhoda, an unmarried woman, had been really helpful to her. Though she had unnerved her with gloomy tales about her having been engaged to a young man who'd been killed in 1917. Then shrugging and saying, 'And now it's all happening again.'

Besides Rhoda, she had colleagues in the typing pool, a lively bunch of six girls, whose fingers went ten to the dozen on their typewriters, a sound only interrupted by the carriage swishing back and forwards.

They typed the invoices and the orders for the warehouse to dispatch, as well as letters — well, at least two of them typed letters as they could take short-hand dictation from Mr Bradshaw, the boss, or from Mr Wilson, the chief accountant.

Mr Wilson was a man of about thirty-five. He was overweight with a round face and small eyes, and sweated a lot, giving the impression he was nervous. But he had a nice way with him.

His nerves, she'd been told, had only developed since war was announced, and sadly had earned him the name 'Cowardy Custard' by the girls in the typing pool.

Jackie felt for him, and wanted to stand up for him, but being new, she hadn't dared to assert herself.

The accounts had proved easy for her to pick up, and this had pleased Mr Wilson. Though she still worried about becoming too friendly with the managers, as she didn't want a repeat of what had happened in her last job.

Yesterday afternoon, she'd been entering a pile of paid invoices into the ledger and checking them against bank entries when he'd called her into his office.

'Jackie . . . May I call you that?'

'Aye, of course.'

'Well, I just wanted to say that you are excellent at your job. And as I will no doubt be conscripted in due course, I think you could take over from me based on what I have seen this week. To that end, I will continue your training in depth for a few weeks.'

'Ta, Mr Wilson. I'm sorry you face going,' she'd told him. 'You must be scared . . .'

As soon as she'd said this, she'd regretted it. It wasn't the sort of thing she should talk to him about.

'I am as it happens, Jackie. Oh, no more than

287

anyone else, but . . . Look, finish up what you are doing and then you can go. But just to say, please don't take any notice of gossip. I know what the typing pool girls are saying and that isn't the case. I have a very sick brother and I am afraid to leave him . . . I don't want to, but war doesn't take into account our personal circumstances. It is that and that alone that is causing my anxiety.'

Having already stepped over the line, she'd made things even worse by blurting out, 'Eeh, I'm sorry. If there's owt I can do, you only have to say.' And then had stumbled, 'I mean . . . Well, I'll see you on Monday. Goodnight, Mr Wilson.' And had then escaped, almost banging the door behind her.

Her face reddened as she tied her laces. She'd done the very thing she'd promised herself not to, and now Mr Wilson may think that he can speak to her on a personal level, and not always about business.

The door knocker rattling sent Jackie running for the stairs. She met a bleary-eyed Marg coming out of her room. 'Eeh, lass, it's Gerald, I saw him out of the window.'

Marg was tying her robe as she followed her downstairs.

'Sommat's up, I knaw it is, Marg, I've known it all night.'

'It might not be, love.'

But Jackie knew Marg was as worried as she was. She glanced at the clock on the mantle shelf and felt even more worried when she saw that it was only six thirty.

'I'm sorry, Jackie, Marg, I had to come. Harry's been taken ill.'

'Come in. Eeh, what happened?'

'I won't come in, Marg, as I've just come off duty. But Harry's had an operation on his appendix, only there are complications. He isn't very well at all and we think having Jackie by his side will help him. I came to ask if you could get up to the hospital as soon as possible, Jackie, but I see you're already dressed so I could drop you off there if you like.'

Jackie couldn't speak, but Marg said, 'Oh God, Gerald, is he going to be all right?'

'We're doing our best, Marg, but I'm sorry, I can't stay, I'll update you later.'

On the way, Gerald told her not to worry too much, that Alice was with Harry and that he was a strong young man.

'My colleague is taking care of him. He should be on duty now and will authorise you to go through to the ward. I'll be back later.'

Still, Jackie had sat in silence. The shock had been tremendous to her and her mind couldn't help but go over horrible scenarios that scared her.

★ ★ ★

At the hospital, Jackie was near to the ward when she saw Alice come out of a door on the left of the corridor. Her voice seemed full of anguish as she called out. 'Jackie. Jackie, eeh, love.'

Alice came running up to her and flung her arms around her. 'I'm sorry to have you called like this. Are you all right?'

'Aye, but what's happening? How did it happen? I couldn't take it all in when Gerald told me.'

As she listened, two fears plagued her — the first terrifying one was that Harry was in danger, but then to hear that he had received his call-up papers floored her.

'Look, love, he can't go into the army, not for a good while, he won't be fit. But our job is to forget that for now and concentrate on getting him better. He's very ill, but he can recover, he needs us to be strong.'

Jackie nodded, the action causing tears to drip down her cheeks.

'Here, lass, wipe your eyes and blow your nose, then take a deep breath.'

As Jackie took the hanky, Alice spoke to the doctor who'd followed Alice out of the room. 'This is Harry's girlfriend, Jackie.'

'Oh, the young lady we're waiting for — or, at least, Harry is. I'm afraid that you will find that Harry's still in a semi coma, Jackie. But he may be able to hear you.' He looked from her to Alice. 'So both of you, speak cheerfully and hopefully to him and that will help. But just remember that the call-up letter may well be playing on his subconscious mind, so be careful what you say.'

When Jackie saw Harry, she felt near to collapse. He looked as though he could die at any moment, he was so ill and waxen. He didn't even look like her Harry. His face had changed; his features seemed more prominent and his eyes had almost disappeared into their sockets.

'Harry, Harry, me love, it's Jackie.'

It was difficult to keep her tears from her voice, but she swallowed hard. 'Harry, you're going to be all right. Me and you are going to go on that picnic we spoke about, remember? Up in the Bowland Hills? You just need to get better, Harry.'

There was no response. Harry lay so still it was difficult to discern that he had any life in him.

For all her brave words, when Jackie heard Alice make a soft sound and she turned to see that Alice was crying silent tears, her fear increased. She put out her hand and patted Alice's knee. The action somehow helped her. Alice needed her, not the other way around. With this thought, Jackie stood and motioned to Alice to follow her out of the ward.

In the corridor, she told her, 'Go home, Alice, love. I'll stay and I promise you I'll make sure they ring if anything changes. I knaw it ain't me place to tell you what to do, but I am doing so. You can't do anything here and you're exhausted. At least you knaw I won't leave Harry's side and I'll watch over him every minute. I've a lot that we were looking forward to that I can chat to him about.'

'I knaw. And aye, I think I will go for a while, but it breaks me heart to see him like this.'

Alice hugged her, then kissed Harry before leaving.

Left alone with Harry, Jackie took his hand. In his face she saw peace, and knew that wasn't often his expression. He never spoke of it, but she sensed that Harry was troubled by his past, and unlike Alice, he hadn't really come to terms with how his da had treated him. Harry had taken the brunt of his da's anger, and had never received a kind word from him until just before he'd died.

She wondered if this was why the Church meant so much to him, for there, he came near to this same peacefulness.

A nurse came in then. 'I'm sorry, I'll have to ask you to step outside a moment, miss, while I do some checks on Harry.'

Jackie didn't want to leave, but she didn't want to cause a problem so she got up and left the room. Then a terror filled her as, after a few seconds, the nurse came dashing out, saying, 'I've to fetch the doctor. Stay with him, miss, try to talk to him.'

Rushing back in to Harry, Jackie could see no change, but knew there must be an underlying cause to why the nurse had panicked.

'Harry, Harry, me love, it's Jackie. I love you, Harry. Everything's going to be all right, but you need to fight, Harry. Use every ounce of strength you have to get well. Then we'll marry. I don't care about our ages; we're of legal age to marry and you won't have to go to the army now, at least not for a long time, so we can be happy together and not have to part. We'll be happy, Harry, really happy. There'll never be anything but peace and love in our home and that's what we'll give to our children — a happy home without problems. You and I have never known that — well, at least not when we were kids. Everything turned out for us in the end, but we can make that even better together, Harry. Please don't die, please, Harry, don't die . . .'

The doctor's voice cut into her plea. 'I'm sorry, Jackie, I will have to ask you to step outside.'

Jackie turned. The doctor from earlier had come into the room. 'Please make him better, Doctor, don't let him die.'

The nurse took hold of her gently by the arm. 'Let the doctor do his job, love, come on.'

Jackie went with her, but felt as though she wasn't whole. She would never be without Harry by her side, as he held her heart.

She sat for a moment on the bench outside the

ward, undecided as to what to do. She'd promised Alice that she would call her if things got worse, which they surely had done, but Alice would hardly be home yet.

Deciding she would wait to see what the doctor said, she stared at the closed door willing it to open. When it did, the doctor smiled at her. 'Harry's a very strong young man, Jackie. His heart rate had slowed dangerously low, but we've managed to stabilise him again. He is on oxygen now for a while, so don't be alarmed by the contraption or the noise it makes.'

'Should I get Alice back in?'

'Not as an emergency, but is she coming back later?'

'Aye, she's only seeing to the boys. I told her to rest a while, but no doubt she'll be back soon.'

'Well, I would leave it at that. There's no need to panic. The nurse will check Harry every few minutes. I don't think he will need oxygen for long, it's just a measure that will prevent his heart having to work too hard. If we can do some of the body's work for it, then it can get on with healing itself. His temperature is up, which shows the infection is still rife, so we've taken some of his covers off and left just a sheet covering him. I'll be back soon with a fan to help further with cooling him. In the meantime, Nurse has put a bowl of cold water and a flannel on the side table, so you could help by sponging his face with it.'

'Eeh, ta, Doctor, it'll be grand to be able to do sommat to help him.'

The doctor smiled at her, and she knew he'd given her this task to help her as much as Harry.

After a few minutes of mopping his brow, Harry opened his eyes. But far from cheering her, this frightened her as his stare was blank and showed no recognition of her.

'Harry? Harry, me love, it's me, Jackie.'

His eyes closed again.

'You're in hospital, Harry. Don't be afraid. I'm with you and you're going to be all right.'

His arm came up, and in a jerky movement he pulled at the mask.

'Naw, Harry, you need that, love.'

But Harry's agitation increased. His body thrashed about. Running to the door, Jackie called out for the nurse and was relieved to see her already coming towards her, carrying the promised fan and with Alice by her side. 'Hurry, Nurse, Harry, he . . .'

In what seemed like seconds she was being held by Alice, and the nurse was inside Harry's room.

'Alice, how . . . ?'

'I hadn't got out of the hospital when I met a colleague.

We were stood chatting when Brian — that's the doctor I introduced you to — came around the corner. He told me that Harry had had a relapse so I came back.'

'He's bad, Alice, I — I'm afraid. He didn't seem as though he could see me.'

When the nurse came out, she told them they could go in now. 'He's more peaceful and I've taken the mask off as it bothers him so much. I'll go along and see the doctor and tell him what I've done.'

They sat together. Jackie held Alice's cold hand in hers as they both stared at Harry. The fan whirred away, providing the only sound in the room.

Alice whispered, 'Gerald told me that Harry's recovery will largely be down to his own strength.'

Jackie just nodded; she knew Alice was trying to

294

convince herself as much as her. But at this moment, the bottom was dropping out of her world as all she could see was a weak, worn-out, very sick Harry who she was so afraid of losing.

Live for me, Harry. Don't leave me.

The thought had hardly died when Harry lifted his head and retched. Alice jumped up and grabbed the kidney-shaped bowl from next to the fan and just managed to get it in place as Harry vomited.

Jackie felt herself wanting to retch, but she swallowed hard.

When the bout passed, she rose and went around the other side of the bed. On this side table stood a jug of water and a glass. She poured some. 'Harry, take a sip of water, love.'

'Aye, come on, Harry. Gerald told me before he went off duty this morning that we must keep you hydrated.'

Harry nodded at Alice and allowed Jackie to lift his head as she held the water to his lips. 'You're going to be all right, love. You'll get through this.'

Harry's bloodshot eyes stared at her as he lay his head back down. It was as if he was pleading with her to give him her strength. 'I'm here for you, Harry. Hang on to me, keep thinking about us and our future together, and Alice and Billy and Joey. We all need you, Harry.'

Alice lay her hand gently on his forehead. 'Your temperature is coming down, lad, the cold swabbing is working. Try to close your eyes and sleep, love.'

A little hope came into Jackie at these words. She touched Harry's head to confirm what Alice had said and knew he was much cooler than last time she'd checked.

Harry didn't react. He kept his eyes open. As Jackie looked into them she saw his pain and it was as if he was begging for their help.

But Jackie felt that they had no help to give him. They could only be with him and try to keep him with them — and pray. She'd never had the strength of faith that Harry had had, but now felt an urge to call on God. Closing her eyes, she begged of Him to help.

When she opened them, something had changed in Harry's expression. He no longer looked pleading, but intense, as if he was joining his prayers to hers. Knowing how much store he put in prayer, she told him, 'We'll make our prayers pay saying them together, Harry. Hold on to your faith, love, and you will get better.'

Harry nodded. This lifted Jackie and she knew it did Alice as Alice smiled. 'That's the spirit, lad, fight back, Harry, love, we all need you.'

To this, Jackie thought, *Need him? Me life depends on him. I'm nothing without him.*

An involuntary shudder went through her body as she knew that even if he did get through this, Harry wouldn't be safe — the dreaded brown envelope he'd received would still hold them under a cloud of uncertainty, and she wished with all her heart that she could pray that away, but knew that she couldn't.

24

Edith

Edith looked at her watch as she saw the postman crossing the road.

Eight thirty.

She and Philip were up early for a Saturday, but Philip had needed to work and had wanted to get it done so that they could spend the rest of the day together.

She'd left him in the front room, sitting at the table. He was marking papers and had a lesson to plan.

Edith smiled as she wondered what he was conjuring up for his pupils. She knew that his lessons were fun, as he tried them out on her sometimes, which meant that through giggles and teasing, she was learning quite a bit of French.

The sound of their letter box opening took her attention from these thoughts and catapulted her into a world of dread, as two brown envelopes dropped onto the mat. From where she stood, she could see the feared words 'Private and Confidential' stamped on the top corner of them.

Going through to the kitchen, Edith made a pot of tea, using the action to keep things normal so that she could compose herself before gathering the letters up and going through to Philip.

When she had everything ready, she scooped them up without looking at them properly and then tapped on the bedroom door. 'Tea, me love?'

Philip didn't look up. 'Mmm, very welcome. Nearly done and then I suggest we go for a drive. I've been thinking that it's time for your first lesson. We'll go into the countryside and stop somewhere where we can have a nice long walk, blow the cobwebs of the week away.'

'That sounds nice. By, I could do with some fresh air. Not sure on the driving, though.'

'You're not chickening out now, darling. Alice will leave you behind if you do. Besides . . . ' He looked up. His eyes rested on the envelopes; his Adam's apple raced up and down as he swallowed hard. 'Oh . . . ? Well, we both know what that is.' Recovering, he lightened his tone. 'Now, no excuses, darling, as by the looks of that post it's become imperative that you learn to drive, now.'

The sound of his paper knife slitting through the crisp paper set her nerves on edge. The unfolding of the yellowish, almost parchment paper made her hold her breath.

'I am to report to the War Office, Horse Guards Avenue, London, on Monday, the twenty-fifth of September 1939.'

'That's on Marg's birthday!'

'Yes, but yours is on the Friday before, so I'll be here for that, darling, and Alice's is near too, isn't it?'

'Aye, the Sunday.'

'Ha, even when born you three made sure you arrived close together. It's always amused Gerald and me. Mind, we love the annual party, and this year we'll all have to make it one to remember!'

Despite his jolliness, Edith wanted to scream, but she held it in.

'Eeh, Philip, we only have just over a week together.'

'We have a lifetime together, my darling.' Philip rose. 'I'll be back, this won't be me gone. It will be briefings, and training schedules, and then home on leave. I'll probably be here for Marg's wedding. And we have the telephone now, so I can ring you every day and every night. You'll hardly notice that I've gone, darling.'

Edith knew this was bravado. Philip's voice was full of emotion and his body trembled as he held her to him. With this, Edith knew that he needed her strength. 'It'll be fine, darling, we'll make your calls our reunion. Now, I'll get my cardi and we'll go for that drive. But be prepared, I might make your hair stand on end.'

Philip chuckled as he picked up his cup but then noticed the second envelope. 'Oh, I haven't opened this one yet — it might be cancelling the first, saying, 'On second thoughts, you're not what we're looking for.' He laughed at his own joke before saying, 'Oh, it's for you, darling.'

'Me? Well, I didn't notice that. I thought it was part of yours and didn't bother to read who it was addressed to.' Taking it, Edith felt curious as to why she should receive a letter. 'It's from the council!'

'Open it, darling.'

'*Dear Mrs Bradshaw, the council have approved your request to house Amanda and Alf Burns and Benjamin Cope subject to an inspection of your home to make sure it is suitable. An official from the Evacuation Department will call on you shortly. We have asked them to arrange a visit between four and five as we understand you are a member of the teaching profession . . .* Eeh, Philip, to get this on the same day you are told to report!'

'Well, darling, I hope it helps to soften the blow. It

will mean that we will be kept busy — we need to buy beds for them and a chest of drawers for their clothes.'

'Yes, and bedding, and a gus-under.'

'A what?'

'Ha, a piddle pot. We can't expect children to go out into the backyard in the middle of the night.'

Philip laughed. 'Oh, a chamber pot!'

Edith would never get used to these differences between them and hated it when they cropped up.

'My darling, I know why you want to live here while I'm gone, but I so wish we had a bathroom. Promise me that when this is all over we'll look at moving. This was only meant to be a stopgap.'

There it was again. She wondered how Alice coped with it, but then, Alice had moved up into Gerald's class effortlessly. She supposed that she must do the same. 'I promise, and if the opportunity arises while you're away, then I'll do it in readiness for your home-coming.'

'Well, I hope it does as life would be so much easier.'

'I know, but for now I'm here, me love, and aye, we need to get busy. Being accepted as a potential guardian of these children is the best thing for them, and me, and I don't want to be refused.'

'Are you all right, Edith, darling?'

She nodded, but the action spilt the tears that had gathered in her eyes with her thoughts.

'Oh, my darling.'

She went into his arms, but though she found comfort it didn't help the desolate feeling inside her. A feeling fed by the hopelessness of not being able to do anything to change the way it was. Philip was going and that was that. He was going into danger, the

300

nature of which she had no idea, and after his training she may not see him, or even hear from him, for years and years, or know if he was safe. It was unbearable.

Philip didn't try to stop her crying, but joined her, his sobs racking his body. This gave her strength more than any pleading of her to be strong could have.

'By, we're a pair of softies, me and you. Here's you going out to fight for this country's freedom — freedom for us and our future family — and we're crying about it, when we should be rejoicing that you're brave enough to do that. You will be a valuable asset to the cause, Philip, me love, and I'm very proud of you. There's none better to do this than my man.'

Philip got out his handkerchief and blew his nose loudly. 'I'm sorry, it just got to me then how much I am going to miss you and that this really is going to happen. I'm all right now.'

Edith blew her own nose and dabbed at her tears. 'You are, you're me hero.'

'Ha! I don't know about that. I don't even know what I'll be doing. I may end up behind a desk in London translating documents and communications into English — not a hero at all but a stuffy old clerk with knowledge of languages.'

'Well, I hope you do, then you can come home regularly, or I can visit you. That would be a wonderful outcome, and yet, such a waste of what you're capable of, as teaching our future generations is a better occupation for you than being a translator — there must be a lot of folk who have the ability to do that.'

'Yes, teaching is a worthy occupation, and that's what you'll be doing, darling, giving the future generations a good grounding in the basics of life to take them forward.'

'By, I feel like the hero now!'

'Well, the pen is mightier than the sword, you know.'

Edith giggled and Philip joined her. They were watery giggles, peppered with rebound sobs, but Edith felt better for them — stronger than she did before. 'Right, lad, this won't get me driving that car.'

Philip burst out laughing. He'd said many times that he loved it when she called him 'lad'. He pulled her closer to him and she saw the love he held for her shining from his eyes, but saw them mist over too, so whispered, 'Neither will what you have in mind, but who cares, eh?'

He kissed her as if it would be their last ever kiss, grinding his lips onto hers.

Nothing mattered but the beautiful expression of their love as they undressed each other and found themselves in their bed in a frenzy of need. A need to change things — to blot out what they couldn't alter and to cement their love in a bond that being apart couldn't break.

★ ★ ★

Lying in Philip's arms after, feeling the calm and complete love that surrounded them, Edith wondered if this time she would be pregnant. In the short while they had been married they'd made love at every opportunity, and even made opportunities to do so, so surely she must be soon. Her period was due next week, and she prayed it wouldn't arrive. That Philip would leave behind a little of him growing inside her for her to nurture.

The same thought must have struck Philip as he rolled over and looked at her. 'What if that family you spoke of is already beginning to grow inside you with our first child having been made and living in here?' He patted her stomach. 'How will you cope then, my darling?'

'Better than I would if we haven't got a babby to look forward to. As then I would have a part of you with me all of the time.'

'Oh, Edith, you're an amazing woman. I think of you as taking after your father. What little I knew of him, mostly from what you have told me, he sounds like a man of courage and insight and someone who always found a way to cope.'

'Eeh, he was like that, and I'd be honoured to be thought of like him.'

'You are, darling.'

Edith rolled over and threw her long legs over the side of the bed. 'We've got a drive to have and look at us, lying here naked.' She turned and picked up her pillow and hit out at Philip with it. 'Come on, get up, we've to wash and dress all over again because of you enticing me back to bed!'

'Ha! Me? You practically dragged me between the sheets!'

Their giggles continued as they dressed once more and prepared to go out. Edith's excitement at the thought that she might soon have the evacuee children with her outweighed her sadness.

'We'll drive down to Lytham and through the village of Wrea Green, one of my favourites, and then back onto Preston Road and back into Blackpool. By that time you should be fit to drive on your own and I'll be starving, so we can call to have something to eat.'

Edith let out a disbelieving breath. Somehow, she

felt really nervous at the prospect of being behind the wheel, but when she thought of Alice doing it, she knew she could too.

'Eeh, that trip sounds a lot for me first drive. Let's just go to Lytham for me first time out, eh?'

Philip agreed and was full of praise for her driving when she eventually took over the wheel. Though there was no one about, she'd refused to do so until they were well away from Whittaker Avenue.

Edith was surprised how easy it was, until a hairy moment when she met with a hold-up of three cars ahead of her caused by a horse-drawn carriage — one of the fun rides offered on the prom, turning around in the road.

'Eek, Philip, what do I do?'

Philip laughed. 'Try stopping, darling.'

Feeling foolish, she stalled the car, causing a lot of hooting and shouts of 'Get out and milk it, if you can't drive it.' She had no idea what they meant.

Philip soon got them going, but to her plea to him to take over, he refused. 'It's like riding a bike — if you don't get on again when you fall, you never will. So, off you go, darling.'

Calming herself, she did just that, and felt her confidence growing.

When they stopped, they decided they would rather have fish and chips and eat them sitting on a bench on the prom than go into a café for lunch.

Philip took the wheel to park the car. With this done they found a bench.

'By, me legs are a bit wobbly after that, Philip.'

'That's just first-time nerves — or a crafty way of getting out of fetching the fish and chips. You sit and I'll go for them.'

Edith knew he was joking, but the feeling was real to her; even though she'd enjoyed driving the car and would carry on with her lessons, her nerves had done this to her.

As she sat looking out at the turbulent sea, familiar smells assailed her to a background of seagulls squawking as they dived for fish, scavenged off folk who sat on the benches eating chips or sandwiches, or just flew in circles above. She was struck by how different the scene was now.

In front of her on the sand, instead of bathers, children building sandcastles and families picnicking, a group of servicemen stood in a circle carrying out fitness exercises.

It was an impressive regimental show, but though she was proud of them she couldn't help longing for normality to never have been banished.

'Here you are, darling.' Philip broke into her thoughts as he handed her the newspaper-wrapped hot parcel. 'I'm looking forward to these, Edith. Huh, I bet they're better than the ones you fry up in that blackened pan of yours!'

Edith forgot the men as she laughed at this and tucked into the delicious fish and chips.

'I put salt and vinegar on as you like them. Well, I did, but it's running down your chin now!'

Edith ignored him and relished the taste of the hot chip she'd bitten into, with its crisp outer layer and fluffy interior. Despite the vinegar dripping through her lips, there was no taste like it in the world.

Philip wafted his mouth as he'd bitten on a hot chip that was too much to handle, making Edith laugh. 'You're not used to this! The trick is to blow on each one before you put it into your mouth, lad.'

His coughing and spluttering drew the attention of the servicemen who were taking a break. One shouted, 'You want to volunteer, man. It'd make a man of you, instead of a spluttering wimp — there's a war on, you know. It ain't for the likes of us to sit on benches with our girlfriends and eat fish and chips!'

Philip coloured. But Edith bristled. She stood and shouted, 'Don't make snap judgements about others 'cause you ain't right! My husband leaves a week on Monday to carry out training in a field you know nothing about. And for your information, he volunteered the moment war broke out. Britain will need more than brawn to get through this, you ignorant pig!'

Unable to stop it happening, Edith's face flooded with tears. There was a silence, and then someone started to clap, and others joined in. Edith looked around her to see a crowd had gathered.

An elderly gentleman piped up, 'We didn't get through the last lot by carping amongst ourselves, young man, but by solidarity and applauding all the different tactics men had to undergo. You have no right upsetting this young lady who is spending the last days that she may have for a long time by the side of her man.'

One of the men on the beach who was seemingly in charge, though not discernible as such as all were in vests and pants, stepped forward and spoke to the soldier who'd shouted the insult. Edith watched as he stood to attention, saluted and marched towards her and Philip with his commander following.

When he reached them, he stood to attention. 'I apologise, sir, and to you, madam.'

Philip's answer shocked Edith. 'Thank you, Private.

306

I am an officer in the British Army. I admire how much effort you all put into your training and understand your sentiments. However, my wife is correct in saying you shouldn't make snap judgements. I hope that you have learnt that valuable lesson today, Private.'

The young man's face flushed with embarrassment. He saluted as he said, 'Sir'. But to Edith his voice had an air of defiance to it.

His superior commanded that he went back to the others, then put his hand on the sea wall and vaulted over it. He saluted Philip. Philip returned the gesture as if he had been doing so all his life.

'Sergeant Proctor, sir, begging your leave.'

'Carry on, Sergeant, and thank you, that apology was much appreciated and will stand the young man in good stead, as will his defiance. We need young men with that attitude. So, while he must learn manners in front of his superiors, be careful not to break him. Do it with his knowledge that it is part of the discipline he must have to make him a great soldier. One that we would all want taking care of our backs and our country.'

The sergeant saluted again. 'Yes, sir. Thank you, sir. I have noted that with Parkinson, sir.'

When the soldiers had gone back to their training, the crowd that had gathered started to drift away, amidst comments of 'Well done, sir' and 'Good to know we have such men on our side.' Philip sat back down. 'Shall we eat, darling? The chips are cooler now.'

'Eat? You said you were an officer!'

'I am. I have been given the rank as an automatic right; it goes with the job I will be doing. The rest I learnt as a natural process of teaching and of my time as an officer in my school army, but Edith, my darling,

307

you were a marvel. You were like a goddess standing up and telling that young man the rights of the world. I'm proud of you.'

Edith sighed. What was the use of berating him for not telling her he was an officer? The fact was, that was what he was, and that's all there was to it. Though she wished it wasn't, as every revelation brought to her the reality of what was going to happen.

★ ★ ★

When they reached home, Marg came out of her house and beckoned them.

'Marg, what is it? Are you all right, do you need help?'

'Aye, Gran's fallen and I can't lift her, and Jackie's up at the hospital with Harry.'

'Oh, Marg, no! But what's happened to Harry? Come here, love, you're shaking and you're as white as a sheet.'

'I couldn't get round to yours to tell you this morning. Gran had a bad night and she was in a state. By the time I sorted her, you'd gone.'

Philip took charge. 'Darling, you see to Marg. I'll get Gran up off the cold floor first.'

As Philip left them, Edith soothed Marg. 'Tell me all about it once we have everything sorted, love. Let's get inside.' Marg leant heavily on her arm. 'Eeh, lass, you're exhausted.'

When they went through the door, Philip already had Gran in his arms and she was saying, 'Harry's bad and it's upset me. Jackie's gone to him and she ain't back. Ta, John, for helping me. I do love you.'

Philip shocked Edith for the second time today as

308

he said in a good imitation of the Lancashire accent, 'And I love you, lass.'

Did she really know this husband of hers? Her heart melted. What a lovely thing to say to Gran. But then, he was lovely. He was special.

'Will you take me to bed, John, love? I could do with a cuddle.'

Edith daren't look at Marg, who she knew, despite how upset she was, would be like herself, bursting to laugh, as now Philip was in deep water. She couldn't wait to hear how he would get out of it — but, full of surprises, he rose to the challenge.

'Not now, love. I've to go to work. You have a nice rest and then you'll feel better. I'll call in on Harry and see how he is.'

'Aye, that's a good idea, give him me love.'

'I will. Now, let's get you into your chair and then I'll get off.'

'I need to pee.'

At this, Edith couldn't help herself. She turned her head and held her mirth, but Marg worried her even more then as she didn't attempt to laugh, making Edith realise that something really was seriously wrong. Before she could ask, Marg said, 'Just take her into the front room, ta, Philip. I have a commode for her in there. I'll see to her.'

When Philip came back into the living room, Edith flung her arms around him. 'I love you, Officer Philip Bradshaw. You're the loveliest man I know.'

He kissed her nose. 'You didn't mind me going off with another woman then? Hmm, that's useful to know.'

He laughed as Edith playfully smacked his shoulder, but then became serious. 'What do you think is wrong with Harry, darling? I'm really worried about him.'

'I know. Marg looked so distraught, and I don't think it was all because Gran had fallen.' 'Look, I think once Marg has Gran sorted, we should all go around to Alice's.'

* * *

Edith was worried sick by the time they reached Alice's house. Marg had told her what she knew, but hadn't been clear as she couldn't remember the name of what ailed Harry. Philip had said it could be peritonitis if it was to do with Harry's appendix, but the uncertainty was very frightening.

Billy's reaction on opening the door to them compounded her worry. Usually strong when faced with problems, he flung himself at her and burst into tears.

Joey, who was just behind him, flung himself at Marg.

Taking the approach she thought best, Edith became practical, and took charge of the situation. 'Let's get inside, shall we, Billy, lad? We could all do with a pot of tea. You put the kettle on and then you can tell us all about it, eh?'

This did the trick. Billy straightened, sniffed loudly, and took hold of Joey. 'Give me a hand, Joey. You can get the cups out.'

Marg seemed reluctant to let Joey go; it was as if it were giving her strength to be caring for him. But Philip sorted this by saying, 'You take Gran's arm from me, Marg, and I'll go and help the lads. See if I can calm their fears a little. Come on, Joey.'

Once inside and with Gran sat in a chair, Marg

turned to Edith, a look of despair on her face. 'Eeh, Edith, whatever will befall us next?'

This was the question Edith had asked herself so many times. At the moment it seemed the world was against them, but she fell back on their stock answer that always cheered them. 'Whatever it is, it won't beat us, Marg. We may be all grown-up now, but me, you and Alice are still those strong girls who took a lot of knocks and came up smiling.'

Though Marg gave a half-smile and squeezed her hand, Edith knew her words hadn't helped her. But she understood this, because they hadn't given herself the hope they usually did either.

25

Alice

Alice filled with relief when the door to the ward opened and Gerald came through asking, 'How's he doing, darling?'

'Eeh, I'm glad to see you. We're both so worried, love.'

Gerald kissed her cheek and smiled over at Jackie. 'I'll check Harry over. Try not to get too distressed, both of you, they would have called me if there was any change for the worse, but the reports have been good.' He picked up the clipboard that was hooked over the end of Harry's bed and scrutinised it. His expression gave nothing away when he replaced it.

'Now that I'm here, darling, I think you should think about going home for a while. The lads need you — they're very upset. Jackie will still be with Harry . . . Is that all right with you, Jackie? Are you coping, my dear?'

'Aye, I'm all right, ta, Gerald. I just want me Harry to get better. You will make him better, won't you?'

'We will, and Brian, my colleague, who I know you have met, has been doing all he can. He tells me that there have been signs of improvement and Harry's chart shows that.'

Gerald took hold Harry's wrist. 'You're a strong young man, Harry, and I know you're feeling rough, old chap, but it's to be expected.'

Harry nodded at Gerald. He seemed too weak to

312

talk, but at least he was communicating with gestures and through his expressive eyes.

After examining Harry, Gerald smiled. 'Didn't I tell you that you're a tough young man? You're beating this. Your temperature's down, which means the infection could be abating. I'll give you something to help stop the vomiting, and some aspirin to relieve the pain. I know you feel terrible, but the signs are very good. Your heart is strong, so keep fighting, Harry.' Turning to Jackie, he said, 'We're winning, my dear. Keep your spirits up for Harry's sake.'

'Aye, I will, Gerald, ta.'

Alice followed Gerald out of the ward. 'How is he really, Gerald? Is he going to live?'

'Darling, that's the hardest question for a doctor to answer. We're doing all we can to help him beat this. That's all I can say at the moment, but I truly believe he will win through. He's improving, not deteriorating, and that is a massively good sign.' Gerald sighed. 'What you and Jackie are doing in giving your strength to him is helping, but neither of you can sit with him every hour of the day and night, so why don't you go home now and rest, then you can take over from Jackie, or be here with her and let her sleep for a while in the chair?'

'All right. I feel better now you are here, love. I'll come back when the boys are in bed. I might drive to Marg and Edith's and take them there for a while.'

'That's a good idea. I expect Marg will have told Philip and Edith and they'll all be frantic for an update.'

After saying goodbye to Jackie and Harry, and promising to come back later, Alice's heart thumped her fear around her body as she walked the long corridor.

Cranking her car — a task that was always heavy going for her — helped her to compose herself. She was glad that it did as she desperately needed to be strong for Billy and Joey — well, for everyone. Taking a deep breath, she felt pleased that she was able to pull herself together when she needed to as this was something she knew she would be called on to do more than ever in the months and years ahead.

* * *

The sight of Philip's car sitting in the drive lifted her as she pulled in alongside it — a bit too close, but reversing wasn't a skill she had mastered yet.

The front door opened before she had a chance to alight and Marg and Edith came out. Marg called over, 'By, you cut that fine, Alice, lass.'

Alice made herself laugh. 'Still working on me parking, but I didn't hit Philip's car, that's the main thing.'

'He'll need a can opener to get out, though.' Edith smiled as she said this, then surprised Alice by telling her, 'Mind, that's nothing to my effort, though you've foiled me now as I was looking to get you to help me, Alice, but on that showing . . .'

'You've had a drive, Edith? But that's grand.'

Marg sighed. 'It might be grand, but I feel left out. You two are leaving me behind.'

'Ha, you'll have to get Clive to teach you, Marg. It'll help us all to be independent, when we'll have to be.'

'Eeh, don't talk of that, Alice. How's Harry doing?'

They were inside the hall, but before Alice could answer Joey came bowling at her, almost knocking

314

her over. 'Steady on, lad. It's all right. Harry's getting better.'

'Let's get Alice inside to sit down, eh, lad?'

Joey nodded at Edith and took Alice's hand. Once in the lounge, she looked down at Joey. 'Ooh, is there any tea left in that pot? I'm dying for a cup.'

Billy, who hadn't come out to greet her, but sat looking pensive, jumped up, seeming to be glad to have something to do. 'I'll pour it, Joey . . . So Harry's all right, then, Alice?'

Before she could answer, Gran said, 'Aye, how's me Harry?'

'Hello, Gran.' Alice crossed the room to where Gran was sat, looking so tiny in the winged armchair. Her face was etched with worry. 'He's getting better, Gran. His temperature's dropping.'

'Nice lad. Did you knaw me John came?'

'Aye, he would. He'd want to look after Harry.'

'Is that where he is?'

'He's sitting with him at this very moment. Harry'll pull through, now.'

'I'm tired, lass.'

'Aw, love, would you like to lie down for a while? I've a spare room.'

'I don't knaw if me legs'll carry me. Do you know me, lass?'

'I do. And your Marg. She's a lovely lass. I'll tell you what, there's a couch just in the conservatory there. Philip can carry you to it and you can lie down and still see us, and can have a nod if you want to, how does that sound?'

'Aye, that'll do me. I've been here before, you knaw.'

'You have, and you're welcome anytime.'

'We had a lass like you across the road. I don't knaw

where she went, but eeh, her da were a bad 'un. Used to knock the living daylights out of her and the lads. I were glad to see the back of him.'

Alice's heart constricted.

'Gran!' Marg shot across the room to her gran.

'It's all right, Marg.' Alice held Gran's hand. 'I knew that lass an' all, Gran, but she's all right now, and her da was sorry before he died, he couldn't help what he did. He had something wrong inside his head.'

'The bravest man I knew, lass. He saved that bloke who's sweet on our Marg, you know. And he could have been killed himself, but he didn't take no heed of that. I tell you, they don't make men like that today.'

This made Alice feel better, and the mood lightened as Gran took to flirting with Philip when he scooped her up.

No sooner had Gran laid her head on the soft cushion than she closed her eyes.

'Eeh, peace'll reign now, Alice, lass. I'm sorry about what she said.'

'No, Marg, never be sorry, Gran says whatever pops in her head, she has no forethought about it, and she don't mean anything.'

Billy helped as he said, 'Gran's all right, Marg. It doesn't worry us what she says. The thing is, how's Harry? Me and Joey have been out of our minds.'

Alice crossed over to her brothers and opened her arms to them both. Billy awkwardly gave her a quick hug, but Joey snuggled into her. 'Eeh, me lads, we go through the mill, don't we? Look, though our Harry's very poorly, he's improving, but he's a long way to go. Gerald thinks he'll be all right, though. So, hold on to that, and ask God to help him.'

'God don't seem to be on our side much, he never

does owt I ask him to, Alice.'

Philip answered this. 'It depends what you ask for, Joey. You see, if you ask for a shiny new bike and another lad asks for his mother to get better, then God will put all his attention to that boy and think to himself, 'You, Joey, can put your mind to earning your bike, I'm busy . . .' Now, He may not make the other boy's mother better, as it may be in His plan to take her to heaven so that she can have eternal peace and happiness, but He'll stay by that boy and help him, or send someone to him to help him.'

'Like when Gerald came to us?'

'Exactly like that. Your da needed to be out of pain, and to be with your ma, who could take care of him and dance with him and make him happy again, but that would leave you with no one, so he sent Gerald to care for you.'

'So, if I pray for Harry, He'll take him and send me someone else . . . I don't want that, I want Harry.'

Joey's bottom lip quivered. Poor Philip looked out of his depth for a moment, but recovered, 'No, your prayers will help Harry to get well, because Harry isn't dying, and will be a priority to God. He will listen and help Harry. We were talking about the difference between you asking for a bike and another boy asking for a dying mother to be saved. In that instance, God had a different choice to make.'

Joey drew away from him seemingly determined to get to the bottom of the question. 'So, if I ask for sommat silly, I should say,' but it ain't important, God, if you've a lot on your plate', then He can get on with sorting the bad things?'

'That's right. So pray for Harry, and God will sort it out, as it is something that really needs His help.'

'I reckon I've got it. But He does complicate things, as He could give me me bike and make someone better an' all. He's just being picky.'

Philip burst out laughing. 'Well, you could say that, so don't stop asking as you never know.'

Joey laughed now and Alice thought how marvellous Philip was with children, and what a pity it was that he had to go away, rather than be doing what he was born to do — give knowledge and understanding to young 'uns and raise his own family with Edith.

She caught Edith's eye and saw the pain in her. She'd been very quiet, as if she had something big on her mind. She needed to talk to her to find out what it was.

'Well, I'll get these cups back into the kitchen, so why don't you lads go and have a kickabout for a while, get some fresh air? It'll do you good.'

'I'll help you, Alice.' Edith rose.

'Aye, and me. Gran's fast asleep now, it'll take wild horses to wake her.'

When the three of them were in the kitchen, Marg said, 'Your Philip's got a special way with him, Edith. He even made me understand how God works, 'cause, by, I've berated Him many a time for not taking notice of me prayers.'

'He has. He's got so many talents . . . only, well, one of them is taking him away from me in ten days' time.'

'No! As soon as that? Eeh, lass, I don't know what to say.' Alice put the tray on the draining board and turned to Edith. 'Aw, come here, lass.'

As always, the hug became a three-way one as Marg jumped forward and joined Alice. 'Aw, I'm sorry an' all, Edith, love. Does this mean he'll be gone for a long time?'

'No, he's hoping to be back for your wedding, Marg.'

'And at least he won't miss your birthday.' Alice knew this was no compensation, but she just didn't know what to say.

'Aye, and Philip said we should have a big party as usual, so we'll have something to look forward to and to remember, but I . . . well, what do you think? Only, I'd like to spend me actual birthday with him, and we do have the wedding coming up, so?'

'Well, I think you should, and it's grand that he could be back for me wedding. I reckon that's enough of a celebration to look forward to, how things are.'

'I agree, but is there more to this, Edith, love? You seem as if you're not telling us it all.'

'Well . . . it's just that I think he knows more than he's told me — or rather, can tell me, as we had an incident down by the seafront.' Edith told them what had happened. 'I found out that he already holds the rank of officer. But what he will be involved in is all hush-hush.'

'Well, that's a silver lining, ain't it? I don't mean the bit about it being hush-hush, but that he can come home and that he's an officer. Officers are safer than the men as they do more of the working out than the doing.'

This from Marg seemed to cheer Edith as she said, 'I have other news an' all.'

When Edith told them about Mandy, Alf and Ben, Alice clapped her hands. 'By, I've thought about them kids day and night. I was on the verge of offering for them to come here, but I so want to do me Red Cross work.'

'Well, these kids must be something special to have

319

you both so concerned for them, so I'm glad for them and you, Edith.'

'They are, Marg. Not that it's just them, all of the evacuees are, and if I could help them all, I would. I'd love to go all around the placements and make sure they're being looked after and are happy.'

Marg broke away from them and sat at the kitchen table. 'I can't see how they can be happy. Imagine when we were kids. We adored our ma's and if anything had happened to take us away from them, or from each other, come to that, we'd have been broken-hearted . . . I am now at losing me ma, and I'm a grown woman. It's tragic for these young 'uns.'

They were all quiet for a moment, and Alice guessed that, like her, they were thinking about their mothers. She remembered Mandy telling her that hers worked the street, but like Marg with her manipulative ma, and Edith with her drunken one, that didn't matter; what mattered was that it was your ma, and no one could take her place.

'Anyroad, Edith, even if you can't help them all, you're doing your bit — more than that, even, and I'll help you all I can.'

'Ta, Marg.'

'I will an' all, Edith, you know that. Well, as much as I can, but something just came to me mind.' She told them about the old lady who'd been sat in the hospital corridor. 'Her name's Heather and I have a mind to go to see her to ask if she'll become a kind of surrogate granny to Joey. Maybe she would be that to Mandy, Alf and Ben, and give you some respite.'

'Eeh, poor woman. I hope she takes you up on it, but I already have one — Sue, Philip's ma. She really wants to be involved, so you can keep Heather for your lads, as I'm sure it'd really do Joey good to have someone of his own.'

'It would. He's always lovely with me gran, as is Billy, and of course, you know Harry's the apple of her eye, but for someone as young as Joey, he seems able to relate to her.'

'So, it looks like we'll all be sorted if Heather agrees . . . well . . . sort of.'

They were quiet then. Each mulling their own thoughts.

Marg broke the silence by changing the subject. 'Anyroad, it's about time we talked weddings. It ain't that far off now and I've such a lot to do.'

'Aw, we're here for you, Marg. How about we go shopping next weekend, eh? We can get your dress and the bridesmaids' frocks.'

'Me dress is sorted. I walked back from work through Layton the other day and nipped into that dressmaker there. She had some drawings and I chose one and paid for it. I want it to be a surprise for you all. But I do want to talk to you about the bridesmaids. I reckon it's a waste to get new frocks. I've still got the one I had for your wedding, Alice, and for yours, Edith, though I did get some use out of that one as I wore it to the Tower last weekend. Anyroad, I wondered if you minded if you and Jackie wore a combination of them? Edith, you could wear the one you wore for Alice's, as none of those we had for yours will be long enough for you. You could wear the purple cummerbund, and then you and Jackie could wear the rose-coloured frocks we had for Edith's, Alice.'

'I'm all for it, I reckon it's a grand idea. Mine were a bit impractical really, whereas Edith's can be worn again.'

'I've had an idea about that.' Edith told them how Father Malley was talking of starting Holy Communion lessons and had asked her to help. 'Some of the mothers struggle to get communion dresses, so I thought, if you don't mind, Alice, the three would make at least six frocks. The Women's Institute ladies'll make them all up and Mandy can have one as she'll be one of the candidates.'

'That's a grand use for them. You can have mine . . . that is, if you don't mind, Alice?'

'No, I like the idea of them being used for that. It's better than them hanging in your cupboards.'

'Ta, Alice, it'll look grand to see all the kids lined up in frocks made of the same material. Eeh, and all posh an' all. It'll make it feel like there's no blooming war on.'

Alice giggled with them both at the thought of the sight of the children, but knew she would know every painful minute that they were at war and that Marg and Edith would too, as they all faced life without their men by their side and with the constant agony of not knowing if they were alive or not.

'So, as soon as Harry's all right, we'll concentrate on me wedding then?'

'We will, Marg, I promise you. It'll be weddings night and day from that moment, won't it, Edith?'

'Aye, we'll give you and Clive the best day ever.'

'I just had a thought. If you've got them kids, how about Mandy is a bridesmaid an' all? I could make her a frock out of the bridesmaid's dress that I wore for your wedding, Edith. Gran would help, she's a good seamstress.'

'Aw, that'd be lovely. And Alf and Ben could play a part, if you'd like them to, Marg?'

'Oh, aye, they could. That'll make them feel wanted by us all. They could hand out the hymnal books.'

Edith laughed. 'Or take the collection. I mean, there's bound to be a collection — Father Malley always has his collections, no matter what the occasion, funerals an' all. He has to get his beer money.'

Alice and Marg joined in the laughter as it was well known that Father Malley liked his tipple.

Alice thought that it was this sense of silly fun that she, Marg and Edith had always enjoyed that had often kept them going when things got tough for them. And as she hugged them both before they left, she knew that their easy humour would always carry on doing so.

26

Marg

Marg couldn't believe the weather as she was putting her pipe clips in the following Saturday afternoon. It had been a beautiful morning, but the wind had whipped up a storm in the last hour. Even for Blackpool, where the changing of the tide often brought squalls, this was unusual.

She looked wistfully at her outfit laid out on the bed. It was one of the three that Alice had given her out of the many outfits left by her ma-in-law for Alice to do what she wanted with. Most had gone to jumble sales.

This one was a pale blue costume in a fine woven fabric. Its skirt was straight, but not what you would call a tight fit, and hung just below the knee — a length Marg loved after years of wearing calf or longer length skirts and frocks. The jacket didn't need a blouse as the bodice crossed over and had two rows of buttons, and the large collar was trimmed with a darker blue velvet.

It was as she popped downstairs with her curlers all in place and still in her house frock to check on Gran, that she heard the bang of the sea flare that put rescuers on guard.

On such a day, when pleasure boaters would take to the calm waters, there was always one that got caught out by the sudden weather change.

A second blast followed, and she knew then that

Clive wouldn't make their shopping date, or afternoon tea that was supposed to follow, as he'd be on his way to the lifeboat station to join his crew.

She'd so needed to see him and prayed that it wouldn't be a long and arduous rescue, and that they would all be safe.

Gran was asleep in the same position she'd left her, snug in her fireside chair, but woke with a start as a clap of thunder seemed to shake the whole house.

'Eeh, Marg, what was that?'

'It's all right, Gran.' Marg explained what was happening with the lifeboat crew.

With this, Gran relaxed. 'Eeh, it's dark early, lass. What time is it?'

'Almost four, and that's the weather making it dark. I'll light the lamp above you, but there's no need to black out yet, one little light won't be seen.'

'I could do with a hot drink, lass.'

'Give me a mo to nip and tell Edith that I won't be going out, eh? She was going to take you round to hers while I was gone.'

'Don't leave me, Marg.'

'All right, love. I'll make that drink for you.'

As they sat together drinking cocoa, Edith popped in. 'What time are you going, Marg? I've been waiting.'

'Sorry, love.' Marg explained why she hadn't been in before. 'Have you any news from the hospital today? I'm worried about Harry and Jackie. I know she's taking breaks and getting a wash and change at Alice's to be nearby, but eeh, I miss her.'

'Aye, Alice has phoned. Harry's making good progress, but they can't persuade Jackie to leave his side for more than half an hour at the most.'

'Aw, our Jackie's a loyal soul, but this won't do her any good.'

'She's young, Marg, she'll cope, love. I'll tell you what, as you don't need me I'll go to the hospital with Philip, and then I'll be able to let you know how things really are. And I'll have a little chat with Jackie if I can.'

'Ta, Edith.'

When Edith crossed the room to say goodbye to Gran, Gran looked up at her with a blank stare. Edith just smiled at her and patted her hand. But when Edith got to the door, Gran said, 'Don't get wet, you'll catch your death, lass.'

Edith giggled. 'That took me back. Gran always looked out for us, didn't she?'

'She did. She's always been a lovely gran. The saviour of me at times.'

They hugged before Edith pulled her cardi over her head and dashed back to her house.

'Put wireless on, lass. Best thing in a thunderstorm — a sing-song.'

'That's a good idea, Gran, it'll block it out a bit.'

When Marg turned the dials, Forbes Robinson, the tenor, was giving a recital, and Gran sang along in her sweet, if crackling, voice. When it came to an end, she looked across at Marg. 'Eeh, Marg, I do love you.'

This filled Marg with joy. 'And I love you, Gran.'

'Do you want to dance? I can still do the waltz, you knaw. Kick the rug out of the way.'

This amazed her. Yesterday, Gran was off her legs; now she wanted to dance!

With the rug rolled up, Gran held firmly in her arms, and the wind and rain clanging and banging, Marg felt the wonderment of having her gran know who she was and having a dance with her. It made up for not being able to have her engagement tea.

Eeh, I wouldn't have missed this for the world.

'So, you and that big fella are going to wed, eh?'

'We are, Gran. I'll sort your outfit so that it's all ready for you. It's upstairs in the spare room.'

'Ta, lass . . . Now, you do knaw how to go on, don't you?'

Marg coloured.

'Now, don't be like that . . . Eeh, let me sit down a mo. That's right. Look, lass, your ma's no good. She won't tell you owt, she's too busy getting it for herself.'

Marg felt the pain of this, never had she heard her gran talk like this of her ma. Yes, she used to tell her to her face in her odd cross moments, but then what she said next made Marg realise that she was off with the fairies again.

'She's out at the moment, probably with that Eric. He's a rum 'un, Marg. Don't have owt to do with him. Anyroad, I'll put you right. Mind, it'll make your hair curl, lass. You'll have no need for them pipe clips.'

Marg's hand instinctively went to her head — she'd forgotten all about them. She sat next to Gran and started to take them out, hoping that Gran had forgotten she was about to give her a talk on the birds and bees — or at least, that's what Marg thought she meant. Gran's next words confirmed this.

'Eeh, me John's a lad.' She looked at the clock. 'And he's late back an' all. One of these days I'll tell him, if he don't come home on time, he'll get no hanky-panky for a week. That'll sort him, as he likes his hanky-panky does John.' She leant over and switched the wireless off. 'Now, when you first get wed, you wonder what's happening to you. But, lass, take it as

327

it comes and leave it to your man. He'll do things to you that'll make you think you're in heaven . . . Eeh, where's me cocoa?'

'I'll make you another, Gran.'

As she escaped to the kitchen, Marg let out a big sigh.

Life's nothing if it ain't eventful, but I just wish me gran wouldn't add to that! Eeh, I'll have to think of something to distract her.

But as it turned out, she didn't have to, because when she returned to Gran she said, 'Put wireless back on and knock the top off that stout I've got left, eh? I feel like rejoicing. I don't knaw why, but I do.'

Marg felt lifted by this. She couldn't guess what had made Gran feel happy, but she was, and that was all that mattered. Putting the cocoa down to drink herself, she fetched the stout.

This time the wireless belted out Vera Lynn singing 'The General's Fast Asleep', and had Marg tapping her toes.

Suddenly, in a really strong voice, Gran joined in with the lyrics, and Marg knew a moment of awe.

Eeh, I'm having a strange night, what with dancing with Gran and having a sing-song with her and the storm not letting up and lashing the windows. It wouldn't surprise me if the blooming German Army marched in on me next!

She smiled at this thought, but then became wistful.

If only Clive would walk through the door, I'd be happy. I've had no time to think about him and what he might be doing, but now, I just want to know that he's safe.

★ ★ ★

It was two hours later, with Gran snoring away, before there was a barely discernible tap on the door and a voice shouted, 'It's me, Marg. Clive.'

As soon as she let him in, she was in his arms. He smelt of the sea and fresh air, and his face looked wind-burnt. But his eyes held love, and that was all she wanted — the good, kind, gentle love that Clive gave to her. It made all her problems fade and made her feel safe.

'Eeh, I could do with a cuddle like that, lad.'

Gran had woken — she never missed a chance with a handsome young man.

'Well, you shall have one then, Gran.'

Marg's heart filled with warmth as Clive marched over to Gran, took her hands and lifted her, then took her in his arms.

'Where's me little lads?'

'I have them in the car. I wanted the door open so I could get them in quickly out of this weather.'

'Eeh, you should have brought them, lad. But have a dance with me first.'

'I'd love to, but I can't leave them. I want to book my dance with you for the wedding breakfast, though, Gran, if I may. I'm going to take my gramophone to the church hall.'

'Are you asking me to marry you, lad? Eeh, you'd better watch out for me John, he'll skin your hide. Make yourself scarce now, and be quick about it, and don't tell him about our dance.'

Marg could see Clive bursting to laugh, but he managed to contain it as he scooted out the door.

Gran had a coy smile on her lips.

Carl and George were full of excitement and hugged Marg. 'Eeh, lads, you look nice, you've got your Sunday best on.' Both wore long corduroy trousers and smart fawn coats with tweed caps. 'Let's get your coats and caps off, shall we? We'll hang them over the chair to dry.'

'I've brought our tea, Marg. I took these biscuit tins to the café and asked her to fill one with sandwiches and one with cakes.'

'Aw, Clive, that's lovely. I'll get me best cloth out and put it on the table. Then I'll nip up and get changed. We'll make it how it should be.'

As she found the rarely used pristine white cloth, Clive asked after Harry, but their attention was taken by the lads showing Gran the toys they'd brought with them.

'I've got a box of bricks, Gran; they click into one another and I can build all sorts. I'll build Blackpool Tower for you.'

'Ha, well, I've got my truck, so I'll run it right into your tower, Carl, and it'll fall over then.'

'No, you won't, you're a nuisance, George. Go and play over there with your baby's truck.'

'Aw, lad, he's only having fun, you should laugh at him. He won't really knock your tower down; he's just trying to get some attention as you're such a clever brother.'

Carl beamed. 'All right then, George. You deliver the bricks to me in your truck, eh?'

When George smiled at Gran, she seemed to get strength she hadn't had for a long time as she bent over and tried to lift him onto her knee.

'Eeh, Gran, don't be hurting yourself.'

'I want to cuddle me lads, Marg.'

George looked embarrassed, but Carl, always the diplomat, said, 'We'll cuddle you, Gran. We're too big

330

to sit on your knee, so we'll do what we do with our other grandma. Look, like this . . . Come on, George.' They both knelt down and put their heads on Gran's lap.

As Gran stroked their fair hair, she looked so content.

'Aw, Clive, I'd like to remember that picture forever.'

'You can. Hold on, I brought something else with me. My camera . . . and a couple of other things. I'll bring them in.'

Marg was amazed as Clive brought in a camera and tripod and had a paper carrier bag over his arm.

'Put this somewhere for me, Marg, and no peeping.'

Marg took the carrier bag and though tempted to take a quick peek, she resisted and tucked it behind the sofa.

Clive had his camera out of his case in no time and began clicking away. 'There should be some good ones amongst them, love. Now, let's get the blackouts down and have our tea, shall we?'

'I'll leave you to do the blackouts — you should know how as you fitted them! I'll do me own room and get changed. I don't want no photo took in me housework frock.'

'Oh, before you do, I want to give you one of the presents I have for you.'

Marg felt like a kid at Christmas — a present? For her? She'd never had many presents off anyone but Alice and Edith. Well, other than the beautiful locket Clive bought her — she must ask about that, see if the photo had been framed.

'Here you are, darling. You might like to try it out.'

331

Clive had fished in the carrier before he turned to her. The lilac box didn't give a lot away, until she saw the gold writing, which said, 'Goldberg's Perfumery.' She looked up at Clive. She'd never ever owned any real perfume.

'Open it.'

From the box, she pulled out the most beautiful pearl-coloured, globe-shaped bottle, draped with gold filigree, with ruby-red stones embedded in it. The top was also gold-coloured in a butterfly shape with more red stones encrusting it. 'It's grand, Clive, I — I don't know what to say.'

'I had the perfume I bought for you — Je Reviens — decanted into it. There's a dabber or some such attached to the lid.'

'Aw, Clive. Eeh, I know what you mean, I've seen the film stars do it at the flicks. Ooh, ta, I'll feel like a film star meself now. It's the nicest thing that anyone's ever bought for me.' She went over to him.

He looked down and told her, 'The lady who served me told me the words meant, 'I'll be back.' I chose it for them as I haven't a clue about the different smells, except that I loved this one. But the words are what I want you to always to remember.'

His eyes held hers.

'I will.' She offered her lips to him.

The kiss was a gentle quick kiss, that brought an 'Ooh, Dada, she kissed you!' from George. Carl just tutted one of his now famous tuts.

'Aye, well, I'm going to be kissing him a lot, lads, so you'll have to get used to it.'

'Can I have a kiss?'

Carl nudged George for saying this, but undeterred, George came into Marg's open arms. She squeezed him tightly, then kissed his cheek before lifting him and swinging him around. This broke Carl's embarrassment and he came and joined the hug.

Clive rescued her. But part of her didn't want to be rescued. To have the love of these two lads was something very precious to her. 'Right, I won't be a mo, you two look out for Gran for me.'

With this she scooted upstairs.

When she came back down, Clive gasped. Never before had she felt beautiful, like she did since she and Clive had declared their love for one another. Always she'd looked on herself as the dowdy or plain one next to Alice's pretty, dainty looks and Edith's elegant stunning beauty.

'By, Vera, lass, you look lovely,' Gran beamed.

George gave Gran a funny look. 'Have you taken the fairies for a walk again, Gran?'

Marg couldn't help laughing. She gave Clive a knowing look.

He looked the picture of innocence as he held his hands up. 'What? Well . . . the phrase might have slipped out once, but I didn't mean anything.'

Marg grinned, but Gran looked bemused. 'Fairies, lad? Do you believe in fairies? I do. They live at the bottom of pretty gardens . . .'

As George listened intently to Gran, Marg thought it time to get the tea onto the table. They'd almost done this, with Marg getting her ma's best china out, when the front door opened.

Marg was shocked and overjoyed to see Jackie and Da come through it.

'Eeh, Jackie, lass!' She ran over and hugged her. 'What are you doing here, and together?' She didn't remark on Jackie's exhausted appearance, but then she didn't have time as Carl and George threw themselves at Jackie.

'Hello, me lads, my, you look smart.'

'Are you all right, Jackie?' Marg hardly dared to ask. 'Is . . . Harry . . . ?'

'Aye, he's all right, Marg. He woke fully this afternoon, and though he's still poorly the effects of the anaesthetic have worn off, so he's fully aware. The first thing he said was that he . . . he loves me.'

'Aww.'

'The second was, 'Go home'. I didn't want to, but he was worried about me and said he would rest easier if I did. Anyroad, I asked the nurse if I could ring Da and he came and picked me up.'

'Looks like we're just in time for a party, lass.'

'And you're not invited, Eric Porter!'

'Right, I'll take them stouts I bought back home then, shall I, Sandra?'

'Eeh, well, you can stay this time then.'

'Ta very much.' Eric grinned at them all.'The way to a woman's heart, eh?'

Clive laughed.'Well, I reckon there's enough food to go around, so it's lovely that you've both arrived.'

'By, I'm happy to have you all. Me and Clive and the lads were meant to go out to tea, but Clive got called out to a rescue.'

'Did you now, Clive? And did you rescue the stricken then?'

'Aye, we did, Eric. They weren't far out, but the police were waiting for them and carted them off. They had a boatload of stolen goods — black market stuff. They offered us some if we took them and their boat to Knot End. Cheek of them.'

Eric shot Marg a glance.'Eeh, lass, I'm sorry, but I

334

can't stay. I've to be somewhere.'

Da looked scared. She'd never seen him like this before, but she didn't have time to ask what was wrong as he made for the door with Gran shouting after him to make sure he brought her stout in before he went.

Da looked cornered; he glanced back at Gran. 'I'm in a hurry, you daft sod!'

'Hey, Da, there's — '

Da looked shamefaced. 'Sorry, Marg . . . Jackie, love, come and get it, will you? I have to go.'

Marg was mystified, but Clive had his eyebrows raised and looked at her with an expression that suggested he knew what was going on. When the door closed behind Jackie, he gestured to her to follow him.

'What was that look, Clive? Do you know something?'

'Eric became agitated when I said the police were involved. I would guess that he had something to do with the consignment that we rescued, and now I'm guessing he needs to make a few phone calls — or disappear for a while.'

'Eeh, no!'

Clive held her arms and looked down at her. 'Look, Marg, you know your da, you know what he gets up to, you know he has protection in place for himself. The last thing you should do is ever worry about him. He's a crook, Marg, and one day, he'll be caught. You just take care that you never get involved with any of his dealings.'

A wet, cold Jackie appeared at the kitchen door. 'Aw, Marg, Clive, I heard what you just said and I — I think I've already involved us . . . I mean, well, when I went with him to get the stout, he asked me to make arrangements to let him in the back gate later. He said he needed to get to the Anderson shelter so I told him I'd leave it unlocked.'

Marg felt as though her lovely evening had been spoilt, and by her rotten da. She hadn't thought of him like that for a while, but suddenly she realised that he wasn't loving towards them for no reason, but because he needed them in his pocket, just like everyone else, so that he could use them for his criminal activities any time he wanted to.

'He said I weren't to say anything. He said it was a surprise for Christmas, that's all.'

'That's what he's truly like, Jackie. I'm sorry, love. But Eric Porter is a lying, cheating, violent criminal. Marg realised it a long time ago and has witnessed it. She's tried her best to overcome it and treat him like her father, but it seems possible that he may be about to throw all that back into her face by using your house as a hideaway. My advice is not to open the gate.'

Jackie looked near to tears. Clive put his arm around her. 'I'm not telling you anything that in your heart you don't know, lass. But we'll deal with it together, eh? Don't forget, I'm to be your big brother. Look, you've been through a lot, so shall we forget it for now and have our tea?'

As they went through to the living room, Marg was relieved that Jackie seemed to be able to cope with what Clive had said, as she cheerfully commented, 'By, Marg, you smell smashing! What is it?'

Marg beamed. 'It's Je Reviens — me posh perfume. I'll show you after tea, it's grand.'

When they were all around the table, the atmosphere lightened and Carl, as if he were a grown man, helped Gran, passing her sandwiches and making sure she had everything she needed, and that his brother did too.

'Now, boys, when you've eaten your sandwich you can have a cake, but no one must take that doughnut. That's for Marg, as the shop only had one and it's her special day. So, you can all choose from the jam or lemon curd tarts. Then after tea I have some presents for Marg.'

George said, 'Because it's her engagement day, Dada?'

Clive nodded. 'That's right. Good boy for remembering.'

Marg gave a little giggle. She felt an excitement in her belly, like she used to on Christmas Eve when she believed in Santa, no matter that he didn't bring her much. He never brought any of the kids in the street much — a yoyo, an apple, and sometimes some toffees — but it was special as Gran always came and stayed over. The front room, which was their Sunday best then, looked magical as Ma and Gran dressed the tree, and she helped Gran to make paper chains to drape over the ceiling. And the fire in the grate roared, smelling deliciously of roasted chestnuts.

'Eeh, let's have a cracking Christmas this year, eh?'

'Ha, what brought that on?' Clive looked bemused.

'It were you saying you had presents for me. It made me feel like I did as a kid at Christmas.'

'Well, that's a great idea. We'll all pray that everyone is still here, and we'll make it special.'

'Aw, but they won't be, will they? They'll be — '

'Let's not talk of that today, Marg, darling. Eat your doughnut, I can't wait much longer.'

There was laughter then as the boys tackled their tarts, tongue first, licking out the jam and ending up with sticky red noses, lightening the sudden doom and gloom that she'd triggered and helping her to forget it as she savoured every bit of her doughnut. Sinking her teeth into the soft dough, feeling the sugar grains on her lips and tongue, and then the discovery of the jam in the centre.

Clive laughed. 'You're as bad as the boys. You've got jam drizzling down your chin!'

With tea over, Clive lifted the bag onto the table. 'Now, here's my first present, Marg.'

'Oh, Clive, I've got nothing for you. I — I . . .'

'No, you don't have to have. It's me who has to woo you on the day we affirm that we are getting married.'

The boys looked on as she opened the beautifully wrapped box. Inside was the locket he'd bought her before, and inside that a tiny photo of them each.

'It's lovely. And we've both been captured perfectly. Ooh, I love it, Clive, thank you.'

She handed it to Jackie.

'It's beautiful, Marg.'

Clive beamed. 'Open the next one.'

Though she guessed this would be the framed photo, nothing prepared her for the beauty of it. The shiny silver frame with a filigree pattern and the lovely picture of them sitting close with Clive's arm around her and looking down at her. Tears of happiness welled up.

'And last, but not least, I had a premonition that we wouldn't make the shopping trip together today, once the clouds gathered, so I made a phone call and then picked this up. Now, if you don't like it, or it doesn't fit, then it can go back, but I so wanted this day to be as planned, and for us to be officially engaged.'

Clive opened the tiny box and tilted it towards her.

338

The most beautiful ring shone out. Gold, with what looked like silver joining it at the top. The silver was in the shape of a bow and glittered with tiny diamonds; where the bows met, one glittering stone sat, not huge, but perfectly formed as if it was a tiny diamond cake.

Marg gasped. 'It . . . it's beautiful. I love it, Clive! Eeh, ta, me love.'

Taking the ring out of the box, Clive came over to her. He knelt in front of her and lifted her hand. For the first time ever, Marg experienced a moment of shame at her care-worn hands that showed signs of the hot water she plunged them into on a daily basis to wash Gran's sheets. Her nails were strong, though, and didn't look too bad. Clive didn't seem to notice as he slipped the perfectly fitting ring onto her left hand.

'Now you have to marry me, my darling, it's sealed with a ring.'

She looked into his eyes as he lifted his head after kissing her hand. 'I love you.'

A round of applause erupted, that she suspected Jackie started, as she then called out, 'Hip! Hip!' and Gran hollered, 'Hooray!'

The next time Jackie did this the boys caught on and they too shouted, 'Hooray!'

Gran clapped her hands. 'By, Marg, when do we get married, love?'

Marg smiled at Clive. Then turned to Gran. 'We get married four weeks today, Gran.'

'Eeh, I need a new hat. I can't wear me old one.'

'We'll get you a new one.'

'That'll be grand. Now, I need me bed, lass.'

'Aw, Gran, you've had quite a day.'

'So has this little one.' Jackie stroked George's hair

as his head flopped forward. 'Come on, let's lie you down on the sofa, shall we, lad?'

George didn't resist. Always one to live every moment to the full, the lad often just seemed to flop as if his energy had suddenly been switched off.

'I'll help with Gran, Marg. She's looks worn out all of a sudden. Then I'll have to take my leave and get the boys home to bed.'

Clive lifted Gran as easily as Philip had done, and sat her in the chair next to her bed. 'I can take your shoes off, Gran, but that's as far as I can help.'

Marg held her breath, waiting for some lewd comment, but it didn't come. Gran was really exhausted. Her eyes were closing. 'I'll see to her, Clive, I'll not be long.'

Slipping on one of Gran's wraparound pinnies, Marg soon had Gran in bed. 'Night, Gran. That were a lovely party, love, I'm glad it worked out that we had it at home.'

'Were there a party, lass?'

Marg sighed. 'Aye, there was. Night, Gran.'

A sleepy voice came back, 'Do you knaw me, lass? I can't remember seeing you before. I usually have a fair-haired nurse, little and very pretty. She's nice, I wish she was here.'

'That's Alice, Gran.'

But this fell on deaf ears. Marg sighed as she closed the door quietly and went back through to the living room. She'd never forget tonight — Gran dancing . . . well, just everything, even Gran having her sudden memory loss, because she wouldn't be Gran without that now.

27

Edith blew the whistle, bringing silence to the playground. 'File into your classrooms in an orderly manner, please, children.'

Today was an exciting day for her for two reasons. Both gave her great joy, but she knew the one that gave her the most was that her home had been approved for Mandy, Alf and Ben to move into that evening. The second reason was that today she was going to take her first lesson on her own.

Mrs Thornton had telephoned in sick. The other teachers had smiled knowingly, saying that Rosamond — Mrs Thornton's Christian name, which Edith hadn't yet been given permission to use — was pulling the wool over no one's eyes. They all knew that she would be taking as much time off as she could as her retirement day loomed.

But to counter the excitement, Edith did hold a small concern. Both Alf and Ben had been registered at this school after she had pointed out that they weren't receiving a Catholic education, and that meant all three children would be in her class. She knew she had to take care to treat them the same way as she did the rest of the class, without upsetting them, or letting them think they could have special favours.

No sooner had she thought this than Alf ran up to her, breaking the instruction she'd just given to the children. 'Will I 'ave to call you Mummy, miss?'

341

Mandy was just behind him. 'Well, I will, Alf.'

'We'll talk about this at home, little ones, but whilst here I need you to remember that I'm one of your teachers, and I've asked you to form an orderly queue, so can you do that? I reckon you can, and learn to treat me as a teacher and not a parent when I'm in school, eh?'

'Flipping 'eck, I won't know where I am, nor will me bruvver.'

Edith laughed. 'Come on, do as you know you should be doing and be good in class for me, as that will be helping me and you'd want to do that, wouldn't you?'

Alf kicked a small stone. 'It ain't gonna be like you said, Mandy.'

Mandy shrugged. 'Well, it ain't forever, is it?'

This put Edith in the doldrums after feeling so happy. She needed to make the children understand the difference in how she treated them at school wasn't because she didn't love them just as much. 'We'll pretend that I'm two different people, the one that takes care of you at home and the one who teaches you at school. But remember, whichever I am, I love you very much. I just need you to carry on at school as you would for any of the teachers. Can you understand that?'

'Yer, I can. Come on, Alf, let's get in line.' The cheeky wink Mandy gave her seemed to make her appear years above her age as it showed her instant understanding of the situation and Edith felt she now had an ally in her, and that was a big plus.

★ ★ ★

342

As she stood in front of the class, Edith was over-come with nerves. She'd been given a couple of hours in the staffroom to sort out her English lesson and wanted to do what Philip did and make the learning simple and fun. At seven years old, she knew it would be difficult for them to grasp things in a formal way. She'd seen their blank faces as they sat watching Mrs Thornton writing on the board, expecting them to understand how the letter 'H' was sometimes silent. Today, the lesson involved reading out loud, a daunt-ing task for them. She remembered only too well the laughter that reddened her face as she'd done this in her day and had stumbled over a word.

She hoped she'd got it right, as at this moment, as she looked around the class, the thirty or so young-sters seemed like monsters getting ready to eat her up.

The door opening gently and the headteacher sidling in didn't help. 'Carry on, I'm just here for a few moments to observe.'

Edith nodded, but wished he'd just disappear. She felt lacking in confidence now the lesson had begun, and the children weren't helping as they were chat-ting and throwing things to each other.

Taking a deep breath, she knew the first step she had to take was to get them to do as she asked. Clap-ping her hands, she surprised herself by roaring out, 'Silence!' and was even more surprised when they did.

'Now, children, by that behaviour you let your-selves and me down. Mr Raven has walked into the room and not one of you noticed or paid him the respect you should have. So please do that now. All stand. . . . Now, what do you say to Mr Raven?'

In unison and in a sing-song voice they chant-ed, 'Good afternoon, Mr Raven.'

The head stood and bowed. 'Thank you, children, and a good afternoon to you, too.' He bowed his head to Edith in a gesture which told her to carry on.

'Veronica and Jean, please come up and take these books to hand out. One between two pupils.'

This done and all still paying attention, Edith prayed that the lesson she'd prepared was to the head's liking.

'The book is nursery rhymes. I'll put you into groups of four. Two of the group will read out a verse each, then the other two will act out those verses with me.'

She could feel the head's eyes on her and felt it was all a stupid idea, but the lesson went so well, with giggles and shyness overcome, and all being able to recite the rhymes at the end of the lesson.

The head remained throughout and afterwards told her, 'I did enjoy that, well done. A very innovative method of teaching, and very effective too. I think you're ready to take a class on a regular basis.'

'Really? Ta ever so much. I enjoyed it an' all. I remember me own school days and how boring it was with the teacher talking at us for ages, and none of it going in.'

'Well, that certainly did, and it taught them confidence, reading skills, improved their memory, and gave them a little light relief. Good luck. And remember, my door is always open if you have any problems.'

'Ta, sir, I'll remember that.'

'Peter, not sir. We staff don't stand on ceremony and you are a full member of our staff now, Edith.'

With this he bowed and left, and Edith did a little skip with joy — she was a teacher! A real teacher and she loved it.

Later, Philip was the nervous one when the knock came on the door hailing the arrival of the children.

'How shall I be with them? I suddenly feel so out of my depth.'

'Just be yourself, lad. You'll see it'll all come naturally. By, you teach hundreds of boys, you'll be better at this than me.'

He winked at her. 'Best foot forward, eh?' And with this, his nerves seemed to have passed.

The official who brought the children — a stout woman with greying hair — gave a few instructions. 'This is where I can be reached if there are any problems, but also inform me when you have registered them with a doctor — their medical care will be paid for, the doctors know where to send their bills. None of them have any health problems that I am aware of, except Alf is a bedwetter.'

'He's not when he's at 'ome, are you, Alf?' Mandy's indignant voice as she defended her brother took the official by surprise.

Edith jumped in. 'Please don't worry, I'll take care of them.'

'Huh, you'll have your hands full by the sound of it. Well, good luck.'

When she'd left, Edith saw that each child had the same little bag they'd had with them when they'd first arrived. At a loss for a moment, she fell back on her usual way of dealing with awkward moments and got everyone busy by suggesting they went up to the rooms first and put their things away.

She was surprised at how little they had — a clean set of underwear, two sets of pyjamas, and one change of clothes.

Philip was too, as he whispered, 'I think another shopping trip is in order.'

She nodded as a voice piped up. 'So, this is me room and it's all to meself, miss?'

'It is, Mandy. Do you like it, lass?'

'I do, ta. Whose teddy is that?'

'It's yours, Philip bought it for you. And see who that is in your bed? I think you'll like her.'

Mandy pounced on the pot doll. She held it to her and looked up. 'She's lovely, ta. Can I keep her and take her 'ome?'

'Aye, you can, love. Now, let's get the boys settled, shall we?'

'Ooh, we've got a football, ta, miss.'

'And teddy bears, Alf. We can 'ave a real teddy bears' picnic now.'

All three giggled at Ben, and at last, the strained atmosphere dissolved.

'I've got an idea. Why don't we all go down to the prom? We can wrap up warm in our coats and have fish and chips on our bench, Edith.'

'That's a grand idea, Philip. I can cool the stew I made and we can have that tomorrow night. What do you all think, me lads and lassie?'

They all giggled, then the three of them jumped for joy, telling her they hadn't been down to the prom yet and they didn't know what fish and chips tasted like.

'I'd give anything for some pie, mash and liquor, though.'

'What? Meat pie, Mandy?'

'Yer, it's what we have down London. There's no taste like it.'

When Mandy explained what liquor was, it sounded more like parsley sauce, but Edith didn't say so. 'Well, you're in for a treat with our fish and chips, there's none like them either. And you can have a few goes on the stalls an' all.'

This was met with squeals of delight.

* * *

Alf turned out to be a great shot with the bean bags as he skittled over the pile of tin cans. He chose a lovely knitted black doll, with beads for eyes, a cross-stitched red nose and mouth and plaited wool for hair. He presented it to Mandy. She hugged him, prompting him to say, 'Gerroff.'

Philip laughed at this. 'My sister used to be exactly the same, always wanting to mother me. You'll have to get used to it, Alf, it's what the womenfolk do.' Then he whispered in Edith's ear, 'I kicked her shins once and she stopped it after that.'

'Eeh, Philip, you didn't!'

Philip pulled a pretend 'shamed' face that made Edith smile.

'I can win. I'd like a go on the goldfish stall, please.'

'Of course, Ben. Here you are.' Philip gave him the farthing he'd need. Ben's face was a picture of concentration; his tongue came out the side of his mouth and a frown furrowed his brow. Edith willed the balls to go into a bowl, but the first one bounced on several and ended up on the floor.'

'I'll do it for yer, Ben.'

'No, Alf, I want to do it on me own.'

Edith looked at Philip. She could see he was willing Ben on too.

Once again, Ben put on his concentrating expression, which made him look like an old man and made Edith want to giggle, but she kept quiet and her fingers crossed.

The second ping-pong ball went the same way. Now he only had one left. *Please, God, let this one go in!*

She held her breath once more, watched the ball bounce on one bowl, then another, then jumped up and down squealing, 'Yes. Yes!' as at last he'd hit target and the ball rolled around the base of the bowl.

Ben turned to look at her, his face a picture of happiness. 'Can I keep it? Please, let me.'

'Aye, you can keep it, lad. What will you call it? It needs a name?'

As the stall holder handed him a jam jar with the fish looking huge as it swam around it, Ben looked up and said, 'Micky. Me dad's named Micky. He's a soldier now.'

The lad's eyes brimmed with tears.

The stall holder bent over. 'In that case, lad, I'll give you a proper bowl for him. Every soldier has to be treated with respect. There you are, lad.'

'Ta, mister.'

As they walked off, Philip carrying the goldfish bowl, Edith put her arm around Ben. 'Don't bottle it all up. It's all right to feel sad, and even to cry if you feel like it. It is sad to be away from your mum and dad. What regiment is your dad in?'

'He's in the Essex Regiment, as he comes from Romford. He met me mam when he came to London once.'

'Well, we can write a letter to him, he'd like that. Philip will tell us where to post it.'

'Ta, miss.'

348

Edith made her mind up to sort out what the children should call her outside of school. 'Miss' sounded so formal and seemed to distance them from her. She'd heard of others who had taken evacuees in who were called Aunty, so she decided to go with that. She'd talk to them about it when she was putting them to bed later.

Mandy didn't seem interested in trying to win anything, and Edith was relieved at this as she didn't think her nerves could take willing another child on, or the awful prospect of her losing. That would be a disaster, especially with her being a girl. The lads would feel they were superior.

Mandy was more interested in the music coming from a barrel organ, as she'd wandered ahead and stood listening.

When they caught up with her all she said was, 'I'm hungry.'

'Right, fish and chips it is. I'll go, Edith, you take the children to the bench where we sat the other day.'

When they were all seated, Edith decided to have the conversation with them. They all loved the idea of calling her Aunty and said they promised not to when they were in school. Mandy sat next to her and after a moment she felt her hand in hers. She held on to it.

'Well, do you like the seaside, Mandy?'

'I do. I want to kick off me shoes and swim.'

'You swim?'

'Yes, in the River Lea. The barge kids taught me.'

'That's very clever, love. I'd like to swim. I see holidaymakers doing it, but I've rarely been in the sea.'

'When the summer comes I'll teach you.'

'You might be able to before that, we still get nice

349

days. Or there's the newly opened Derby Baths — we could go there. Can the lads swim?'

'They can, Alf is really fast.'

'Eeh, you'll all put me to shame, but I'm a quick learner, so we'll see.'

'I wish I 'ad a dad like Ben's got. Ben's dad's nice. Could Philip be our dad?'

Philip returned at that moment. He glanced at Edith. He looked taken aback.

'No, love, Philip has to go away soon, to help the war effort.'

'You mean, we won't see him?'

'No, we won't . . . we . . .'

'You'll see me every few weeks for a start as I come home on leave, I promise you.'

Edith was glad that Philip had taken command of the conversation. A large lump had formed in her throat and she'd felt she might break down. Somehow with the happiness of completing her first lesson and having the children come to stay, his looming departure had left her mind for a while. The stark reminder had now jolted her emotions.

Philip winked at her and grinned. She smiled back as she busied herself giving out the food.

'I won't have mine for a moment, darling. I'll nip to that photographer and see if the film I left with him is ready.'

Edith nodded — she'd forgotten all about the photos.

The photo was beautiful, and she saw that she had achieved her aim of being as brave and strong as Eloise, the woman in the photo they'd copied.

The sun had picked up the blue lights in her hair, bringing memories of her da, whose hair had been the same colour. Tears pricked her eyes as she looked at the image of Philip, smiling widely, looking so handsome as he sat with his arm around her shoulder, looking like a man in love, and she knew she would remember the moment they'd shared on that bench forever.

Philip's voice was thick with emotion as he echoed her thoughts. 'It's how I want to remember you always.'

A shiver ran through her, frightening her as the gentleman's words came back to her — he'd recounted the tale of when he'd sat on the same bench for a photo with his love, Eloise, and how it was marked in his memory as a special moment and one he treasured as he'd lost her forever when he'd gone off to war. She didn't want that same thing to happen to her and Philip but felt helpless to stop it.

'I'll get your copy made bigger and framed for you, darling, but mine will stay in my wallet forever and go everywhere with me.'

Edith couldn't speak. She was in danger of breaking down and weeping her heart out. Mandy saved her then, as she hoped she and the others would always do. 'That bloody seagull nicked me chip out of me bleedin' 'and!'

Philip put his head back and roared with laughter. Edith couldn't help but join in with him but felt torn as she didn't want to be seen as condoning Mandy's swearing, so she sobered herself quickly. 'Eeh, Mandy, love, I don't like that language.'

'Sorry. It just came out of me mouth.'

'She's been good till now. You should 'ear 'er back 'ome. Gran threatens to wash her mouth with soap. But she don't mean it and Mandy tries not to.'

'Don't talk about Gran, Alf!' Mandy got up, plonked her chips down and ran away from them.

Philip went to get up, but Edith stopped him. 'Stay with the lads, love. Make them understand that they will see their families again. I'll talk to Mandy.'

Her own troubles forgotten, Edith was desperate to help the little girl who thought herself grown-up and able to deal with everything.

When she caught up with Mandy, she found her in floods of tears.

'Mandy, love, it's all right to cry, I do it all the time. Only, like you, I try hard not to, but sometimes it overwhelms you.'

'I miss me gran, so I try not to think about 'er, and then idiot Alf keeps mentioning 'er as if she's just around the corner or something! I 'ate 'im and wish he weren't me bruvver.'

'No, you don't, lass. You're just cross with him. Look at the lovely doll he won for you. I'll tell you what we'll do, we'll write to Gran as well, and ask her to hop on a train and visit us. How would that be? There's loads of trains come into Blackpool carrying folk from all over the country. Would she do that?'

'Like a shot. She's afraid that London'll have bombs dropped on it. She wanted us all to move, but me mum wouldn't; she said there's plenty of trade for her on the streets of London and she wouldn't know 'ow to earn 'er money anywhere else.'

Edith thought that there'd be plenty of work for women, but had the impression that Mandy's mum liked what she did. 'Well then, if Gran's willing to come, we'll soon arrange it. We'll write to her giving her me telephone number and then she can ring you from a phone box.'

Mandy looked up into Edith's face. 'You're the best bleedin' aunty in the world, you know.'

Edith decided not to say anything about the 'bleedin' part. Now wasn't the time for correction, but for hugging, so she took hold of Mandy's hand and squeezed her. 'And you're the best little girl to care for in all the world, but your chips are at the mercy of the seagulls and I reckon you were enjoying them an' all.'

'I were. I ain't never ate anything out of newspaper before, and the fish with that batter on were good an' all.'

'Come on then, I'll race you back.'

Mandy showed she was up for a challenge as she took off like the wind, leaving Edith purposely lagging behind.

When they arrived, Alf stood up and said, 'Sorry, Mandy, I just can't forget Gran, I 'ave to talk about 'er.'

'Well, you can now as she's coming to stay!'

Philip looked quizzically at Edith. 'Aye, we hope so, we're going to invite her to come up on the train.'

Ben asked, 'Aunty, can me mum come too?'

'She can, love. And you can send her me telephone number so she can ring from a telephone box an' all.'

'What about me dad?'

Philip took charge of this. 'Like Edith said, Ben, you can write to your dad, but he won't be able to telephone you. But your letters, and especially if you include some drawings, will really help him to be the brave soldier he is.'

'But I want to talk to him.' Ben's lips quivered once more.

Philip took him in his arms. 'You see the outline of the moon? It's faded, but trying to take over from the sun, but it isn't time yet. It isn't time for you to see your dad yet either, but just as surely as the moon will take over from the sun, you will one day talk to your dad. In the meantime, write in your letter that you will look at the moon every night when you go to bed and you'll say, 'Goodnight, Dad, I love you,' and ask him to do the same, and then for that moment, you will be connected.'

Edith was left with a feeling of pride once again at the exceptional talent Philip had with children. The thought came to her that this war wasn't just robbing her of his presence, but robbing the many children he would normally have filled with his wisdom and seen on to the next step of their lives.

She sighed. 'Well, this won't get the babby bathed, nor you children into bed for a goodnight's sleep.'

This led to her being plied with questions as to whether she had a baby at home.

She laughed. 'No, it's just a saying we use up here in the North. It means that we're delaying what we should be doing.'

'Will you 'ave a baby as you are married?'

'One day, Ben, one day.' But though she batted the question away, she did sneak a little rub of her tummy and told it, *You would do me the biggest favour ever if you held a babby for me.*

28

Marg

Waking early on the Tuesday morning after a restless night, Marg sat up feeling bleary-eyed. Bringing her left hand out from under the covers, she stared at her beautiful ring, trying to recapture every moment of when Clive gave it to her, but it was what they had all done on Sunday that had filled her head with thoughts of the changes they faced.

With talking of Christmas on Saturday night, she'd woken on Sunday determined to carry on as if Christmas were going to be normal, and so had gathered all her ingredients together and mixed her Christmas pudding ready to leave it to stand with a damp cloth covering it at the back of the cold slab in the pantry. With this done, she'd had half a bag of dried fruit left, so she'd poured the last of an old bottle of sherry over it that had been left by her ma and left it to soak ready for the mince pies Jackie wanted to make.

They'd both cried as the smell of the sherry brought their ma back to them.

Swinging her legs out of the bed, Marg started to dress for work, but the thought of Christmas wouldn't leave her and she wished it were sooner so she could be certain everyone would be there. With this thought a sudden idea popped into her head.

Eeh, why not? Why can't I have Christmas early?

An excitement crept into her as the idea began to grow until she couldn't wait to talk to Edith and Alice

355

about it.

It could be our birthday celebration. No one has fixed anything up this year with all that's going on. And Edith wants to spend hers on Saturday with Philip. What a send-off that would be!

Plans began to form and fill her with anticipation, until it suddenly struck her that Harry wouldn't be able to be there and everything about the idea shrivelled like a popped balloon.

It was a silly idea anyway; everyone would laugh at me!

Once downstairs, Marg groped her way to the window to pull up the blackout curtain and let in the light. She was shocked to see her da standing outside. As he caught sight of her, he moved towards the front door.

Not wanting him to knock for fear of waking Gran, Marg dashed over and opened the door. 'Da? What're you doing here? Why did you leave me party? It would've been nice to have us all together for me engagement.'

'Get inside, lass, I need you to do sommat for me.'

Marg's guard came up as she remembered Clive's words. 'No, Da, I'm not getting mixed up in any of your dealings.'

'I suppose it were you who stopped Jackie from leaving the gate open, eh?'

'It was Clive, actually, after Jackie told us what you'd asked her to do. He thought that you maybe had something to do with that boatload of black-market goods he helped to rescue and warned us not to get involved with anything you were up to. What were you planning? 'Cause, I don't reckon it was to store Christmas presents, not in September it weren't.'

'Well, Clive can keep his bloody nose out of me

business. I've a right to put stuff in me own Anderson shelter.'

'But you had that built to keep me, Jackie and Gran safe!'

'Ha! If you believe that, you'll believe owt. No, me idea was for a safe storage place, and that's what I'm going to use it for.'

'Da? Where're you going?'

'To open the gate, where'd you think? I've me car parked in the back alley. I need to stash me stock before the whole bloody street wakes up and the coppers start to sniff around me lock-ups. One of them blokes they picked up might start talking to save their skins and this is the first chance I've had.'

'No, Da. I don't want you to do this. Please. I could get into trouble.'

'Look, Marg, there'll be plenty in this for you, lass. You'll want for nothing when the shortages begin to bite.'

'I'll tell the police!'

The darker side of Eric came to the fore then as he reeled round and stared at her, his face an ugly mask of evil.

His hand shot out. A vicious punch sent Marg reeling across the kitchen. The pot sink dug painfully into her ribs. Her face smarted. Drips of blood splattered the flagstone floor.

'Da!'

'Don't Da me, you bastard! Snitch on your own, would you? Eh?' He stood with his fist raised.

'No, Da, I won't . . . I won't tell anyone, I promise.'

She watched his fist rise again, felt the impact of it sinking into her stomach.

As she gasped for breath at his feet, he snarled, 'See

that you don't, 'cause if you do, I won't be in prison forever, and you'll be a dead cow the minute I get out.'

Just managing to stand, Marg slumped against the wall as her da turned the key in the back door and let himself out into the yard.

She didn't move while she watched him through the open door, taking box after box into the shelter. Then without coming inside again, he drove off.

With the relief of him having gone, Marg's body began to tremble, her strength left her, and she slithered down, not feeling the bump as she hit the cold floor. Her world went into a black, all-consuming darkness.

* * *

When she woke, she felt disorientated. Nothing was familiar to her.

'Ah, Marg, you're awake. You've an entourage waiting to see you. How're you feeling?'

As her focus cleared, Marg saw the nurse who'd attended to Alice. 'Am . . . I — I in hospital?'

'Aye, love, you look like someone beat you up. Your sister found you on the floor of your kitchen and phoned for an ambulance. I'll just fetch the doctor, lass.'

A few minutes later, Gerald came through the door. 'Marg! What happened? I've only just come on duty and seen that you were brought in this morning.'

'Me . . . da . . .' Her eyes flooded with tears, which spilt over as she took in a gasp of breath.

'Eric Porter did this? Dear, dear. Look, Marg, I've been told that the police have been called as it was

358

obvious to my colleague who admitted you that you had been attacked, so save it all for them. I don't want you getting too upset. You have other underlying issues that we need to deal with.'

Marg didn't know what to ask first, but questions about what else was wrong with her won.

'You're what we call anaemic. In your case, it seems to be related to low iron in your blood. My colleague has suggested a blood transfusion. Do you eat much red meat? Especially liver?'

'Eeh, it ain't often we can afford much meat, but we've had a bit more lately since me da . . . well, he's been helping us out a bit more. Is that what causes it?'

'Not caused it, but could help prevent it. Look, Marg, I want you to forget that I am your friend for a moment and look on me as a doctor only, as I must ask you a couple of embarrassing questions about what could be causing this.'

'Aye, I understand, Ger — Doctor, but can you give me something to stop me head pain? It's really bad.'

'I will. Ah, here's Nurse . . . Nurse, once you have the stand up, will you fetch aspirin, please? I'll administer the blood.'

While Gerald stuck a needle in her arm and attached the blood to flow into her, his questions made Marg cringe with embarrassment.

'Are you pregnant, Marg?'

'No! Me and Clive ain't never done anything. I can't be.'

'Right, what about your periods?'

Never did Marg see a day she would talk about something so private to one of her friends' husbands. Her cheeks reddened, and she tried to concentrate on Gerald being just a doctor.

'Are they heavy? Light? Regular?'

'Well . . . the last three have been really heavy and . . . well, I sometimes think they're not going to stop.' She recalled how she'd had to change her rag twice during the morning at work the last time and try to conceal the offending, smelly thing in her bag till she could get home. Marg felt even more embarrassed at the thought. She'd been glad when it had stopped.

'I see. Well, this could be the cause and will have to be looked into. But let's get you better first. When this is flowing nicely and you've had your aspirin, would you like me to let Clive, Gran, Alice and Jackie in?'

'They're all here? Even Clive?'

'Yes, Jackie rang the ambulance from Edith's phone and then they rang Alice and Clive.'

'Yes, let them in, ta, Gerald.'

Gerald smiled at her. 'You did well, Marg. As for your injuries, they are nasty, but will soon clear up. If you feel sick at all, ring the bell and call for the nurse as that could indicate that you may have concussion. I'll leave now. I want to have a word with Clive before he comes in.'

'Gerald, before you go, is this a private ward? Only I should be on the voluntary ward as I ain't got the money to pay for this.'

'I know. Don't worry, Marg. Clive wanted you to come here, he told Alice on the phone.'

When Alice, Jackie and Gran came in, Jackie was crying.

'Aw, it's all right, Jackie, love, I'm going to get well.'

'But how . . . how could our da . . . ?'

'I know, love. He's done a bad thing, he —'

'He's shown his true colours, that's what. I warned

360

you, Vera. But you'd never listen. I remember when he hit you before, but you said it were your own fault.' Gran began to shake. Alice caught hold of her.

Marg tried to reassure her. 'Gran, Gran, it's all right . . . Oh, Alice, help her to sit down, please, love.'

She looked over at Jackie. Jackie showed the same shock on her face that Marg felt. To think that Eric had hit her ma!

'Come here, Jackie, lass, don't get too upset. Eeh, me little love, you've had it rough lately. Sit on the bed and hold me hand, lass.' Jackie's hand felt cold in hers. 'We did know our da had an evil side, love, but we ignored it — wanted to, I suppose. But we can't ignore it any longer. The police are coming to see me and I'm going to tell them everything Da said and that he's stored a lot of stuff in the Anderson — stolen stuff, I reckon. And we can't let him do that, even if telling on him means he has to go to prison.'

Jackie let out a sob. Alice went to her and took her in her arms. 'Marg's right, love. Go and see to your gran. She needs you, she's confused and frightened.' Alice sat on the bed once Jackie had moved towards Gran. 'Eeh, Marg, lass.' She took her hand in hers. 'That this should happen to you after your lovely weekend. Edith told me on Sunday what a grand time you'd had and I can see your ring, it's beautiful. Everything'll work out. You'll see. I'm sorry about your da.'

'I hate him, Alice. He's evil. I never want to see him again as long as I live. I want him to go to jail and I think Jackie will too, she's devastated by this.'

'By, I don't know what to do to make everything right. What with Harry an' all.'

'How is he, love? Jackie said he was a bit better

361

again yesterday.'

'He is. A lot better and Gerald thinks he could come home in a couple of days. He'll not be right for a long time. He'll be weak, and have to build his strength, but Gerald reckons he'd recover better at home.'

'That's grand news.'

'Aye, and you need to get better for your wedding, lass.'

'Ha, I ain't thought a lot about that since Saturday night, me mind's been full of Christmas.'

'Christmas! What, dreaming of your first one after you're married?'

Jackie came back over to the bed and looked a bit brighter. 'Ha, she even had us making the pud and we never usually do that till after her birthday.'

'I know, but I had the strangest idea . . .'

'What?'

'You'll laugh at me, Alice, but I wanted us to have Christmas early — a pretend one that's just like a real one. Before Philip goes. On your birthday.'

'What? Ha!'

'I knew you'd laugh.'

'No . . . actually, I'm not . . . Could we . . . ? I mean . . . well, I don't know what to think. With all that's going on I haven't arranged anything for me birthday, but well, with Harry coming home now . . . But what if you have to stay in hospital, Marg?'

'I don't think I will. Gerald said I should be easily mended and sorted. He did say something about if I feel sick, but I don't, just very sore and weak.'

'Eeh, and daft in the head, Marg. I've never heard of anyone having Christmas in September, have you, Alice?'

'No . . . but, well, Marg's idea ain't a bad one. I

mean . . . well, all the men could be gone by Christmas, then what sort of a do would we have? This way we'd have the memory of a lovely day . . . But we've only got a few days . . . could we get it ready by then?'

Marg felt her earlier excitement return. 'We could. Well, we could try. Edith could get them kids on making paper chains . . . But where would we get a tree?'

'There's one in me garden. It's the one we've had these last two Christmases. We keep it in a pot and Gerald has kept it trimmed to keep it from growing too big. And I've me box of decorations for it in the loft, and we've got holly in the garden an' all. Its berries are only just turning orange, but they'll look lovely anyway.'

'Aww, we can do this, we can.'

Jackie sounded excited as she answered, 'We can, we've the pudding made, Marg. It won't have stood long, but I bet it'd do and I could make the mince pies . . . Eeh, it's a grand idea.'

'Aw, so you really think it could be done, Jackie?'

'Suddenly, I want it to happen, Marg, especially with Harry coming home. It'll be a welcome home for him and, like you say, a Christmas we can all have together.'

'That's the spirit, lass. Let's show Hitler that he can't beat us. He's up against the Halfpenny Girls now.'

'Eeh, am I one of them now then, Marg?'

'You are, Jackie, join the gang, lass.' They all giggled, but then, suddenly, the excitement that had kept Marg going ebbed away as she felt so tired. She lay her head down heavily on the pillow.

'Aw, you've had enough now, love. We'll go, eh? I can nip Jackie over to be with Harry, and then I can take Gran home. I'll see that Ada knows she's back, then I'll come back later . . . Ooh, with all the excitement, I haven't told you that Edith'll be round in her dinner break from school.'

'Aw, that'll be good. Bring Gran over to me before you go, love.'

Marg took Gran's hand. 'Gran, Eric won't be able to hurt us again, he'll be in prison, so don't worry. Alice will take you home and see that Ada can come over to check on you. Then if you feel up to it, Clive will bring you back to see me later.'

'All right, Marg. Eeh, I'm tired of him and his antics over the years. Ruined me family, he did.'

Marg didn't say that Ma had had a hand in that; she didn't want to think that way anymore. She was missing her ma more than ever, especially as her wedding day approached. 'Well, he'll be gone from our lives, love.'

Gran bent down and kissed her. 'I should have been there and stopped him, me little lass. I used to look out for you.'

'Now I'll look out for you, Gran. I love you, and I'll see you later.'

Jackie gave her a kiss, and as weak as she felt, Marg put her arms around her sister for a moment before Alice said, 'I don't want to hurry you, lass, but I don't want to leave Harry too long.'

As she kissed Marg, she told her, 'We'll make that Christmas happen, love. I'll come in to see you when Edith arrives and we'll talk about it then.'

Clive came in the door as they left. He smiled a lovely smile, though she could see his concern in his eyes. He rushed over to her. 'My darling, how are you? I wanted to come in straight away, but Gerald needed me to sort something out . . . Marg, we've spoken to the police . . .'

'Eeh, that's good.'

'Oh, I'm glad you feel like that, love. I wanted to come and ask you first to make sure, but Gerald said you were of that mind, but didn't think you well enough to see the police just now. You will have to later, though, darling, and they will go to the house. Gerald's going to get Alice to take Gran back to hers and get the key off Jackie before they leave. I'll go over there now to meet the police and come back later.'

Clive took both of her hands in his. 'Everything's going to be all right, Marg. I'm going to take care of you. I can't believe this happened to you, my darling.' Tears misted his eyes. Marg felt so emotional she couldn't speak.

'I love you so much, Marg. I'm going to look after you from now on, and that means making sure you have enough money. I never want you to want for anything ever again, nor to work another morning in that factory.'

'Eeh, Clive, I don't know what to say.'

'Don't say anything, Marg, just accept it. In a short while you're going to be my wife, when this will be natural for me to do. I just want to do it now because this has happened. Gerald said that until they build up your iron levels you may feel very tired, my darling. Going to work and struggling on with no help from your da would mean you won't recover quickly.'

'I don't want to think of him as me da ever again, Clive.'

'No, I don't want you to. He needs to be out of your life. And he will be.'

'Clive, ta. What you've done for me is beyond any

words, but I'll make it up to you. I'll be the best wife ever . . . I mean, well, as good as Harriet was.'

'Hey, it's not a competition that you have to win. I just think of myself as a lucky man to have a second chance at the happiness Harriet brought me, and I hope making you as happy, too.'

'I know, I shouldn't have said that. I just want you to know that I love you and want to be with you.'

He stroked her hair. She heard him swallow hard. Knew he was fighting tears. Closing her eyes, she allowed the gesture to comfort and soothe her as she drifted off to sleep.

★ ★ ★

When she next woke, it was to the sound of Jackie calling her name.

Marg opened her eyes, and it seemed to her as though the world had changed, as she felt a peace that she hadn't felt for a long time settle in her. She looked at the three beloved faces of Jackie, Alice and Edith and smiled.

Edith held her hand. 'By, you look a lot better, lass, you've got some colour now. You've looked really pale and tired lately.'

'I've felt it, love, but now I feel grand.'

'It'll be the blood they gave you, love.' Alice sat on the bottom of the bed. 'Anyroad, we ain't got long, so can we bring the Halfpenny Girls' meeting to order, ladies?'

Jackie giggled.

Marg looked at her and told her, 'Well, I think the newest member should go first.'

Jackie winked. 'Well, I think we should do it — we

366

should have an early Christmas. I've been getting more and more excited about it all morning.'

Edith piped up, 'Well, I think you're all mad, but then I am an' all, so aye, Sunday is Christmas Day!'

'By, we've a lot to do, lasses.'

'We have, Marg, but I think we can do it. Is everyone agreeable it should be at mine?' Alice looked from one to the other of them. All nodded. 'Right, I say that we get all the men to do the decorations on Saturday — during the day, as Edith and Philip are going out to dinner in the evening.'

Marg thought to herself that more than a few things were changing in their lives. Not long ago Alice and Edith had found it hard to call their tea their dinner, but she didn't remark on this. 'That sounds grand to me.'

'I'll take on the cooking.'

'Well, we'll all help you, Jackie. There'll be a lot to do, but you can direct operations.'

They giggled at this and Marg could hear the excitement in their voices. 'What about Santa for the kids?'

'That's a good idea, Marg.' Edith took charge of this. 'We can buy them some gifts and put stockings on the end of their beds, and then have a present-giving hour before we eat our Christmas dinner. If we all buy each other something, not expensive, we can wrap it and put it under the tree.'

'Time's what we're short of and we don't want to tire Marg out.'

'Aye, you're right, Alice. So how about we make a list of everything we need, then see what we already have, then me, you and Jackie divide the items we need between us and shop when we leave work each day?'

'No. Well, I mean, the list is fine — a great idea — but I'm buying the food . . . No, I won't take any argument. I wanted a birthday party anyway and would have bought it then. I can easily drop a list into the grocer and have it delivered. And ring the butcher and ask him to get me a cockerel and deliver it. He deals with a local farm for his poultry, so he'll be able to do it.'

By the time they left half an hour later, so much had been organised that Marg felt a mixture of excitement, tiredness and joy. The tiredness won and she drifted back off to sleep, hardly able to believe that she was going to have a September Christmas.

This was one birthday she didn't think any of them would forget and they'd had some good ones over the years — street parties; jam butties in the park with the three of them and all their siblings when they were younger; oh, and so many more — but a Christmas one! This was going to be a party to end all parties. It would mark the changing of all of their lives, for who knew what the future held for them?

29

Edith

When the weekend arrived, Alice's house had become a hive of activity. The tree was put up and decorated in no time, and Alice had dug out a few packets of crêpe paper in different colours that had been left over from last Christmas and had set the children making paper chains.

'Eeh, look at this!' Joey's excited voice as he rummaged in a box that Gerald had found in the attic had them all looking in his direction. 'Crackers! Real crackers! I ain't never pulled a real cracker.'

'No, but we used to love the ones Alice made, remember, Joey?' Billy had walked over to him. 'They were all colours, and we had to shout 'bang' when they gave way to our tugging, and we found all sorts in them — a sweet or a footie card.'

'Aye, we did, but to pull a real one and hear it bang, by, that'll be something.'

Edith felt Philip's arm around her giving her a gentle squeeze as he asked, 'How many are there, Joey?'

'A dozen, all packed tightly, so they ain't damaged.'

'Well, Alice, it looks like you'll have to make two. Now, who should have Alice's, that is the question?'

From Billy down, the young 'uns all had their eyes cast to the floor, not wanting to be picked to go without a cracker. And Edith noticed that even Jackie was keeping very quiet. None of them had ever seen, let alone pulled, a real cracker — she hadn't herself, but this first time belonged to them. 'I think the names of all of those over twenty should go into a hat and we'll pull out two to have the last ones.'

There was an audible releasing of breath.

'Ahh, but wait a minute.' Philip lifted his hand. 'Why don't I give my mother a ring — I bet you that she has a box in her loft too, but if she doesn't, then we'll do as Edith suggests, eh?'

Edith clapped her hands together. 'Aye, that's grand — hooray, kids, you're all going to pull a cracker.'

A cheer went up as the tense moment passed, only brought to an end by a knock on the door. Clive had arrived. He was to take her, Alice and Marg to the shops so they could do the present buying for the children.

* * *

Linking arms and giggling like schoolgirls, they made Woolworths their first stop. They all loved Woolies, and while there they browsed the toy counter and picked out jigsaw puzzles, yoyos, colouring books and crayons. Wooden train sets for Clive's boys, and for Mandy a doll's house. Roller skates for Alf and Ben. A protractor and easel and large drawing pad for Joey.

Clive had seen to sourcing a bike for Billy and, lastly, they went to the photographer's and bought Harry a camera.

The girls were loaded down by the time they made their way across to the promenade to what they all knew now as Edith's bench where they were to wait for Clive.

'What's that smell?' Edith sniffed the air. 'Chestnuts!

Eeh, the spud man is roasting chestnuts! That's a bit early, ain't it?'

'What? Earlier than our Christmas, you mean?'

They all laughed at Marg, who then reminded them that this was usual. 'The first ones drop off their trees about now. They're not always ripe, but Spuddy don't care, he'll roast anything on his spit.'

'Christmas wouldn't be Christmas without roast chestnuts.'

Whatever took Marg, Edith didn't know, but she suddenly burst into song. '*We wish you a Merry Christmas, We wish you a Merry Christmas . . .*'

A passer-by looked astonished, and even more so when Bendy came over and promptly did a cartwheel in front of her, leaving the three of them in fits of giggles.

When they calmed down, they said a quick hello to Bendy, who had his usual crowd to get back to.

'Eeh, hold on a mo. Ripe or not, I'm going to see if Spuddy will sell me some chestnuts. They'd make tomorrow perfect.'

★ ★ ★

The house was transformed, but they didn't stop to inspect it all as they hurried upstairs, with Clive carrying some of their purchases and Philip and Gerald close on their heels.

Once in Alice and Gerald's bedroom, the men wanted to see what they'd purchased. All went mad about the camera and were like kids over the train sets — one with a red engine and the other with a blue one.

'Now, we have a surprise for you, darling.' Gerald

371

took Alice's hand.

As they went to leave the room, Gerald said, 'You come too, Marg and Edith.'

He took them back downstairs. '*Voilà*.'

There in the living room was the sun lounger from the summer house.

Edith looked at Marg and saw the same blank expression on her face as she saw on Alice's as Alice asked, 'What?'

'For Harry. He's not well enough to come down and stay down, but with this he can be brought down for a little part of the day, and then again for a bit longer. You girls can make it comfortable for him. We menfolk will be responsible for carrying him up and down depending on his needs.'

'It's perfect! Ta, Gerald. Let's go up and ask Harry what he thinks.'

As they followed Alice, Edith really hoped Harry agreed and wanted to join in as she knew this would make Alice's day.

It was lovely to see Harry sat up in bed looking so much better. He grinned at them and then at Jackie. 'By, Jackie, are we in trouble, lass, or what? It's the big sis brigade.'

They all laughed.

When Alice explained to him, he said, 'Sounds good, sis, I really want to join in, even though I can't get me head around it all . . . We'll be the talk of Blackpool, you knaw.'

'Ha, it won't be the first time, lad.'

This made for more laughter, but Edith was so glad to see the happiness spread over Alice's face.

* * *

Philip was like a kid himself that evening as they filled three of his socks just before they went to bed and crept upstairs to fix them to the bedposts of their three sleeping charges.

They stood a moment, gazing down on each of the boys and then went through to Mandy's room, and fixed hers, in a stealthier way as so far they'd noticed that she would wake up at the slightest noise.

When the floorboard creaked as they stepped inside, they both stood like statues, but had to retreat quickly as they took a fit of the giggles.

Outside the bedroom door, they held their mouths and bent double with the agony of suppressed laughter.

Edith sobered first. She took the stocking and went inside the room once more. At the creak of the board, Mandy shot up. 'Mum?'

'No, lass, it's Aunty. I was just checking that you were asleep.'

'I were. I were dreaming of me mum and gran.'

Edith detected a sob. She ran over to Mandy with the sock behind her back. When she sat on the bed, she laid it behind her and took Mandy in her arms. A sobbing Mandy clung to her.

'Your gran will come as soon as she gets your letter, I'm sure, love. And from what you've told me of her, she'll get Ben's ma too and they'll be on that train in a flash.'

Mandy didn't speak. Edith rocked her backwards and forwards, humming the lullaby 'Rockabye Baby', which is what she remembered her own ma singing to her.

Gradually, she felt Mandy relaxing and heard her breathing deepen. Laying her down, she tucked her in before quickly fixing the sock onto her bedpost.

Outside the room, Philip stood with his arms open. His expression was such that he didn't have to speak. She knew many emotions were assailing him.

They hugged one another, then crept back downstairs.

★ ★ ★

With the dawn chorus came pandemonium, as whatever magic wakes kids on a real Christmas morning woke Mandy, Alf and Ben.

Edith lay by Philip's side listening to their squeals of delight and was transported back in time. She could see her young brother, Albert, rushing into the room — his striped pyjamas falling down, as he could never tie the cord properly, his hands in the air waving a yoyo, his smile hindered by his mouth being full of toffee, but his face a picture of joy.

Taking a deep breath, Edith turned into Philip. 'Can you hear them?'

Philip giggled. 'Perfect. I wouldn't have missed this for the world. How clever of Marg to think up this scheme. I'm going to give her a big hug today.'

Edith laughed. 'Come on, we may as well get them in here with us, they'll not sleep again now.'

'But it's only four thirty!'

'By, you've got years of this, lad, when we have our own. Now's good practice.'

Philip sat up and grabbed her. 'Let's have another go at making our own family now, eh?'

'Philip! You daft apeth, the kids will be through that door any minute!' She wriggled from his arms, laughing down at him.

The pandemonium continued when they arrived at Alice's, amidst everyone calling out 'Happy Birthday' to Alice, and 'Merry Christmas' to everyone else.

The house smelt Christmassy as Jackie, who'd stayed the night, already had the Christmas pudding steaming on the stove and the large cockerel in the oven.

Noise levels were so high it was difficult to hear themselves speak, but they wouldn't have it any different.

Gerald shouted over the noise, 'Come on, teacher, get some order, Alice wants to do the present giving.'

Philip clapped his hands — the sound oozed authority and brought the room to order.'Present opening time is on us, but only good children who sit crossed-legged on the floor will get something from under the tree.'

Billy sat down and called to George, 'Come and sit on me knee, lad. I'll help you open yours, eh?'

George went willingly and looked honoured to do so. He seemed to have really taken to Billy. Jackie did the same with Carl, who hesitated for a moment, but then grinned as he sat between her legs and let her put her arms around him. Joey sat with Ben and Philip and Edith with Mandy and Alf. But peace didn't reign long as the presents were handed out and paper ripped off in a frenzy of excitement.

As Gerald pulled them out one by one, he came to a soft parcel that Edith didn't recognise. 'Ah, this one's for Gran.'

Carl jumped up.'May I give it to Gran?'

As he handed the parcel to Gran, he said, 'My other

grandma knitted it for you, Gran.'

Edith looked at Marg; her face was a picture. She still hadn't met Clive's family and it was a source of worry for her. Gran opened the parcel and the fluffy knitted item inside swelled as it was let out of its restricting wrapping. Gran opened it up to reveal a beautiful blue shawl. Her lip quivered. 'Eeh, I love it. Tell your grandma ta from me, won't you, Carl, lad.'

'Put it on, Gran, I'll help you.'

Carl took the shawl, and somehow managed to tuck it around Gran with a little help from her.

'You look lovely, Gran, like a queen.'

'Aye, well, I feel like a queen, lad. Ta. So, do you think you could put up with me then, when your da marries Marg?'

'I can, Gran. I'm going to look after you, only . . . I wish that you'd come and live in our house. We don't have to go outside to the lavatory.'

The room was quiet, except for the kids, who carried on comparing gifts. Edith held her breath and knew everyone else was doing so too. She glanced over at Marg standing with Clive, and part of her wanted to say, 'No, don't go.' And yet, a large part of her wanted to beg Gran to say she would.

'Can I bring me chair with me, lad?'

'Course you can, Gran, we've got a lot of room.'

Gran shocked them all then as she spat on her hand and held it out to Carl. 'Right, shake on it, lad.'

Carl looked unsure. He looked around the room till his eyes rested on his dad. Clive stepped forward. 'That's my job, Gran. I'm the one to seal the deal.' He took Gran's hand gently and shook it.

Gran looked up. 'Is this what you want for me, John, me love?'

Clive looked over at Marg; Marg nodded.

'Aye, it is, lass. I want to know that you're with Marg and Clive, and Jackie and them lads. They need you, Sandra, love.'

Edith saw the tears running down Marg's face. Saw the look of astonishment on Carl's little face and then watched Jackie move closer to the sunbed and take Harry's hand.

'Well, I'll have to wait until they wed, but eeh, Marg's got a good 'un.'

Alice cheered first, then the whole room joined in.

She and Alice went to Marg's side. Marg looked a bit bewildered for a moment, but Edith made her laugh. 'The power of a shawl, eh?'

When they finished giggling, Marg said, 'What about you, Edith? You'll be left in Whittaker Avenue without any of us.'

'We'll see. Philip wanted to get me a place. Maybe we'll look around for one when you're all settled.'

Alice didn't give time for this conversation to continue as she said, 'Well, you won't be so nervous at meeting Clive's parents now, will you, Marg?'

Marg agreed, but to Edith something still wasn't right. Yes, Clive's mother had made this gesture, but for Marg to be a friend of Clive's for over two years, and now his betrothed, it seemed strange to her that Marg hadn't been invited before now.

This was forgotten as the last of the presents were given out, and she and Marg gave Alice her birthday present — a replica perfume bottle only in purple, a different colour to Marg's.

'Marg tells me that eventually, we will all have one and they will be the symbols of the Halfpenny Girls making good. While we each own these, wherever life takes us, when we use them, we will think of each other.'

'Eeh, that's a grand thing to say, Edith.'

Their three-way hug held such love that it brought a tear to Edith's eye, something she was trying to avoid today.

After a rendition of 'Happy Birthday', the kids went off to various rooms, or out into the garden, to play with their toys. Billy went for a spin on his bike, and Joey set up his easel in the conservatory.

'Time for a pre-dinner sherry, I think,' Alice told Gerald.

'Make mine a stout, lad.'

'I will, Gran, we've got some in for you.'

'Eeh, Gran, you'll be asleep before your dinner.'

Gran laughed. She looked at Marg with love as she said, 'You've done all right for yourself, lass.'

Marg went to her and hugged her.

★ ★ ★

Dinner was delicious. Jackie was a marvel, and though they'd all mucked in and helped, she'd remained at the helm.

The afternoon was a quiet affair: Philip, Clive and Gerald played chess, Gran dozed, the children were anywhere but in the lounge, though their happy voices could just be heard, and Harry had been taken upstairs for a sleep.

Edith, Alice and Marg sat together on the bench in the garden.

'Ta for this, Alice, it's been a grand day.'

'No, thank you for thinking of it, Marg.'

'Aye, Marg,' Edith told her. 'There was no better

378

way we could have spent today than having a Christmas Day and we've still got your wedding to come.'

It was Alice who asked the question that had puzzled them both. 'Will you meet Clive's parents before the day, Marg?'

'Aye. Clive told me earlier, when we sat together after Gran said she'd come to live with us, that he'd trodden carefully as his ma suffers with her nerves. But that she really wanted to meet me and me family. He said she was hurt badly with losing Harriet.'

'Ah, it's understandable. And I think it's good that Clive has taken his time then. And not just with his ma, but with you an' all, Marg. But, eeh, love, I'm that happy for you. It's going to be a grand wedding, and for you two to be able to live together properly is lovely and how it should be.'

'Ta, Alice. Clive told me something else an' all. Me da . . . Eric Porter's been arrested, and the police told Clive he was looking at going down for a long time, so that's something else that's put me mind at rest.'

Wanting to take the conversation away from anything bad, Edith said, 'So, everything's coming right for you, lass. I'm glad, you deserve it, love . . . Hey, I've had an idea. Let's do this thing properly and end the day as we do all our Christmases by singing carols around the tree.'

'Eeh, can we? I mean, it ain't really Christmas — you know, the celebration of Jesus's birth and all that.'

'It's our real Christmas, Marg. Yes, let's do it. I think it's a grand idea, Edith, love.' Alice stood. 'I'll go and tell the men and get Billy to light the fire — it ain't Christmas without a log fire.'

Edith stood too. 'And I'll ask Joey to rehearse Mandy, Alf and Ben. He's such a good lad with them,

379

they hang on his every word.'

With tea over, they all gathered around the tree. Alice and Gerald had closed all the blackouts and lit the standard lamp, giving just enough light for the flicker of the fire to dance shadows onto the walls.

Edith closed her eyes, wanting to impress this memory to keep forever. She opened them as the piano music began. Philip was playing 'Silent Night'.

The most perfect rendition of the carol filled the room as Mandy stood next to the piano and sang. The other children joined in the chorus.

Edith looked around the room and saw Marg standing in the circle of Clive's arms, one hand holding a seated Gran's hand, and looking serenely happy. Then at Alice and Gerald. As they swayed together looking into each other's eyes, Edith couldn't imagine what they were thinking, but she hoped it was good things. They'd come out the other side of a traumatic time, that had nearly broken them, but their love was stronger than ever now.

Her gaze went to Jackie, sitting next to the sunbed that Harry lay on, holding his hand. What a lovely young woman Jackie had become.

As the music came to an end and everyone applauded, she slipped across to stand by Philip's side.

'Can we sing our next one, Aunty?'

'You can, Mandy. Which one have you chosen, lass?'

George ran forward. "Jingle Bells', and I'm going to ring the bell.'

'Eeh, I can't wait for this.' Edith winked at Philip. He laughed his lovely laugh.

A pain clutched Edith's heart as she thought that tomorrow he would be gone from her and she didn't know for how long. Oh, how she wished tomorrow wouldn't happen. But she brushed the thought away and determined to do as Philip had said and enjoy every moment of today.

Smiling her widest smile, she joined everyone as they belted out 'Jingle Bells' to the sound of little George marching around with a dinner bell — something Alice had as an ornament. Its shining brass glittered in the firelight, matching the joyous, glowing faces of all those she loved.

Today was for rejoicing and it had been so wonderful. She knew they would all treasure the memory of the last day of their life as they'd known it till now and take it forward to help them get through whatever life threw at them in the future.

A Letter From Maggie

Dear Reader,

Hi.

Lovely to have spent these hours with you as you read my book, I hope you enjoyed reading it as much as I did writing it. Thank you from the bottom of my heart for choosing my work to curl up with.

The second in a trilogy, as this is, is always such a pleasure as I revisit characters I have created and who by now have become like friends.

From the moment they begin to people my story, in the first book, they are in my heart. My emotions are in a turmoil as they battle through life in some of the most difficult of times for women. Their pain is mine, their joy is a salve to me, and their triumphs make me proud. I hope I have conveyed this on the page so that you felt it too.

If so, one of the best things that can happen for me that connects you and me in a personal way is if you take the time to leave me a review on one of the many online outlets — Amazon and Goodreads to name two.

Reviews are like being hugged by the reader and they help to encourage me on to write the next book — they further my career as they advise other readers about the book and hopefully whet their appetite to also buy the book.

Don't worry if you missed the first in the series,

I always try to write each book as a standalone, but if you would like to step back a little in the timeline of the lives of Marg, Alice and Edith, *The Halfpenny Girls* is available from many online outlets.

Next and coming in springtime is *The Halfpenny Girls at War*. How will each of them fare? What heartache is in store for them?

This is a work in progress and as I sit and write, I am once more having my heartstrings tugged, crying buckets, and yet laughing and filling with pride. Marge, Alice and Edith are doing the country proud. They are strong for themselves and for others. They will not waver. What they are doing, our female ancestors did. Lest we forget.

As you wait for this next in the series, have you read my other books? You will see them all listed in the front of this one. If you like trilogies/series they are there, and if you like standalones, there's a choice for you too. And if you would like to chat to me, I love to interact with readers and would welcome your comments, your emails, and messages through:

My Facebook Page:
https://www.facebook.com/ MaggieMasonAuthor

My Twitter @AuthorMagsMason

My Website: www.authormarywood.com/contact

Here you can email me and receive a personal reply and if you subscribe, you will also be entered in a draw to win my latest book personally signed to you and receive three-monthly newsletters giving you all the updates and many chances of winning lovely prizes.

Love to hear from you

Much love
Maggie xxx

Acknowledgements

Many people were involved in getting my book to the shelves and presenting it in the very best way to my readers — my commissioning editor, Rebecca Farrell, who works tirelessly, advising on structure of the story and editing my work, besides overseeing umpteen other processes my book goes through. My agent, Judith Murdoch, always in my corner as she deals with so many things too numerous to mention but all vital to giving me support through the minefield of the publishing world. My editorial team headed by Thalia Proctor, whose work brings out the very best of my story to make it shine. My publicist, Francesca Banks and her team who seek out many opportunities for me to showcase my work. Her innovation in doing so during lockdown has led to short stories in magazines, appearances through the virtual media in my local library, and online promotions. My cover designers who do an amazing job in bringing my story alive in picture form, producing covers that stand out from the crowd. The sales team who seeks outlets across the country for my books. My son, James Wood, who reads so many versions of my work, to help and advise me, and works alongside me on the edits that come in. And last but not least, my readers who encourage me on as they await another book, support me by buying my books and warm my heart with praise in their reviews. My heartfelt thanks to you all.

But no one person stands alone. My family are amazing. They give me an abundance of love and support and when one of them says they are proud of me, then my world is complete. My special thanks to my darling Roy, my husband and very best friend. My children, grandchildren and great grandchildren who light up my life, and my Olley and Wood families. You are all my rock and help me to climb my mountain. Thank you. I love you with all my heart.

We do hope that you have enjoyed
reading this large print book.

Did you know that all of our titles
are available for purchase?

We publish a wide range of high
quality large print books including:
Romances, Mysteries, Classics
General Fiction
Non Fiction and Westerns

Special interest titles available in
large print are:
The Little Oxford Dictionary
Music Book, Song Book
Hymn Book, Service Book

Also available from us courtesy of
Oxford University Press:
Young Readers' Dictionary
(large print edition)
Young Readers' Thesaurus
(large print edition)

For further information or a free
brochure, please contact us at:
Ulverscroft Large Print Books Ltd.,
The Green, Bradgate Road, Anstey,
Leicester, LE7 7FU, England.
Tel: (00 44) 0116 236 4325
Fax: (00 44) 0116 234 0205

Other titles published by Ulverscroft:

BLACKPOOL LASS

Maggie Mason

Blackpool, 1932. When Grace's Ma passes away and her Da's ship sinks with all hands, Grace is utterly alone in the world. She's sent to an orphanage in Blackpool, but the master has an eye for a pretty young lass. Grace won't be his victim, so she runs, destitute, into the night.

In Blackpool, she finds a home with the kindly Sheila and Peggy — and meets a lovely airman. But it's 1938, and war is on the horizon. Will Grace ever find the happiness and home she deserves?